Spirit of Haiti

SUNY series, Afro-Latinx Futures

Vanessa K. Valdés, editor

Spirit of Haiti

Myriam J. A. Chancy

SUNY
PRESS

Cover credit: Rice field, Haiti, 1995 © MJA Chancy

Published by State University of New York Press, Albany

First SUNY Press edition 2023

For information, contact State University of New York Press, Albany, NY
www.sunypress.edu

Library of Congress Cataloging-in-Publication Data

Name: Chancy, Myriam J. A., 1970– author.
Title: Spirit of Haiti / Myriam J. A. Chancy.
Description: Albany : State University of New York Press, [2023] | Series: SUNY series, Afro-Latinx futures | Includes bibliographical references and index.
Identifiers: LCCN 2023002649 | ISBN 9781438495125 (pbk. : alk. paper) | ISBN 9781438495118 (ebook)
Subjects: LCSH: Haitians—Fiction. | Haiti—History—Coup d'état, 1991—Fiction. | LCGFT: Historical fiction. | Novels.
Classification: LCC PR9260.9.C43 S65 2023 | DDC 813/.6—dc23/eng/20230323
LC record available at https://lccn.loc.gov/2023002649

10 9 8 7 6 5 4 3 2 1

Note to the Reader

Dreams are reality at its most profound, and what you invent is truth because invention, by its nature, can't be a lie.

—Eugene Ionesco

In 1804, the island of Haiti successfully established itself as the first Black Republic of the Western Hemisphere after at least two decades of slave insurrections. By the beginning of the next century, due to American interventions and global trade, Haiti was fast on its way to becoming the poorest nation in the Western Hemisphere, which it is today. Economically poor but rich in heritage, Haiti has been further marginalized through the demonization by non-Haitian writers of *vodou* spirituality, a spirituality which is based on West African animist belief systems. Further, between the years 1957 and 1986, Haiti was governed by François Duvalier and son under a brutal dictatorship which stripped Haitians of personal and political freedoms such as basic human rights. In the years following the fall of the regime, Haiti sought to establish itself as a democratic nation. Its first freely elected president, Jean-Bertrand Aristide, came to power on December 16, 1990. On September 29–30, 1991, President Aristide was ousted from the country by a military junta. The following novel takes place during the weeks preceding the coup.

This novel is a work of art and is in no way intended to be read as a historical or spiritual treatise. It is a work of fiction which relies on the framework of Haitian history and culture yet the author has taken creative licence with historical details, Haitian geography, and myths related to Haitian *vodou*. The reader will find that the spirituality conveyed in this work is closely related to West African belief systems rather than to the specifics of *vodou*. The author trusts that readers will forgive these liberties.

The author thanks the *loas*, in spirit and human form, who assisted the birthing of this text.

An excerpt from this novel appeared in *Hayden's Ferry Review* 24 (Spring/Summer 1999).

Our greatest challenge is to find the one true rhythm of freedom—
something like the wind that allows a bird to fly, or a new language
more powerful than speech, that holds you.

—Susana Baca

Prologue

The Myth of King Christophe and the Citadel

She watches as the midwife carries the bloody sheets across the room to a basin filled with steaming water. She imagines the liquid turning scarlet, soaking through the fabric yellowed with use, the midwife's long, bony fingers pained by the sudden shift in temperature from the cold air to the scalding pool. Positioned on the bed, head held up high by straw-filled pillows, caramel-hued shin glistening against faded white cotton sheets, Taffia can see the midwife's elbows rising and falling like the brown, beaten husks of wooden ships against sharp-edged sea waves as she scrubs the sheets clean. The midwife is singing a song, a spiritual, a blessing . . . like wings . . . flying above these hills . . . tight skins of drums . . . sounding out . . . sorrow . . . hiss of the whip . . . against my breasts . . . I wear yellow . . . like the sun. Taffia hums along even though she feels too tired for such uncertain acts of hope; her body aches, an open sore. Taffia closes her eyes to listen more clearly to the midwife's voice: . . . a signal to the tree spirits . . . I have not forgotten . . . my hands balance . . . the weight of the wind . . . my arms embrace . . . the weight of the world.

The words move her to the memory of her mother's house, a small clapboard dwelling on the outskirts of the plantation where she was mistress to the landowner but mother to all her children, a rare luxury in those times. Her mother too sang songs that spoke of sadness, despair, and sometimes of hope for the children she had borne into a world filled with anger, hatred. Taffia remembers her mother's voice sounding out, a chiming bell in the wind, filling the space between the walls of the house with such pained love that, as a child, she had wanted to tear those walls down. At other times, Taffia wanted to sit very still beside her mother, hold her hand, caress her face. Listening to the midwife, she forgets for a moment that her mother has died long ago, her body laid to rest in a field for coloreds, far, far from the plot reserved for the family of the man with whom she had conceived all of her children, each a different shade of brown than the other. Taffia remembers her mother's smile, her tenderness, her tears. .

The baby lying beside Taffia's thigh stirs, begins to cry. She brushes a finger against one of his damp, chestnut cheeks. He is beautiful, Taffia thinks. His skin reminds her of damp trees, a forest alive with the sounds of maroons crossing to enter a clearing where they have carved imprints of their souls into the sediment. He stops crying for a moment and his eyes look deep into her own. She knows her son will be a warrior. Her heart skips a beat. She closes her eyes against the fear that has crept up in her at the thought of her son's future, a vision of hundreds of stained sheets hung up to dry in the thick haze of a field where the smoldering ground has been ploughed over in battle by the feet of soldiers and the hooves of their horses. She pushes her fright down a dry, scratchy throat and hums along with the midwife whose back, hidden beneath the folds of a starched linen dress, is betrayed by muscles dancing softly against the stiff fabric.

The midwife, a former slave, is a woman Taffia has come across before, in those days when her innocence remained protected by the embrace of her mother's voice. Taffia remembers her, wonders how she survived those merciless days. Taffia remembers the moment she had first seen the midwife as if no time has elapsed. That day, like Taffia, she had been but a child, not the midwife with the strong, saving hands, but a girl-child whose body had just begun to break softly from its shell of infancy. Taffia had been six or seven, ten years the midwife's junior who was then perhaps sixteen or seventeen. That day, Taffia's mother had taken her to town to buy cloth and thread to make clothes for the household and left her waiting on the storefront porch, looking out into the main square. Taffia liked to watch the passersby. She liked to try to give them a history, a narrative of their hidden lives. A copper-colored man with a top hat was a gambler with a brood of five waiting at home for his coins. An elderly man, skin pale as bone, with a curly moustache and a gold tooth, was a prospector living out the end of his days in his private version of a Caribbean paradise after having made a fortune in the American West. A young ebony-skinned woman with a bag of laundry tied around her chest protruding like a humpback was, just that, a laundry woman. Taffia wondered what else that woman could have been: a princess from faraway Africa? A vodou priestess? The woman looked at her as she passed, a smile in her eyes, though her lips were a tight, straight line, pressed firmly against each other. That smile contained a world and Taffia followed the woman with her own eyes, understanding, perhaps for the first time, that nothing was necessarily as it seemed.

The sky was a striking deep cobalt blue. At least, this is what she remembers now: that the sky was unnaturally placid, not a disturbance in view across its wide expanse. As she continued to wait for her mother, whom she could hear behind her rummaging through the cloth shop, she noted that the passersby were thickening into a throng of loud folks, mostly white, who were waiting to see the animal being tugged along at the end of a long yellowish cord behind the flanks of two fine-looking brown-red mares.

But it was not an animal that was half dragged into the square, legs folding under the body like matchsticks. Taffia watched as a young woman, in a torn and muddied dress of calico cloth, was led to the whipping post in the center of the square; the soft promise of breasts spilled from a straining tear in the fabric across her chest; the crowd drew closer around the post; the few colored faces in the crowd, stonelike, reflected the placidity of the sky. The whip ignored the tenderness of the youthful body, cut into the buds on the chest like a scythe cutting flowers in bloom. The soft skin burst upon contact, fell from the body in narrow ribbons; one nipple tore from a breast and hung limply against her breastbone. (Taffia shudders to think of it now; her eyes closed tight against the memory, she feels her own milk-full breasts and wonders if the midwife had ever had her own children and, if so, if she had been able to bring their small mouths to the breast in mothering, the nipples composed of weaved scar-tissue, bursting with milk they could not pass through the hard, rubberized webbing into a newborn's mouth. Or had the breasts stopped to function altogether, a knot of scarred flesh replacing their roundness?) That day, blood streamed from the young woman's nostrils and mouth. Bruises rose in lumps beneath the exposed skin. The colored folks trembled, imagining what would come next before it occurred. Cords were tied to each of her ankles and wrists. Four executioners pulled on the cords until the body rose from the ground as if by its own will. The girl, suspended in the air, let out a scream to wake the dead and, for a moment, all was still in the universe except for her vocal cords issuing their final cry. A shudder went through the body. For a moment, their eyes locked. Then, as if they were connected by some secret force, Taffia became, somewhere deep within herself, the young woman before her. Every pore on their skins filled with pain, strained against the air for deliverance. Their mouths dried with fear; their eyes closed to greet their souls which had begun to drift from their bodies like clouds intent on holding up the sky. The crowd around them had quieted and then, very quietly, a murmur of song erupted from the lips of the colored, slave and free alike. . . . My arms embrace . . . the weight of the world . . . each newborn spirit . . . holds each against my scars . . . fly above these hills. . . . Taffia, the child, opened her eyes to look at the young woman whose chest was covered with the deep gouges left by the whip. The song enveloped the young woman in a sweetness to counter the bitter bile filling her mouth.

When they cut her down, she was still alive. Having absorbed the dreams of her people transmitted by the air to her in song, she became a midwife to all their hopes. Later that day, she burned her master's house to ashes in a great circle of fire. Later still, when they saw her walking through the square, they found that the young woman had been transformed. The girl with the scarred chest had become a woman who restored life to the living dead. She walked, straight-backed, head held high, a fire in her eyes, body cloaked in the saffron yellow dress of Ochún, protectress of children, prophetess of the sea.

Taffia looks down at her son, his small body swaddled in freshly laundered cloth. Her body still aches dully from the delivery. The midwife turns to her, wipes her hands on a dry cloth, turns to the counter on her right where Taffia keeps honey for their tea in a glass jar the color of sand. The midwife opens the jar, tips it over so a small drop of honey falls on her left index finger; she brings the honey to the lips of the child on the bed who eagerly suckles the sweetness from her finger.

"Your son," the midwife tells Taffia, "will be as strong as my woman's back, hidden from sight, waiting to be unleashed, quietly powerful until his time arrives.

"Let him remember the gods, his ancestors, when he acquires his full powers," she says, eyes closed to Taffia's fear. "Should he fail to remember," she adds, "I will return." She slips into Taffia's hand a necklace made of seven large olive-shaped stones. "When his time comes, these he should wear. And he shall be protected always."

In an instant, so quick a moment that Taffia feels that the words have all been a dream, she sees the midwife's cloaked back bent over the birthing sheets soaking in the steel basin across the room, drawing them out one by one from the red water and singing her song of lament.

The sheets emerge from the water dripping yellow light into the room until the midwife moves them out of doors and hangs them in the night air where they will stay until morning to announce the birth. Taffia looks down at her child. Her son seems to smile at her . . . sprout wings . . . of freedom . . . She closes her eyes against the midwife's song and, fingers still touching her son's cheek, beads palmed in her left hand, dreams his true, true name: Henry Christophe.

Twenty-eight years later, on the Turpin Plantation, an enslaved African by the name of Boukman sounds the first conch, dances the first dance against the soil that reminds him of his native Jamaica, the land he fled, for too few fires had been lit there, beneath the porches of the whites. He flees on foot, then on ship, and comes to his newfound homeland, hunted. He blows the sounds of his freedom into the pink conch shell resting between his palms, a shell so large he has to hold it tightly with both his hands. It tremors against his fingers and pushes out the blessings of the gods. It is said that when he lowers the shell, Boukman feels a wetness thick as blood sticking to his fingers. When he tastes his hands and his lips, it is to find the salt of tears staining his fingertips. Before turning to the maroon rebels he has vowed to lead into battle, down from their enclaves in the mountainous hills and into the urban centers of the island, he kneels and weeps, face turned to the ground, tears lodging themselves into the dust like heavy droplets of rain.

When he rises, it is to turn a face of steel toward his comrades in arms, men and women, guns and cutlass in both hands, muscles tensed against the cool night air. They descend quietly through the plantations, stretching themselves between the mountains and Le Cap, the city on the harbor. Fire lights their way from house to house, spreads through the fields of cane they have been forced to work for generations. The thick and pungent smell of burned sugar rises in the air, envelops them with sweet victory. All that stands between the rebels and the sea is the city filled with French troops lying in wait for their arrival.

The smell of smoldering cane energizes Boukman. He looks to the east, then to the west, and feels his blood boil at the sight of the burning fields. His head swims in a torrent of red. So inebriated is he with the dream of victory that he forgets to sing to the gods for guidance as he swings a cutlass over his head in a wide arc and yells to his troop to follow him through the city walls.

The commanders of the French army are a godless crew; they do not have to look east or west before fighting the motley crew of Africans descending upon them. Bullets fly through the night air, splicing brown skin much like machetes hack through stalks of cane during cultivation.

Boukman strides through the hail of bullets, holding the conch shell of the slave's emancipation in his right hand and a cutlass in his left. Gray steel slices through the air. Boukman feels the cut deep, deep, the instant of his dying, the instant of his body collapsing in two against the beaten ground, blood seeping into the earth his tears have showered only hours earlier. Boukman's head lays severed from his body in one, clean, clean stroke.

The French soldiers place Boukman's shriveling head on a spike in the middle of the town square. They do not know that the dead have a way of rising again. This fact Henry Christophe has learned in the cradle of his birth, in Grand Anse, Grenada, years before the Revolution has even begun. He has encountered the dead long before thinking of crossing the waters from his own native land to this land of negritude where men and women of dark hues could govern their own minds and their fates.

Some eleven years earlier, in 1780, Christophe had felt the first pounding yearnings for freedom in his heart. He had felt destined for greater things than his father's life as a metalsmith, more than his mother's life with her household duties. He had heard murmurings concerning the uprisings in the neighboring islands, especially in what was then known as Saint-Domingue, what was to become Haiti. He was presented with the opportunity to join a French regimen headed for Savannah, Georgia, to fight on American soil. His father had refused the French officer's request, pleading that he needed his son's hands as the wars raged on and more arms were needed, as were shoes for the horses of battle. In that moment's refusal, all had seemed lost.

As he heard his father's "no," Christophe ran away from his father's house, his mother's hands, spirit on fire. He ran to the sea for comfort. Only the sea had the effect of calming him. In a gesture of youthful frustration, he threw himself against the damp, beige sand, fists pummeling the ground like a man who had reached his Mecca after days and days of travel. The mountains rose on both sides of the harbor, to his right and left, ears at the ready to listen to his sorrow. The sun was falling slowly beyond the horizon, sending plumes of orange shimmering across the sky and the undulating waters. He watched the outlines of ships, cut-out pantomime figures thrown against the half-light. The beach was deserted. Stray dogs, consumed with the task of licking themselves free of roaming ants, sat beneath the shade of twisted tree trunks. Christophe was filled with despair, and the tranquility surrounding him oppressed him all the more. He had had enough of waiting, enough of watching the ships go in and out of the harbor without him on board.

Christophe stood at the lip of the ocean, spumes of water licking his feet tenderly. He felt his arms plunging through the salty liquid, up and then down, down and then up. He swam like a man possessed. His body pushed him on as if it knew some unfathomable secret, and Christophe followed his limbs into the warm water, followed his arms beneath the milky surface, guided his legs in the same, smooth, rhythmic motion. He sank into the murky depths of blue-green waters, schools of multicolored fish gliding past him, algae clinging, then melting, against his smooth legs. He found himself swimming parallel to the belly of the sea, pink shells imbedded in her soil. He did not know how he breathed, how he continued as if gliding on air.

A dark expanse before him pushed Christophe to fight the currents of the water that had been holding him up. It was a battle to move but he inched forward slowly, wanting to know what was hiding in the murky pitch. There, he heard the rattle of heavy chains. The sound was cavernous like air being pushed through a conch. It rippled through the water endlessly, deafening. The sound filled his spirit with an unquiet terror of the depths. He tried in vain to swim back, back with the current, and up, but the water swirled around him in a spiral. He spun toward the sound, the chains grating against the sea floor. When he stopped fighting the forces of the waves, he saw her: long black hair akimbo in the water like the branches of a strange tree reaching for sunlight. Her face, masked with a blue veil, moved softly in the water. The veil rippled, leaving him with the impression that white stripes ran the length of her long, oval face, a face dark like coal, eyes black like midnight, a necklace of indigo blue stones fastened to her neck resembling those his mother wore daily, telling him often that they would be his someday, someday when he was ready to face the world. The mermaid (for that is what he thought he saw though no scales graced her lower body, no fins her feet) danced on the sand of the ocean floor, her bare feet brushing away weeds and shells; her arms raised above her head; her body a candle flame flickering against the blue-green of the water. The chains, fastened to her ankles and wrists, moved with her like serpents to music. When she raised her head from her dance to look at Christophe, his heart stopped, and his lungs filled with water. He wanted to surrender to her, to the water, to everything his body knew that he did not know consciously. There seemed nothing beyond that moment. It was all.

A sound forced Christophe's eyes to close, to break the current holding him captive to the chained woman dancing against the ocean bed. It was a voice singing, softly, so softly *fa, fa, shhh, hahahha, shh, tah.* Then there were words in a voice he remembered from another time, another place, a voice from his childhood: *remember the ancestors when you leave this place. Remember that it is they who have given you great power. They will guide your vision. Stay close to the gods, Christophe. If forsaken, we will haunt you.* The words faded with a tremor of the water and his body was released from the spiraling waters. He rose to meet the shore. The sea spat him out into the tangle of his wet clothes.

To the day of his death, in the monumental palace he had built as a testament to his power and vision, Christophe wondered if it all had been a dream. When he returned to his parents' home, his mother held out the blue stones, telling him she had had a vision the night before. She explained that Ochún had been his midwife. In her dream, she had seen him wrestling in water, faced by Ochún's deathly half-sister, Olokún. *Your waiting has at last ended*, she said. *You must go where the spirits want you to go*, she continued, *to Saint-Domingue*. His father sat outside the front door of the house, on a bench set against the wall, smoking on a pipe to measure the passing hours. From that day on, the eyes of the woman he had seen beneath the sea would haunt his days on earth, they who bore a forbearance of his own, untimely, death. He had put the necklace on to please his mother but it left him feeling as if there was a chokehold on his very breath. Once the ship left the harbor and his mother was out of sight, he slipped the necklace into his pocket, later into a velveteen pouch, promising himself to wear it again when its time had come, fearful of the powers invested in it by the goddesses of the seas, fearful of the powers they had seen fit to lay across his shoulders.

Christophe had seen many things since that time of naivete, of innocence. He had left his parents in Grenada and followed the French into Savannah, fighting at their side almost like a free man and then onto Saint-Domingue in the midst of chaos and revolution. He had worked for years in a hotel and eventually joined the rebel forces when he heard about Toussaint L'Ouverture defecting first from the French army and then from the Spanish to lead the slaves. He had become a soldier for the cause and risen in the ranks to hold his own alongside Toussaint and Dessalines. All the time, he saw himself closer to the riches he desired. The blue stones lay tucked away and out of sight. He dreamed now only of dizzying power and, as the colony crumbled, the French losing their power day by day, it seemed within his reach, just beyond the shadows of Toussaint and Dessalines both. Two men he admired and resented simultaneously and, in Toussaint's case, sometimes did not understand. Dessalines he understood clearly. The man was crazy for blood and revenge, inebriated with his own power. Christophe recognized that same desire flowing in his own veins. He had come to understand the source of the madness when he had heard of the ways in which the bodies of Africans and mulattos alike were being tortured by the French, who saw the continued resistance of the former as a sort of aping, unnatural violence. Christophe saw things he could never have conceived in his own mind. He wrote notes in his journal: *The French invented a new machine of destruction, in which victims of both sexes, heaped one upon another, were suffocated by the smoke of sulphur. What could they do against such tactics? Perhaps Dessalines was not so crazy after all. In the end, Dessalines died as he lived, by the cutting of the sword:*

Without the sounding of the conch, without the beating of the drums, the men gathered at the foot of the fragrant eucalyptus trees lining the hills and conspired against Jacques I, their new Emperor, their once treasured Papa Dessalines. They summoned the great man out of his plantation house for a meeting in the capital. Dessalines traveled far from home, south from Marchand, down the coast to Saint-Marc, where he stopped to look at the sea, not knowing it would be his last time. The troops converged to meet him on a footbridge leading to the capital, a bridge called Pont-Rouge, red bridge. They were surrounded by fields of rice, sparse patches of young cane. As Dessalines was forced down from his horse, a young man cried out: "*Liberté ou la mort!*" and shot the old warrior through the heart. The soldiers cut into Dessalines' flesh, severed the head from the neck, limbs from torso. The men had had enough of war. Someone set fire to the dried stalks of cane, the thin shoots of rice. They took the jewels from his severed fingers and left him to the crowds, who pummelled his body, eventually dragging it through the emptied streets leading to the capital before his soldiers took it upon themselves to bury the remains.

"Slaughtered like a dog," a country woman had observed. They say she was clothed in thick skirts, a multicolored, patchwork apron, a red kerchief losing itself in the wide umbrella of the flamboyant tree above her. She stood there, they told Christophe the news as he sat in a luxurious hideaway, smoke billowing from the fields in front of her and repeated to no one in particular, "just like a dog."

Christophe went on to lead the north of Haiti into a period of hitherto unknown prosperity. He built sumptuous palaces to prove the worth of Africans in the New World. One of these was called the palace of 365 openings because it had 365 windows. His favorite, at the foot of the Citadel, was called Sans Souci, because, there, he found no worries to trouble him in the beauty of the imported Italian marble and commissioned frescoes decorating the high ceilings. But nothing was to equal the Citadel itself, perched atop the mountain La Ferrière. It was meant to stand in defiance of outside attack but never served a day in war. Civilians were enslaved to create its glory; soldiers were walked off its high walls in a pageantry of power and fell to their deaths. Too many lives were lost in the making of its glory. But nothing could stop Christophe, except those eyes, the eyes that came to haunt him from the bottom of the sea. Those eyes came again in the form of an assassin, a young man named José forced to work on the Citadel beyond his capability, who watched others fall to their deaths to satisfy Christophe's ego. Like Christophe before him, he too had been a man of modest means. He too had cleaned dishes in a hotel and tried to take up arms for a good cause. But nothing could have prepared him for what José saw in Christophe: a man whose once good nature became distorted by the myth of a common good, a Black kingdom that none could enjoy but the few with power, the few who now obstinately defied the ancestors and gods who had blessed their resistance and seen them through to victory. *Why had they forsaken the gods?* José wondered to himself, plotting revenge on behalf of sea and sky.

Christophe, recognizing his own death in José's eyes, killed the young man first, the year being 1820.

With the same gun he had used that night against José, Christophe stands beneath the arch of his palace, the most beautiful place he could have conceived in his life. The Citadel is complete and will stand through time. Christophe kneels beneath the arch and seeks mercy from the spirits he has, with one shot to his heart, abandoned. As the blue stones of the necklace his mother had given him long ago spin out of the pocket of his long coat and hit the ground, he hears his wife, Marie-Louise, then expires.

Marie-Louise speaks to the guards, who have entered the room before her. They are crying. "It's now that you cry," she says, thinking of the months of decline her husband has endured since the heart attack that left him weak as a newborn chick, a heart attack he suffered after an attempt had been made on his life.

"It's now that you cry," she repeats bitterly, stretching out the words, leaving the room with a flourish of her skirts as she kicks away the blue stones from beneath her feet and makes her way to the corpse, as if they alone are responsible for her breaking heart.

Léogane, a blind man of Christophe's employ, upon hearing the stones clang against the cold marble of the palace floor once the body has been picked up on a cloth stretcher to be buried in the Citadel, Christophe's monument to immortality, scoops them into one hand and into a lined jacket pocket. No one notices his quicksilver gesture; Léogane is not a man who attracts attention. His blindness makes him useful, with his acute sense of hearing. He stays out of others' way and is rewarded with his own silences, his thoughts, an awareness of more than those around him would allow, of their habits, their flaws, and better points. They do not know he is a seer of sorts, blind as he his. Hours later, standing among the throng paying their last respects to the king, Léogane feels a strange heat coming from those stones.

Christophe is buried, a bronze plaque fastened to the slab placed upon his grave with the words: I shall be reborn from my ashes. No one would wish it so, thinks Léogane.

Léogane forgets the stones until he returns to his living quarters in the palace. His wife, corpulent and overdressed in her muslin skirts, sits in her rocking chair after a long day of packing the royal family's belongings; the family is preparing to leave the island of their father's death for the sparkling Mediterranean shores of Italy. Léogane will forget the stones until his sighted daughter, only eight years of age, a thin sapling of a girl, midnight-blue hues in her skin, pulls them one by one from his coat pocket and strings them on a piece of burlap twine. Once all seven olive-shaped stones are strung together, separated each from the other by a nimbly made knot, she drapes the newly assembled necklace around her already long-stemmed neck, murmuring her awed thanks for such a gift on a day of burial. Léogane smiles, "What color are they?" he asks.

"Blue," she says, her small, high-pitched voice impish, pleased.

"Blue for the sky and for the sea," Léogane says. "Blue for love and for desire."

"Look, Manman," she says, running to her mother already falling fast asleep in her rocking chair. "Look what Papi has given to me."

"Que Dieu nous bénisse," her mother says, awakening, recognizing the king's jewels, stones that seemed to have no value but that the king often hid away under lock and key, taking them out only on days of fretting, days when he would talk long to himself, pacing the halls of the palace, trying to determine how to outmaneuver enemies imagined or real. She makes the sign of the cross in quick reflex and looks to her husband, knowing that he has no thoughts of returning the necklace. Perhaps it has found its rightful owner.

"En vérité," Léogane sighs from across the room, as if hearing her very thoughts. May the truth protect us always, he thinks, bulbous lids falling over glassy eyes.

Almost two hundred years later, the Citadel stands there still, atop the Pic Laferriere. Pilgrimages are made to it yearly by citizens of nations from around the world. Christophe, as he had wanted, is remembered for his Black reign and extravagances, for his rise from pauper to leader of a nation. The palace of his death, Sans Souci, is eulogized far and wide. Yet other things remain: the whispers in the eaves of the ruins of his palaces, the haunting eyes of a young man cut down before his time, and the blue stones, meandering through the ages, finding their way back to the sea and then to shore to find a new bearer, someone worthy of their power, someone who will bring relief to the poor and justice to the land.

What is invisible and yet still lives is more powerful than monuments or words engraved in stone.

September 7, 1991

Alexis

As hard as I try to keep them still, my hands keep moving, sometimes to brush away the mist on the windowpane, where I can see myself reflected against the darkness of night, sometimes to reach out to grab something from my backpack, or to brush down my hair, forward, with the grain, toward the contours of my wide forehead. They are anxious, my hands. They save me and dishonor me. I fold them in my lap, fingers lacing each other in short, thick braids of brown flesh. I want to be still. If it were not for these hands of mine, I could forget, just for a moment, the chaos I have left in my wake, in a piece of island so small as to be insignificant to anyone I would encounter on this swiftly passing road. If I could forget, I could feel exhilaration with nothing to fear. For now, this road seems to be leading toward nothing. There are miles and miles of nothing before me.

My fingers unclasp themselves. There they go again, with minds of their own, reaching for pencil and paper. Tracing a line here and then one there until another landscape from memory emerges: the tall walls of the Citadel standing at the top of the mountain where my village lies cradled at its gargantuan feet. We, the descendants of those who survived the Citadel's making, who survived King Christophe's egomania at the turn of the century. And yet we revere him, our King, our Savior. Without him, we would not have had a road leading out of the mountainous wilderness to the city by the ocean, Le Cap, once named Cap Henry, for him. Without him, I would not have gone to school and learned to draw these things: outline of Ayiti chérie in the shape of a scorpion's claw; faces of those left behind: Philippe, Mamie Leila, my mother, my father, Marthes. The Citadel loomed above us all of our days, a reminder of what the muscles of men can do and what the want of power can destroy. We suffer still under the shadow of what Christophe left behind. My itching fingers know this truth. They cannot rest for anger of what cannot be changed, what they wish they could redraw and remap. The world pilgrimages to our shores in search of the lost kingdom former slaves built from their own sweat and love of freedom. The world comes to see and delights in the colorful hues of our huts at the base of the mountain, at our strange accents pronouncing the words of its native tongues. The world gapes at us as if at curios in a shop and then turns its back on us, amused at our poverty, amused at the ancient splendour of a kingdom that failed to live up to its promise. They wash their hands of us and go back to their foreign lands with their forked tongues. We are left behind to gather up their rubbish in piles between the falling rose bricks of all that is left to mark the site of Christophe's best-known palace, Sans Souci. We gather up the rubbish and let it burn along with our dreams of never having to set eyes on a pale tourist again. But they come again and again and we are none the richer for their visits. We look down in shame at our clothing, at the torn remnants of our roads, and eventually we turn from each other, not understanding what has brought us the aching in our chests and bellies, the vacancy in our eyes.

I am far from home and I think of those I have left behind in the echoes of the past. Am I to see them again? I wonder. I try to clench the pencil tighter so that my hands will stop their broad strokes. It will take practice for them to unlearn these movements. But I will have to teach them silence. The truth is this: if I were to follow my hands, I would have to stop running. I cannot stop running. I will have to teach them to be still. But I do not know exactly why I am running, and to where, and to whom. I should be asking myself, from whom? from where? I am too tired to think. My fingers draw in answer to the chaos of my mind.

It is difficult to explain. I have found no one yet who has understood the story of my life. What it has meant to me to be born under an unforgiving sun, in a village where poverty is a way of life. I was born to parents who thought they could change the world, if not in their own time, then through me. My father owned land and hired many of the villages for their labor; he paid them a fair wage. My mother taught drawing lessons in the harbor of our kitchen. They are modest people, my parents. Class has kept them from mixing with the villagers in ways that get closer to the bone, closer to the self. Yet, they sent me to the public school of the village so that I would be one with the people, so that my mind would be as one with the hearts of the villagers. And they allowed me a best friend I have had since the earliest days of my childhood. His name is Philippe. Philippe is the son of no one. His father is unknown, his mother long dead. His grandmother has taken care of him through the growing-up years, his grandmother the laundry woman who washed our clothes and returned them blanched and pressed early on Sunday mornings. Our parents hardly knew each other, but Philippe and I, we are as close as brothers who have suckled milk from the same breast, who have been born from the same womb.

My parents have made sure that I have learned to read, to spell, to count, to apply my mind to all worlds of things. But I do not know how to plough the earth open, to make it yield its fruits. I am as unconnected to land as a fish in its water. I do not know where my stream lies. I am running, swimming over land and sea to find it. Yes, I will admit it: I am running away from Ayiti and all of its misery, all its broken promises and terror of a history.

You see, I was there. I am not talking out the side of my mouth. I was sheltered by my parents and the Jesuit priest, our schoolteacher Pè Joshua, with all my book learning and staying indoors. But I was there. I was there sitting in front of the local Tele at the Lotto stall when Baby Doc and his wife Michèle sped past the international reporters on their way to the airport only five years ago. *Was it possible?* I asked myself, *Could they really be leaving?* My friends and I thought it was a *truc monté*, a joke, like those shows where an unsuspecting common person is duped into believing something they know cannot be true, like those photographs in American magazines that someone has made up in a lab to sell their rag, but it was true. The next day, all the papers carried the headline: Bébé Doc ousted, gone! And the people in Port-au-Prince danced on his father's, Papa Doc's, grave, and wished him and his wife dead too. Up here, near Le Cap, there was not much we could do. But we watched and listened to the radio, and when it was clear that the Duvaliers were not returning, we turned on those who had been the instrument of their destructive powers.

Macoutes were dragged out of their cars and burned alive in the middle of the street, others were beaten, denounced, houses of the Duvalierists looted and turned inside out. I saw these things with my own two eyes. I was frozen to the stool while all this was happening, on the TV, on the streets behind me. I did not know whether to stand, whether to turn right or left. I did not know if I had the power to loot or set a building on fire. I had learned for too long how to be quiet and still against all the things that went on around us, all the invisible things

3

that transpired, the *teledjòl* in the street letting us know who had been imprisoned, whose limbs twisted out of shape in Duvalier's prisons.

In those days of terror, especially those before my birth, when François Duvalier reigned supreme, our own angel of death made flesh, villagers came home looking like *zonbi*, like all the lifeblood had been drained of their bodies, and we knew without knowing that something had gone terribly wrong. My mother's older brother was one of the unfortunates who came home like this one day, beaten down, feet dragging in the dust, shoeless, as if his spirit had been driven out by some force of malevolence that had caught him off-guard. The family arranged to have him sent away to Canada, to the home of some villager who had gone before and would make some room. I do not know how they got him out or what he had done to deserve to be driven out in this way. I had not yet been born.

The year was 1986 and finally, finally, it had all come to an end, the lies and the half-truths, the disappearances and the bones broken beyond repair. Bébé Doc was driving himself to the airport. Who would have believed it? He was driving himself! No chauffeur, no smoked glass. He was in plain sight, with his wife at his side smoking like a chimney. Were they afraid we would stop them? Had our fear died with their Papa Doc, the great *Baron Samedi*—the *vodou* god of death? Did they even have souls? All these thoughts traversed my mind as I watched these incredible scenes unfold. I was sixteen, seventeen, and the world of Ayiti I had known until that day was coming to an end. What would follow? What would come? What could we expect? My mother had told me that the Duvaliers were like nothing we had known before, and yet, as she looked up to the Citadel, its prow hanging over us with all its splendid grandeur, she would pause and say, "Of course, the history of these mountains paved the way." For a long time, I did not know how to take in those words. If Duvalier was the worse thing that had ever happened to us, then how could we have known what he was capable of doing? I read and read in order to understand the wisdom of my mother and of the ancestors before her. I read about Henry Christophe and the lengths he went to to secure his empire. Machiavelli was right: absolute power corrupts absolutely. So it can be, even for former slaves.

I would like to believe that things could be different in my homeland of Ayiti, but what proof do I have that anything will change? So I am running, but my hands, these narrow fingers, will not let me go freely. They drag up pieces of my memory even as I tell myself to forget family, landscape, and everything in between. But if I were to forget, then I would not flee and perhaps I would return. Do my hands know this? I watch them making quick strokes of pencil against paper, thumbs spreading out the soot to create the illusions of shadows below the nub of a nose, the length of a jutting jaw. I refuse to see the face there and quickly blacken the whole so that the face is lost beneath thin layers of powdered lead. If I can break this connection between mind and hand entirely, I will be free.

My mother once told me that my hands move so much because they are the recorders of my every dream. When I draw, paint, attempt a hand at sculpture, what emerges is always the product of some other world where I have ventured, unconsciously, in dream. My hands remember what my waking thoughts will not.

I am fearful of my dreams.

Philippe

Philippe sways back and forth and the sky appears to undulate like a pool of clear water in which a stone has been thrown in the luminous halo bending itself around his head. He closes his eyes against the brightness of the morning light streaming over the mountain ranges. A soft breeze touches his cheek. It reminds him of a mother looking in on her child as it sleeps, though he can hardly remember his mother, much less the feel of her fingers. He has a vague memory of the outline of her hands. When he thinks of those hands, he imagines wood splinters: uneven, fissured, rough and broken edges of nails. He would have liked to have imagined her fingers round, smooth, bordered with a healthy rose glow, but those imaginary fingers could not have been those of a washerwoman as she had been, like her mother before her. His mother's fingers were tired and Philippe does not know if they were ever more than that.

Philippe inhales deeply. He feels deflated. The air is thick with the scent of the sea, ponderously saturated with salt. For a moment, he feels peaceful. He stands very still, still like the few trees left uncut on the balding, deforested mountaintops surrounding him. Nothing had been the same after his mother's return from the capital, where she had gone in pursuit of her heart, dreams that a man had promised her and seen fit to destroy piece by piece. Even in death, she was the speculation of endless rumors about the man who had brought her home and the wife that had sent a curse to take away her spirit. His grandmother was grief-stricken by the loss, cutting back on her laundry clientele one by one over several months until she almost never left the house. It was as if the rumors and questioning glances of villagers had caused her to shrivel up inside, pushed her up the dirt road leading to her small hut of a house lying dormant below the shadows of the mountains above, behind the cloak of the vines growing wild in her front yard. She grew rounder from inactivity even though she continued to take in loads of wash to make a living, leaving clean and pressed basketloads by the gate to be picked up, waiting for dirty loads to be brought in by Philippe on his way home from school. She grew quieter and quieter over the years. The only noise she made was with the creaking of her rocking chair on the porch where she watched the comings and goings of the villagers. She would make the effort to raise her hand "hello" when she saw someone she knew from her own growing-up years. The old people still came to exchange a word or two, but the young stayed away, spreading the lie that the house and all within it were cursed. Then, some years later, when Mamie's own health began to fail, Philippe began to take time from his studies to make sure they had decent food on the table. New rumors started about how he was making ends meet.

Philippe is thankful that those rumors have never reached Mamie's ears, and yet it also means that he lives with the secret on his own, especially now that Alexis has gone. Even though that secret, he feels, is part of the reason Alexis chose to leave.

Eyes closed, Philippe wonders what these hills would have been like in King Christophe's day. Philippe feels his feet upon the ground, so soothing. He breathes in and out. All this is his, for the moment: the rolling hills, the canopy of sky overhead; the flamboyants a carpet of red along the paths leading out from the mountain to his village. There the houses are painted bright colors of mauve, indigo, azure, so the tourists will think that they are not poor like the others in the neighboring villages but happily entertaining their thirst for history and new discoveries. Tourism is the biggest magic trick ever invented, he thinks, a sleight of hand made possible by the blindness of the onlooker, his or her inability to see reality as it is, the willingness he or she has to see only one's own image in the distortions of the carnival mirrors offered by marketwomen in their stalls as they whittle "authentic" images of Arawaks or braid straw into pleasing hats or bags. Philippe feels the king on this bright Sunday morning. He understands clearly why Christophe would have chosen these hills to build his palace, Sans Souci. No worries. As if such a name could have changed the course of their history.

Philippe sighs, opens his eyes. He feels blinded by the blue-green of the sea and sky embracing the coastline of the sprawling city down below. The sea appears to cling to the earth like a parasitic crayfish, like a scorpion ready to fold its manacles upon an unsuspecting prey. The sea has reclaimed, slowly, the shoreline, chipped away at the mass of concrete that used to buoy a promenade very popular in the early days of the city, so popular that the city dwellers took to saying that its present erosion was due to the weight of the tourists, that the sea had had nothing at all to do with it. Philippe prefers to think that the sea is their secret ally, breaking things down that only remind them of a past ensnaring them all in this senseless cycle of giving up dreams for the pleasure of the colonials, old and new. *Damn them*, Philippe thinks to himself, *damn them all to hell.*

As Philippe walks along the shore caught up in his thoughts, he stumbles on a crack in the pavement. *Ah*, he thinks, *the sea is bringing me back to earth.* But as he looks up, he is startled by a woman rising from the depth of the waters a few feet below him, beyond the broken concrete of the dissolving promenade:

Her wet body rises, a piece of ebony driftwood spat out from the lip of the sea. Foam tongues lick her bare feet. She does not notice the stir she has caused. Her body glistens, shimmers, a knife blade hit by a ray of sun. In her hands, she carries her clothes folded neatly one on top of the other as if she has simply walked out of her house earlier in the morning with the intention of doing the laundry. But her clothes are dry as bone, her hands marking them with the wetness of raindrops, a necklace of blue indigo stones, a webbing of transparent seaweed wrapped around her throat. An apparition, this is what she is. The woman pays him no attention even though her naked body draws closer to Philippe with each of her sure steps advancing from sand to broken rubble. It is then that Philippe notices her unblinking eyes. *Léah*. Léah, the daughter of Léogane, the old man who has no eyes with which to see, who can remember anyone in the village from a scent they carry in the marrow of their bones, a song in their way of speech, a dance in the way they set their feet against the ground for walking. Léogane tells stories of these hills, of his own great-great-grandfather who once worked in King Christophe's Sans Souci palace, a man as blind as he.

Léah is not a storyteller like her grandfather, and yet, somehow, the family's genetic predisposition to blindness had successfully skipped her mother's generation and alighted upon her, perhaps a welcome gift. Léah is a seer, or so Léogane says. Léogane claims a great many things. He often speaks of ancient documents that have been handed down to him through the generations from the king's court in Sans Souci. Who knew what to believe. But Léah is a different matter. Her presence is sufficient to inspire confidence in all of Léogane's pronouncements and mutterings.

Philippe has not seen her in years, not since long-gone schooldays. She had always been the freest being Philippe had ever encountered. He recognizes now the stiff way she has of holding her shoulders back, the

8

swooping curve of her wide forehead, the skin dark as winter plums, the full, pinkish lips. Lips that once closed against his in a butterfly-winged kiss, on a school bus returning from a long trip to the capital, the trip that had been his unmaking, especially in Alexis' eyes, a trip he was forced to remember more often than he liked.

Her silence, her beauty, keeps him from crying out her name.

Some in the village are frightened of Léah's mouth, seemingly emptied of words, her still eyes that seem to bore right through her onlookers. Some say she is one of the undead, hair cut close to the scalp as it is, wearing a string of thick, olive-shaped blue stones around her neck that resemble a necklace it is rumored once belonged to King Henry Christophe. *Well*, Philippe remembers hearing the villagers say, *wasn't that the same as drawing a curse upon your neck, cursing yourself?* Philippe wonders what the villagers thought they knew about Léah. They whisper terrible things. They say she likes women, *that* way. He wonders about the kiss the two of them had shared. He wonders what the villagers think they know about him. He tries not to look too long at Léah's lean body, the roundness of her breasts, hips swaying like palm fronds, the muscles of her thighs tight and long. He wonders. She glistens like a dark pearl finely smoothed by the muscles of the rarest of sea oysters. Her beauty stills him, moves him. That morning, Léah does not appear to him to be of this world. She glides past him like a ghost, without a sound.

In an instant, the rutting through the rubble of a monstrous black pig the size of a mule with a smaller hybrid pig at its side shatters the moment. Glancing at the pigs, Philippe smirks to himself. The hybrid had been produced by crossing an indigenous Haitian pig with a gluttonous pink breed from Iowa, USA; rather than increase the income of peasants who relied on the black pigs for their survival, the Americans had succeeded only in spreading unlikely diseases in the indigenous species while the pink sows died from heat, or starvation, or mutated into these mottled grayish pink survivors that scavenged the streets alongside human companions.

The tableau strikes Philippe as an unlikely pairing of the mundane with the spiritual. The meaning of it all beyond his grasp. Every time he feels himself coming close to a revelation, it escapes him. Something in him understands that he will always be brought back to this broken piece of ground, that he will always remember Léah rising from the sea, their common mother, each of them wordlessly slipping by each other, leaving the scavenging pigs behind. She has taken his breath away, quietly, noiselessly. He fractures the silence with a raucous cough. He clutches at his chest and doubles over with his eyes closed against the pain. When he opens his eyes, it is to see frothy, bright red splatters of his own blood against the broken pieces of concrete between his feet. Philippe straightens up and wipes his mouth against the back of his hand. He will have to be careful from now on or else he, too, like his mother, will be accused of having *move san*, some affliction of the blood. But in his case, unlike his mother, the accusation will have some basis in truth.

Philippe sighs against despair. He will remember, always, this moment, and yet return as if something might change, as if the road will appear repaired and the scene replaced with the ancient, turn-of-the-century promenade, pristine, filled with nothing more than relics of this history they seem unable to escape, as if no blood has ever been spilled against this concrete from his own mouth or anyone else's before him.

Clinging to this hope, Philippe starts off to meet a new group of tourists, wondering which of his five languages will be of use today.

Carmen

"I've never asked for help from anybody," the woman whispers. She rocks herself, almost imperceptibly, back and forth, the back of her chair propelling her forward each time she makes contact with the worn, cracked brown leather of its cushions and remembers where she is and why she has come.

Carmen looks across her cluttered desk at the woman and pities her. She wishes she felt something else, something deeper, more compassionate, but her heart feels encased in a box, admitting nothing else but this, a shallow beat of recognition, a numbing nod for the woman's humanity.

The woman looks up, swallows hard. Her neck is swollen around the Adam's apple where the shadow of fingers held her firmly days ago, perhaps only a few hours hence. The wrinkled skin is purpled pink, bluesy. She clears her throat, "You are so young," she says to Carmen, a slight note of contempt in her voice. She means too young, too young to know the workings of the world, its ugly, scabbed underbelly. Then the woman's voice fills with resignation, "There are things that no one understands. *Ou pa kab konprann, ti fi.*" She has shifted to the familiar tongue of the island, the comfort of the Kreyol that filled her childhood days and nights, that breathed life into her tired limbs after school and days helping her parents at the family pharmacy in Port-au-Prince before they sent her North in her twenties in the hopes that she could do more with her life than toil for dictators in her home island. She has yet to escape the confines of this city which has been the site of her rebirth so far from Caribbean shores.

"Try me," Carmen says evenly, not moving an inch in her seat, not sitting up against the desk, elbows propping up a concerned chin, or hands sorting through the mounds of paperwork to create a landing strip for the story yet to come. She sits, almost primly, bracing herself mentally for the words about to spill from the woman's mouth, like tears too long held at bay, the fragments of a lump of pain rising vomitously from the abyss of a clenched throat.

"He's not a bad man, Carl," the woman begins. She looks up at Carmen with expectation written all over her face, a wrenching need for approval and compliance with her own denial.

Carmen has seen it all before. She refuses to acquiesce. Instead, she makes a point of taking a long look at the bruise extending itself from the woman's right cheekbone up toward the circumference of her right eye. The eyelid is swollen and barely open, revealing a sliver of brown floating in a watery bloodshot whiteness. She interrupts, "Perhaps your name?"

The woman's left eyebrow arches, "My name?"

"Yes. You haven't told me your name."

"Is that necessary?" the woman asks, the hesitancy creeping back into her voice.

"Yes," Carmen says. "But completely confidential."

The woman sighs. "This is what you all say and then your name finds its way into the papers or some newsletter or memo and everybody knows."

Carmen half-smiles. The woman is suspicious of her even though they are sitting in the Haitian Community Centre off Henri-Bourassa Avenue, the front window emblazoned with the Haitian coat of arms and the motto "L'Union fait la Force." Perhaps no one can be trusted anymore. Perhaps faith—for Haitians born during the thirty-odd-year reign of the Duvalier family which took up power in 1957—died long ago. Everyone is simply trying to survive now. Carmen gauges the woman's age and thinks to herself, fifty, fifty-five, no more than that. She speculates: born in the nineteen fifties among the wretched of the earth, scorching sun above and the waiting blue arms of the sea, awaiting drownings of a new age of despair. Boat people. Tuberculosis. Ringworms. Tapers. Diseases of the skin too numerous to name. Tortures in Fort Dimanche. SIDA aka AIDS. Market stalls overflowing with American contraband. Guava jelly. Chicklet packs in rainbow colors sold at market in straw baskets. Cane stalks. Wooden figurines whittled by the roadside. Paintings more beautiful than dreams. *Akasan* porridge served with strong morning coffee black like the midnight sky. Roosters crying out with the breaking sun. All this Carmen imagines the woman would have left behind—a one-way ticket to Canada from a well-meaning relative, or from a prospective employer promising room and board, a good wage, in return for cleaning the house, looking after the children, grocery shopping, and cooking the three meals a day for four (not including herself)—her ticket out of the nightmare of Haiti's impoverished dirt streets and houses broken down, walls crowded with too many unfulfilled dreams, their scent of despair burning the lining of her empty pockets, burning holes into her memory.

"Your name?" Carmen asks again.

"Gladys," the woman answers finally.

"*Mesi anpil*," Carmen says, moving a hand to a piece of paper jutting out from beneath a large pile of odd-sized sheets set before her to write down the name. "I don't need the last name for now," she adds, "So, you were saying, about your . . ." she reached for the right word, thinking of the practice of *plaçage* in Haiti, women and men cohabiting or setting up house without the benefit of formalizing their union, ". . . your husband?"

"Yes," Gladys replies, neither confirming or denying the form of the arrangement, "Carl is not a bad man but sometimes he does have a temper. As you can see." She looks down into the palms of her hands lying open in her lap. "But I am not here for myself. I am here because of our children. We have three: two boys and a girl. I don't want to raise them to see this kind of violence between their father and myself. I don't want his violence to spill over into their lives and tear them apart at the seams like overfilled sacks of rice."

Carmen smiles grimly at the image Gladys conjures up for her of rice sacks piled one on top of another at the docks in Port-au-Prince. She wonders where all that rice goes, how it fails to make its way into the ballooned stomachs of the young children standing by the sides of dusty roads, begging with the rotund emptiness of their eyes, the cars and jeeps speeding by.

Gladys looks across the desk at the young woman, with expectation for some solution. She has seen Carmen around the neighborhood this past year, walking to and from work along the narrow streets of Montreal, cocooned in her dark blue felt coat in winter, a gray windbreaker at other times. Gladys is thankful for the coming of winter despite the coldness that numbs the extremities of her fingers and pains the joints gnarled by arthritis induced prematurely by her work as a seamstress in a factory on the outskirts of town. She is forced to take the day off from work because of her bruises. Carl is at home sleeping off the alcohol that had turned him into a maelstrom of conflicting emotions, all of which came pouring out onto her, scorching lava. She had sat in the front room, looking out through the gauzy windows to the heaps of fallen leaves after she had got the children off to school. She had sat there and considered her options when she saw the gray of Carmen's fall coat go by the window. Minutes later she was putting on coat and scarf, the running shoes she had been wearing to and from work for the past five years without change, and followed Carmen's footsteps down the sidewalk to the community center. She had never been there before for a reason such as this. She had brought her daughter to playtime once or twice and her sons to weekend films. Most of the time, she spoke to no one except to utter a greeting of "*Koman ou ye*" here or there, a smile or two. She did not know other mothers, other women in the community to whom she could have confided. They always seemed so happy, their husbands more or less responsive to the needs of their families if not of the particular women they had wed. Some complained but always with such joviality that Gladys could not imagine their faces being slapped, shoulders punched, bones broken as hers had been, on occasion, over the years.

"We can help both you and the children," Carmen says then. "We can have you in a shelter by end of week, if you're willing. Or we can offer counseling." She peers at a leaflet on her desk, folds it, hands it over the piles of papers to Gladys, "We have individual and couple's counseling, group counseling. There's also a battered women's group."

Gladys looks up from the leaflet at Carmen in surprise.

"Yes, I know," Carmen says in response to Gladys' arched eyebrows. "It's something no one talks about at the luncheons and gatherings. But it's there in the community. It's there. And some people, even the men, are trying to change things for the better. What do you think, Gladys, do you want to be one of those people?"

Gladys is at a loss for words. She reads the flyer over and over again as if it would reveal the answer suitable to Carmen's question. What would she say to Carl if she agreed to counseling, even just on her own? What would he say if he found out that she was taking their problems out into the street? What she was doing was like hanging dirty sheets in the wind for everyone to smell. "*Je ne sais pas*," she says finally. "I don't know. I came here because I thought you could tell me what to do, for the children mostly."

"We *can't* tell you what to do, Gladys," Carmen replies, emphasizing the "can't," trying to keep the impatience she feels creeping up her spine from spilling out into her words. Why does she suddenly feel as if she can help no one? As if these women have got themselves into difficult situations of their own accord? Where is her compassion? "We can only help you once you've made a decision. The ball is in your court, so to speak." She tries to think of some way to encourage Gladys to take one of the options presented. The wrong thing said could send her scurrying away. "Perhaps you can go home, rest, give it some thought." She hesitates before adding, "Remember that whatever you do for yourself, the children will have to live with your decision. If you stay where you are, your children will have to be silent witnesses, or worse, if it hasn't already happened, victims themselves."

The woman nods. A thin stream of liquid squeezes past the swollen tissue around her bruised eye. She slumps into the chair, letting the chairback come into full contact with her own. "My feet are tired of walking," she says, "I spend all my days walking, from home to work and back again. And at work I am sitting all day, pushing pieces of cloth through needle and thread on the sewing machines, my right foot pedaling in time to the stitching. I am tired. You are too young to know how tired a body can become."

Carmen does not interrupt. She is thinking of how tired she is herself. She wonders if everyone conceives of their own body's pain, their life's worry, as isolated from the pain around them, carried in bodies not so different down narrow alleyways and cramped apartments. The small of her back has been aching since mid-afternoon. Thankfully, she had managed to hide herself behind her pile of papers, busying herself with administrative tasks until Gladys had been ushered into her office. She had barely looked up, offered a curt smile, and turned to the business at hand of attempting to help a woman who clearly was in need but did not want the help she had to offer. Fear was standing in her way. Nothing more than that.

Gladys sighs. "Do you know the name of Marie-Josèphe Angélique?"

The terms of the discussion are shifting. Carmen is unsure of where this is leading. She glances at the flyer in Glady's hands and wonders if the woman will choose one of the alternatives by the end of the interview. And here she has become the interviewee. "No," she says finally, "I can't say that I have."

"But you've heard of the fire of 1734? The one that burned down a part of Montreal?"

"Vaguely, yes," Carmen replies.

"Marie Angélique was my great-great-great grandmother. She was the one who set fire to the city."

Carmen leans forward. Her breasts graze the top of her desk. She keeps both arms folded across the steel border of the protruding front drawer and lets her weight sink into it. She thinks she has perhaps heard Gladys incorrectly, that she has not been paying good enough attention to the woman's words. "She what?" She has misjudged Gladys for Haitian, or is she a mixture of heritages, Canadian and Haitian like herself?

"She set fire to the city. Yes, she did," Gladys nods and her eyes fix upon something slightly to the right of Carmen's head as if she is talking to someone standing directly behind the young woman.

Carmen does not move.

"Marie-Angélique walked the streets of this city long ago, not knowing whether to head east or west. All she knew was that she had to leave to escape being sold away from her family by her master. She set fire to his house and burned it and the city down." Gladys' gaze returns to the soft features of Carmen's face. She smiles, "They won't tell you things like that in the history books when you're growing up. But I know where I came from. I know what strength I have. I can tell you this: one day, my feet will set to walking on these streets. When my children are grown . . ."

Carmen sits back into her chair, trying to stifle disappointment.

". . . I will burn his house down with everything in it. Everything except an old rug we have in the living room. It belonged to Carl's own great-ma. A woman who burned down a plantation in Grenada. Carl told me the story before we got married. His sister gave him the rug as they sent him out of the country. It convinced me to look beyond his bitterness, past the reasons that had brought him to Canada, expelled from his country." Gladys looks across the desk at Carmen: does she know Carl's past? That he has been involved with Duvalier's secret police? Even she does not know the whole story. "I wanted to believe our destinies were locked together as one. We come from strong women, my husband and I. Resisters and survivors. But all we've managed to do is create more pain for ourselves in the world. How is that? How does such a thing happen?" Real tears began to flow from Gladys' eyes then; she seeks to hide them in her wide palms, both hands flying up to her cheeks in unison. The skin on the backs of her hands are ashen, dry and cracked. They shake as they cradle her face.

Something within Carmen moves then. It is a strange sensation that rises from the depths of her belly and the life newly growing there, to her solar plexus, to the base of her throat, propelling her up from her seat, hands balancing her body to an upright position as she holds on to the arm rests. She makes her way around the desk, upsetting piles of paper as she goes.

She kneels clumsily by Gladys' chair, her body leaning away from the woman at an odd angle. She hands Gladys a folded tissue that has been stored away in one of the many pockets of her blue corduroy jumper.

Gladys takes the tissue from her hands into her own and continues to cry. Carmen holds an elbow and waits for the water to subside. She feels as she had as a child when watching the tides ebb away on a lakeside beach or at the mouth of the sea, wondering how long it would take for the tide to lower so that she could walk safely along the edge of the water, without worry. It makes her think of her mother, who has moved back to Haiti after divorcing her husband of twenty plus years, Carmen's father, only five years ago. Her mother who stayed in a marriage that only caused her pain year after year but who refused to leave because she was more worried about what the community would think than what her own children's eyes were witnessing, their mother's death, her shame cloaked in silence. What made life all the more difficult was the fact that Carmen's father was British Canadian; the chokehold on his wife's life was hidden behind a cold, civil propriety that he had learned at the side of his own father's knee, an immigrant from England who remembered the old country with fondness, who felt that Canada was the next best thing to being home. The fights Carmen had witnessed between her parents, followed by the long spells of quiet—like the quiet after a snowstorm when one wakes to snowbanks blocking front doors and garages and is left stranded on the edge of a white-blanketed world—had shaped her own existence, her ability to efface herself in gatherings and live buttressed within her own silences.

They sit there, ribboned by Gladys' gasps for breath and flow of tears. It seems that the tears will never end when Gladys finally sighs heavily, wipes them away, and looks down at Carmen, who is still looking at her with questions in her eyes, wondering how to help. It is then that Gladys notices Carmen's slightly rounded belly. She pauses, then smiles.

"*Wap pote bebe*," she says in Kreyol—you are with child. Gladys has only noticed because she too had hardly shown for months into her pregnancies. She suddenly feels a kinship with Carmen that reminds her of those mornings she had seen Carmen walk by their house. Their paths have crossed for a reason, but she does not know if she is ready to hear the answers this young woman has to present. She does not know if she is ready to walk away from her marriage. Then there are the children. Can she deny them their father? And who is their father? What good could they see in a man who looked right through them, his speech and actions betrayed by the alcohol he set flowing daily through his veins?

Carmen nods, smiles weakly. "Yes."

"When are you due?" Gladys asks, attempting to keep her thoughts clear of the confusion in her mind.

"A few months yet. Just getting out of the first trimester."

"Ah," Gladys replies, "You have quite a ways to go."

"Um-hunh," Carmen mutters. "It's my first. Sometimes it feels like it's nothing at all. Today it feels like a mountain I'm carrying." She laughs, "But I'm sure it will be worth it in the end."

Gladys' face turns to sadness once more. "Yes," she says, "children are a gift from above." She suddenly looks at her watch, reminded of how long she has been away from home. "I must go." She shoves the tissue into a coat pocket and helps Carmen to her feet. She smiles and puts a hand on Carmen's stomach, "You take care of the both of you," she says. "But . . ."

"I must go. Carl will be wondering where I've gone," Gladys interrupts.

"But what about the counseling?"

Gladys takes a last look at the brochure and sets it in front of Carmen's nameplate on the desk, "I'll think about it. I really will." With those words, she turns away from Carmen and retraces her steps to the front door.

Carmen watches as Gladys negotiates the slippery walk in front of the center, her bruised face hidden by a thick scarf. There goes Marie-Josèphe Angelique's *great-daughter*, she thinks. How long do the effects of slavery last? she asks herself. How many generations does it take for people to realize they have something to live for, even if the memories of the past are too painful to face? Was it the lack of turning to the pain that created more pain, more violence, more despair? Carmen returns to her seat at the desk. She is uncomfortable in her body, not large yet, not obviously pregnant. Like most of the women on her mother's side of the family, she hardly shows, especially if she chooses to wear dresses. She wonders what she will have to give to her newborn child when she comes, for she is convinced it will be a girl. Her dreams have told her so. She reaches across the desk for the flyer and writes "Gladys" on it, in case the woman returns.

Philippe

The last time he remembers having seen his mother well, she had just climbed into the back of a tap-tap on its way to the capital, a whole day's journey away. He remembers crying for her, with one hand outstretched and the other held back in the firm grip of his grandmother's large and calloused hands.

It was as if his whole world was disappearing into the crammed bus. All he could see of his mother before he fell and twisted himself around his grandmother's ankles in a small heap of defeat was a piece of her best calico dress. She had made it herself for the trip, and then to wear when selling goods at market in Port-au-Prince. It had been early in the morning, dusk, and the shaft of light falling between the trees into the clearing where a handful of the villagers had gathered to see off their relatives made everything seem bright through the cloud of his tears. The calico danced before him, scarlet bright like the skin hanging off a rooster's proud beak. Philippe remembered this every morning after her departure when the rooster pecking through the soft earth of his grandmother's plantings in their front yard would crow them to wakefulness. Then he would pray for his mother's safe return.

It took four years for Philippe's prayers to be answered. He was five years old and about to start school on the hill facing the Citadel. His grandmother had told him to expect his Ma soon, before school had even begun. He waited impatiently day after day when the tap-tap made its final stop at the foot of their hill and day after day he was disappointed. He would slowly make his way home in the dust lifted by other feet gladly welcoming their family member's return. School had already started and still there was no sign of her. He had wanted to show her off, to prove that she outsold all the village women who had gone before her and made a name for herself in the capital. The other children accused him of having made her up, all except for his closest friend, Alexis.

He was sitting on the front porch with a chalk plate in his lap working on his additions with a piece of chalk Pè Joshua, the schoolteacher, had given him for a whole week of practice when he saw a man and woman coming up the road to the gate of the house. His grandmother was not home yet and he wondered who they might be. The man was almost six feet tall and wore a stained gray fedora on his head. His shirt, open to the waist and exposing the muscled chest and stomach of a laborer, cascaded over faded green trousers. The woman was slumped into him, half-walking, half-dragged in the circle of the man's left arm. When they reached the gate, the man pulled a crumpled piece of paper from a back pocket and seemed to read something on it. He glanced at the gate made of painted-over, flimsy white iron. Among the vines created by the iron was the number of the house, 383. The man seemed satisfied, pushed the paper back into his pocket and removed his hat from his head. With his hat in one hand, and the woman in the other, he pushed the gate open with a nudge of his foot. It creaked open. Philippe jumped up against the boards of the porch. He felt a small sliver enter a muscle in his right thigh. The chalk fell out of his hand and between the boards of the porch to the ground below.

"*Ti moun*," the man gestured toward him, "*Ti moun. Vin ede m.*"

Philippe stayed glued to the porch, not knowing if he should advance or retreat, rubbing his thigh where he could feel the tickling of the sliver beneath the skin. Mamie would be along any minute now. Perhaps he could just stand there quiet until she appeared and told him what to do.

The man was standing before him in no time. He scowled up at Philippe. "Don't you recognize your mother?"

Philippe dropped the slate. He heard it crack. He hoped it had not broken in two.

"Is your grandmother home?"

Philippe shook his head back and forth, no. He looked furtively at the woman who this man claimed was his mother. He looked from her back to the fence where some of his schoolmates were gathering and tittering among themselves. This woman looked nothing like his mother, nothing like he had described her. This woman was frail, cheeks sunken in, eyes bloodshot and yellowed around the irises. Philippe noticed that she was wearing a calico dress but it bore little resemblance to the one his mother had been wearing on the trip to the capital. It was faded and ill-fitting, a dull orange and fraying along the hem. This could not be his mother.

The man smiled wearily. "Don't be frightened," he said, "she's not as sick as she looks." But before he had even finished his sentence, the woman clutched at his arm and coughed into one of her hands, bony of spent flesh, the remaining skin a dullish brown. Her whole body trembled as she coughed. The man grew serious once more and frowned. "I must get her lying down." He looked beyond Philippe and into the house for a sign of where to lay his charge. The woman was sagging at his side and breathing with difficulty, as if drowning in deep waters.

"*Sa k pase!*" a voice exclaimed from beyond the gate. Mamie was pushing her way through the crowd that had gathered there. As soon as she saw her daughter, one hand came flying up to her mouth and covered up her surprise. With the other, she waved the gaping bystanders by. She tried to recover her calm and turned to the adults standing alongside the children. "Aren't you ashamed," she said, "to let your children watch the ill as if they were at the circus? You should be ashamed!" She turned back toward the house and rushed as quickly up the path as her ample body would let her. She was a short woman, plump all around, and deeply proud of her small house and garden. She could not stand that the neighbors were looking upon them as if evil had fallen across the door to the house. She pushed by Philippe and invited the man in, helping him with the woman until they had her lying down on the bed with both her own and Philippe's pillow keeping her head high. She yelled out to Philippe to find sprigs of fresh mint and parsley in the garden and to bring them back as quickly as he could. When he brought them back scrunched tightly between the palms of his small hands, she took them from him and placed them in a pot of boiling water set upon the stove.

Philippe could smell cinnamon and sage in the air. The woman was very quiet on the bed. She seemed to be asleep. The man sat on the edge of the bed with the straw hat held stiffly between his knees. He was looking down at the slats of the floor that the grandmother had covered over with scraps of cloth sewn together for a carpet. Philippe stood out of the way, below the only window in the house, to the left of the main and only entrance.

"How did this happen?" Mamie asked the man, "I thought you were taking good care of her there."

"*Kisa konnen,*" the man shrugged his bulky shoulders, "*Je ne sais pas. One* day she seemed fine. The next day, *pouf,* she was coughing up blood."

Mamie slapped her thigh with a fist and turned on the man, "How can you say one day fine, one day *pouf*? How can you say this? You who were there every day."

"Mamie," the man tried to explain. His eyes were filling up with water. "Mamie. I did everything I could. I took her to the clinic. We got the medicine they prescribed. Nothing seems to work. We even went to see the *houngan*. You don't understand."

"No!" Mamie cried out.

She was ready to kill the man. Philippe had never seen Mamie so angry. Not even the time he pulled out one of her favorite flowers by the roots to see how it drank its water from the ground.

"You do not understand. This is my only surviving child and I sent her to you because you promised to keep her and marry her. You did neither. What did you do to her?"

"You don't understand," the water spilled out of the man's eyes.

"What?" Mamie continued to bounce her fist on her thigh. "What don't I understand? Explain to me!"

"My wife. My wife." The man seemed at a loss for words. His hands parted, one holding up the hat, the other balancing itself against the air thickening with mint and sage, fever and anger. The woman moaned beside him and seemed to be waking. He looked up at Mamie, looking as helpless as a child.

"*Seigneur,*" Mamie exhaled. "*Seigneur, Marie, Joseph.*"

"Yes. My wife. The *houngan* told us my wife must have had a powerful curse put on her because she hasn't been getting better even with the medicine from the clinic. She has only been getting thinner and her joints hurt her so much she cannot walk to market or sit in her stall all day if she can make it there. We've just been getting by with my work on the roads." He looked at Mamie again. "I know I should have brought her to you sooner but I was working, and at first she seemed not so unwell. You know the roads are slow to build these days. I was lucky to be working at all. She didn't seem so bad, even after we saw the *houngan*. I thought she could hold on for a while and things could get better." He paused. "I lost my job a couple of days ago. Something is going on with the military and there isn't any money to be made anywhere. I came as soon as I could get my affairs in order."

"Your affairs? You mean your wife," Mamie whispered.

"Yes," the man replied.

". . . and your children."

"Yes. I have two."

"I see," Mamie said. "I understand. You did not wonder about her child." She looked at Philippe then, still standing quietly beneath the window, holding his breath so he would not disturb them. "You did not wonder after his health or how he longed to see his mother again. This is how you have brought her home." Mamie slumped against the oven and remembered the tea. She poured the yellow-green liquid into a chipped cup her daughter had bought for her the month before her departure, the month she had spent all her nights laboring over the making of the calico dress in the orange light cast by the only oil lamp she owned.

The man stood up and moved away from the bed. He walked the length of the short hall toward Philippe and looked down at the child. "I'm sorry," he said. "I'm sorry." He walked out to the porch and sat on the uppermost step.

Philippe watched the man's back, the muscles stretching the weave of the cotton shirt between his shoulder blades, then turned his attention back to his grandmother and the woman on the bed. Mamie was holding the cup up to the woman's lips with her left hand and holding the woman's head and neck up with her right so she could swallow. The woman's lips touched the warm liquid. Philippe could see the steam rising above her forehead. Mamie made soft cooing sounds that he remembered from the last time he had come down with something. When the woman had finished drinking from the cup, Mamie eased her back into the pillows and patted her cheek. Mamie cleaned out the cup right away with water and a sliver of soap. As she set it to dry on a wooden cutting board, the woman started to cough once more. It sounded to Philippe as if her body had been taken over by an invisible force that compelled her to sit up as it hit her chest walls from the inside. Mamie tried to soothe the woman by rubbing her back but this only seemed to make the demon inside the woman shake harder. When the woman finally stopped her shaking, her dress was soaked through and in the space where the roundness of his mother's stomach would have been, there flowered instead an uneven, scarlet stain. It was the only part of the woman that Philippe could see as Mamie bent over the woman and began to disrobe her. "Out, Philippe," she said. "Out."

Philippe went out to sit by the man on the top step of the porch. His mother had come home. He knew it by the piece of calico on her dress that had turned scarlet with her blood. It was then that he remembered the red of the dress before it had faded and torn. It was then that he recognized the dress as hers. But he did not understand why the rest of his mother did not look like her. Why would a diabolic spirit have decided to take hold of her? As if guessing his thoughts, the man put an arm around Philippe's shoulders and squeezed him close. "She's cursed," the man said. "A *bokor*, a witch-doctor in the capital did it." Upon hearing the words, Philippe burst into tears.

The man was gone by morning.

Before and after school, Philippe helped his grandmother to take care of his mother. Sometimes neighboring women would come by with something to eat and they would look down at him with pity in their eyes. Everyone knew that a spell had been cast on her and that, because of it, she was *pwatine*. Her lungs filled with a sickly mucous and blood. They took her to the small clinic in the next village with the help of Pè Joshua. The doctor told them it was tuberculosis but there was nothing left to be done. She was too far along in the illness and if she had taken the cures offered in the capital and nothing had helped, then it was just too late for him to try. As soon as the villagers heard this news, that even the medicine of the white people could not help, they were confirmed in their suspicions. The spell was too hard to break; it had been cast through a *bokor* whose magic was too dense to be broken. Philippe's mother seemed to accept this. She lay on the grandmother's bed and awaited the Angel of Death to take her away. She spoke very little and lived her remaining days in great pain.

Philippe would read to her after school, and once she smiled as he read her a short poem from his primer by a man named Jean de La Fontaine, a poem about a crow who liked to eat cheese but lost his *rondèle* to a fox waiting at the bottom of his nesting tree. His mother smiled at him and held the point of his chin between two clubbed and stubby fingers. "There's a good lesson," she said to him, looking straight into his amber eyes so much like her own, "Don't try to grasp too much out of life."

Philippe would remember those words always. The same way he remembered his grandmother growing quiet and still every night her daughter did not sleep easily. The same way he remembered doing laundry after laundry to keep his mother in clean sheets between her night chills and day fevers. The same way he remembered emptying bowl after bowl of spat-up blood and streams of diarrhea into the ditch out back. He remembered his mother growing thinner and thinner as he grew inch by inch and began running races after school with his friend Alexis and the other boys. After four long months of these endless repetitions, she was dead.

Philippe remembers that his grandmother had spent the last weeks of that time patching up the calico dress after cleaning it in a solution of borax to enliven its reddish colors. That calico was the last thing he saw as the casket was closed over the tight lines of her emaciated face. It was the last thing he saw every evening before going to sleep and the first thing he saw upon waking as he stumbled in the soft blue of predawn darkness to help his grandmother prepare their day's coffee. Mamie had added a patch of the reddish fabric discarded from the calico dress to the rug they kept on the floor between the sink and her bed to keep the worn boards out of view. It would remain the first thing that came to his mind when he thought of his mother.

From that moment forward, in Philippe's mind, hope and death were forever associated with a taint of red recalling the flame and heat of burning fevers sent on the wings of curses no one had the power to stop, not even, it seemed, the very gods in their heavens.

September 8, 1991

Alexis

Sometimes, I swear I hear Philippe, the heart and soul of my childhood, speaking to me in my dreams. I feel as if I could open my eyes and there he would be, standing in front of me, arms folded against his stomach, rocking back and forth on the balls of his feet, laughing at me or laughing with me, as was his habit when we were children and all life seemed so clear to him, so opaque to me. I always felt as if I was walking ten paces behind him. He would always insist that we walked in each other's footsteps. The further I get from my beloved Haiti, the more I doubt his words. I have never doubted him more. I think it is because I have never doubted myself more. I have never had to look at myself so closely as now, for there is nothing of me reflected in the landscape rolling by as the bus makes its way through the South, nothing of me reflected in the faces of the other weary travelers by my side.

I rest my head against the windowpane of the bus and the dreams come, the memories, like a filmstrip unfurling itself against the dark screens of my closed eyelids.

The moment he could walk was the moment Philippe had found me, or I him. He was sitting on a mound of earth in the front yard of his grandmother's house watching ants crawl in and out of the ground in a wild frenzy as he tried to cover them with loose dirt. I had come through the open gate, unsteady on my newfound legs, attracted by the sight of Philippe covering and uncovering himself with earth and singing softly in that breezy way children have before they have mastered language and are told to hush their babble. We sat together for more than an hour, discovering each other's limbs and tickling places, until Mamie Leila discovered me and quickly returned me home. There had been rumors in the village that someone was stealing the children for months that year, even that someone was poisoning those that could not be carried too easily away. All the mothers paid the children close watch, so that theirs would outlive the shadow of death lurking around the edge of Haitian children's fifth year of life. But it was not so easy to keep track of the adventurous with work to be done all day to eke out a meagre living, the pile of fresh laundry to hang, pots of food to be cooked for the men returning from laboring in faraway fields; the women who labored alongside them had to do all for themselves and often for young children left in their hands for upbringing. Mamie Leila hurried nonetheless as she did not want to be suspected of ill-doing. She scooped me up into her strong arms, Philippe following after her, anchored with a fist wrapped around a corner of her work apron, and returned me to my mother down the way.

My mother and Philippe's grandmother did not have a lot in common. Even in a village there is such a thing as the barrier of class, even if the differences between individuals are slight. My own grandmother had been a market woman like Mamie Leila. Perhaps it was the memory of that old woman that kept Mamie Leila's fear balled up in her pocket and out of the way as she walked the road leading to our house. The families' fortunes had changed over the generations. My mother had been to school, and her brothers and sisters had gone away from the north to the capital or, better yet, far from Haiti to the continent. They led quiet, professional lives. My mother had married a laborer. This is what had kept her in the village. That day, for the first and last time, the two women shared a cup of tea.

"I hope he was no trouble," I imagine my mother saying in her French-accented, lilting Kreyol.

"No, not at all," Mamie Leila would have answered in her quiet way. "And how are your brothers and sisters?"

"All well, thanks to the gods. They send a little something once in a while. But we are doing all right."

We lived in a house twice the size of Mamie Leila's. Hers was no more than a dignified shack surrounded on all sides by wild greenery that she tried as best she could to tame and put to some use in her own concoctions and remedies against illness and spells. Sitting across the table with my mother that day, she had no clue that her work in that untamed wild would come to nothing when faced with the illness of her own daughter who had left so long ago to return only a ghost of herself to her childhood door. Mamie Leila was perhaps strangely comforted, in the absence of her daughter, by this neighbor of whom she knew so little.

Our house was shaped like an "L"; the main door led through the kitchen to an elbow-turn to the right leading to a small sitting room and a bedroom beyond it.

That day, the bedroom door was closed and light streamed in through a window Mamie Leila could not see. The light cascaded over our chairs made of wicker, and pillows neatly embroidered with folkloric scenes of cane cutters and women with wares balanced on their hands in brilliant colors.

"You have a lovely house," perhaps Mamie Leila would have said.

And my mother would have nodded, "Yes, we do what we can." Then she would have hesitated, thinking of the grandson playing at her feet with her own son and the clothes he wore, patched over here and there. "I give lessons to the children after school."

"Lessons?" Mamie Leila may have inquired.

"Drawing, mathematics."

Mamie Leila would have smiled, dimples flashing in the half-light of the kitchen. "Ah, that is very nice. Very good for the children." She may have wished she could have sent her grandson to this woman when he got older and could hold a pencil in his hands.

"Your grandson is welcome here any time," my mother would have said, sensing the old woman's discomfort. "Any time," she would have repeated with a nod of her head.

Above our heads, fresh bread covered by a thin piece of white terry cloth hung in a basket made of the thickly braided stems of green reeds. The green watery smell of the creek beyond the houses from which we pumped our drinking and bathing water emanated from the basket. The scent made my mother sigh in remembrance of days when things seemed easier than they were now, when her brothers and sisters had been there still and they were one of the most prosperous families in town, next to the mayor.

They would have spoken of the dreams they had for us as we sat on the floor, playing, looking like negative mirrors of one another. As a child, my complexion was the color of stewed sweet plums with the same golden glow of the preserves when spread upon crisply toasted bread. My eyes were then, as they are now, a deep brown, dark as night. Philippe was as light as I was dark, a red-brown like the earth we soon trod in the mountains, his eyes an amber that changed colors like a river reflecting prismed sunlight against a smooth riverbed lined with pink, black, and copper stones.

We clapped at our mothers and smiled wide toothless grins. The two women joined in, with their laughter flowing freely from the deep recesses of their open throats.

In that moment, when the worries of each woman seemed lifted by the presence of the other, they did not foresee that, in time, other things beyond the control of each would slip between them and divide them, as quietly and persistently as wind trailing so close to the ground as to swirl about the ankles and pick up force at the onset of a deep and destructive storm. Philippe and I were too young to ferret out the troubles lying ahead of us.

We learned to stand on our wobbly feet together, tracked mud through each other's houses, and sat at each other's kitchen tables day in and day out. My mother offered to teach Philippe to paint and sketch the things he saw in the mountains as she conducted her sporadic art lessons in her tiny kitchen. Mamie Leila taught me to cook in their small space. I took to cooking as well as I did to drawing; my hands loved the activity. Philippe left more than one blank piece of paper on my mother's kitchen table as his thoughts drifted off to other things, like where fruit flies came from and whether the stars shone during the day. Philippe liked to daydream with his eyes wide open, and I could often tell from looking at the changing intensity of the colors reflected there and the faintest of smiles animating his lips that he was in a world of his own that brought him great comfort in ways that I could never understand.

As we grew older, I lost myself in a world of drawings. I learned to speak to people in the village that way, across divisions of class and caste. I liked to draw things better than they were, the proportions often awry, objects far away seeming near enough to touch and objects close up drawn in deep recession. I called my style the "Alexis effect." It enabled me to keep close things at bay and draw close those things that seemed the least important to my person. It was about illusions and deception. But I used it to good purpose when I drew portraits, never accepting money from the poorer among us; I traded drawings for star apples and sweet, ripe mangoes, accentuating the positive in a man's face made hard by sun and work so that it would seem wise beyond the bearer's years, or making more beautiful in appearance a woman who had never had the time to take care of external things but whose spiritual presence was beyond words. When I wanted to, I could see deep into things and bring them out to the light. I did not always want to see deep into things, the way Philippe so naturally could, as he moved about the world. I grew up afraid of my own talents, fleeing from them, distorting them, laughing them off. All the while, Philippe spoke to spirits I could not see, stilling his spirit to quiet in the storm of my terror.

He would come to me, sometimes, nights I would be tossing and turning in my bed against a nightmare, and wake me. From the earliest of our days he would do this, as if my spirit had called out to him and he could do nothing but come to my aid in answer. When we were seven years old, Philippe had walked in the dark, down the dusty village street, the white of his nightshirt moving in and out of moonlight like a small, earthbound cloud, and climbed through the open window of my room. I had been dreaming of a light shining relentlessly in my eyes, causing me a blinding pain. I woke to Philippe tapping at my arm asking if the light had gone away. As Philippe slipped under the covers with me, I told him of my recurring nightmare in which something had been holding him down while snakes were trying to furrow through every orifice of his body.

"But how do you know they were snakes?" Philippe had asked.

"It just felt like that," I answered.

"Did you see them?"

"I told you, I couldn't see a thing."

"They weren't snakes."

"How do you know?"

"Because I was there," Philippe answered. "The light was the moon and the snakes were water. We were dancing beneath a waterfall and you were afraid of drowning so you fought the water spirits."

"What are you talking about?" I asked, but I knew there had been water somewhere in the dream and I remembered laughter.

Philippe, lying on his stomach, put an arm around my shoulder and turned his head away. I heard a light snoring as I asked myself how this could be. How could Philippe have entered my nightmare and turned it into the stuff of fantasy, of dreams?

It just is.

Startled at the voice I heard coming from nowhere, I lay very still, feeling the straw of the mattress beneath my back more sharply than I ever had before. The voice was Philippe's but Philippe was certainly asleep.

It just is.

The voice came again. Philippe's hand was limp against my shoulder. I thought about waking him. Then I thought I should just answer back in my mind: *It's all right.*

This I heard in answer: *It just is.*

31

I fell asleep.

In the morning Philippe was gone, and when I saw him later as we trudged down the dirt road on the way to school, neither of us mentioned what had happened. But I noticed that Philippe's eyes had taken on a sparkling golden hue, like pieces of amber polished by rainfall.

And now I miss the summer rains the way I miss Philippe, my brother of the sun, and yet I haven't changed since the moment I left Port-au-Prince. I just want to leave. I want to believe that my faith has been buried beneath the belly of the earth like the eyes of the young man I had been told had tried to kill Christophe in the last year of his reign. I didn't believe in the story. Why should I? It had so little to do with me, so very little.

I huddle against the window and pull my baseball cap with the initials NY down over my eyes to block the lamplight from my eyes. I am simply tired of traveling. I am tired of life. I cannot explain such tiredness to anyone. Each of us has a weight that must be carried through the world. This tiredness is mine. Even Philippe has not understood this about me. Even he questioned my departure only weeks ago as I told him of my decision. The world of our village had changed so much since the departure of the Duvaliers. I had been working with the grassroots organization associated with an American mission in Millot called "Deliverance" for almost two years. We had been successful in getting our candidate elected to the presidency. But everything had been falling apart. We had heard that Aristide would be deposed by the military within weeks. The military had been going through the villages roughing up those associated with Lavalas for some time now. If we did not get out now, there would be no telling who of us might survive. If I could get out, then perhaps my parents would be left alone. Perhaps we would all get to survive.

"Why go so far, frè?" Philippe had asked as we walked the narrow path leading away from the village into the bush of the mountain and the ruins of the Citadel shortly before I had accepted Pè Joshua's offer to leave the country with Deliverance. "There is everything here for us, don't you see?"

I stopped behind him and watched him move further and further away from me. This is what I remember of him most clearly: the way we left only one set of imprints in the soil when it was damp with rain. For the longest time, I had thought we were on the same path.

"Because," I resumed walking, "because I don't want to live and die here like our ancestors have. You hear the spirits, Philippe. I don't want to hear their moaning. They tell us about this boy who tried to assassinate King Christophe. Do we want to end up like him? This place is a burial ground." I gestured with my hands, that sideways movement I had learned at my father's knee. "This is a place where dreams are swallowed whole."

"What are you talking about?" Philippe threw back at me over his narrow shoulders that moved up and down like the two blades of a scissor. His body had death written all over it. Why did no one see that? He was a twenty-year-old man who looked like he was still fifteen, thin from undernourishment even though our parish was "blessed" by being zoned in a tourist area. Thin from the SIDA I suspected coursed through his veins. He had the long legs of a gazelle, and I had seen him run like one in the schoolyard when we raced as children. I wanted to leap toward him that day and make a joke, embrace him, but I felt a tiredness creep into my limbs and every step I took seemed filled with lead, almost impossible.

"I am talking about the future."

"There is a future here. If no one stays," it was then that he turned to face me, and I looked up at him from my position lower down on the path, holding my hand up against the sun so I could see the outline of his head peeking into the clouds, "then there will be nothing."

I laughed mockingly, "Who has ever been trying to stay, Philippe? If they could, people would be rushing to board every American Airlines plane that stops here and filling them to capacity with their calabashes stuffed full of herbs and chickens in wire cages. Look, look," I pointed down to the harbor, "there are ships, tiny little boats, down there by the docks, being plugged up with chewing gum so that they will hold ten bodies against the crashing waves. Everyone is leaving. Open your eyes, Philippe, *merde!*"

He turned back to the trail, "It is you who needs to open your eyes, *frè*. I'm not the one who's blind."

We were quiet for a time after that and our silence filled itself with an anger that felt to me like thunder. I could see the side of his face and it was like watching a streak of lightning move through the sky from east to west, from our beginning to our end. I turned to take a deep breath of air to rid myself of my resentment (I wanted him to understand: I wanted him to wish me well), and it felt to me like smoke was entering my lungs. He never stopped walking ahead until we arrived at the entrance to the Citadel. And then he turned toward Le Cap and looked hard into the distance.

"You see," he said, "that boy they say tried to kill King Christophe, Pè Joshua told me his eyes were buried down there somewhere. That means his spirit knows no rest." He turned to me then with eyes of sorrow. "And who will put his spirit to rest, my brother, if not us?"

"I . . ."

"I don't want to hear it," he said, waving a long finger into the air and walking the rest of the way into the Citadel.

"How can I explain to you if you won't listen?"

"Talk to the wind, *frè*. The wind always has an ear and it's to her that you owe an explanation, not to me." His voice rose and I could feel all his rage hit my body like one of those cannonballs Christophe had never had the opportunity of launching. "If you want to abandon your brother, like all the rest of them, then go ahead."

"But I'm not abandoning . . ."

He disappeared behind the thick walls made of huge, overlaid stones. No one knew exactly how the monument to Christophe's monarchy had been built. In school, they could hardly recount the number of men who had died making it, so they told us little else but of its greatness. Most of us swallowed the fable whole, without question. We were hungry for heroes . . . as we are still. It was something to be proud of when most of us were sitting on the hard wooden benches with our stomachs making noises like small, wounded animals. It was something to call our own.

The wind whistled into my ear. *Leave him be.* Then there was the emptiness of soundlessness and I understood for the first time that there is no such thing as a true silence. I understood for the first time that there is always something alive, moving: this gust of wind, touching our limbs each on his side of the wall, reminding us that we too are part of the world we so often choose to control and possess: this body that breathes, exhales, and breathes again because it has no other choice but to desire its own continued being. It too makes its own sounds: blood swirling through the veins, pumping through the heart, soft murmurs of bones moving against one another, muscles pushing and pulling in an intricate pattern of movement. These sounds moved through me then like a cyclone, a tempest, even though it seemed that all was still, quiet. *Leave him be.* My anger turned the wind away even though I listened to the words it carried to my ears. In that moment, I heard all the sounds rushing through my body, all the sounds this mountain had carried within it since before my day of birth and I hated Philippe like a fury. I hated him, of course, because I loved him like one does one's own self.

When it came time for me to leave the village, I walked the familiar terrain between the shacks of the village from the door of my mother's kitchen to Philippe's back door, remembering the first time my legs had carried me this far in search of a voice I could hear laughing in the distance, a boy my own age playing with delight at the sight of ants clambering over red earth with the spoils of war on their backs, the remains of a chicken's dinner. My feet, then, were heavy with the knowledge of no return, that this was the last time I would walk this path for some time.

"*Onè!*" I called out with hesitation, catching the word in the back of my throat as I stood at the back door of Mamie Leila's house. The door, steel twisted into a grid of palm leaves and painted an unlikely yellow, yellow like tarnished copper, had been left open; it swung on its hinges. Mamie Leila stepped out of the shadows of her front porch into sunlight that brightened her round, angelic face, the color of purple plums. "*Respè*," she said. Honor. Respect. These were the words that signaled true kinship in the parts where I grew up, the words Philippe and I used with each other to signal our brotherhood.

Mamie Leila came out into the sun hesitantly. She had a habit of staying out of the sun for fear of getting darker, a fear bred into her by an aunt long ago who had been as fair as the days were long. In those days, it was not so much the sun Mamie Leila was afraid of but the changes that had taken place outside her door. She could not face the brutality surrounding her: it pained her, physically. She spent many of her days lying down, resting, singing softly to the pain so that it would desist and leave her body in flight.

Mamie Leila was resting against a post on her porch. The post creaked softly against her weight. Slivers of white paint fell against one arm, looking like flecks of pollen against her dark skin. She sighed, looking at her garden that had gone to ruin. Everything around her had taken on an irreparable sadness. As she took in the sight of her garden, I hesitated to step past the broken gate of the fence, as had been my habit for so many of my childhood years. I stood by my bag, quietly.

"He's not here, Alexis," Mamie Leila said.

"Where is he?"

Mamie Leila shrugged, "I don't know, Alexis. Probably, he is in the mountains, walking. Did he know you were leaving at this hour?"

We both knew that he did. I looked to the mountains. The trees hid any human form from sight. I felt tears waiting to spill from my eyes. I kept my eyes wide open so that the tears would stay where they were, like secrets lying dormant in far corners of the mind. I turned back toward Mamie Leila. I felt her sadness, wanted to make the final walk to her stoop and embrace her. A tear fell from my left eye and I brushed it away, quickly. "The sun," I said to Mamie Leila, "It's the sun."

"Yes," she said, "The sun has its way with us."

"Well," I replied, "I should be going."

"Come here, son." Her voice struck my shoulder blades, already turned away from her. I turned to face her. I missed Philippe already. I was angry and sad at the same time. How to defy time, space? I urged my tired legs to make the final steps to the porch where I first met the boy who would become the man whose body housed my spirit mate.

"Come," she repeated, her eyes two beacons of solace.

I walked down the dirt path. The gnarled vines of wild bushes threw themselves against my shoes to stop my progress. It was a long walk, an arduous walk. I arrived at last at the porch. I faced Mamie Leila, who took me in her arms and rocked me back and forth as if I was still a small child. "Be safe," she said, "be safe always."

The bus screeches to a halt in a truck stop in Tallahassee. All these foreign names. They mean so little to me. Do we know anyone who settled here? With that name, I doubt it. I check my papers again. They clearly say: Nashville, Tennessee. What do I know of Tennessee? I know only that there are four hundred Haitian refugees there dispersed through the city. Will there be anyone there to take my hand, I wonder? Will there be anyone there I recognize? If Philippe is right, that none of us leave Millot for America, then there will be no one from the village and I will feel truly alone.

I sit in the bus, too afraid to venture outside. I don't know what the customs are here, even though, like everyone else, I have watched the American films in the cinema and have watched *Dynasty* on television. I have seen *Pretty Woman* twice and I know the actress in it is a goodwill ambassador to our nation, though this makes no sense to me because the film has nothing to do with us. This is a thought that keeps me in my seat as if I am in grade school and afraid to lose my spot in a row. There is such fear in my soul I begin to wonder why I ever left Haiti.

Eventually, the other passengers come back to the bus. There is a McDonald's there, and a woman with skin dark as a coffee bean with two young children in tow has brought me back a hamburger and cola. I thank her with a smile. She smiles back. Perhaps there is more here, in America, than meets the eye.

I eat in my seat while the bus finds its way back onto the highway, a long strip of gray ribbon that never seems to end.

Philippe

The rumors about Philippe had not yet begun to spread like a virus through the village, moving from one child to the next as would a summer cold, when the two were twelve and had shared a great many things since that first day in the dirt of Philippe's yard with scrambling ants for company. They had run school races through the streets of the village one behind the other, spat pieces of sugarcane in the canals behind the school after sucking the cane clean of its sweet juices. Despite the occasional unease between them, they remained like brothers, wearing each other's clothes, sleeping in each other's beds, until their households began to wonder if two healthy boys should be so free with one another. Curfews were imposed, but Philippe alone disregarded the rules, walked the mountains after dark, and sat beneath the trees to listen to the whispers cascading over one another through the fleshy leaves of the eucalyptus trees.

He had begun then to hear a voice, distinct from the other sounds rising out from the belly of the mountains. In response, Philippe carved for himself a place of solitude where all the things that others thought strange he would hold close and dear, hidden from others' fears.

Once, when he sat very still and tried to make out a new voice from the others, he saw a shadow fall in front of him. It was like no shadow he had ever seen before. It was a fog-filled light that sparkled in the moonlight as if lit by a dozen or so teeming fireflies. The shadow of light moved in front of Philippe dancing with itself or with something else that Philippe could not yet see. For several nights, Philippe would come to the clearing and wait for the shadow to reappear and it would come as if they had set an appointed time.

On the fourth night, the light was there but there were also words riding the wind.

Philippe. The voice was gentle, low. A man's voice. *Philippe*, it murmured again. *Ou tandém? Do you hear me? Can you hear me?* Beads of sweat dripped from Philippe's face and onto the compact red earth of the clearing floor. *I have been trying to speak to you in the mountains. Ummmh. Don't you recognize me, Philippe?* The voice faded, seemed to hover about the leaves of overhanging branches, returned, touched Philippe lightly on the cheek, wiping away a tear trailing down the line of his cheekbone.

The light took on a shape and Philippe's eyes could finally make out a thin young man. A man who could not have been much older than he was. Philippe smiled at the young man and put out a hand but the boy only laughed. His laughter rang out like a chime in the wind. It was so clear that Philippe felt he could reach out and touch it as he would water spouting from a spring.

In that moment of recognition, they began to speak:

I have traveled through time to find you, speak to you these words that have no weight but the importance you attach to each.

But who are you? Philippe spoke back, without uttering a single word into the air.

I was one of the men who built the Citadel from the labor of my back, carried stones, broke them with nail and spike, ate what was given me and kept my thoughts quiet in a hole buried in my chest.

Do you have a name? Why have you come?

My name is José. It is time for me to take the words that shape those thoughts out of that abyss, one by one, to hold them up to the light so that you can see your true value.

I see you, Philippe, every day, taking the tap-tap to the water, walking aimlessly through the streets, watching. But what do you see, Philippe? What is your hunger?

I hunger to be free from this place, José. I want to be free. The only time I feel free is when I come to walk the hills under the cover of night and talk to whatever moves with me, alongside my very own steps.

Shackle, Philippe. Shackle. I worked the Citadel in the days when hope, for the darker ones among us carving it out with our raw fingertips breaking rock away from the mountain, hope for us was a forgotten memory. King Christophe wanted us to work the land, turn fruits into coins. And we did it, blinded by the fantasy of recognition from the outside world. And where were we, Philippe? Dying in the mountains . . . dying in the mountains.

You lived then, way back then? How did you survive? How can this be?

I tell you Philippe, I hold no gods above me. The sky is your only salvation, and even that, too, is an illusion.

We worked for King Christophe like dogs, like dogs. My mother sent me to help build the glory of the kingdom.

I was light-skinned. She thought I would have an easier life even though I had no schooling. And so I worked for the glory of the kingdom.

The father at the school taught us that many of you were killed. That the king would walk you off the sides of the Citadel to prove to his enemies how faithful his followers could be.

Ahhhh . . . let me tell you, Philippe . . . in those days, men fell from the sky. They fell, like, like birds . . . their feet slipped off the black stones, tumbled the two hundred feet down the mountainside, noise hushed by distance immeasurable by the eye.

We fell like manna out of the sky.

The Citadel moved away from the flying bodies like a ship sinking through green waves. The mountain receded.

We fell like manna out of the sky.

I was a bird, and like you, I watched the men I was chained to in the worker's village fall off the mountain one by one, blood pouring from their ears, bodies turned soft like rubber, bouncing into crevices, bone of skulls shattering.

When you look at the Citadel, Philippe, remember us. The clotted blood of our bodies have nourished the soil of the mountains.

We fell, manna out of the sky.

Without us, the walls would have crumbled long ago.

Do you hear, Philippe? Without us, the ground would not hold you up; you would be swallowed into it.

You hear the voices on the wind, Philippe, I know. Why has it taken you so long to hear me? You and I are made of the same spirit . . . the sun blanches my bones . . .

A week later, Philippe tried to explain the sighting to Alexis, but it had been of no use.

"There are too many voices here," Philippe had said, trying to start up the conversation when they were sitting beneath the trees as was their habit after a long day of study, followed by chores for their households. "They are searching for rest. There is no rest here."

Alexis could hear something in the wind but he could not make anything out. They seemed like a jumble in his mind, or like trying to make out the sound of a single raindrop during a storm. "How do you know?" he asked Philippe. He turned to his friend.

Philippe's eyes were closed, the long lashes resting softly on the upper reaches of his cheeks. His lips pursed in concentration. "Shh," he said.

Alexis strained to hear the voices in the wind but nothing came to him clearly. Something in him resisted hearing what the voices had to say, this much he understood, and nothing in him desired to unblock the path for the words the air lifted to the eaves of his ears. The wind in the leaves of the trees, brushing against the thick foliage of the trees, began to worry him. Worry filled his soul and, eventually, fear. He wanted Philippe to stop this mad listening, stand, and turn with him to leave the mountains to their buried secrets. He stood. Philippe grabbed his arm and pulled him back down on the slab of granite rock they had warmed with their bodies.

"You'll scare them," he whispered, eyes still closed, ears open in concentration. Philippe's fingers left pink imprints on the surface of Alexis' skin. Alexis watched them fade as he crossed his arms one on top of the other and rested his forehead against them. This way, the voices would drift over his back like a river over a rock. He would be spared the jumbled words, their demands, their sleeplessness. He could feel them brushing up insistently against his body, then making their way around to reach Philippe. He wanted them gone. He sang to himself a song he had heard his mother sing in her kitchen, a song about putting the dead to rest . . . *my hands balance . . . the weight of the wind . . .*

You'll scare them.

Alexis lifted his head. Philippe was staring at him with otherworldly eyes. The amber in them had turned a deep gold that seemed to glow in the dark, outlining his dark irises in a burst of sunlight. There was something else in those eyes that Alexis could not put his finger on, as if Philippe had gone and someone else had taken his place. Alexis had heard his mother talk of the dead returning in human form. For a moment, Philippe looked to him like one of those returning spirits. His eyes were filled with a force not his own. There were shadows racing in that circle of fire, chasing each other down. Alexis looked away, frightened.

Philippe heard José's voice in the distance. He would come no closer with Alexis there.

"There's nothing to be scared of," Philippe said to both.

The wind had died down. The leaves hardly moved. They could hear the sounds of a tam-tam coming from below, in the village, rising up the mountain with the cries of children running through the narrow dirt strips in front of the shacks. Philippe put an arm around Alexis' shoulder. His eyes had returned to themselves. Alexis could see the old mischievous glow, the squint that told him that he was safe under Philippe's gaze and that anything they attempted to do together would turn out all right in the end. "I just don't hear them," Alexis said.

"Of course you do," Philippe took his arm away. "You simply don't want to hear."

"Well, what are they saying?"

Philippe paused. "You know the stories the women whisper across the wooden fences as they taste each other's soups with wooden ladles, thinking that we are too far, too small, to hear? The stories the priest tells us when we study in the schoolhouse on Saturday mornings?" Philippe continued with an impatient strain in his voice. "You know, the stories about the tortures in Fort Dimanche down in Port-au-Prince . . . how they sever the fingers one from the other, mutilate the privates, gouge the eyes out . . ."

"I don't want to hear any more," Alexis' chestnut brown face had turned pale. The hot sun had fallen behind the straight line of the horizon beyond the harbor. There was a strange glow covering the mountains, outlining the peaks of the trees. The rock beneath them was growing cold as the earth cooled. The voices in the distance had quieted. How long had they been there? Time had escaped them. "I don't want to hear about . . . about all those things."

"Well, frè," Philippe sighed in answer, "there's the problem. The voices in those mountains, they are older than Fort Dimanche, older than the horrors of our fathers' times, our time. And this is all they talk about. That and the beauty of this place as it used to be, before all that. If ever there was a before." He continued, "And still, there are terrible things happening here every day."

Alexis knew that Philippe was right. There was the woman down the street who had been raped in plain daylight in her backyard by Duvalier's

Macoutes as her two children watched, crying, sucking their thumbs. Everyone gone to market and too late to help. And would they have? Could they have? Alexis had eyes even though he tried as best he could to plug up his ears. And he had a mother who said she was as old as the sea who would tell him dream-stories that filled his mind with wonder about the people who had been here before, who had survived so that he and his mother and father could live on, in this time.

"It's not enough to have your eyes open, *frè*. Not enough," Philippe said, reading Alexis' thoughts.

"Dakò," Alexis frowned against the darkness. It seemed impenetrable to him, foreign. His skin was beginning to pucker against the coolness hanging off the night air. "Can we go?"

"Ay," Philippe said, shaking his head back and forth sadly like an old man who has seen too much and has had enough of youth, "all I want to tell you is this, Alexis. The mountains are speaking to us, all right. The spirits here are as old as the Revolution. As old as that. And they will haunt us until we honor their deaths."

"Enough," Alexis stood up. He tried to smile in the dark, to move his friend into another space that would exclude the spirits and tie them together once again.

Philippe stood up slowly. "I just want to tell you one more thing."

Alexis waited. If he just listened long enough, Philippe would be done and then they could go on as they had before, laughing, thinking of nothing else but the next prank they would play on a neighbor, the priest who taught them their lessons, or Léogane, the blind man who made his way to the foot of the Citadel from Cap-Haitien to tell stories to the tourists at the bottom of the footpath. If he could just be still long enough and feign interest. "Tell me," he said.

"You see that wall there?" Philippe pointed to one of the great walls of the Citadel which hovered above them like a dark and heavy stormcloud. "I come here at night, sometimes, by myself. I walk all the way up the path and through the bushes," he smiled, "sometimes I get scratched to death by the low branches and bitten by red ants if I stop too long. I walk and I meet a boy up there. Well, he's not really a boy. He's more like a man. He's much taller than either one of us but he still looks like a boy. Maybe sixteen, seventeen. I don't know. He comes straight out of those black rocks. But when he stands there in front of me, he is all flesh and bone." Philippe held his arms in a hug as if to prove that his own substance was as solid as the apparition he was attempting to describe to Alexis, whose slight body postured in disbelief. "It's true, Alexis. I'm not lying. When he came the first times, he was like a ghost and he came to me in the clearing. Now he comes out of the walls and he speaks to me about the things he's seen. He says his eyes were buried where the high walls make a corner, just where the footpath meets the road to the old gates.

"He is the color of sunlight, golden, and he has eyes gray like steel. He wears pants the likes I've never seen before, muslin maybe, tied around his waist with a rope, unraveling at the bottom. He wears no shoes, no shirt, and there is a jagged scar on his chest like something clawed itself through him as it reached in for his heart."

"What does it tell you," Alexis interrupted impatiently, "this thing?"

"It's not a thing. He's a man, I tell you. Flesh and bone. Just like you and I standing here. And he talks about the days when the Citadel was being built. He talks about the people who were forced to die inside the walls after building the monument. He talks about the people who were forced to leap from the thick walls and meet the ground beneath in death. He talks about not having enough to eat and a small corner of the world in which to sleep. He talks about the wind's fingers holding him like a newborn infant, reminding him of his mother when he was young and lived across the water on La Tortue. He talks of many things. But mostly he is silent, telling me his story by the way he snakes his body through the trees to show me the graves of those who were ordered to leap to their deaths, their thin bodies slapping the air like thunder as they fell." Philippe smacked the palms of his hands together for punctuation. Alexis jumped, startled. "He's not that much older than we are, Alexis. And the things he's seen . . ." Philippe drew out the last word languorously, like a sweet too long kept in the mouth. "It's his voice you don't want to hear, Alexis. But there are many others, just waiting, just waiting," Philippe inhaled deeply.

"He comes every time you're out here?" Alexis asked, suddenly curious.

The voices of the children below were replaced by the sound of men sitting in the shadows of the wooden shacks, shouting insults across the porches in between puffs on their pipes, laughing.

Philippe turned to Alexis, a blank expression on his face, and then stepped quickly past him down the path toward the village. "Last one down is a dirty rooster!" he shouted. Alexis had no choice but to follow.

After that time, they spoke little of the spirits. When the voices slid on the wind to greet them on that cold slab of stone in the mountain, Alexis sat quietly and thought to himself to keep the voices from entering his mind, or he drew scenes of his mother's stories on the blank pages of his schoolbooks, while Philippe breathed deeply and listened, always nodding in agreement with whatever it was he allowed himself to hear.

Carmen

She sits in the dark of the office, papers on her desk glowing from the light drifting in from the front windows. She does not know what she is still doing there, letting time get away from her. The office is quiet, the others having gone home fifteen minutes or so ago, leaving Carmen to herself. The front door locked behind the last of her coworkers and, afterward, she had seen something moving in the darkness from the corner of her eye. The movement had been quick, furtive. Carmen looked toward the blur at the edge of her cornea and peered into the darkness of the office. A little girl stepped out from the doorframe leading to their makeshift meeting room. The girl was dressed in a pretty pale yellow frock, matching ribbons tied to twisted locks of auburn black hair. She smiled shyly. Carmen returned the smile. They stood there silently, gazing at each other, speaking silently across the doorjamb, where the girl stood across an invisible threshold that divides the living from the world of the spirits. Then the girl left as quickly as she had appeared, leaving Carmen to peer into the darkness wondering when she would see the little girl again.

The first time Carmen had dreamed of her daughter—in fact, it was not a real dream at all but wake-thoughts that had come to her in the full light of a sunny day—she had been walking through thick leaves piled up on the sidewalks on her way to the part-time job she had held at the library before taking on the domestic violence counseling position at the Haitian Community Centre of the city of Montreal. There she would reshelf book upon book alongside others that were musty with age, dust-covered, hiding between their sticky pages dreams long ago released by their authors but taken up by next to no one for kindling to their own fires. Carmen had been thinking about these forgotten and hidden treasures as she slipped a history of the Canary Islands between two thin plastic-covered working papers issued two decades ago by the center for International Studies of a college she had never heard of, south of the border, an American university, somewhere in the wilds of Minnesota.

She had been thinking of all the places she had never been, of all the faces she had yet to meet, and with one hand poised in midair over the history book bound in a green pebbled leather, she saw the little face she had come to recognize as her daughter's own peering at her from beneath the shelf above her hand.

She saw soft brown doe eyes and thick, long eyelashes, a sparkle of mischievousness and long, flowing curls of auburn black hair. The girl laughed, and as Carmen laughed in response and began to pull the book back off the shelf in order to see fully the face she expected would end in an oval peek about the chin just as her own did, it disappeared, ghostlike, into thin air. Carmen, nonplussed, had simply pushed the book back into the gaping hole that had held, if for only a moment, the face of one of her beloveds, and then smiled to herself before standing up straight to turn to the cart at her side. She continued to push its load of books in and out of the aisles, placing one book there and another here until the task was done. Later, as she was readying to leave the building and plod back through the heaps of leaves that had suddenly fallen from the trees to announce the inevitable turn from the erroneously named "Indian" summer to the cooling fall weather, her daughter had returned to peer at her from a mirror as she tied a bright colored kerchief her mother had sent her from Haiti months ago but had never used, the summer being too hot, over her curly locks of hair. Their laughter had again mingled in the air like two leaves falling from the same tree, colors complementing the other as they fall in the amber light of the falling sun. The joy between them formed a warm blanket of protection around Carmen's shoulders.

That first visit had occurred only two months ago, on a dreary day that had begun with a fight with her ex-boyfriend Nick. Carmen remembers the scene with bitterness still.

"What do you want me to do?" Nick had said, his droopy eyelids seeming to flutter in the falling light. He stood in the kitchen in his underwear and white T-shirt while she made herself a cup of tea. He spread out his long, thin arms, and his vocal cords seemed to strangle his words as he spoke again, "Carmen, what do you want?"

"What do I want?" she had said slowly, every word carefully enunciated so that he could not say later that she had mumbled something out, a defence he had used against her often, her shyness breaking down her ability to communicate.

Nick dropped his arms to his side. The hairs on his legs seemed darker than usual against the pale of his skin. "Did you enjoy yourself,

Nick?" she asked, thinking about who had touched those thighs, in her bed, while she was away at work putting in as many hours as she could at the library so she could support his unfulfilled dreams.

"What?" he asked. The droopy lids and bushy eyebrows she had once loved now appeared grotesque. She wondered how she had ever loved him.

She looked up at him. "I asked you whether you enjoyed yourself."

He looked pained. She smiled, empty of feeling.

"Why are you smiling? You think this is a joke?"

It had taken her some time to get it, that even in her own home she was dispensable. "I'm pregnant," she said.

"My god," he replied, staring at her in disbelief.

"Maybe you'll have twins," she said, thinking again of who had touched those thighs and where and when.

"What do you mean?"

She smiled again and looked down into her tea cup. She wished then that she had learned something of the occult arts, the reading of palms and tea leaves. Maybe she could have avoided this scene, a scene she remembered witnessing between her mother and father years ago, except her father had denied his betrayals and her mother had chosen to stay, cocooned in the pain.

"You know what I mean," she said.

"You didn't answer my question," he tried to get the conversation back on track even as he shivered in his underwear, looking guilty as sin: she had come too early, the someone in her bed still there, escaping through the back door as she turned the key in the locks and entered what she thought of as her safe haven. He had scrambled to put on his underwear, a T-shirt, thought of his excuse, but she had seen through him, right to the bed and its uncovered sheets, right through to his heart which was lying to her. "I think we can work this out," he said. He started pacing the length of the kitchen floor, thinking of what next to say. He was going to be a father?

"I don't want anything from you," Carmen replied as she watched the tea leaves floating in her cup, moving in circular motions, following each other in the wake of the stirring of her spoon.

"What?" he asked, more as a statement than anything else. "What are you saying?" His face was turning red from the neck up, the red disappearing into the stubble of his chin. He rushed toward her and she felt the waves of air lifting all around her as if a sudden gust of wind had broken through the window before she saw his fist strike down on the table, sending her cup clattering off its saucer, the tea spilling over from the sides and onto the wood of the table and off its rounded side onto the tile of the floor.

She stared at his anger, eyes bloodshot with bewilderment. What had he expected? In the past, she would have recoiled from his fists in fear, they may even have fallen on her skin as Carl's had fallen on Gladys' one time too many. She was glad for his indiscretion. It meant she was free from those droopy eyes and unshaven face, free from those fists. She decided to ignore him. "I don't need anything from you," she repeated.

He was still half-bent over the table, his naked legs looking vulnerable. like those of a child's, his T-shirt damp with sweat. "You can't mean that," he blustered, "and with our baby on the way."

She had advanced toward the sink in search of a rag to clean up the pooling tea on the floor, to wipe down the table, but the word "our" stopped her dead in her tracks. He had said it plaintively, as if this fact only would keep her there, ignoring what her eyes had seen just minutes prior. "Our," she said, almost mockingly, "*our*? Are you kidding? This baby is mine, Nick. From day one you said you were better off without children. Has anything changed? We slipped, something went wrong, and now I'm pregnant. So what!" Her voice was escalating, her own anger spilling over, "So what." She wanted to hit him with the wet rag, or anything. But having been exposed to violence throughout her childhood had kept her from lifting a finger against anyone. She was not going to start now. "After what I've seen, Nick, I think you had better hope that I let you see her once she's born."

Nick's arms hung limply at his side. He appeared defeated.

Carmen jumped at the only opportunity to say what she really felt: "I want you to leave."

He only nodded and walked past her and into the bedroom to gather some of his things.

"I'll send the rest to the radio station," she said as lightly as she could.

He said nothing and went on gathering items from the bedroom, living room, bathroom. She was still wiping up the tea, endlessly stroking down the tile and wood long after the liquid had been absorbed by the rag, when she heard the front door open and shut. Hearing the familiar creak of the door moving on its hinges, she cried, wondering what would become of her with a child on the way.

It was on just this day that her daughter had made her first appearance.

After Nick's departure, she had felt her life broken in two. It was into that torn space that all of her deepest dreams had escaped and from that space that the ghost of her daughter had emerged to keep her company throughout the day, holding on to her hand into the deepest of sleeps at evening. Then she had gone, and Carmen's mind had turned to other things, like her impending return to once familiar shores, to Ayiti or Quisqueya, depending on which side of the island had recorded Hispaniola's history. To her, it would always be Haiti, betraying the colonial French that was nonetheless her mother tongue. She had pondered whether or not to pack up and see her mother. She had not made up her mind then.

The very next week, the very minute she had carried Nick's Samsonite out of doors (he had agreed to pick it up while she was out, saving her a trip to the radio station where he worked), something like a window seemed to unhinge itself in her mind and she began to think of what she ought to do with the life stretching itself before her without a compass. She went back into the house and dialed the eight hundred number for Air Canada to book herself a flight home to Haiti. Why put off now doing what she had waited to do for more years than she could count? For the last year, she had tried to convince Nick to come along with her, so that he could see where she had been born and her mother before her. There was always something tying him up at the music station or with his on-again, off-again band. And from month to month she was putting off her own dreams, one as simple as working in the Haitian community of Montreal. She had not yet begun to dream bigger dreams. She had waited too long, or so it seemed. She did not want to have a child and not know what to hand to her, what to tell her about the past, her heritage.

She had been pondering her options when back at the library busying herself with the shelving and cataloguing.

"Daydreaming again, I see," a pleasant voice chided her as she was preparing a book for its bar code.

Carmen looked up and saw Yannick's angular face looking down at her. She was smiling broadly, "How are you doing?"

"Yannick," Carmen said, "I haven't seen you in the longest time. How have you been doing?"

"*M la*," Yannick replied with a laugh, her Kreyol thick. She rolled her eyes. "You know how it is. How's Nick?"

Carmen's hands froze over the books Yannick had set in front of her to check out. She had selected books on African dance and theater. Yannick was completing a master's degree in performance art at McGill, taking a couple of night classes a semester while she worked days at the Haitian Community Centre. They had met at an evening of Black arts sponsored by the radio station Nick worked for a year ago and had become friends over that time. Sometimes they would share an evening with Yannick, her girlfriend, and Yannick's young son, but it had been some months since they had shared a drink or a conversation. Of course, Yannick could not know what had just happened. Carmen sighed as her hands fell on the books. She would have to start telling people sooner or later.

"Trouble in paradise?" Yannick asked, sensing Carmen's disarray.

"Yes," Carmen said and ventured a smile. "Nick and I broke up last week."

"I'm sorry," Yannick said, "You two seemed so . . ."

"Happy?" Carmen laughed, "I don't think so."

"What happened?"

"Don't ask," Carmen waved the question away as if shooing a fly, then quickly processed the books and handed them back to Yannick.

"We should get together," Yannick said as she took the books from her. "Rona would be happy to see you and so would TiDavid."

Carmen smiled remembering the evenings they had all shared together and TiDavid, Yannick's son, who was the cutest little boy she'd seen in a long time, "He must be quite big by now."

"Getting bigger day by day," Yannick chuckled, "and getting into heaps of trouble. It's been a long time. Why don't you come to dinner this weekend and we'll try to cheer you up?"

Thankful for the gesture, the distraction, Carmen had accepted and found herself at Yannick's dinner table the next Saturday telling her and her partner about Nick's infidelity, her pregnancy, her feeling lost and detached from family, from anything that mattered.

"My lord," Rona said as she finished her story, "that is a lot." She had been washing dishes while Yannick and Carmen talked over cups of mint tea. "What are you going to do?"

"Well," Carmen replied, "I've already ended the relationship." She frowned. "And I know I have to change apartments, maybe get a second job."

"Yannick," Rona said, "isn't there an opening at the center?"

"Yes, there is," Yannick tried to gauge Carmen, "I don't know if you'd be interested. It's an assistant counseling job."

"Counseling? I don't have the experience." Carmen felt suddenly as if all was impossible, that perhaps she had made the biggest mistake of her life. They had played games with TiDavid before dinner and she had felt her heart open to the joy of having her own child soon. Now she felt miserable and unprepared for what was to come.

Yannick gave Rona a glance. "I'll leave the two of you alone," Rona said. She took off her apron and let it hang over the kitchen sink. As she passed by Carmen she hugged her from the back, her long braids brushing against Carmen's cheeks. "Hang in there, baby," she said calmly, looking past Carmen at Yannick. She remembered when things had been difficult for the two of them, trying to make a go of things without support in the Caribbean community for their union, with a child to bring up whose father already made life difficult for Yannick. Now there was another child on the way and more pain than love already surrounded it.

"We need people from the community, Carmen," Yannick resumed. "You used to talk about wanting to know your roots, going the distance. Nick is gone and you know he never supported anything like that in you." Now that the relationship was over, Yannick felt she could be clear, not mince her words. She pushed on, "We need young women at the center who can be role models, who can help other women get on their feet."

Carmen opened and closed her hands, "What kind of example would I be?"

"A live one," Yannick smiled kindly, "A role model is anyone who is making it in this world with their head up high, you know? And you're going to keep your head up high. The job is part-time. You come in in the mornings, talk to clients if they drop by, let them know about the counseling services, do some paperwork. It's not as hard as you think." She pointed to her heart, then her head, "You just have to use your heart, your mind, and help people out a bit in their lives. It will help you too."

No sooner had a door closed than a window had opened. Her mother used to say clichéd things like that. Carmen smiled to herself. The window was open and she felt the breeze from the life awaiting her in the great outdoors reaching her on the wings of Yannick's words. "OK," she said. "Okay, I'll give it a try."

Yannick smiled and lightly patted Carmen's hand, "*Tu vas voir*," you'll see, "everything will turn out."

That evening's meal, quickly following on the heels of her daughter's first appearance, had brought her to the doors of the Haitian Community

Centre located on a side street perpendicular to the main thoroughfare, Henri-Bourassa Boulevard. The new job had brought her a sense of awakening and hope.

Now, a few months later, Carmen is still holding on to this hope, even as the work becomes more difficult and her faith in her ability to help others begins to wane.

Carmen looks around the offices of the center making sure that all the lights have been turned off, the coffee maker unplugged, and the front and back doors locked. A few weeks ago, they had been broken into and lost what little computer equipment they had. It was the reason her desk was teeming over with paperwork. She walks out onto the sidewalk and heads home with the secret of her daughter lightening her step as she goes. A breeze lifts seemingly out of nowhere and accompanies her, brushing past her feet as they strike the sidewalk. Today she will not be heading back to the apartment she had occupied with Nick but to a rented room in another Victorian house on Rue Leblanc owned and run by a Ms. Alberta, an elderly Black woman who had been born in the Southern United States but had emigrated to Canada in search of her roots.

"It took me forever to get myself on up here," Ms. Alberta told her the day she signed her lease, "Never thought I'd see the day." Then she slapped her knee as her rounded body quivered with laughter sending little splashes of tea spilling from the cup teetering in a little puddle in the saucer she was holding primly in one hand.

Carmen had smiled then, watching Ms. Alberta's face as it creased in delight, her eyelids closed. She bit down on her upper lip as her cheeks expanded with stifled air and a dimple revealed itself in the hollow between cheek muscle and bone. "What took so long?"

Ms. Alberta waved her free hand at her and opened her eyes. "Child," she said, "If I told you that story, you'd be here 'til doomsday!"

"You see me going anywhere, Ms. Alberta?" Carmen shrugged and smiled, "I'm all ears."

The old woman laughed. "Well then, I'll just get us some more tea, don't you think?"

She returned with a pot of steeping herbs and set it between them on the walnut coffee table she had brought all the way up from the South with her.

"This here was a gift from my brother, Louis. A good man, Louis. A good man." For a moment, Ms. Alberta seemed lost in thought. "Hasn't made it up here yet. But seeing how long it's taken me, child, I don't blame him."

She looked across the table to Carmen and squinted. "You know anything about the underground railroad?"

"Wasn't that how slaves came to this country for their freedom?" Carmen replied.

"Yes," Ms. Alberta's eye brightened up at the thought of talking to a young person who knew something about their history, "That's just right. Now you understand we weren't born no slaves. That's what they made us into. And some of us resisted all the way across the sea in the belly of those ships, in the cotton and cane fields. We watched what they did to our mothers and fathers, our children, all the atrocities and pain and then we made us some plans." Ms. Alberta's voice had dropped an octave or two until it was deep as a river.

Carmen thought about the stories she'd heard about the Mississippi and slaves following it to freedom or sinking to its depths when found and killed. She thought she heard its great red waters flowing beneath Ms. Alberta's words and a chill went through her spine.

"You all rright, child?"

"Yes," Carmen almost stuttered. "Yes, please go on."

"Well, my family was living dispersed through Tennessee in those days, where my brother Louis still lives. And the great-grands heard about a Harriet Tubman, this feisty woman who had escaped slavery and was helping others to go up North. You could go straight through to Canada. You understand there wasn't any railroad. That's just what they call a . . . a . . . euphemism, see. We just ran from one place to the next. Sometimes we'd have to change our plans if someone told on us, a white sharecropper or something else would give us away, a torn piece of clothing here, a lost shoe there. Sometimes there was nothing to do but give up." Ms. Alberta's eyes clouded over with the pain of history. She waved her hands in front of her. "But that's an old story. Old. Old. You don't need me to prattle on about all that." She sighed and they sat quietly for a few minutes. Carmen sipped her tea. Ms. Alberta had set her teacup down long ago. She stared into the brown of the walnut as if it held some old secret she was wondering whether to say or keep.

"It's funny how we carry objects with us from one place to another," she finally said, "as if they could speak to us in the middle of the night. Give us some in-the-dark comfort. Funny, isn't it?"

Carmen shrugged. She had sold off most of her belongings in order to fit into the one room plus bath she had just signed for. Did she have any old talismans to carry up to the third room floor? She thought of the wooden boxes she had kept since childhood, bought at the sides of roads in Haiti by her mother on visits home. Sometimes it was like they could speak. At least they brought back the memories.

"We need them more than they need us," she said to Ms. Alberta.

"We sure do," Ms. Aberta sighed. She sagged in her chair, looking suddenly all of her seventy or so years, gravity pulling mercilessly on her body. "I came up here because there are some things down in the South that don't change. You wouldn't know anything about this," she smiled sadly at Carmen. "You're too young to know. But I've seen what it can do to you. Louis loves it down there. Never left the soil that birthed him. I understand why he stays. But me, no sirree, I needed to follow my blood the way rivers don't flow all the way North. That's what I did. My name isn't Alberta for nothing!" She laughed quietly into her chest. "That's where the great-grands settled. Had themselves some land. Farmed it. Sold their produce. Put clothes on their children's backs, food on the table, shoes on their feet. Had everything a body could have and yet they didn't feel like they were free. You know, they had that kind of freedom that makes you feel uneasy in your skin, like you're never home. You know?"

Carmen did know. She nodded. She was living between two worlds, her mother's in her heart and mind, her father's in the traits he had left imprinted on her face, her blood, the very land where she stood. She put a hand on her belly, thinking of the unborn child to come. What would she have to tell her about herself? What legacies to give?

"When are you due?" Ms. Alberta asked then, interrupting her story.

"Six months or so," Carmen smiled.

"You're not so young after all," Ms. Alberta said. "You're no baby having a baby. You are a full-grown woman." She paused. "Glad to have you under my roof. You'll be safe here."

"I know, Ms. Alberta. I know." She felt safe already. She put down her teacup alongside the other on the table. "Have you told me the whole story, Ms. Aberta?"

"Well, child," Ms. Alberta resumed, "there's a heap more to tell or nothing at all. Can't tell you which way I'd rather go. Let's just say that some of us will never find our way home. I came to find out what the place I was name for looked like. I wanted to touch land that my people owned. We didn't own nothing in Tennessee, still don't excepting for Louis and that plot of land. No fields though. No forty acres. No mule. Sometimes you have to go far from everything you know just to find out there isn't any promised land."

Ms. Alberta's words made Carmen feel like crying. Her mother had warned her against emotional excesses. *You don't want your girl to cry her way into life, do you?* she'd asked Carmen over the phone a few weeks ago. *Don't you want her to be strong?* Was crying weakness? Carmen wondered as tears welled up in her eyes.

"All right now," Ms. Alberta said, rising to her feet and brushing down her black dress across her wide thighs. The fabric was wrinkled in wide stripes from left to right from below her breasts down to her knees. "Don't want you crying your first day here. There'll be other times. Come, come, let me show you your room."

Carmen quickly wiped at her tears with the back of her hand and followed Ms. Alberta as she clambered up the steps to the third floor. Hers was the only room there. It was large and had a bay window with stained glass at the top that let light stream in like a multicolored fan across the floor. "It's lovely," she said.

"I knew as soon as you walked in that this was your room. Just had a feeling in my bones." Ms. Alberta smiled. "I told Mr. Gillespie that we had just better take down the 'For Rent' sign when you walked on up here."

Mr. Gillespie was an old arthritic cat who liked to nap in the front window on the landing. Carmen smiled.

She would hear later about Ms. Alberta's journey through western Canada, how Ms. Alberta had come to understand that the white Canadians she met were afraid of what they did not know so she gave up trying to understand the absence of people with her color there and sought out places where she could see herself reflected in the faces she encountered, people with faces of brown just like hers. She headed east and finally came upon Montreal, with its rich mixture of peoples from Africa and the Caribbean, Asia and Europe, and she found she liked it and remained. Carmen had sensed from the very first that here she would be safe and perhaps she might even be able to speak of her daughter's visits before her birth into this world, of the way she materialized out of nowhere then disappeared, without having to think that perhaps she had begun to lose her mind, as her mother would have told her had she been there to talk to. *Foli vin tout jan,* she had been fond of saying when Carmen was growing up. Craziness arrives in many guises.

It was in sitting with Ms. Alberta that she had begun to realize that there was no crazy bone in her body and that her unborn daughter had truly begun to speak to her, soul to soul.

September 9, 1991

Philippe

As is his daily routine, Philippe rises with the sun at his back, whistling to himself as he walks the long miles to the harbor from the village. It is early morning, and the air is already thickly humid, announcing a sweltering day. The waters are calm. The right side of the harbor is lined with a row of scraggly looking palm trees onshore and a dozen small fishing boats with their masts pulled down. Philippe sits on the edge of one of the docks and watches five of his former schoolmates on a larger boat preparing their nets for a day at sea. He wonders what they will bring back. They are taking longer than usual this morning but it is still early so Philippe stands in his usual place on the rocks by the shore and watches.

"You call that work!" he yells out to his former schoolmates; his voice is tinged with a note of good humor.

"Don't you have some tourists to guide, *en haut là*, in the mountains?" Jean, one of the crew calls back across the water, waving toward Millot. He is wearing a large, oversized T-shirt with a golden-hued face of Bob Marley screenprinted on the front. The others are all barebacked and in jeans.

Philippe laughs, "Got nothing better to do than watch you."

"Un-hunh," says Ti Boule, another who has gotten his name because of the roundness of his shape as a child. "We are beautiful, aren't we?" They all laugh then, tying ship to shore with their humor.

It has been a long time since Philippe has been to the shore to watch his friends on their fishing boat, readying themselves for a day out at sea. He has not done so since Alexis left earlier that fall. They had stood next to each other, that one last time, their friends' wooden boat painted in the blue and red of the traditional Haitian flag, rocking against the waves. *Why don't you come?* the young men had yelled out to Philippe and Alexis from the upper deck, *the sea desires your labors.*

They had spoken the word "desires" almost licentiously and Philippe had grown tense and wild in thought. What did they know of him? What did they suspect? But their good-natured laughter had reassured him, and he imitated Alexis in gesticulating wildly back. What would the two of them have done on a boat? He was the son of a laborer and Alexis was on his way to becoming a man of letters. They were tied to the earth. In this, and many other ways, they mirrored each other. *No, no*, they waved back, *we are happy where we stand*. There was another round of laughter. *You'll be sorry*, the backs of the ship's crew seemed to say as the light of the sun danced upon their sinewy muscles.

As he stands alone onshore, Philippe feels a strange and sudden emptiness at the thought of this lost ritual. Alexis is no longer there to protect him from the taunts of the other boys who accuse him of being a *makoumé*. The name-calling had begun on a school field trip organized in secret by Pè Joshua.

Pè Joshua was unorthodox. Born himself in the high hills of Ayiti, he loved her culture as much as he did the cloth. As a young man, he had decided that he would make use of his faith to teach. He was willing to part ways with the Church when it came to making the children feel good about themselves and where they came from.

Pè Joshua thought it was possible to hold two things in the mind at one time—that it was possible to love a Christian God while venerating the pantheon of those that had come before—the African *loas*. He continuously put himself at odds with the Church and his own congregation, but he was young yet, and they assumed that, with age, he would put first the God that he had promised to love and serve. Pè Joshua, however, seemed to move through the world unaware of the fuss he was causing. He knew well enough to keep a low profile, to smile and shake the right hands. But he kept on doing what he felt he must, despite the conflicts of faith it presented. Pè Joshua refused to see conflict in himself and assumed that others could rise to the challenge of also holding more than one thing in their minds at once.

Pè Joshua liked to take the older children on field trips to outlying communities. He often received permission to combine groups from the villages with schoolchildren from Cap-Haitien, and he would rent out a rickety school bus painted a dull gray for those festive occasions. He thought it useful to have the urban and rural children mix and know each other. He wanted to create a sense of community in them so that they would grow up to change the course of their own history. Pè Joshua, however, was notorious for telling the children one thing and their parents another. On this particular occasion, he told the parents that they were all on their way to a variety of church buildings south of Le Cap and that the children would be engaged in repainting them in an effort to boost morale in the outlying parishes. It would be a two-day adventure. After he had done the rounds of the village schools and then took the bus bouncing along the rutted highway to Le Cap to pick up the last of the schoolchildren whose parents still thought trips with Pè Joshua could have some value, he informed the children that they were on their way to Saut d'Eau, the sacred *vodou* site. The bus grew quiet for a moment and then the excitement between the children grew as the bus made its way carefully along the creviced dirt roads like a blind crab rising from waterlogged sand.

On the bus, Philippe watched as Alexis joined the other boys in teasing the girls by pulling off the ribbons from the ends of their fat braids while the girls screamed their disdain. Then the boys took to imitating zombies and rolling back their eyes until the whites of their eyes showed. Philippe could see faint blue and pink veins along the edges of their pupils.

Philippe looked around the bus to see who else had joined them. At the back of the bus his eyes fell on a thin, dark girl. She sat with her back quite straight as if she was in a Church of some kind. Her eyes were closed and she ignored all of the ruckus around her. Philippe tried to get Alexis' attention to point out the strange girl but Alexis only pushed his hand away. The girl opened her eyes and startled him. Her eyes were milky and dark as a night sky. She stared emptily ahead as if she was hearing something all her own. Philippe concentrated and tried to pick up on whatever it was in the air that she could hear beyond the din. He could not make it out clearly because Alexis was screaming beside him and he could not get him to quiet down. He looked at the girl again. Her hair was cut close to the scalp and curled softly where the hairline met the muscles of her neck behind the ears. She wore a simple yellow blouse and green skirt. A girl next to her held her hand and pointed at things outside the window but she said nothing in reply. Philippe then realized that the eyes did not move to see what was being pointed at beyond the window. Sometimes she nodded or shook her head but her eyes never moved. And when she grew tired of her companion's chatter, she would close her eyes again and listen to something that seemed so entrancing that it must have been like a symphony in her mind. Philippe closed his own eyes and tried to see what he could hear despite the loud banter of the other boys.

As they came closer to the site, Pè Joshua gave them all a sidelong glance in the oblong rearview mirror. By then, some were sleeping while others were playing word games across the torn vinyl of the seats. The bus lurched to a stop alongside a mud-filled ditch and they all tumbled out to follow the diminutive priest on a narrow path into the bush. They knew they had arrived at their destination when Pè Joshua's back straightened up and shadows of leaves fell across his white crinkled shirt to cut out a half-moon shape between his shoulders. Pè Joshua clasped both hands behind his head, rubbing his closely-cropped hair back and forth. Philippe could tell he had forgotten them for a moment and that the lines of his long face had broken out into a smile as he looked out onto a scene that their imaginations could not have created alone.

Philippe watched as the other children rushed forward, unable to contain themselves any longer. He waited, alone, on the footpath, half-hidden in the shadows. Pè Joshua's white shirt became a blur as he indicated where the children should stand. Philippe advanced quietly. When he arrived at the end of the path, it was to see bare-chested men and women calling out for Damballa and Ayida Wèdo. Others were scrambling down through damp and bright-green moss with plastic red and yellow containers to fill them with water. Philippe looked up to see what looked like rain from a storm pouring out of the sky. A waterfall emptied itself out from the lip of the mountain and thundered down onto large red-brown rocks. Pè Joshua explained the sacredness of the site to the group and then the meaning of the chants. Philippe could tell that he was pleased with himself for having brought them there. He could tell also that there was something about the pilgrims that spoke to something in his soul much more clearly than did the sermons he gave at the Church near the school. Philippe wondered how Pè Joshua could reconcile the two in his mind, in his very soul.

As if reading Philippe's mind, Pè Joshua turned around and smiled. "Here," he said, looking directly at Philippe, "here you may begin to find your ancestors." Pè Joshua did the sign of the cross and bowed his head in silence.

The group had grown serious by then. They watched as Pè Joshua proceeded to unbutton his shirt and strip down to his underwear, hanging each piece of clothing carefully in the branches of trees all poised like arms ready to receive each piece of cloth. The trees were filled in this way with clothing and many were girded by sashes of blue and white. Pè Joshua disappeared into the waterfall and Philippe watched as Alexis and the others followed suit until they were all enveloped in a thick white mist.

There were people already bathing at the foot of the falls. There was an old man who had laid his crutches where the water and land made like soup in a terrine, the water lifting up and down slowly against the sodden earth. There were young children pulling down the soaked undergarments of their mothers who were throwing up their hands into the falling water and asking the gods for deliverance from so many things that their words made a stew of song in Philippe's mind. He smiled. He knew then what the girl at the back of the bus had been hearing all along the way, ears finely tuned to something that lay ahead on the journey. He looked for her through the fine mist rising from the cool waters and saw the girl that had been sitting next to her in the bus leading the way. The two were walking toward the foot of the waterfall, clasped hands forming a bridge of stretched tendons and brown flesh over stream and stones as the girl pointed out to the other where to place her feet with a few words that sounded out softly like feathers falling from the sky. Philippe advanced then, his feet falling against the soft earth, slipping on wet leaves. His mind raced as voices rushed the canals of his ears. He was hearing the pilgrims and the voices of the ancestors answering. He could see hands rising and falling against flesh as bodies became possessed by what could not be seen with the naked eye, palms cupping breasts and smoothing backs, every touch sacred, unchallenged, unquestioned, inviolate.

Philippe advanced until the stream ran over his feet like hundreds of slow-moving, slithering coils of snakes. He felt covered over by scales as his skin responded to the wet like a fish first taking to water. He plunged forward, into the waterfall.

After that, everything that happened seemed so much like a dream that he could not quite remember it all in a sequence of images. Everything was out of order in his mind.

Covered by the water snaking itself over his body and around each of his limbs in quiet succession, Philippe's eyes clouded over. He could see only a light of pale blue before him. A great happiness filled his soul and he heard incantations to the gods swirling through the water with the force of ten hurricanes. Words fell from his lips involuntarily as he joined in, each foot lifting itself up and then down against the stones in a slow-motion dance, arms rising against the water. He reached out a hand and felt about with fingers splayed like the thin oblong threads that hold together the meshings of a spider's web.

He was reaching out into air and it felt to him that he was being taken back to a time long gone when there had stood no one here but perhaps wild and colorful birds singing out their songs, leaping from branch to branch overhead only to fly through the waterfall from the folly of their own joy. Philippe laughed and felt the laughter rising up from deep within his chest as if he had never in his life laughed before, as if he had just fallen from the sky like the *loas* themselves and come to inhabit a human form for the very first time. At the same time, his hand fell upon a raised shoulder.

Philippe's fingertips roamed and he felt both water and smooth skin beneath his fingertips. He marvelled at the shape of tendons and the edges of bones. He opened up his hands and the water rushed through his fingers and cooled the skin his palms cupped with abandon. And then, suddenly, every touch brought with it a piece of a puzzle until, without even opening his eyes, he knew who was before him by the shape and length of the muscles, the barely hardened bones. It was Alexis. Philippe did not open his eyes. It was the first time he had touched Alexis like this, even though they were so close. It was the first time he had wanted to touch someone like this. The sensuality of the waterfall made his hands alive with desire and his fingertips sought out Alexis with renewed urgency, the innocence of the touching he had felt until then dropping away like the water pooling at his feet. Alexis was so still, Philippe forced himself to open his eyes. Could it be that they were trapped in a dream? Philippe could not see Alexis through the white cloud of falling water rushing between their bodies, hiding them from the other worshippers bathing each other in the water, with no thought of eroticism pulsating between the slick bodies as it was beneath Philippe's hands. Philippe's hands fell on empty space. His whole body leaned in to feel again the magic of touch beneath the waterfall. He leaned forward and it seemed to him that everything then happened at once: the thrill rising from his toes and up through his thighs into the depth of his stomach, up through his chest, to his spine, and into the cranium; that, and the way Alexis slapped away his hand that had gone on to claim the soft tissues of his stomach and the faint scars of childhood scrapes at the elbow. Then three pairs of eyes belonging to school chums turned upon them both and it seemed to Philippe that, in that briefest of moments, all was lost.

Those eyes claimed that Philippe's hands were different. *Makoumé!* Philippe heard them cry out. They could tell by his eyes that he was different. *Makoumé.* They could tell because whatever was wrong with what he had done must be showing in his face. *Makoumé.* Terror and fear overcame him when Philippe realized that his fingers, the palms of his hands, had just confessed a longing he had yet to put into words, for the very best friend he had ever known in this world.

It was then that the girl with the vacant eyes from the bus appeared, as if the waters had just newly given birth to her. She walked between the boys and touched her hands to their lips until they were quiet. The water cascaded over their bodies in a deafening roar. The boys looked at her, stunned, forgetting Philippe and what had just occurred. As quickly as she had appeared, she melted away beneath the water, leaving Philippe to run from the group, eyes streaming their own salty water, feet slipping against the rocks.

In the end, Philippe could not remember if they had really called him *makoumé* at all. All he remembered was the strange feeling that had passed like a bolt of lightning through his body as he had touched Alexis, and that the others had seen it. Then, running from the waterfall and hurtling into bodies with hands upraised to the sky, all eyes turned away from his own frightened form cutting a path toward brilliant green moss and his pile of clothes thrown behind a tree jutting over the stream at the bottom of the falls. The tree hid him from view of the others as he changed.

It was there that he met Léah face-to-face for the first time, sitting alone, hands one on top of the other in her lap, eyes closed, ears open to the wind.

"I feel you there," she said in a quiet voice.

Philippe looked about and saw her sitting on the trunk of a felled tree just opposite him. At first, he made as if to cover up but there was no reason to do anything of the sort so he just continued to dress.

"You were in the waterfall?" Léah asked.

Philippe had lost his voice.

"Why are you afraid?"

"Why do you ask?" Philippe retorted, trying to hide his fear. He felt truly naked, as if her milky blue-black eyes could see right through him and into his soul.

"You shouldn't be afraid of yourself," she said then.

The words made him want to fall to his knees and cry.

Léah continued to speak across the space that divided them. Philippe could hardly make out a word she said, but the hum her voice made in his ears gave him a strange comfort. It reminded him of the sound of his mother's voice when she had still been well and living with them in the village, in the days before she had sewn the dress of calico and flown away to the capital, where it seemed all the darkest spells lay in wait for those who sought too much from life, too much beyond the village walls.

He began to cry.

When he was spent from crying, Léah told him that there were ways for him to survive. It would not be easy, she told him then. Léah went on to explain how he might find others like himself in shadow places and edges of clearings. Philippe's mind reeled. Léah's words came to an end as she gave him her name and where to find her in Cap-Haitien. She gave an address up on the main street of commerce, and Philippe recognized it as an ice cream shop owned by Léogane, the storyteller. He thanked the young girl who had helped Léah from the bus as she came to fetch her and guide her back. Philippe knew at the moment she departed that he would not get in touch with her.

As they sat on the bus heading back north, and a blanket of darkness grew around them with each passing hour, Philippe thought on how a moment in time could change everything. Alexis sat away from him with the cluster of other boys. They sometimes furtively looked his way and made obscene gestures or pursed their mouths until Alexis finally told them all to keep quiet, that Philippe was his friend after all. Philippe was only slightly consoled. The rift between them suddenly loomed large before him and he felt as if he were standing on the edge of some huge precipice over which he would fall with only a word from Alexis, a goodbye or hasty, dismissive glance. He looked out of the windows into the night's darkness. The moon's glow bounced off the dust-streaked windows. He realized then that the nightmare Alexis had had all those years ago when they would share each other's bedding had come true. There had been snakes in the form of water and touch so powerful it hushed words.

The bus grew quiet in time and Pè Joshua seemed lost in his own thoughts as they lurched homeward like some huge and extinct dinosaur brought back to life from the forest floor. When they stopped to let the children from Le Cap out by the harbor, it was already midmorning the next day. Léah came over to him and kissed him on the lips, softly. This softness he remembered always.

From that day on, Philippe had retreated even more so to his solitude and cared for his grandmother as he searched for the key to his own future. He found life in the *vodou* circles he encountered but it was always a cloaked life at best. His friendship with Alexis had gone on but differently than before. Alexis excelled in school as the rest of them found jobs to support their families and eventually dropped out of school altogether.

September 9, 1991

Alexis

The city is slumbering like a giant when the bus, its wheels spinning with noisy trepidation, lumbers down the main street. It could be that it is my owns anxiety I feel moving through the wheels and up through the rubber-covered floor, metal walls, these wheels that have transported me this far, right into the mouth of the American South I have read so much about in my school books: Christophe fighting on behalf of the French in the battle of Savannah, Georgia, in 1779. What would our great king have thought, I think, of the time it took for the American slaves to be freed? He would have been pacing the floors of one of his palaces, up and down the long halls, thinking through how not to be overthrown when they would have been cutting the throats of their masters' dogs, walking north to liberty. But what does it matter now? Here I am, one of the sons of the first Black Revolution in this hemisphere, son of unrelenting misery, making my way North just as they had. What does it matter now? Perhaps this is it: there is hope. There is the hope that things are different enough on this American continent for a man with the color of my skin to journey with his head held up high. There is the hope that once I have made it here, I will be able to leave again, one day return to my country with pockets lined with money, and sweets for the children of my village. There is nothing left to me but this.

The bus stops with a resigned gasp of exhaust in a terminal marked "Greyhound." The woman with the two children pats me on the shoulder.

"We've arrived," she says softly, a murmur of fatigue escaping from beneath her simple words, burying each syllable in the rasp of her throat. It is the first time that I hear her voice. She has not spoken to me before or after giving me the food from the last stop. She has only smiled and I have smiled in return as if that is all the language needed. She surprises me with a twang in her voice similar to the white man's who had given me my plane ticket in Port-au-Prince, who had left me to take this bus with only a letter of introduction for when I reached the end point of this journey. He does not know that I will keep walking even if I stay in this South of his for years, that I plan to go on to what has always been spoken of as the promised land: North, North, North. I am going to make it to freedom even if I have to crawl on my hands and knees like a baby. I know all about Harriet Tubman and the underground railroad. I want to see what her eyes have seen, what all the slaves have seen.

"We're here," she says again. I close my eyes against the warmth in her voice which reminds me of my mother and father both. She takes her hand away from my shoulder and my shoulder nearly aches from her sudden absence. I nod my understanding, not trusting my voice yet in this new place that may cut out my tongue with its foreignness and hand it back to me in ribbons.

The woman gathers her children and their bags and they go clambering down the corridor of the bus with the others. I watch them all go and wonder if I have the strength to leave the seat that has been my sanctuary for so many hours. I have risen only to move to the back of the bus, to wait my turn in line to go to the bathroom, and returned, and sat. What am I afraid of, I wonder? What is there to be afraid of? America has sold all her goods to us in Haiti. We have it all: Coca-Cola battling Kola Champagne, Malibu Beach battling the long stretches of sand below Jacmel south of the capital, dreams of New York City and Los Angeles, jewels for the women and handguns for the men. We have been taught to love this America and we believe in its promise of equality. The proof: Michael Jordan, Jesse Jackson, Babyface. It's all there for us to get, even if we have to fight our way in. So what am I afraid of? I take a deep breath, nod to my reflection in the glass, and grab my bag.

I walk out of the bus into air thick with sticky humidity even though it is the middle of the night. I have several hours before the pickup takes place and I am taken to my new, temporary home. I sit in the bus station for a time but the green of the fluorescent lights bouncing off the dirt-streaked squares of linoleum makes me feel sick to my stomach. I double over and cough, closing my eyes to keep the room from swirling about me.

"You all right?"

I squint upward to see an old man attired in a green jumpsuit, mop in hand, staring at me. His face betrays years of hardship and heartache in every fold of his skin.

"You all right, son?" he says again, this time peering up into my face. "Is there something I can do for you? Something I can get you?"

I say nothing. The room continues to spin.

"Maybe you need some fresh air." He puts down the mop and says a word to someone further off whom I cannot see. Everything in front of my eyes is distorted. "I'll put your bag in a locker, see?" He disappears from view then returns, placing a key in my hand then leads me out of doors. "Breathe in son. Breathe. I told the night watchman I was taking my break." He laughs a soft, warbly laugh. "I'm going to take you downtown for a drink and something to eat. Looks like you could use both."

I breathe in deeply and my senses slowly return as if I have just broken through the surface of a large body of water and am gasping for breath, light streaming through, the shore coming into focus, palms swaying. But here, what my eyes take in is a muted darkness, the faint yellow glow of streetlights, and the scent of damp earth. There is a light mist in the air. I shiver.

The man laughs and reveals gapped front teeth. "You must've come from somewhere hot, son, if this place makes you shiver."

I smile back and look into the dark, revealing eyes of a youthful soul still contained within the brittle frame of an aging man. "Yes," I say, "It is much warmer in my country."

He slaps me on the back then holds out his right hand, "Louis," he says. "Name is Louis Brown."

I shake his hand. "Good to meet you. I'm Alexis."

"Know where you're going from here, Alexis? You waiting for family?"

"Not exactly," I say. I fumble for the letter and show him what it says. "I think someone is supposed to pick me up here later but I'm not sure when."

Louis shrugs and smiles again. "Well, I've got thirty minutes to get something to drink and eat. They'll wait for you."

With that said, we set off down a street called Broadway, a wide street with old churches made of stone. I think back to what I had been taught in school about the South. I cannot imagine Christophe here, or in a place so much like this one, especially in a state of war. Of course, none of this would have been here then, or very little of it. Louis takes me down to the banks of the Mississippi, passing bars with their doors wide open, music and alcohol slip-sliding into the air, intoxicating us.

It is too dark to see much of anything. I smell the water, flat, lifeless; I sense its brownness, thickened with earth, remains of bloated corpses, excrements, modern pollutants. This is a river that knows no rest. But its smells are foreign to me, somehow more pristine than anything I know of home with the streets crowded with people standing shoulder to shoulder, sweating out their worries and hurry, mounds of garbage being burned out in the open, singeing the air with decay, and, encircling it all, the raw, acrid scent of the sea. Sadness fills me because I know this water's history is also my own, like ancestral blood in the veins.

We take our time walking up the main street; its old brick buildings stand guard sleepily. Most have their windows boarded up and graffiti scrawled against their walls. There are men wrapped in layers of torn clothes, long beards moving softly in the evening breeze, lying across door frames. Some lie on gratings in the middle of the sidewalks. Most of them are white men and I wonder at this poverty that knows no color line as I step over them. I wonder if I will be like them one of these days, my dreams like pieces of broken crystal brushing against each other with soft, musical noises in the middle of my chest that only I can hear. Best to keep on walking.

"Here we are," Louis finally says. "We've reached the promised land." He leads the way into a restaurant filled with people, the beat of a bass guitar shaking the large windowpane of the storefront in a slow, undulating rhythm. The name of the bar is "Relax Blues."

I follow Louis into the dimly lit eatery. I smell boiled potatoes and the grease of grilled steaks. The air is laced with stale smoke and liquor. The music seems to be pulling us further in with a low crooning of drums and syncopation. Then a voice sings out and moves me as nothing has for such a long, long time. Louis smiles back at me as he sits down at a table with four other men and pulls out a chair for me. But the voice keeps me in a trance. It is a voice deep and smooth as scarlet velvet. It stops me dead in my tracks then pulls me past a man with skin the color of eggplant seated at the bar, tapping out the beat with the toe of his shoe. On the stage, the man with the velvet voice is singing the blues, a deep kind of blues, a blues that makes you stop and take notice as if your name is being called but. It is the voice of the Mississippi lying just a few yards away: it is the voice of all those whose bones are embedded in its underbelly: it is the voice of shattered dreams and hopes beaten underfoot from fleeing.

I watch from the edge of the stage. I watch the man with the velvet voice and the leathery skin, his bony fingers moving over the strings of an old guitar worn down to the wood in the tapping places, lips moving over the holes of a harmonica resting around his neck from time to time when his voice needs a rest from all those blues. He wears an old suit that reminds me of my father when he prepares for Sunday mass and dons his gray-black wool, too hot for any Southern parts let alone the Antilles. I watch this man sing with his eyes closed as if he is possessed, feet moving up and down against floorboards marked with scuff marks from a dozen boots like his own. For a second time on this journey, I cry.

This time, I cry because these men and women here assembled are my brothers, sisters, and, for the first time, I feel I have not arrived in a foreign land.

"It's all right," I hear Louis say as he grasps my elbow and stirs me back to the table where his friends sit with compassion in their eyes. Each of them slaps my knee and then they turn to each other, telling the best and worse part of the story of their day. I sit and let them order me a shot of whisky, steak and potatoes. They let me cry for a moment and then we all sit and listen to the blues man sing the songs that have kept us all moving, dark bodies swaying like stalks of sugarcane, stronger than steel, through the passage ways of a long and foreboding history that has not yet come to an end.

When Louis and I finally make it back to the bus station, light has begun to rise and I can see the downtown as it really is, a shamble of low-rise buildings. There are placards on some announcing renovations and a "Planet Hollywood." I have read about those in the American magazines in Haiti but I am sure that is one franchise that will never make it to our shores even if we have become one of the most faithful consumers of American products on this side of the world: Stallone, Bond . . . all those cartoon figures playing on the movie screens of the Rex Theatre. Who knows what they can be about with all their death and destruction? As if we don't already have our own to deal with. But the American version always seems much more desirable.

"You have your key?" Louis inquires.

"The key?" I say, momentarily confused.

"For your bag, man." Louis' eyes are red-rimmed and puffy. "You got to get your stuff."

"Oh yeah," I remember now that he put my bag away in a locker. I hand over the key.

Louis returns with my bag, sets it down, then shakes my hand again. "It's been a pleasure meeting you, brother. A real pleasure. If you ever need me, you know where to find me."

"Relax Blues?" I smile.

"That's right, son. There's no better place for miles for brothers like us. And I guarantee it won't be here for long after they're through with their remodeling, if you know what I mean."

I nod. "I'll look for you."

Louis eyes me with a measuring glance. "I hope you will son. I hope you will."

He leaves then, after a word with the night watchman. I watch him go home, wherever home is, missing him suddenly, a man who only hours ago had no resonance in my memory, no face in my imagination.

I straighten myself out and look for my ride.

There is only a man in blue jeans and a white shirt with a straw hat in hand in the waiting room. He smiles. He must be waiting for me.

He puts out his hand and introduces himself: "Jean-Pierre, from Jacmel." I nod, note the absence of a last name even though I had done the same with Louis. It seems odd coming from a Haitian, when it was common knowledge among us that your last name could reveal who you were, from whose loins you had emerged, if your family owned land or worked for others, if you have a name worth holding on to.

Perhaps things are different here in America, I think to myself.

Jean-Pierre has my name in his hands as well as a picture of me; I can see both on a piece of paper he holds gingerly. There is nothing for me to hide. He directs me to his car, a new model Toyota I have never seen before, and we are on our way. Jean-Pierre drives in quiet, face stonily set. I stare ahead at the road and wait to arrive at my final destination.

"Here we are," Jean-Pierre finally says, pulling into the driveway of a housing complex with a gray brick exterior. He points out one of the units on the second floor; its windows are curtained with pieces of paper. "You'll be staying here with four other men, all from Haiti." He explains how things will work from this point on, how the volunteers with the Jesuit order that has processed my paperwork will come in the morning and take us all to the main center and train us in different jobs before placement. Placement will take at least two months. It is going to be a lot of hard work, he says with a toothy smile, but worth the effort.

The interior of the apartment is nondescript, and cramped. The men I meet there as I enter are sullen, quiet, and I recognize nothing of myself in them.

I am suddenly struck with the thought that, sometimes, when a plant is uprooted, it can wither and also die.

The weeks at the Jesuit center are long, as long as the strip of road called Charlotte that the complex overlooks where I take walks to clear my mind after supper. The road is lined with pawnshops, places to change checks into dollar bills, small convenience shops with names like "Papa's" and "Mama's" painted in red on their clapboard fronts, shops that are closed with chains at night. It reminds me of downtown Port-au-Prince: the men squatting outside the shop doors, passing smokes from one to the other, braided hair falling across their faces or held back by red, green, and black berets, colors of Africa stamped on their foreheads, all over their brown skins. Their eyes are tired, and my heart goes out to these men every time they say hello or ask for money which I don't have because none has come to line my pockets. They seem to know I'm not one of them and they must wonder why I insist on walking their street every night as if I could be. I don't explain. I have no words for their world or to explain my world in theirs. But soon, in not very much time at all, and as quiet as a whisper, I become part of the fabric of their days.

Charlotte becomes my street. Neon signs and all. Every day, I walk past heaps of tires, boarded-up houses, a house standing on its own between heaps of metallic debris, a yellow dog tied to a cypress tree. The weeping willows and magnolia trees release their pungent scents into the air. All this reminds me of the hills of Haiti; the vegetation is much the same except that there are few fruit trees sweetening the wind. But I will not cry in this land of the dispossessed. I will not shed tears any longer.

I want to become hard as the pavement beneath my feet, hard as stone. A lonely way to live in a place not your own, that plays with your memory like an old record, like a Billie Holiday song.

Philippe

It was not until their high school graduation that Philippe broke through the layer of difference between himself and Alexis which had birthed a profound silence.

That night, the skies had a look of foreboding. The wind whipped through the dense trees with a ferocity that tore limbs from their hardy trunks. The village paths were filled with people walking to and from each other's homes carrying buckets, candles, loose pieces of white clothing for the dance that would take place later, celebrating the end of twelve years of schooling for the luckier children of the community, an end they hoped would bring rewards, some hope back into the heart of the village that had seen too much poverty to be able to put scarcity into words.

The women stood against each other's fences and laughed, shared spoonfuls of broth, commented on the contents of meals. The men sat on the porches, smoking pipes, cutting the air to ribbons with their laughter. The younger children ran through the yards, screamed at each other, danced in anticipation of the revels. Philippe sat with Alexis on Mamie Leila's porch and together they watched the comings and goings of the villagers with a keen eye. They commented on the girls they knew from school, yelling insults at them that were actually meant to make them feel as if their notice was worth the price of a little good-humored abuse. If they went too far, which was usually the case more so with Alexis than it was with Philippe, who preferred to smile and wave when there was someone he liked walking across their field of vision, Mamie Leila stepped out from her kitchen and waved a wooden spoon at him in warning of what was to come if he did not hold his tongue in check. "Respect where you came from," she would often say.

And so Alexis held himself in check, especially when Marthes, a girl from their school, walked by in an indigo blue dress with matching ribbons in her braided hair. He elbowed Philippe and pointed with a quick thrust of his chin in Marthes' direction. Philippe waved. Alexis elbowed

Philippe again but this time to make him put his arm down. He wanted to appear nonchalant with Marthes, as if he really didn't care one way or the other if she waved back. She waved back.

"How are you?" she said.

Alexis looked at Philippe then down at his shoes. "Oh, fine."

"Just fine?" she asked, a pout hanging in the air.

Philippe felt his anxiety turn to disgust.

"Yep." Alexis answered, Just hanging out with my friend here." He put a gangly arm around Philippe's thin shoulders. Philippe slumped into Alexis' side, feeling the warmth of his body. Alexis squeezed his shoulder; it reassured him. He forgot his defenses and smiled at Marthes.

The scent of blooming magnolias was in the air. It would be a lovely evening. Marthes breathed in deeply. She made as if to walk away. Her left hand lingered against the top edge of a fence post. "Well, I hope you can tear yourself away to make it to the dance," she said, back turned to them both, her head positioned sideways, angular planes of skin shining in the sunset's glow, mouth pursed with some hidden intention. She squinted her eyes into thin dark lines, faced the boys again. "You the painter?" she asked Alexis.

Alexis smiled, proud that his status as artist was becoming recognized in the village. "Yes," he said. "That's me." He looked to Philippe who was scowling at him, moving out of the curl of his arm.

Philippe spat against the ground. Mamie Leila stretched out her neck to see what was going on. *"Pitit mwen, pa krache nan legim mwen yo, non,"* she hissed like an old tired hen.

Philippe waved her back into the alcove of the kitchen with a loud, "Uh, hunh." He turned to Alexis, "Are you going to talk to her 'til nightfall?" He suddenly felt threatened, as if the space he shared with Alexis would grow smaller until it disappeared if he allowed the flirtation across the porch, the yard, the fence posts, to go on any longer.

"No, *frè,*" Alexis replied, cocking his head to the side, eyes languidly filled with sunset colors. The amber of his eyes absorbed every hue of the falling sun, streaks of purple, oranges tracing shadowed lines.

Looking into his eyes, Philippe wondered how Alexis could see anything around him clearly. He wondered if Alexis held the whole world in his eyes or if he was blinded by the splendor they reflected at odd times during the day, times when everything around them shifted in shapes, appearance, brilliant colors dimming to pastels, light colors naming themselves in fire.

Alexis stared back into Philippe's eyes, registering the uncertainty that lay dormant behind the heavy eyelids. What could be so frightening about a girl? He turned to look at Marthes. She was pretty: skin a sienna red, black coarse hair with hints of purple highlights tinted by the sun, eyes narrow ovals like grapes, a plump mouth he could draw from memory with a piece of soft colored charcoal or with nothing at all, with only the tip of his fingers against the red soil that matched the color of those lips. His thoughts were interrupted by Philippe's impatient knocking of his knee against his own. "We'll see you there," he said to Marthes, and as she made a show of straightening out her skirt which fell softly against her thin, bare thighs, he yelled out, "Maybe I'll paint you someday."

Her laughter carried itself on the pulse of the purple night air that grew thickly around them even though she had already regained the street and disappeared behind other human forms that had none of her allure.

Philippe sighed, delivered. Alexis was all his own once more. He smiled at his friend, "What shall we do now?"

Alexis stood up, shook off the dust from his jeans. "Nothing to do but join the festivities."

They kissed Mamie Leila on both her chubby cheeks, picked their way through the food she was preparing for later that evening. She tried to reach for Philippe and hug him to her. He pushed away her hands, pointing to the white shirt he was wearing that she had ironed for him. They left the house in a loud flurry of boy-turned-to-men steps. Their laughter joyous anticipation of the evening's revelry. They walked out into the streets and joined the fevered bustle.

The villagers were decked out in their Sunday best, some in the robes of *vodou* initiates, and were heading to the school on the hill in small groups as the evening enveloped each house in its own private and somber cloud. Philippe and Alexis stumbled through the crowds and arrived at the school out of breath.

The main hall had been decorated with colored streamers. Drumbeats sounded out from the stage, making the walls tremble with a syncopated rhythm. A *ra-ra* band from the village filled the platform with quickly moving fingers, flat palms, an occasional shout, the twisting of a waist, heads snapping back, teeth holding tongues, lips smacking with the taste of a well-sounded out beat. And the people who arrived early were already snaking across the makeshift dance floor, flesh loosened from the bone, frowns thrown out to the wind still whistling the murmur of an impending storm. Philippe and Alexis joined the fray until they were being held up against each other by the other bodies on the floor. There was nowhere to move but upward, and the crowd threw up their hands to heaven as the band sped up the tempo. Philippe and Alexis were two small ships riding an invisible but powerful sinewy wave.

"This is how we dance in the clearings," Philippe yelled at Alexis, alluding to the *vodou* ceremonies that were held in the forest. But Alexis could not hear him. He was listening to the beat of the band, watching the hands fly up and up, and his eye had caught a flash of blue to his right that he followed until Marthes materialized in her dress, looking as fresh as she had been on the other side of Mamie Leila's fence.

Alexis touched Philippe's arm lightly. "I'm going," he said.

Philippe watched Alexis move through the crowd as if oiled. He himself could not move to the left or right. He was being held up by the other dancers. It was some time before he realized where Alexis had gone, and with whom. He was too caught up in the crashing of hard, sweaty palms against the stretched hides of drum. He felt the beat against the soles of his bare feet. He closed his eyes against the droplets of sweat sliding off his forehead and emptied his mind of thought.

It felt like hours later when Philippe ventured out from the heat of the dance floor to look for Alexis. It had only been minutes. The party was in full swing. The drums could be heard from miles around. At the center of the storm, the beat clapped like thunder. Fat droplets of rain fell on the corrugated tin roof, dancing along with the villagers to their own peculiar rhythm. When Philippe stepped outside, he was startled by the water falling on his face. It was raining as hard outside as the feet were falling upon the ground penned within the thin walls of the school. The blue-black skies were illuminated by sudden flashes of white lightning. Philippe threw back his head, opened his mouth, and drank in the rain, gurgled laughter. He heard the snapping of twigs behind him, a soft folding of pliant branches at first, then a number falling prey to some unforeseen weight. The lightning flashed again and when Philippe turned around to see where the distant noise was coming from he saw the edge of a blue dress thrown back over thin brown thighs. The rest of the body was hidden from view. He saw the green-and-red plaid short-sleeved shirt that Alexis had been wearing earlier, blue jeans fallen to midthigh, fabric bunching in unnatural folds against soft skin. The lightning disappeared and all returned to darkness. Philippe's eyes could see nothing more. His ears could hear nothing of the two whose bodies he had seen entwined, locked in a passionate embrace. The rain fell again, harder. The dancing behind him, in the hall, had taken on a maddening cadence. The feet leaped into the air, fell with purpose onto the ground, and somewhere in the dense cloud of darkness, branches crackled beneath invisible weights and bodies swayed like the fallen fronds of palm trees. Philippe stood in the rain a long time, feeling numb beneath the trails of water. Then some of the dancers burst out into the rain and took him in their arms back into the hall.

When the sun rose, the hall had been cleared of its revels for hours. The village was already quiet with sleep. The drums had been carried away on the thin hips of the men with the flattened palms, the long fingers on hands that seemed no more delicate than stalks of cane but which could strum out rhythms to make pollen drift out of newly opened flowers.

Alexis had walked Marthes home after their encounter in the shadows of the hall, drumbeats holding them up against the wall of the building, rain anointing them with secret blessings. He had returned to the hall to find Philippe staring into space, glassy-eyed, body wet from rain and sweat. They had walked from the hall to the shed behind the school. Alexis had taken Philippe in the half-circle of his arms. Philippe had wept in the space between Alexis' neck and shoulder. Alexis had buried his fingers in his friend's hair, a gesture of consolation, of grief for having pained him in a way he did not know. They did not speak until Philippe's tears stopped flowing and it seemed to Alexis that Philippe had fallen asleep, standing up, braced against his body as if to an anchor.

September 10, 1991

Carmen

Trudging up the wooden steps to the Victorian house after a long day's work, still thinking about Gladys and her plea for help of a few days earlier, Carmen feels a sudden lightness in her body. She is pleased that all of the sudden changes in her life, post-Nick, have included this refuge. She checks her mailbox and finds nestled between a stack of bills and flyers a letter postmarked from Haiti. The multicolored stamp grabs her attention and she glances at the writing. Her name is written in the familiar curlicues of her mother's hand, a style she had acquired from the nuns at the French primary school she had attended in Port-au-Prince. Carmen had always envied her mother her childhood and the strict discipline of the Haitian schools she had had the privilege to frequent. Her own handwriting was the product of a liberal education in Canada, where individuality was stressed over penmanship. Carmen felt that her own schooling had fostered in her a sort of lackadaisical approach to life, no *t*'s had to be crossed or *i*'s dotted. Her writing was hardly legible, her mother often complained when she wrote back. Carmen wonders if her mother has ever pondered the difference in their upbringings, of all that had been lost in the crossing of the waters to Canada.

Carmen sighs to herself and unlocks the heavy front door. Once inside she takes a deep breath and makes her way up the creaking steps that comfort her with their aged presence. She will open the letter after preparing her supper, an activity which always soothes her spirit and makes her feel as if she can withstand any news, good or bad, in a state of quietude. She does not know what the letter contains, but since she has finally announced to her mother that her engagement with Nick has been broken—the breaking apart she has left unexplained—she knows her mother would have something to say about her unmarried state and her age. She wants to be seated when reading the critical words in her mother's hand. At least she does not have to speak to her face-to-face.

When Carmen finally opens her mother's letter, her dinner of rice and kidney beans completed as she read through her bills and made a mental note of how to begin to get rid of the final remnants of her debts, it is to find a very brief note and a photocopied excerpt from a faded typed manuscript titled "The Diary of a Madwoman." The note, in French, read simply:

Très chère,

Je suis désolée d'avoir appris que tu as cassé avec Nicholas.
Tu devrais venir nous voir. Je t'envoie quelques pages d'un manuscrit que j'ai découvert chez Mr. Antoine ou je travaille comme secrétaire libraire depuis quelques semaines. J'ai pensé que cela pourrait t'interesser. Je pense à toi souvent, ma petite, et je t'embrasse très fort.
Le pays est en voie de transition. Ce n'est pas terrible comme progrès mais je crois qu'il y a quelque chose qui t'attend. Même, j'ai vu Léah dernièrement. Elle n'a pas beaucoup changé.
Viens nous voir. Tout le monde veux te revoir.

Je t'embrasse,

Mamie

Carmen is surprised that her mother seems so understanding about Nick, whose name she had, from the very beginning, chosen to alter to its French equivalent. Nick had thought it was cute, liked to think of himself as a Frenchman "manqué" or one who should have been born French. Her mother has volunteered that she has finally found work as a secretary/librarian for an old friend of the family, Mr. Antoine, who has one of the most extensive private libraries in Port-au-Prince. It had been said to contain unedited and unpublished manuscripts from famous Haitian literary figures, many of whom died young or were forced into exile by Duvalier père, leaving most of their unfinished works behind in their haste to flee the country back in the late fifties and early sixties. It was in Mr. Antoine's archives that Carmen's mother must have found the "Diary of a Madwoman." It was probably there, too, that she had found the manuscript titled "The Myth of King Cristophe and His Mighty Citadel," which she had forwarded a few weeks prior and which Carmen had read just recently as she let curiosity about her homeland stir her toward the mimeographed sheets that reminded her of the ways Haiti was still behind the times, still using outdated technology yet progressing nonetheless. Twice in the letter, her mother urged her to return to Haiti for a visit. The family wanted to see her, she wrote. And she had run into Léah, an old childhood friend of Carmen's, a girl blind since birth who had scared everyone but Carmen because she could see without sight and was unafraid of darkness. Carmen wondered what Léah looked like now, what she had made of her life. She remembered her as a beautiful young girl, skin dark as winter plums and eyes black and bright as lit coal.

Letter in hand, Carmen tries to think of what it would be like to set foot in Haiti once again, what it would be like to turn new eyes on a country that had birthed her, and her mother also, only to become a forgotten jewel in the crown of her memory. The only thing that had kept her tied to the island of her birth throughout her childhood had been telephone lines, umbilical cords made of twine and wire. Her father, born and raised in New Brunswick, the son of a fisherman, had no interest in the small island and discouraged family trips to his wife's and daughter's birthplace. Once they settled in Montreal in the midseventies, any mention of Haiti would send him furiously out of the house even though he had allowed himself to fall in love with a Haitian woman with copper skin, had even agreed to spend their honeymoon on the island, and had let his wife go home to her family to have their one and only child.

Carmen had been conceived in a Club Med along the western shore, a few miles north of the capital. In the photographs Carmen had seen, few had been taken outside of the resort. Carmen had never been able to ask her father what about Haiti had made him hate it so. Perhaps it had nothing to do with Haiti itself but with the marriage he had entered into, knowing so little of himself that he was unprepared to meet the challenges of another so different. Now that he was gone, dead of a heart attack at age fifty only a year ago, it was too late to try to find answers to those questions.

Carmen wonders if some of the answers are awaiting her in Haiti. She wonders if her mother's letters and pieces of manuscripts are fragments of some giant map to the future she has yet to understand. She puts the letter down and begins to read the mimeographed pages that had been folded and tucked into the envelope along with her mother's letter, in search of her mother's voice, of home.

From the Diary of a Madwoman: Northern Haiti, 1805

Lafolle gathers wildflowers in her fists as if they are clumps of shorn hair. Weed-like, their thin roots squeeze through the openings between fingers prematurely gnarled and scarred from the healed-over cuts she has suffered in the cutting of cane. She gathers the wildflowers in her heavied, trembling hands, tears streaming from half-shut eyes.

From the side of the road, stragglers stand and watch her hummingbird flight from one tiger lily struggling to stand above the parched earth to the other. They will say later that her eyes had been clear as glass, that she had foamed at the mouth and nostril, that she had eaten the petals in her hands in a frenzy before she began to gather the remaining pieces of the dismembered body into her patchwork apron.

Those who, unlike her, knew how to wield the cutlass through bone and flesh, who knew how to snap fingers with one sharp blow of rust-colored steel to remove the gold and stone-studded rings of the Emperor, watch her behind hooded eyes. Her feet guide her away in rhythmic steps, from the hands trembling around the worn wooden handles of foot-long machetes, the blades leaving sweeps of red against blue-black veined, muscled calves.

Smoke rises into the air in slow-moving, bilious clouds of orange, yellow, and gold. Waves of heat snake themselves between the ground and the fumes rising from the burning cane and rice fields that hundreds of feet have plodded through not an hour earlier. They have lost count of how many days, months, calendar cycles have gone by. They blink in unison, unbelieving.

It had taken hours for the crowd to assemble in the fields, to descend upon their leader, pull him from his horse, bring the machetes down from the blue sky overhead and into his plum-brown flesh, to set the fires around the carnage, to wipe the blades clean against the brush rising from the sides of the road.

It took only minutes for the crowd to disperse, some to spread the story beyond the valley and into the villages rising into the mountains, others disappearing to forget what they had witnessed, others still, remaining, shadows of regret hovering about their brows.

At present, stray dogs skitter in and out of the now barely moving throng on their way to the capital, nosing here a severed thigh with the knee hanging limply at the bottom by a thread of tendon, licking there the blistering skin of a purplish-brown arm lopped off at the socket. Two men with machetes tied with twine against their wide backs drag behind them the torso in a burlap stained purple with blood, stopping their unsteady progress down the dirt road only to kick the enfeebled jaws of the strays away, to scoop up the chewed remains into the bag.

At least an hour's walk behind them, on the outskirts of the thinning crowd, Lafolle follows the strays from piece to piece of what remains of their leader's dismembered body: a finger there, another here, until she reaches a count of ten. A ghost, she moves in and out of the clouds of smoke and dirt, full skirts bunched at the waist, stained apron twisted up into a makeshift bag, starched muslin shirt wetted to the skin with her own sweat, a bright red, silk kerchief tied about her head, tendrils of hair encircling her exposed, cauliflower ears. She does not see the troubled, clouded-over eyes following her in her wake.

They call her *Lafolle*, the Madwoman, for her habit of living always on the edge of villages, accepting nothing but the dried necks and feet of chickens from the women who talk about her strange ways loudly around the black pot at dinner, from the way she smiles and talks to the spirits in the air all the day long, twisting her hair away from her wide, sunken cheeks only to plunge the tips into her full mouth as if tasting the sweetest mango, lips cracked from heat and lack of care. Her aloneness frightens them.

Her real name is fragile, simple, brief, to the point. She used to whisper her name in her daughter's ears: Défilée. That is, when her daughter was still alive to hear her voice, when her daughter was still a slave as her mother had been.

She is proud of the way Papa Dessalines wore a red flag around his neck for the blood he set to flow in the roughly carved paths leading way onto way, proud of how he ordered his men to cut the throats of anyone who foolishly dared stand in their way. She used to murmur Papa Dessalines' exploits to her daughter, ending her stories with the words *"Souviens toi."* Remember. Always.

When she murmured those words, she thought of how she could have lived the rest of her life in the canefields with her feet splitting open from the raw skins of the stalks. She would think of her daughter following in her footsteps made red from the bloodstained earth. At least the yellow fever took her daughter away, quickly, but not without pain, as it did so many of them only a few years ago.

Défilée abhors pain: she does not like to see the human body torsioned out of shape, suffering.

If it had not been for her brother in the spirit, if it had not been for their furious, former slave of a leader, Papa Dessalines . . . terrible Papa Dessalines . . . she would not have been able to place a stone with her daughter's own true name on her small grave when she died at barely nine years, the age when a child begins the process of flowering into her own bright and beautiful future. Papa Dessalines, she thinks, how could they do this to you? How could they tear you limb from limb and leave you to rot in the dust you saved us from? How could they forget that you freed us from the cane fields, the singeing whip? How could they forget that without you, we would still be drowning the children at sea? She hears the sucking of teeth, the heavy sighs laying a hard road of gossip into the sullen mountains. . . . *Un-hunh, he make himself Emperor. . . . He putting jewels on his fingers for us to kiss like he some precious something. . . . He think he King? Christophe waiting for him to die to make monarchy. We going to let it happen? . . . What we letting happen? . . .* Défilée shuts her eyes against the bitterness.

Défilée gathers the emperor's ten dismembered fingers into her apron along with the wildflowers. The fingers are not unlike her own, misshapen, swelling in the heat, turning odd shades of purplish brown. She strides through the dust-laden streets with determination, the burned fields laying in waste on either side of her, the air thinning of its smoke, the wind gathering about her face in a gesture of compassion.

The mound in the public cemetery where the remains have been hastily buried, the emperor stripped of his fineries, dust returned to dust, is fresh. She digs at the blood-red earth, buries the flesh and bone she has carried to rest and pats the loose soil back into place with tenderness. She strews the wildflowers over the grave that will be left to ruin, unmarked, to hide their communal shame.

The crowd still assembled at the grave site watches Lafolle giving Papa Dessalines his due. They watch her kneel in prayer: *Mesi Pa Dessalines. Mesi. Se te ou ki livre mwen nan lanfè. Mesi Pa Dessalines.* Thank you for delivering me from the hell of this land. *Mesi Pa Dessalines.* She sings him a song of praise, palms falling against the other, sounding out like drums: *Papa Dessalines, ou tankou Bondye. Koupe tèt, boule kay! Papa Dessalines, ou tankou Bondye.*

Repeating her refrain, clapping her hands turned hard like claws from the blood and white pieces of flesh staining her own dark skin, her feet glide around the mound in a soft two-step—*hushhh, hushhh*—stilling the crowd to quiet.

The air stirred by Lafolle's feet glances about the crowd's naked ankles: They ache to fall beside her and join in prayer. They are shamed by Lafolle's piety. They deny themselves the pleasure of the dance. They do not want to admit that it does not take much for the mad to become sane and the sane to become mad in the world they have all conspired to create. Their despair is a thick morass they dare not move through: they are bogged down by the memories of the fires, of the bloodshed, of Papa Dessalines falling off his horse, mouth closing and opening like a fish drowning in his own still pond. How will they atone for his death? How can they put his desecrated body back together again? They note the red kerchief on Lafolle's head—Papa Dessalines' flag. The putrid smell of the decaying body, the heady scents of the freshly plucked flowers, gather about their heads in soft clouds of hope.

When the smoke clears and the sky returns to its placid blue, the stench of death dissipated by the salted sea air drifting in from the harbor, they will tell her that this country, this half of Hispaniola that faces toward the vast and unbeckoning continent to the north, took the shape of the scorpion's claw to fend off those who wanted to conquer her wide shores, plunder her robust mountains, squat in her deep valleys in blind contentment.

Défilée can see what they mean when she stands at the harbor and looks out to sea, but she prefers to see in the shape of the mountains and the shoreline an open mouth speaking, a flower in bloom, or a sliver of moon as its crescent wanes. Yet she knows too well that the spirit of the scorpion lives on in this land, in the hearts of the men who descended upon the shores and attacked the bands of Arawaks, their common and fast-forgotten predecessors, who called the island "Ayiti," "Land of the Mountains." She knows that after a time, the scorpion's bite became that of the slaves who were brought here with their backs bent over blood-caked chains of iron binding them to others who did not speak their tongues. Those slaves stood tall, eyes boring into that of their enslavers, revolted, and attacked. Fresh blood was spilled on this soil, seeped into the land.

Christophe will soon ascend in the north. Like Toussaint before him, and Papa Dessalines, he will seek to make them believe that the future is paved with riches, gold and diamonds, that all is within their reach. Défilée knows already that Christophe will be lethal.

As she picks up her skirts and sweeps the ground with her hems, her feet continuing to move to their own rhythm against the hard wall of the crowd's fear, Défilée can see that nothing will change these ways of blood letting blood. She dances her dance and sings her songs day onto day onto day, night after swirling night.

When her dance is done, she falls asleep with the damp earth of a grave against her cheek for a pillow, her reborn daughter's voice pulsating like the wings of a butterfly against her ears, pulling her into a hum of spirit voices, each drawing maps in the wind for her to follow some hundred years into the future. She smiles in her sleep, content. Her daughter, like the dawn, will return. So that what she has just witnessed will not rise again like dust to wind. So that the wretched of the earth might do better than eat hope in place of daily bread and tears at the table for their wine.

September 11, 1991

Carmen

"Girl," Yannick clicks her tongue, "You have a case of the homesick blues. Why don't you go see your mother? Hasn't she been telling you to go home? Sometimes our mothers are envoys from the heavens. Like it or not, they know more about us and the world than we give them credit for sometimes."

Carmen nods though she isn't sure she agrees. For days now this has been the subject of ongoing conversation between herself and Yannick as they sit at their desks at work. She asks questions about Yannick's memories of Haiti, wonders whether or not she should go. She is indecisive yet she knows deep down that she does need to go home.

But is Haiti still home for her? Is it her father's memory haunting her that keeps her from buying the ticket every time she calls Air Canada? Or is it the ghost of Nick? Nick, who calls her every Sunday for updates on the pregnancy. Sometimes she sits at the kitchen table and listens to him talk to her through the answering machine. She rarely gets up to answer his calls. When she does, they seem to have nothing to say to each other.

Maybe home is everywhere you've left and aren't any longer. Maybe this is why she needs to see Haiti once more. "You might be right," she says to Yannick.

Yannick looks at her with sympathy in her eyes. "I know it's hard. It's hard for all of us, I think. Especially those of us who were forced out under the Duvaliers. I haven't been back in years. Don't know what I would find there." She straightens some papers on her desk, puts on her glasses in a gesture that marks the end of her side of the conversation. Talk of returns makes her uncomfortable even though she is often the one to bring it up. If it weren't for her son and girlfriend, she knows she would have found her way back already. "Just give it some more thought, okay?"

"I'll do that," Carmen replies, realizing that Yannick has slipped out of reach and that she needs to get back to her own work as well. "I'll see you."

Yannick smiles absent-mindedly, her mind already thinking ahead to the caseload on her desk. "Maybe lunch?" she asks as her fingers go through the piles of paper.

"Sure," Carmen replies.

"Carmen!" Carol calls out as Carmen makes her way to her office cubicle at the back of the center. "There is someone here to see you." Carol's voice is serious, more so than usual.

Carmen looks into Carol's eyes and enters her office quickly to see what has placed so much concern in the dark irises set far apart in a round oval face which is usually lively and ready for any challenge.

There, she finds Gladys sitting in the chair in front of her desk as she had been sitting only days ago, face pummeled again. This time, her eyes are a glassy dam against her tears. Yet she shakes in her chair as if a simple touch will send her falling to pieces.

Carmen stands in front of her desk, leaning as far forward as she can in order to make out what the woman is telling her, so Gladys can sense her concern in the space remaining between them without her touch or words.

"*J'essaye*," Gladys whispers, "I am trying to change things. But things are only getting worse."

"Yes," Carmen encourages her to go on.

"But nothing is helping. Nothing. Do you understand?" She looks up at Carmen with despair and fire in her eyes, the layers of skin around each puffed and reddened.

"As I told you last time you were in, Gladys," Carmen responds slowly and very quietly, "there are ways we can help you."

"You don't understand," Gladys replies in a slow hiss, pain oozing out with the words as if she is expiring within. "You don't understand," she reaches out and grasps one of Carmen's arms at the elbow. "I feel like killing him." She looks away furtively as if fearing that her words have been overheard then closes her eyes against the pain of being shamed or, worse, understood.

Carmen stands very still, then places her right hand over Gladys' calloused fingers gripping her left elbow. At this moment, there are no words to offer, only a brief gesture of solace.

When Gladys finally lets go of Carmen's arm, it is to pull out from a sleeve a crumpled tissue, folded carefully over and over again to extend its paper life. Gladys is from the old world, a world where nothing, not even a square of tissue paper for a dripping nose, can be undervalued. Everything has its use and can be used over and over again until it literally falls apart. It is this way of thinking, in the end, Carmen thinks, that has got her into this situation. How to get her out of it?

"Will you wait for me a minute, *sè?*" she asks quietly, politely, letting the weight of the word "*sè*," sister, speak of its own the respect she has for this woman's pain, her bruised, battered body, and all the secrets she transports from one place to another trying to outlive the prison of her own mind, of her own fears.

Gladys nods, "*M la, wi.*" I'm not going anywhere.

Carmen nods and quickly makes her way back to Yannick's office. She closes the door behind her as Yannick looks up, startled, from her paperwork. A pencil is stuck behind her ear. "What is it?" she asks, trying to decipher the strained look on Carmen's face.

"I don't know what to do for this client," Carmen rushes into the office, sits in the chair facing Yannick's desk, and buries her face in her hands. She bursts into tears, not knowing why she is crying, suddenly lost.

"What is it?" Yannick asks again. She has come from around the desk and is kneeling by the chair, striking a pose so similar to Carmen's the first time she had met Gladys that Carmen cannot respond and her tears continue to flow.

"*Ti fi,*" Yannick continues, "It's all right. We'll find a solution but you have got to pull yourself together." Yannick has seen this kind of reaction to clients before in younger case workers, usually interns fresh from college who expect everything to go by the book, clients responding to their entreaties to enter counseling programs and halfway shelters, problems solved with their signatures on three-by-five cards admitting the needy to welfare privileges around the city. She is surprised at Carmen, however, as she had imagined her stronger than the average coed.

"Too much on your plate?" she says to Carmen finally, trying to bring some lightness to the situation, thinking that it must be the hormones, the early morning imbalances every first time mother experiences.

Carmen shakes her head, no, and tries to pull herself together.

Yannick hands her a tissue from the box sitting at the ready on the edge of her desk for crying children with skinned knees, burly men with bruised egos, wives or live-in girlfriends with bruised hearts, all in need of a good ear and a friendly face. "It's okay." Yannick smiles as Carmen wipes at her tears. "Who's the client?"

"Her name is Gladys," Carmen begins, "she was in here a few days ago wanting to get help. She's a battered woman."

"Did you give her our flyer?"

"I showed it to her but she didn't take it. She said one of her ancestors was a woman who set fire to Montreal when she was still a slave."

"The woman trusts you if she gave you that kind of information," Yannick murmurs. "Clearly. Do you know the husband?"

"No. She calls him Carl, or Kiko, I think."

"Oh," Yannick catches in her breath. "I know who you are taking about. There are rumors about him all over the neighborhood."

Carmen frowns, perplexed.

"Didn't you know?" Yannick sighs, "Of course not. You're new to the scene. New to everything." She remembers their earlier conversation; Carmen is a woman struggling for her identity and all of a sudden life has presented too many answers for her to handle.

"I'll take care of it, if you want," Yannick offers.

"Not everything is new," Carmen says in reply. "I've seen these things before."

"Well, it's a lot of what we do around here, dealing with domestic abuse cases."

"No, I mean I grew up with it."

"Oh," Yannick is silent. "You mean your father . . ."

"Yes."

"Your British Canadian father?" Yannick feels confused. She had assumed Carmen had escaped the worst of what it meant to be an immigrant in this country, especially a Haitian one. Sometimes the abuse of Haitian women in Haitian households took place because the society permitted it, here and back home. Women were always at the bottom of the heap. It wasn't strictly a cultural thing. But over the years of working at the community center, watching women in her own family battered throughout their lives and never making changes, having gone through it herself with her son's father, she realized that some of the violence was born out of despair. That good, decent Haitian men who would have turned their backs on the violence had they had a chance to learn to love themselves, had they had the opportunity to make a living with some dignity, not cleaning other people's messes, shining their shoes or serving them in other ways, then, then they might just have come home to their wives and girlfriends and daughters and helped with the cooking, or cleaning the dishes, or kept their hands for nothing but acts of love after a long day's work, an offering to the women in their lives who worked just as hard and long as they did day after day in a world not their own.

But because they did not have those opportunities, because their shame was laid bare for all to see in the foreign streets of a cold, northern city, the confusion of their hearts laid out in the sun like the entrails of a pig slaughtered for the evening meal, their children watching in hunger at their sides, they turned closed fists into the flesh of the women who stood by them not knowing what else to offer these men who felt like children in gruesome disguise. And the women almost never left because they understood the pain, its source, and hoped for its unmaking—an unmaking that never came.

"Yes."

"But he was born here wasn't he?" Yannick asks, still in a state of confusion. She has pulled out her chair from behind the desk and sits next to Carmen as if speaking to a client. At the back of her mind, she is thinking quickly of how to help Gladys and reaches for the phone out of reflex, calling Carol in on the problem so that Gladys will not be left sitting alone for too long. "Carol's on her way," she tells Carmen. "Do you want to talk some more about your father?"

"I don't know what to say. I'm sorry for breaking down like this in your office. It's just that . . ." she chokes back fear. "It's just that every time I see Gladys, it's as if I'm my mother's daughter again, holding her hand after a fight with my father."

"These things must be coming back to you because of your situation," Yannick says, "And you have been feeling homesick. It's all hitting too close to home."

"I don't know. Maybe. I don't know." Carmen knows that she has been thinking more and more of home since Nick's departure and her mother's letters reaching her door at unexpected moments. "I thought I'd forgotten about it. All those years have faded from my memory, more or less faded. But Gladys has brought everything back. I really can't explain why. There's just something about her that brings everything back with such clarity."

Yannick nods. "You know," she says, "we all go through some form of what you are feeling right now. Some days you feel nothing at all for these women dragging themselves in here as if it could be their very last day on earth, and sometimes it might just be. Other days you feel as if your heart is just going to tear through your chest walls."

At that moment, Carol walks into the office. "What's going on?" she asks.

Yannick quickly explains the situation.

"I think you should go home," Carol says, "and take some time from your pregnancy leave. However long you need. We'll take care of things on this end. Is Gladys still in your office?"

Carmen nods.

"Okay. Let me see how she's doing. We'll take care of it. Just go home and take care of yourself."

As soon as Carmen enters her rented room and closes the door behind her, she calls her mother in Haiti.

It is already midday on the island and her mother's voice crackles through the phone line, weary and thin like rainwater collected in a cistern emptying slowly through the copper pipes of the shower stalls newly installed on the second floor of her grandfather's house to make do during water shortages.

"*A-llo*," she says. The line crackles.

"*Maman?*" Carmen asks, knowing full well it is her mother. "*Ou tap domi?*"

Her mother laughs. They converse in French with smatterings of Kreyol. "If I had time for sleep, darling, I wouldn't sound so tired."

Carmen imagines her mother holding the telephone receiver cocked between chin and shoulder bone, sitting on a creaking bed covered with one of her grandmother's embroidered chenille throws. Her mother's slippered feet would be softly moving back and forth across the crocheted rug next to the bed. She listens to her mother's breathing. Lord, she misses her.

"How is the country?" she asks finally, setting the line on fire again. It crackles and pops and her mother's voice returns followed by a hollow echo.

"*Li . . . la,*" she says. *Li . . . la.*

"Difficult?"

"*Ti fi,* it's more of the same except now every one it seems has guns and nobody knows how to use them." Her mother laughs wryly, "They're giving Titid and his clan a hard time." She was alluding to the newly elected President Aristide, whose term in office was becoming increasingly difficult.

"*Kisa?*" Carmen wonders who is responsible now for the renewed chaos.

"*L'armée,*" her mother seems to spit the word into the phone.

Carmen is awed at how freely they are speaking. When she was a child, political discussions were left out of conversations with folks remaining on the island. No risks could be taken. Had things so changed even as they appeared to have not changed at all?

"But things are not so bad," her mother resumes, "I think we're going to make it."

"I think I want to come visit," Carmen allows.

"Oh," her mother says. Carmen can hear her smile and then hears her call out to her grandfather . . . she wants to come . . . "You don't know how much we have been wanting to see you!"

Carmen wishes that her mother had spoken for herself rather than in the collective, wishes she could be certain that her mother misses her as well.

"Well," she says, "I haven't bought a ticket yet."

"Do it soon," her mother replies, "if you are going to do it. Fewer flights are coming in. It's not clear how things are going to work themselves out."

"Is it safe?"

"Has it ever been?"

Carmen finds herself nodding at her mother silently, understanding. The chaos the country has been suffering since the departure for France in 1986 of François Duvalier's son, the overweight playboy Bébé Doc, seems so much worse because no one knows what will happen next. Allegiances unclear. Agendas ambiguous. For years, her mother's family has survived by remaining uninvolved in politics and now, all of a sudden, everything can be interpreted as a political act: what one wears, where one buys food, eats, sleeps at nights, goes to church. But the country cannot be said to be any more dangerous than it had been under the Duvalier patriarch in the late fifties through the early seventies. In Carmen's mind, it was simply a matter of what one was used to. After thirty years of dictatorship, she felt Haitians were used to living a certain way, of being suppressed and unfree to speak their minds; they were even used to the Macoutes and their killing sprees, people disappearing in the middle of the day under a bright sun. Even the most unexplainable persecutions found their footing in the madness of the times. Every occurrence had its place. Now, with the advent of democratic processes through which a new president had been elected and freely so, everything had been rearranged. It was like trying to walk through an unfamiliar room in the dark, bumping into furniture, glimpsing the light from another room beneath its closed door and stumbling toward it, not knowing what will be on the other side, salvation or continued loss.

"I'll keep thinking about it," Carmen says.

"Just do it soon if you are. We would love to see you. Who knows how long your grandfather will be with us. Most of the cousins are not home this time of year but you can see the country."

"Yes, *Maman*. I think I will."

Carmen wants to ask about Léah but she keeps the name locked inside her like a precious jewel. There will be time, she thinks. There will be time.

After hanging up the phone, Carmen ponders buying her ticket right away, heeding her mother's warning about unrest in the country. The thought of being cut off from her mother because of suspended flights frightens her. She compromises and makes a reservation.

"You have twenty-four hours to make a decision," the saleswoman says on the other end of the line, which is as clear and crisp as if the woman were calling from the next house. "Then it cancels on its own. Is there anything else I can do for you?"

"Yes," Carmen says, finally resolute. "I'd like to purchase the ticket."

"Credit card?"

"Yes."

They go through the ritual of the exchange. All the time, knots tie themselves in Carmen's stomach.

"Do you have a passport?"

"Yes," Carmen says, "Canadian."

"You'll be fine, then. Things seem pretty quiet this week in Haiti," the woman volunteers. "But I would be careful if I were you. Stay tuned to the news, you know?"

"Yes," Carmen replies. She wishes the woman could instruct her on what Haiti is like this time of year, this year of all years, how to gird her heart.

"Is there anything else I can do for you?"

"There isn't. Thank you."

"You'll have your ticket express mailed to make the flight end of week. Have a safe journey."

Carmen hangs up the phone and hopes the woman's words will ring true, then she calls back her mother to tell her she is coming home. She begins to pack her suitcase, the trip now only days away, and thinks of all that awaits her on distant shores. She wonders if she will see Léah again.

When they had met, Carmen had been twelve and graduating from elementary school. Her parents had fought over what high school she should attend. Her father had wanted her to attend a public school, no fees. Her mother had insisted on a private Catholic school that would have them scraping by after paying for tuition, bus fares, and school uniforms. Her mother had argued that it was the least they could do for their only child. Secretly, though, Carmen knew that her mother wanted to give her something of a Haitian upbringing. If they were going to live far from the Haitian community, as they did then, then the closest thing she could give her daughter was a Catholic upbringing as she had had in Cap-Haitien. Her father sought her mother's submission through a volley of accusations that still rung in her ears some ten years later: *If you had wanted money you should have married money . . . Why can't you just leave it all behind . . . Why didn't you just forget . . . Why can't you teach your daughter to assimilate . . .* He had not been aware of how assimilated she was despite her mother's own resistance to her mixed identity. Carmen wondered what he saw when he looked at her honey-toned skin.

She had his gray eyes and thin mouth. Her toes splayed out like his, each digit webbed to the other; he used to tell her that Maritimers were descendants of strange sea lions who turned into humans during the day, their webbed feet giving them away when they took off their thick woolen socks after a day out fishing. *You're mine, that's for sure,* he would say in his thick New Brunswick brogue. As if there had ever been a doubt. The argument had gone on for weeks as Carmen had graduated from the sixth grade. She avoided her parents, stayed locked up in her room until the voices died down or the muffled noise of her father's slaps against her mother's skin broke to the dead of night or a knock at the door when a concerned neighbor would try to intervene, feeling sorry for her mother. One night, her bedroom door burst open and it was her mother who stood there, a strange shadow against the shaft of light leaking in.

"Get your things," her mother said, her words strangled as if the words were too large for her vocal cords to pass. "We're leaving."

"Maman?" Carmen asked. She had been sitting on her bed looking through the flyers of the high schools her parents had been fighting over.

She favored neither and tried to see what they saw, what they were fighting so hard to win. "But what about . . . ?"

"Don't argue with me," her mother said. "Just don't argue." She had won in the living room that night. As her mother retreated from the door, Carmen could see her father sitting in the lounge chair in front of the television, fingering the buttons of the remote control even though the television itself was off. He was replaying some faraway scene in his mind. She wondered if he was thinking of New Brunswick and his parents, whom she had only met once. Both her grandparents had smiled at her but refused to pick her up. Before they left for home, her grandfather had told her father, "You're on your own now, son. You're on your own." Was it this rejection that had turned him into this shell of a man who could not love without hurting, who loved like a bull in a china store, breaking anything fragile placed in his path?

"Are you ready?" her mother had returned, smartly outfitted in a navy dress and matching hat. Her peach nut brown complexion shone in the half-light. "I don't have all night. Have you packed?"

"Yes, *Maman*," Carmen said. She had packed a suitcase hurriedly with underwear and her favorite clothes. "Where are we going?"

"Home," her mother said, as if Carmen knew what that meant. "We are going where we are wanted."

They filed out of the house while her father sat very still in front of the television, slumped over in defeat. Or was it despair she saw in his eyes? Carmen had never seen her father cry. He covered his eyes with one hand and waited for them to leave. Carmen tried to go to him and kiss him goodbye but her mother pulled her away with one hand while she gathered their luggage with the crook of her free arm, leaving the door wide open for the neighbors to see into their commotion.

Outside, a taxi awaited them at the curb and they climbed in. The next night they were in Haiti. Carmen met cousins long forgotten who resembled her mother more than she did, with rounded heads, long angular cheekbones, and brown skin reddish like pomegranates. Her mother turned into another woman before her eyes. She became like an older sister or aunt, wearing fashionable dresses instead of the thick polyester suits she wore to work or church in Canada. She played barefoot with her cousins and neighbor's children in the street in front of her grandfather's house.

"Come," she would say to Carmen, "don't be shy. This is where we belong."

Carmen would smile and wait until one of her cousins would take her hand and lead her out toward the street where much fun was to be had. They skipped rope or played hopscotch. Sometimes other children from the neighborhood would come running over to join them and they would play stickball or hide-and-seek. Her mother had never been so much fun at home.

At the end of the days, her mother and she would share her childhood bed. Curled up next to her mother, Carmen would listen as her mother read to her in Kreyol. She repeated the words silently, trying to catch the flavor of each on her tongue as if tasting a new fruit or a piece of sugarcane freshly cut, oozing its sweet juice. She began to forget her father's tired face, his body so still in his easy chair, hand covering the tears in his eyes. She began to forget the cold, the snow, the sullen white faces of the teachers who refused to help her through the bewilderment of being cut out of the games the other children played at recess because of her skin and accented English.

"*Tu t'amuses?*" her mother asked. Having fun?

Carmen nodded childishly and fell asleep against her mother night after night, hoping this idyll would last longer than any rainy season.

It was during that summer that she had met Léah for the first time. Léah who never stopped to join in the fun but who made her way up and down the streets by some strange radar that no one else could decipher unless they too were blind since birth and had developed similar skills of second sight. She avoided jeeps careening through the pitted alleyways at risky speeds and made her way from home to destination unscathed.

"You don't want to get involved with her," one of her cousins, Natalie, said to her, noticing Carmen's interest in Léah. Natalie was the oldest of the cousins. Her long, smooth hair hung in thick plaits against her back. Her skin was a rich yellow-brown like cocoa butter, her lips full, pink, and the envy of the other girls who had just begun to become interested in boys.

"Why not?" Carmen asked innocently, "she's different."

Natalie eyed Carmen incredulously, "Ay, and that's why you want to know her?"

"Why not? I'm different from you and you seem to like me well enough."

"Yeah, but that's because you're family. I'm forced to like you." Natalie flashed a wicked smile that distorted her pretty features.

The other children had begun to gather around them, abandoning the hopscotch square scrawled onto the pavement with the help of a pink piece of chalk the housekeeper had found in the laundry room below the house. Carmen's grandfather had recently hired a tutor for the ladies in employment in the house.

"What's going on?" Paul, the next door neighbor's son, asked. At thirteen, he was already taller than them all and towered over the girls like a giant. Carmen began to feel sickly.

"Nothing," she said.

"We're talking about that blind girl," Natalie said. She could just as well have stuck out her tongue at Carmen, whose face flushed in front of Paul, the most handsome of the boys they played with.

"Who?" Paul asked.

"Her," Natalie said, pointing out into the streets. Léah was making her way up the alley, hands feeling their way before her, fingers interpreting the cracks and nubs in the cement walls, the splintering doors hung on rusted hinges.

They all looked. Paul laughed. "Hey, blind girl," he called out. "Where you going?"

Léah continued on her way. She was dressed that day in the rough calico of a peasant yet her hair was smartly plaited, and ribbons tied to the end of each braid waved in the air colorfully, defiantly.

"You dumb?" Paul lashed out, irritated. "Cat got your tongue?"

In that instant, Carmen lost all respect for Paul and resolved never to speak to him again. And she hadn't to this day, though she had heard through the grapevine that he had attended university in Canada, perhaps even in Montreal, and was there still.

One of the smaller boys then threw a stone in Léah's direction. Léah stopped where she was against the wall in front of their house, on the other side of the street. She turned her head in their direction. Everyone stared across the way. Léah was beautiful. She frowned toward them and the smooth skin of her dark face was made brilliant with sweat, shining like a jewel in the dust of the street.

"*Ou pa gen anyen pou fé?*" she hurled back at them. Bunch of lazy nothings.

Natalie sucked her teeth. The younger children stepped back in surprise. Carmen stepped forward. Paul put a hand out and grabbed her arm as her mother had done when they were leaving her father behind.

Then, all of a sudden, the cousins were all yelling insults at her. Dumb goat. Blind bat. Shoeless girl. Poor dumb idiot girl. Carmen stood there and watched the girl's face crumble, then turn away.

"*Sak pase?*" The housekeeper stepped out of the laundry room and across the front yard where the cars were parked at night and into the street to see why the children were yelling among themselves.

A car rounded the curb at the end of the street and sped quickly past them. When the dust cleared, Léah was gone and there was nothing left to explain.

Carmen and Léah met face-to-face when her mother took them all to the ice cream store and Léah was sitting on a stool telling a customer his fortune. He was a pink-faced, fattish Canadian. Whatever she had to say evidently made him very happy because he reached out toward the old man behind the counter, Léah's grandfather, Léogane, also blind, and gave him some extra *gourdes*. The money had darkened with use and rubbed-in dirt. The man tipped his hat in her mother's direction as he glanced past them, smiling. Her mother smiled back. She was still a beautiful woman.

"Now," her mother cautioned the children, whispering. "Remember what I told you. Don't stare."

They fidgeted as they gave their ice cream orders to Léogane, whose eyes were clouded over, making them seem blue in the dim light of the parlor. One of the smaller cousins, a boy of six, pointed at Léah. Natalie slapped down his hand. "*Mal élevé,*" she hissed and smiled sweetly across the table at Carmen's mother. Carmen, revolted, left the table brusquely.

"*Ou vas-tu?*" her mother asked. Carmen shrugged and kept walking. Her feet led her to the stool next to Léah's.

"*Y'a quelqu'un ici?*" she asked. Anyone sitting here?

Léah signed that it was okay for her to sit there. "*Tu veux ta fortune?*" she asked.

"Non," they spoke in French and Kreyol, "I just wanted to say hello. My name is Carmen."

"Léah." Léah stuck out her hand like a boy for shaking. Carmen shook it. She could hear her cousins laughing behind her and her mother hushing them. "So you don't want your fortune?"

"No."

"That's good," Léah smiled, "Because it would take too long."

"Too long?"

"Yes. You're going to live a long life."

Carmen grew pensive, quiet, and they ate their ice cream silently until it was time for her to go. She touched Léah on the arm to let her know she was going. The skin she met beneath her fingers was smooth and soft. She wondered why Léah had worn a peasant dress through the streets if she was the granddaughter of a merchant.

"Nothing is as it seems," Léah whispered, reading Carmen's mind.

Carmen's mother led the way out of the ice cream shop. When they were out in the street, she took Carmen's hand and whispered into her ear, "I am very proud of you." It was the first time Carmen had heard her mother say such a thing.

That summer, her mother had been so unlike herself. She disappeared sometimes at evenings and there were whispers from the cousins that their aunt had gone to see *vodou* ceremonies. She rarely made it to church outings Sunday mornings. Tongues wagged. Carmen finally asked her mother what was going on.

"Would you like to go with me?" her mother asked in response, "One of these days?"

Carmen nodded, not entirely sure what she was agreeing to.

"*D'accord*," her mother smiled. "Tomorrow I will take you someplace very special. You will remember it for the rest of your life."

And she had. It was mid-July. They took a jeep and made their way inland into the dense, mountainous bush south of Cap-Haïtien. In a day's time she found herself standing knee deep in the water at the base of a large waterfall, surrounded by men, women, and children from all walks of life.

"This is Saut d'Eau," her mother whispered as they made their way past half-clothed women singing incantations to Erzulie, the *vodou* goddess of love, past old men with glazed-over eyes or crippled feet.

Carmen watched as her mother advanced into the foam, feet sure of themselves in a way she had never seen her mother, so strong, so self-full. She heard women asking Erzulie to make them pregnant. Most were asking for boys. Strong as the days are long, they pleaded. They prayed with eyes closed, full breasts exposed to the air. No one but she was startled at their nakedness. Ashamed, she looked away. Her eyes fell on Léah.

Léah was sitting on her own by a pile of rocks next to the waterfall. Her feet dangled in the water and two bright yellow jugs of water with red lids sat at her side. Carmen made her way through the throngs of people to reach her. Trees girded with white and blue sashes rose up from the embankment, making a canopy with their branches over their heads.

"*Bonjou*," Carmen said. "Do you remember me?"

"Um-hunh," Léah nodded, "The girl who didn't want her fortune read."

Carmen blushed, then realized Léah could not see her.

"Changed your mind?" Léah continued.

"No. I'm just here to . . ." Carmen paused. Why was she here? Her mother had explained the importance of the site along the way. She had told her how women came to the site to increase their fertility, as did the men.

"Purification," Léah said. "This is why we are all here."

"How did you . . . ?"

"Ah," Léah laughed, "You do not yet know who you are."

What could she mean? Carmen felt frustrated. Perhaps Natalie was right. Léah was a silly girl.

Léah became suddenly sober. Her laughter stopped short. "Don't mock what you don't know," was all she said as she stood, her dark legs glistening with water, and took up the jugs of water by their oblong handles. "The water will do you good," she said over her shoulder.

"But," Carmen started again. "I'm sorry."

"Don't be sorry," Léah said, "Just do what you came here to do. You and I will meet again."

Just then, Carmen's mother called her back into the water. She had run into the *vodou* priest who had invited her to the site.

Carmen remembers that she underwent some sort of ritual then as Léah disappeared among the trees. A baptism beneath the falls. Her mother's face shone like the moon on a clear night above her. Carmen was happy for her but they had only a week remaining before they returned to Canada and her father, who had been calling every night for the past week. She was going back. They were both going back.

Léah had been wrong. They had not met again.

Five days later, Yannick holds her hand at the airport as they wait for Carmen's flight to be called. "I wish I could come with you," she says.

Carmen nods.

They are both feeling sad. Earlier that morning, Carol let them know that Gladys and her children had returned home after staying in a shelter for a night. Nothing they had tried to do had worked. The couple refused an intervention, no counseling, no halfway house. Carol was going to turn the case over to social services. It was all out of their hands now.

"You'll be okay?"

Carmen nods again. They embrace.

"When your feet touch the ground," Yannick whispers into her ear, "say hello for me."

September 12, 1991

Alexis

Not long after I arrive in Nashville, Tennessee, the Jesuits find me a job. I'm one of the lucky ones because I came speaking English. They put me to work at a Kroger, a produce store on the same street where I live with these men who crouch in the dirt. I notice that almost all the workers at the Kroger have brown skins. My job is easy; I stock the shelves; I sweep and mop the floors; I'm the guy who runs to check the prices on items that don't ring up on the register. It's an easy job but sometimes I wish it were harder because I can think of nothing else but Millot and Philippe, of nothing else but the *mornes* and the way the Citadel looks after it has rained and we danced in the gray shroud of mist enveloping its walls. I write to Philippe, hoping to receive a saving word back from him. No words from home come to greet me on this alien shore, and without them I begin to sink into a morass of homesickness, something close to despair.

Every night, I have dreams. No, they are truly nightmares. Philippe appears in them, a ghost of himself, as I knew him as a child. He is always harmed in some way, with a bleeding gash somewhere on his body. I always wake without remembering exactly what the dream was about except to know that something is not well, a foreboding of something ill to come. I wake with this unease in the pit of my stomach, and the scent of Mamie Leila's *akasan*, her morning porridge sweetened with cane syrup, lodged in the nostalgic pores of my nostrils.

Je suis comme un zombie qui travaille pour d'autres dans un nuage de sommeil sans fin. I am without compass, without solace, a zombie who can be controlled by the whims of others.

I see now with my own two eyes what all those Black American poets we were taught in school were trying to write about, longing for a mother Africa that was too far away to put into words that could contain their longing. I feel that longing—sharp—for Haiti, Philippe, my mother and father. When I work, I think of those poets' words and the way our schoolteacher Pè Joshua had tried to impress upon us their desires.

"Langston, Countee, Zora," he would say, moving his delicate fingers over their photographs in a book from his own library, "they all came here, here to Haiti, at one time or another."

Who would have imagined that Black Americans would have come to Haiti at the turn of the century? "Why did they come?" I had asked.

"They came to see their Haitian brothers and sisters. To learn about the people who had been able to carry out the first successful slave revolution in this hemisphere." He sighed, "I suppose they also came to show us that they had managed better than we had, in the long run."

He once showed me a book by a young poet named Countee Cullen. *Color* was its name and the cover of the book was the orange shade of a *giromon*, a squash we have in Haiti that resembles a pumpkin. I remember touching the book as if it would break if I held it too close; the pages were delicate, the edges browned with age, and the words on those pages sounded out like trumpets in the morning air. But somehow, now, it wasn't the words that had stayed with me. It was the color of the book, and its title. Both were imprinted on me like a second skin.

On the same day Pè Joshua showed me that book, he pulled article after article written by Haitians back then in the twenties and thirties when these giants from Harlem had come to pay their respects. The articles spoke of the Harlem movement as a "brother" movement like our own *"indigénisme"* movement, getting back to African roots. I would read those articles quickly, marveling at Langston Hughes' desire to know us Haitians. He would refer to us in his writing as "the people without shoes." I wondered if he had talked to the people without shoes in his own native land. I wondered if he had walked to the South like I had or if he had stayed in New York, where the living seemed to have been easy, in a way, then. Langston, wearing his fine suits, even when he was a young man, suits that men today could hardly afford in Haiti, let alone had ever seen. I remembered one picture Pè Joshua showed me then so clearly. It was a picture of Langston taken in 1920, the eyes full of charm, the hair curly but soft-looking, cut not too short against his head, the lips refusing to close in a smile. But he was still smiling, somehow. His face was soft, too, as if he had yet to see hard times. The suit, beautiful, white shirt, narrow tie tucked into a vest, wide cuffs, large hands. "Remember this man," Pè Joshua had told me. "He is one of the greats." And so I read his works from beginning to end as I had read Countee. Working in the Kroger day after day, smiling into blue eyes that are marble cold, I remember this line from one of Langston's poems most of all: "I, too, am America."

Still, it is Countee who has stayed with me most clearly on all my after-dinner walks in the streets. I think of all his attempts to contain his anguish, his hopes, his mixed-race heritage that was stamped all over my face too. Countee and his traditional verse burst at the seams and declared: "Here I am, America, like it or not. Even here, here I am." But walking those vast Southern streets, magnolia trees blooming overhead, I find I am going nowhere. What is America to me? I flounder in the sea of her contempt. I walk the streets to stain the trunks of elm trees with my tears.

I try to remember that those were hopeful days, days spent with Pè Joshua, who had eyes like moonlight, always looking back, to the departed day, knowing that the good one took of the past and present formed a bridge to the unknowable future. I could tell that he wished he had lived in those days, that he could have shaken hands with the likes of Langston, Countee, and even Zora with her cutting eyes and quick tongue. He wanted me to feel his passion for those visitors and he played me records in his rooms next to the old school: Duke Ellington, Billie Holiday. Billie's velvety voice, a brook falling on smooth, round stones. It could go one way or another; it could hold you or let you go; it had a broken quality to it. I did not understand her voice, then, all its layers. I can feel that there is something here that will teach me the secret of that voice, its sources of pain. I am weary of the lesson to come.

My superior at work is a young man in his twenties. We seem to be about the same age. He is very tall and thin, towering over me when we stand face-to-face in the food aisles; he makes me think of a scarecrow planted in a field to keep away the clawing birds. His name is Darren.

Even though he is very young, with barely a full beard covering his angular chin, I respect his directives. It is clear to me that he knows what he is doing as he tells me how to stack produce on the shelves and how to price them for easy sell. He is certain of his narrow field of knowledge, and this confidence is enough to awe me as I stumble through the days.

My other coworkers ignore him as much as they can. They tell stories behind his back and mock what they take to be his effeminacy; rumors swirl around the fact that he wears a perfume of rosewater. Their lack of respect endears him to me in a strange way, reminding me of

Philippe in his much younger years, reminding me of how I failed to protect him as he had protected me, like a brother, all those growing years. His perfume reminds me of Haitian colognes, of Friday evenings preparing to attend a ballet, a dance in downtown Cap-Haitien, though few dance halls remain, and the lovely girl you had dreamed for weeks of escorting there.

Lately, I notice Darren keeps an eye out for me, urging me to take my lunch break, breaks at midmorning and midafternoon. If these efforts fail, he tries to convince me not to stay overtime. But where does he imagine I might go? I smile in response and wave him off, knowing that all that awaits me after work is a room shared with another Haitian man, our mattresses set on the floor and a few photographs of loved ones left behind in Haiti taped to the walls at awkward angles a bit above eye level. Missing bits of paint, squares peeled away by aged adhesives, reveal how many other lost souls have been cramped into those quarters. Oracles, they shout that we are not the first: we will not be the last. We have been following the news in the papers announcing the growing hold of the military on our homeland but not much more information is forthcoming than that. It is as if the papers here have blocked us out or blacked us in. We live always on the edge. Those who can afford to call home do and then they report back to the group what general information they have. The news is never good: reports of deaths, tortures, looted homes. But then, always, the hope that President Titid will bring us through the hard times. Our country knows no rest. There is nothing I can do but read and wait, read and wait, and hope for the best.

Then, one of those days stretching itself mundanely into night, work without end in sight, a faint odor of rosewater wafts up the aisles and seeks me out as I wonder what is to become of Ayiti, of me. The news in the papers that day held no piece of comfort. There are tales of brutal murders by the army. President Aristide's life, it seems, is being threatened; he is contemplating leaving the country to seek out aid from his archnemesis, the United States of America. His followers are being harassed. It is a good thing that I am not home at this time and yet the news has unsettled me and makes me wonder after those I left behind. I was the only one anything would have happened to because I too was a supporter of the new government before I left, but I could not hold on long enough. Unlike Philippe, I have never been certain of staying to usher in transformations. By the time I left, only days ago, it seemed to me that even in the face of change, the success of the election, my future was elsewhere. I am not sure of this any longer. Thinking about the world I have left behind, growing more chaotic day by day, every item I place on the shelf before me feels like a mason's brick as it leaves my hands. There is no use in trying to hide my exhaustion.

Darren stands next to the boxes of detergent I have yet to unload. "Hey," he says, speaking to me directly for the first time. "What did I tell you about taking some time, man?"

I smile at him and shrug. How to explain that this empty work is the only thing left to fill the void between my open palms, the only honest thing I have been given in this foreign wilderness to hold?

"Don't you have a home to go home to? A warm meal waiting, maybe?"

I turn away from Darren to hide my shame. I nod.

"Okay," he says, "I'll stop bothering you."

He turns to leave, then pauses. "Look," he says, "I know something about your situation. I mean, there's a file in the office on every employee and supervisors have the right to know who they're supervising. And, anyway, people talk, you know. I'd like to invite you to dinner tonight. Ah, that is, if you don't have ready plans. Dinner at my house."

I feel sudden panic. What is he asking? What if the rumors about Darren are true?

"My grandmother's a great cook!" Darren exclaims with a grin that lights up his face so that the smooth brownness of his skin takes on an amber glow.

"Wouldn't she mind?" I finally ask awkwardly, "I mean, wouldn't she be wary of having a stranger in her house?"

Darren laughs. "Now, I already told her you'd be coming. And I told her what I knew about you, the little I know about you. She's already set an extra plate at the table. You know, she's one of those old folks who's always prepared to pull up a chair for the wanderer who knocks unexpectedly at the door."

I smile. Darren's brief portrait of his grandmother reminds me of Mamie Leila when I had first come to know her as a child, stumbling into her yard to find Philippe playing in the dirt, at a time when she could still be seen calling on her neighbors, straw hat perched on her head, balancing her corpulent body gracefully as she walked the dirt roads of our village.

"All right," I concede. I am grateful for the invitation, more grateful than I would have expected at lost moments in my shared quarters in the apartment, staring at a ceiling or peeling wall. "Let me finish this . . ."

"Of course," Darren laughs again. "I wouldn't expect you to leave anything undone."

". . . and I'll be right with you." My words lace his. I turn away.

Thirty minutes later, we are walking side by side down the sidewalk of a residential street. The houses lining the street are modest, no larger than cottages. The front lawns of each reveal that the occupants have resided there for some time and taken great pains to enliven their surroundings, to make them feel like home.

A breeze picks up around us and rustles through the golden autumnal leaves of the elm trees forming a sparse canopy above our heads. The air is free of pollen and still I think I can smell the faint scent of jasmine and magnolia in the air. As I zip up my jacket against the coolness of early evening, I am comforted by the thought that I am about to enter a real home, that even if just for this once, I can put aside the armor I carry to and from work and even in the place where I lay down my head to sleep.

"Here it is," Darren gestures toward a house to the right of the street. It is small like all the others, painted white with yellow and red trimmings around the windows and doors. The door is painted a muted rust red. Potted plants adorn the porch, and bushes, trimmed around the edges, rise like sentinels against the wooden floorboards. Darren leads the way and soon we are standing inside the little house which only minutes before had seemed impenetrable, like all the other houses I walk by on my way home from work, wondering what is going on inside, wondering if I will ever find a home of my own.

I take in a deep breath. The air is saturated with oven warmth, the scent of bread swelling and browning in their pans, chicken roasting, onions braising, rice and peas with bacon for tasting. I close my eyes to keep from crying. After weeks of wondering what will become of me and why I had left Haiti with such haste, without a final word of goodbye to the one person who knew me best in this world, I can look forward to one evening's respite, one evening of rest.

"Let me take your coat," Darren says, smiling at me with all the beatitude of a favorite uncle. Now at home, he seems older than his years. I take note of faint lines around the edges of his eyes, lines that can only have been etched there by some deep tiredness or worry on the face of a man so young.

I hand over my coat. I wait in the doorway and look ahead into the house cluttered with old, comfortable chairs, knickknacks on tables, a piano with marks of wear and tear above the keys, standing against a far wall, a bouquet of dried flowers hung upside down on the wall above it.

"Is that you, honey?" a woman's voice, low, tired, calls out.

"Yes, ma'am." Darren answers, "I brought my friend." He winks at me, "Come on, let me introduce you."

I follow Darren into a narrow kitchen, brightly lit. I see a small, plump woman standing there, back turned, stirring something in a pot simmering on the stovetop. Darren hugs the woman from behind and she jumps, surprised.

"You going to keep doing that to me, son, in my old and feeble age? What if I burned myself, right here, right now? Who would cook you dinner? Tell me that."

Darren laughs. "You know no one can surprise you like I can," he says.

The woman joins in the laughter, her laugh more like a girlish giggle. She swings around, wooden spoon still in her hand, and hugs Darren with both arms wound tightly around his thin upper chest. Then, quietly, she says, "Good to see you back."

They are hugging for what seems a long minute to me, lost in the sacredness of their embrace, an embrace that speaks everything that their hearts feel, what words cannot say even in speech or poetry.

They remind me of Philippe and Mamie Leila, of the deep love that can sometimes bond a grandparent to a grandchild, especially when the child has been abandoned and the grandparent is forced to be both elder and parent, employing a soft hand and the wisdom of long life to discipline and foster the child's growth. I stand very still, waiting, and in that long minute remember myself and Philippe as we had been once, before the world which lay beyond our dirt yards and mountain paths divided us.

I remember a day bright with sun and finding my way out of my mother's house to travel the dirt path that led closer to the village center. I remember stillness in the air and the first childhood hint of my own freedom, the room to move, to explore, to make my own way. I found myself in a yard grown over with wild weeds and a boy my size playing on a dirt mound. I had found Philippe for the first time. The very moment I sat with him to plunge my fingers into the red earth was the beginning moment of our lifelong connection. I remember him still as he was then, round and plump as toddlers are when they are fed enough rice. We were both lucky enough to have been born in homes in which there was always a bag of rice or cornflour in the cupboard and other staples fresh from market or from our very own backyards. We began to talk then in a language all our own, as if we had been born from the same womb and shared the same mother's milk.

I am still thinking about that first encounter when Darren's grandmother introduces herself by giving me a huge hug to welcome me into her house. I am encircled in the soft warmth of her plump body and the pungent scent of sweet rosewater. I realize then why Darren carries that odor with him to work and I feel a twinge of shame at having wondered if the rumors about him were true. I hug her back. I remember Mamie Leila's arms around me then, the strength of her arms as she had pulled my infant self up from the ground and away from Philippe, the dirt beneath us, and strode out of the yard, down the rutted road linking our two houses together like pearls on a string. She had held me in her two strong arms, her ample bosom a pillow beneath my head, lavender water spilling into my throat like a fillet of smoke, and returned me to my mother. Philippe, agile on his two-year-old legs, trailed behind as he held on to the edge of her skirt and soon we were together again, sitting side by side on the floor, laughing at the flurry of activity we had engendered and picking up where we had left off in our conversation. Our mothers had their tea and looked at us with concern for the years ahead they could not yet discern written in the dark pupils of their eyes, smiles arrested by the worry only a mother's love can know.

"Welcome," Darren's grandmother says, holding me at arms' length then and squinting up into my face. "My name's Eulah but everyone calls me Grandma. I won't mind if you do, too, seeing as you're my little boy's friend. But you can call me Miss Eulah." She put an arm around Darren's waist and looks me over. "This boy needs some fattening up, don't you think?"

There is an extra place setting at the table when we sit down to dinner. I assume it is for the stranger who never comes knocking at the door, symbolic. But no later have the prayers been said, than a scratchy voice comes bellowing through the screen door from the front porch; the wooden door had been left open to let some cool air into the house overheated from the oven.

"Come right in, Louis," Miss Eulah replies.

In comes the same man I met that first night in the city, who had taken me to the blues bar and pulled out a chair for me to sit and drink alongside brethren. I stand.

Miss Eulah looks at us both. "I guess you know each other."

Louis' face breaks into a wide, toothy grin and he reaches to shake my hand. "That's right," he says. "I met this young fellow a while back." He turns to Darren, "Friend of yours?"

"Just a friend," Darren says.

Louis takes his place at the table and for a moment it seems to me as if I could have been in my own house in Millot, mother and father seated, Philippe at my right sharing in a family meal. Thinking of Philippe and all the memories that remain, rendering the distance less painful in the bearing, I smile at Darren as I eat a forkful of Miss Eulah's honey roasted chicken. Chewing, my taste buds firing like pistons in a well-oiled machine, I am grateful beyond words. Darren pretends not to see my smile and asks for the mashed potatoes sitting in a clear bowl set in front of Louis. Louis obliges. Then we eat in silence, so good is the food, and the company.

Later, while Miss Eulah and Louis sit on the front porch, catching up on each other's news of the day, Darren and I clear the table and clean the dishes.

"So," Darren says as we are halfway through the job of straightening the kitchen up, "want to go out?"

I am almost startled at the thought. "The last night I went out," I reply, "was the first night I was here, when I met Louis."

"Bet he took you to the blues bar downtown, right?"

"Yeah," I smile.

"Well, place I hang out at is kinda different," he gives me a quizzical look, the kind that reminds me of Philippe when he would try to judge whether or not I was ready to hear about the spirit voices he heard in the mountains, or if I was up to the challenge of walking the mountains one late night or early morning. The look sends a chill through me. Darren senses my apprehension. In that moment, I understand everything, that the rumors are based on truth. That, like Philippe, Darren is *makoumé*.

"I'll go on ahead by myself," Darren says, smiling tightly. "I can drive you home if you like."

I nod. The sudden realization of Darren's orientation triggers a part of my memory long left dormant, purposefully so. A memory of a day when, waiting for Philippe and I to take to the mountains and walk the paths as we thought up some mischief, Mamie Leila came to the house to tell us that Philippe was missing. He had not returned home for supper after school. She did not know where he could be. We were perhaps eleven or twelve at the time. I ran through the streets of the village to find Philippe but he was nowhere to be found. I finally decided to hitch a ride on a *camion* heading to Cap-Haitien as the day was turning to dusk. I walked the city streets, looking in all the places I thought he might be, all the places we had come to discover together, on field trips or while trying to make some money on holidays from school. I knew that Philippe traveled there more often than I did, out of necessity. I remembered that he had once told me that he would work for tourists at a main hotel in Le Cap, and my feet took me there, out of desperation, despite the fear of what I might find. What I found was Philippe, standing against a wall behind the hotel, an older man pressing him against the concrete, his face contorted with pain, eyes closed. I stood there, unknowing whether to call out or run or hide. I stood there and saw the man pull away. I could see them fumble with their clothing. The man gave Philippe some money and Philippe, head down, took the money, pocketed it, and walked toward me without seeing me standing there. The man took a cigarette from his pocket, lit it, and straightening himself out, found his way back into the privacy of the hotel. Philippe was still walking toward me, head down. When he saw me (he literally walked into me), his head snapped up and fear cloaked his eyes. Tears were streaming down his face. Though every cell in my body wanted to denounce what I had just seen, reach into his pocket and take out that money and burn it, my arms went out and he cried into them like a baby. We stood like that for a while. Then something in me turned cold, unforgiving, and I pushed him away. "What you are doing is dangerous," I said. I didn't know why those were the first words that came out of my mouth. I knew some of us had to make a living this way, sometimes. I thought Philippe had more choices. I didn't know what it meant about Philippe. If he was doing what he was doing because he thought it was the only way to help Mamie Leila make ends meet or if there was something more to it. Rumors about Philippe circulated already then, just as they did at work about Darren. I did not know what to believe, what my eyes had seen. We didn't know then about a thing called SIDA. We didn't know then that taking risks with one's body, even if it was just to make money, could literally kill you. I didn't know then that Philippe would become infected, the signs so clear when I left the country, that the dangers he would face were far greater than I could have imagined. Philippe nodded at my words and said nothing, wiped his tears away. I watched him as he straightened his spine and stood a bit taller, becoming the Philippe I knew and loved in my village.

The Philippe who was fearless and heard voices speaking to him from the world of the ancestors.

We made our way home, told Mamie Leila some lie about Philippe cleaning a shop on the main road and being kept late. We did not speak again about this incident. And I grew afraid of the rumors that swirled among our peers. I grew afraid of being stained by those rumors. I did not know how many knew about the way Philippe made money. Truthfully, and to my shame today, I did not want to know. We maintained our daily rituals as best we could, but I was careful now, in a way I never had been before, of how we touched, of embracing him as I had when he walked out from the shadows of that alley with eyes downcast. I would not give anyone the satisfaction of distorting our bond. The result was a growing discomfort between us, a discomfort that grew alongside the virus in his body, overtaking us silently, quietly, undetected, until it was too late.

And here I find myself, having made my first friend in America (the first if I did not count Louis), only to have come full circle to the past I have fled. The present is my past and there is no way around it.

The ride home is quiet, uncomfortable. Darren fiddles with the radio tuner as he drives, clearly nervous.

"I thought you knew," he finally says when we reach my apartment complex. He parks the car in the street, along the curb. There are no lights on above, no signs of life. "I just thought you . . ."

"You thought I was like you. Isn't that it?"

"No. Yes. I mean I didn't have any way of knowing one way or the other. You just haven't treated me like the other employees."

I remain quiet.

"I just wanted to make you feel at home, in the ways I feel at home."

I nod. I want to say something about Philippe. I want to say that this is not all new to me.

"Is this why you live with your grandmother?"

Darren has never said anything about his parents. I assumed they had passed away.

Darren nods, "My parents kicked me out when I was fourteen. When I told them I was this way." He turns to me as the car comes to a stop in the apartment complex parking lot. "Sorry to have disappointed you," he says.

"No," I say, stepping out of the car. "Nothing to be sorry about. I'll see you at work."

I enter the apartment with the feeling of being weighted down, waterlogged, asphyxiated. I feel trapped, cornered, as if I am in a cell without enough room to move, without air to breathe, sunlight to absorb. My fingers itch from worry, looking for a way to relieve my anxiety. I lay down on my bed. My roommate, exhausted from his own day of discoveries and hard labor, snores on the next bed. I pull out my notebook from below my mattress and let my fingers lead pencil over paper in wide strokes. I remain poised over the paper, spine curved like a palm branch, one elbow digging into the hard mattress, until dawn breaks. My roommate turns toward me then, yawning.

"*Sak pasé?*" he asks.

"Nothing," I answer in English.

"No-ting," he says, "No-ting. *W ap betize.*" He laughs and rubs the sleep out of his eyes, then rises to prepare for the new day.

I stretch my back and look at what I have drawn. It is the portrait of a child, a young girl. Someone I've never met, hair full of wild curls. A girl I used to see in my childhood dreams, eyes round, deep as rivers. I look at the drawing several times, then to my hands.

My roommate returns from the bathroom and looks down at the picture. "*Ti moun ou?*" he asks. Yours?

"*Non,*" I say, "*M pa gen ti moun.*"

I have no children, know no children.

He shrugs. "*Se yon bel pitit kanmenm.*"

Why have I drawn this picture? How do my fingers know this face? This child does not even look like anyone from the village And what does she have to do with this past long night, finding a place of belonging with Miss Eulah and Louis, then the club and remembering Philippe's secret, my own?

I want to tear the picture but, instead, my hands move to hang it above the head of the bed, so that she may enter my dreams and begin to provide me with some answers.

I go to work sleepless not thinking about what I will say to Darren when I see him, not thinking much further than the ache of my muscles, the numbness of my spine from staying crouched over the drawing paper in the early hours.

When I see Darren, the evening rushes back to my memory. I try to avoid him as I work from one aisle to the next. I try to avoid catching his eyes. When I do, there is something in them that I recognize from days gone by, a look Philippe would give me when I was too afraid to walk the mountain paths in the deep of night, too afraid to participate in the *vodou* ceremonies he began to attend regularly, secretly, after Pè Joshua had taken a group of us on a weekend field trip to the waterfalls in Saut d'Eau. It is the look of a prey captured by its hunter, suffering its wounding with stoic grace.

At the end of the day, Darren finally approaches me. I am getting my things ready to head back to the apartment and get some much needed sleep.

"Alexis," he says, "I'd like to say that I hope yesterday doesn't change anything, that we can still be friends."

I'd been thinking about just that all day, concluding in the end that there was much more to be gained in getting to know Darren and his family than there was to lose.

"Yeah," I agree, "we can be friends. Maybe I'll join you at the club sometime. But just for drinks, okay?"

"That's cool. That's cool," Darren answers. He smiles sheepishly. "It can be a trip, I know."

"Yeah," I say again. I hesitate, "Aren't you worried about . . . SIDA?"

"SIDA?"

"You know, AIDS."

"Oh, that," he says. "Not to worry. I take all the necessary precautions."

"I hope you do," I say, thinking again of Philippe and all the others at home, men and women, who could not afford the precautions or who thought that marriage vows would protect them from a disease that knew no boundaries.

"Friends?" Darren asks again.

"Sure," I reply.

Darren puts out his hand and we shake on it.

"Want to come to dinner again?"

I beg off. "Too much excitement for me," I say. "And anyway, I didn't get any sleep after I got back yesterday. I stayed up drawing and lost track of time."

"You draw?"

"Yeah. One of my many gifts," I smile, "I used to draw portraits of the people in my village." The thought makes me sad. Darren takes note of the shift in my mood.

"Maybe you can draw me, or Grandma, someday."

"Sure," I respond, "Maybe I'll do that. Well, I have to go get that rest."

"All right," Darren says, "Just so you know, you're welcome to dinner anytime. Okay?"

"Okay." I smile wearily.

We go our separate ways.

I regain my lonely room. The others are not back yet and I find myself cleaning the kitchen and making myself some rice and peas. For once, there is hardly a thought in my mind. I am enjoying the quiet, the simplicity of the rice, my sense of having passed some test on this foreign ground.

After eating and cleaning the dishes, I shower, then retire to my bedroom. As I slip into bed, I take a look at my drawing. It gives me a strange feeling of comfort, strange because I still do not know who the girl could be. Yet, as I had predicted earlier in the day, as soon as I close my eyes and drift off to sleep, she is there, drifting in and out of my dreams. Sometimes she is smiling, hair flying and sending off sparks of light from auburn strands buried in the blue-black coils. At other times, her eyes are full of tears. In the dream, I find her often standing by or watching a fire. I toss and turn in my sleep. I see people walking down long dirt roads. I can smell cane burning somewhere. The people walking pay me no attention. They carry long machetes and are dressed in ragtag clothing. It takes me some time to realize that I have gone back in time. That I am near Pont-Rouge during the time of the Revolution. Someone says something to me about Papa Dessalines being brought down from his horse and dismembered. I see trickles of blood staining the pathways leading to the capital. I see the girl in my drawing walking through the cane stalks like a ghost, untouched by the fires. She is following a woman whose apron is weighted down with objects I can not make out, and wild field flowers. I follow the old woman and the child. We end up in a cemetery surrounded by onlookers. There has been a battle. I search my memory for the date all this must have happened. I see dismembered fingers fall from the woman's apron onto a fresh mound. The name *Dessalines, Dessalines* is whispered through the crowd, then *La Folle, La Folle*. The crowd does not seem to see the little girl. The woman sees her, talks to her; the small arms encircle her neck. Then, suddenly, I am walking through a long tunnel of light. When I come into the light, I realize it is only snow, a deep blanket of white, brilliant snow. Smoke is in the air here as well. Dogs bark furiously as a house burns to the ground. I find myself standing in a crowd of onlookers; I have the feeling I know the people in the house but I am confused because I do not recognize the house. Smoke blinds me as the fire is put out. The sky is made red with the swirling lights of screeching sirens. For a moment, I think I see her, see the flying curly hair. I am moving through the crowd toward her. She disappears. I am too close to the fire. I feel as if my skin is burning. I think I am in the fire and wake up screaming. My roommate is holding me down, pinning my shoulders against the mattress. I am drenched in sweat from head to toe. I realize where I am and tell my roommate I am all right. He tries to read my eyes, then nods and goes back to his cot. I turn to look at the picture and it seems to me that I am not looking at a drawing at all but at a photograph, something closer to real life, and that the little girl is smiling at me as if to say that she knows who I am, even if I do not know her.

September 16, 1991

Carmen

From her window seat, Carmen looks out and sees the purple-green ridges of the Haitian hills fanning themselves out below the plane. A rush of excitement fills her and she grips the plush blue arms of her chair as the plane makes its descent toward the city of her birth. The electricity in her palms stays with her as she places a palm against her forehead, against the hot rays of the sun. She descends the glinting steel steps leading from airplane to tarmac carefully, balancing handbag in one hand, bottled water beneath an arm, a carry-on piece in her other hand. She follows the other passengers waiting in their queue to pass immigration, some pointed to by men in brown and khaki uniforms, passing the checkpoints with ease because of this or that connection. The lethargy of the past days seeps from Carmen's body into the surrounding heat. The electricity continues to pulse only in her hands. It becomes a dull throbbing echoed beyond the limits of her body's own cells by the frown on the face of a woman in the line ahead as she balances a thick, round body in 1940s low-heeled leather shoes bulging at the seams, her fleshy feet spilling over the weathered sides like water-clogged boats capsizing at sea. A felt hat pinned to her straightened, bouffant hair, the whole of her squeezed into a polyester suit and faux-silk shirt, she rummages through a black purse in search of documents proving she is now a resident of the United States of America.

The throb continues to make itself felt in her hands as Carmen passes over her passport and watches it scrutinized, stamped, returned to her with a flourish. All around her, the air is thick with worry, bodies pressing up against one another, momentarily stripped of class and caste even though they watch each other carefully for signs of otherness—a gold watch here, the scent of fine perfume here, a French Parisian accent rising above them all, amulets hanging from the neck—*bokor* spells hanging on some, religious medals sanctioned and blessed by local priests on others.

There are no smiles shared, no stories of how many years spent in exile, the taste of return in the mouth putrid, laced with fear. Men in army uniforms parade by the glass looking out into the hills. Then she is free and walking into the throng of baggage handlers hissing for American dollars as baggage carts or taped boxes of American goods imported for resale are unloaded from the conveyor belt. Carmen finds her bag easily and hears her name called as she straightens up.

She sees her grandfather and mother waving to her from the other end of the terminal, just beyond the last checkpoint, a table where exiting passengers are asked to place their baggage and uniformed young men set about examining the contents uncritically. She will place her case on the table, take note of the already broken lock as the contents are strewn upside down in full view of the others milling about, watching each other carefully, still. The man going through her things sweats almost imperceptibly, a small row of beaded perspiration clinging to his hairline. He wipes away at the crown of his head with one hand and, tight-lipped, with another hand waves her on, watching her still, yells "*Suivant!*," eyeing her still as she finds her mother and grandfather in the crowd behind the yellow line painted against the asphalt separating inside from outside, looking away as he fingers the contents of the next piece of luggage, looking back as she disappears.

Carmen feels the man's eyes against her body as an extension of the throbbing within her. She feels everything two, no tenfold, as if her skin has been peeled back to expose the underlying nerves to the stinging of the salt air, to the dust covering over the cracked cement below her feet.

"*Ça va?*" she hears her mother say as she embraces Carmen on both cheeks.

Carmen kisses her, then looks beyond her mother's shoulders as they hug lightly. Her eyes scan the crowd calling out to the passengers from behind barbed wire, most wearing what she imagines to be their best clothing: pressed pants, gaberdine shirts, women with bright kerchiefs, heavy skirts in the thick heat of the day.

Shining aluminium containers have been set up beneath the shade of sickly flamboyants, water and Kola stands. Everything for sale. They stand behind their offerings with defiance, below a sign reading: *no merchandizing allowed.*

She shifts to her grandfather. "*Koman ou ye?*" he inquires, white moustache lifting up and down with his smile.

"*M byen*," she laughs at the sight of his polo shirt with an alligator decal stitched over the right breast that has long gone out of style on the continent, a baseball cap hiding his balding head, jeans neatly ironed, "*et ou même?*" She has never mastered the intricacies of the Kreyol language; hers remains stilted with French, almost indistinguishable one from the other.

"*Byen.*"

They sail through into the parking lot, her grandfather holding her largest case firmly at his side. She and her mother carry the rest.

"Louise!" he yells back to her mother, "stay close."

They walk in a line, refusing politely the hands reaching out for their baggage, the hands asking for some small change.

Carmen has a habit of looking people in the eye. She avoids it here, not wanting to be misread. When she forgets to look away, it is to catch the eye of a man resting against a tap-tap. His eyes bespeak contempt. His tap-tap is decorated with paintings of Erzulie and the words "*Toujours L'amour*" painted in blue and red letters outlined in white. There is no love in his eyes. She looks away, disconcerted.

"*Maman*," she says, "It's good to see you."

"Uh-hum," her mother mutters, concentrating on keeping up with the pace of her father who, at seventy-five years of age, is as sprightly as a young man. She could never keep up with him.

The air is thick with humidity, and the scent of burning waste mingles with that of *marinades*, savory pieces of dough frying in pans of hot, overused oil. The long tables have been set up some ten feet away from the terminal, between the twisted trunks of two flamboyants that have lost most of their brilliant color and appear to be dying of thirst. Both men and women stand behind the tables and continue to call out to those emerging from the concrete building to taste their confections or touch their wares of plastic utensils for the kitchen.

The site is so different from those Carmen has seen in history books, of the days when the Duvaliers reigned supreme, when corpses of opponents were left bleeding, tied to the trees in front of the terminal as a warning, to all those who stayed or departed, of what one man could do who ruled all within the country. Carmen had not seen such things with her own two eyes yet she could feel the pull of history beneath her feet, swirling about her ankles with the dust. Things had changed in the last five years and were still changing.

They reach the car and are surrounded by children asking for a *kob* or two, Haitian coins worth next to nothing on the open market.

"*Pa peye yo okenn atansyon,*" her grandfather says with a backward glance, taking the rest of her luggage from her hands and pushing both her and her mother before him with his right hand against the small of their backs. Don't pay them any attention.

She has seen this before, of course, had seen the poverty and the outreached hands of children like herself as a child. But she does not remember ever seeing so many hands, so many people in need of a quick reprieve.

"*Papi,*" she says, as she sits in the passenger seat of the jeep. She smooths the shredded cloth of the seat beneath her wraparound skirt. "*Pourquoi?* So many people?"

"*Oui,*" he nods, "Who would have believed that things could get worse after the Duvaliers left?"

Her mother nods in agreement. "It's more of the same, but always worse, always worse." She looks out of the jeep's window at the children clustered around, "*Quel pays de misère,*" she says. "*Quel pays.*" What a country.

Carmen follows her mother's glance to the children who have now encircled the jeep, hands reaching up toward her as if to rain falling from the sky in a time of drought. Her grandfather slips three two-note *gourdes* into her hands and she rolls down the window to hand them over to the tallest of the children, a boy with dark, plum-colored skin and knotted hair. "*Divize-l.*" He nods and the children turn toward him in expectation as he hands two of the three bills over to two other children. As her grandfather puts the jeep into reverse and then finally makes his way out of the parking lot and onto the paved strip of road that will take them home, she watches in the rearview mirror as the same scenario repeats itself over and over again with sometimes less orderly results and scuffles.

The next days, Carmen divides her time between her mother and visits to her grandfather's restaurant. She watches as the maids in the house rush from one end of the large house to the other with loads of laundry in one hand or dust rags. They answer the phone when it rings, shoo the dogs out back into the courtyard when they try to enter the kitchen, where it seems there is always something boiling atop a burner. She has only to ask and the boiled, white purple-veined sweet potatoes she loved as a child materialize, or fresh-squeezed lemonade in a chilled glass.

It would seem a charmed life save for the deep cracks running through the walls, old bullet holes that have cut their way through glass, days without water to shower, and the cutting out of electricity at all times of day. There are long evenings spent on the front porch hidden behind a tall wall, letting them look out onto the streets but not admitting intruders.

It is on just such a night that Carmen begins to ask her mother questions about her final departure for Haiti five years earlier, her departure from Canada coinciding within months of that of the Duvaliers from Haiti. Her mother, who in her midfifties has within the last year regained her youthful zest for life despite the conflicts in the country. She bears little resemblance to the woman Carmen knew as her father's wife, who wore ill-fitting clothes and sometimes stayed in bed for days on end, depressed, searching within her mind for a way out that never materialized except for her escapades south, and even then, temporary. Today, her mother looks like the woman who had spent that summer long ago with her in Haiti showing her how to read the cultural signs all around her, how to see beyond sight the workings of Erzulie, the goddess of love, between a man and a woman as they walked arm in arm down the street, how to see Legba in the eyes of a man selling shoes by the side of the road, and the power of Ochún, *Ochún*, the churning sea, in the women all around who refused to be satisfied with the position society ill afforded them, who could make the sky tear into rain and cure viruses in their children with knowledge so ancient the naysayers thought it had been lost in the Middle Passage. It is this woman she sees sitting before her, hands wrapped lightly around a tumbler containing golden rum poured over cubes of ice, her smile distorted by the shadows falling all around them as the electricity fades. They watch as lamps and candles begin to be lit up and down the street. as the merchant women continue to sell their wares into the dark of the night.

"Are you happy?" she asks her mother.

Her mother nods and closes her eyes. Carmen wants her to speak some more, to be there, present with her. It is seldom that they have such an occasion to see each other face-to-face. "There are some things I've been wondering about," she tries again, "I think you may have some of the answers."

Her mother looks at her, sips at her rum. She senses the seriousness of her daughter's glance. "All right," she says, "fire away." She can't help herself from trying to be light, to bring humor, to their conversation. What is left these days aside from humor?

A wind sweeps through the veranda, lifting dead leaves and dust from the corners of the porch floor. The skirts of their dresses lift in unison, then fall. "I want to know why you left and didn't take me with you." The words, sounding childish and naive, slip out of Carmen almost against her will. She isn't sure where the question has come from but there it is. Perhaps it is all that she has wanted to know all along.

Her mother sighs, "You're a grown woman now," she says, Wouldn't you have been too old? You were nineteen, if I recall, when I left." She was trying for humour again.

"Eighteen," Carmen replies. They are speaking a formal French suddenly, as if they are two strangers trying to impress on the other their worldliness, "and not old enough to fend for myself. You left five years ago. I just turned twenty-three. Daddy died last year. You didn't come to the funeral. And you left me. I could have come with you. I could have helped. It might have been good for me to be here, to get to know my cousins."

"You never liked your cousins."

"But did I even know them?"

"Don't you remember the summer you met Natalie? The two of you were like fighting dogs, always at each other's throats."

"Where is Natalie? I've been here for a few days now and haven't seen her."

"Didn't I tell you? She and Paul are in the States. They moved there shortly after the wedding to continue their studies."

Carmen had forgotten that Natalie had married the haughty, handsome next-door neighbor who had made such a negative impression upon her that summer long ago when she had first met Léah. Well, she thinks to herself, they deserve each other.

"But I met Léah. We were friends. I could have . . ."

"What would you have done with Léah?"

"Our friendship could have flourished."

Her mother laughs, "You were afraid of her. As you were afraid of so many things." She eyes her daughter, "and still are."

Something inside Carmen wilts at her mother's words.

Her mother catches the look on her daughter's face, the same look she had always seen there when she had fought with her former husband. When things got too difficult to bear, Carmen had the habit of withdrawing inside herself. She straightens out the flounces of her dress and peers out into the darkness of the street as if the words for an apology might be dancing in the pooling light of a flickering candle. Women talk about their men below the wall in front of the house. The women laugh.

"I don't mean to hurt your feelings, Carmen," her mother finally says. "But this was no place for you. You are a Canadian girl. Your father is British Canadian. Half of you belongs with me. The other half does not. I wanted you to be safe. That was all. The Duvaliers had just left. The *dechoukaj* had just taken place. This was no place to bring you, don't you think? And there, with your father and all the things familiar to you, I thought you would continue to do well."

"I haven't," Carmen says bitterly as she thinks of her broken relationship with Nick, of the daughter on her way, her job and her inability to help women like Gladys so in need of guidance and a stable personality. She feels utterly lost in herself.

Her mother sighs, "I'm sorry to hear that. I did the best I could."

"Isn't that what all parents say? We did the best we could. What if the best isn't good enough? Where does that leave us?"

"While you are here, Carmen," her mother's voice is suddenly deep, serious, "I want you to take a good look around. There are things here that you will see that will make you understand why I did not bring you at the end. I brought you when you were younger. You remember? We went to Saut d'Eau, the waterfall. You were baptized in those waters. Whether you drink from the water is yours alone to do."

Who is this woman speaking to her in this way, full of mystery? Carmen wonders. Where has her mother garnered such strength? When she was growing up, Carmen's mother had always seemed so weak in her eyes. She thought of Gladys and if she too made use of the same rationale, if she thought that staying with her husband would make her children's life somehow better. Haiti, for Gladys, was her husband's land, even though part of her family had also been from Haiti. The forgotten island presented no opportunity. They were of two different classes, her mother and Gladys. Gladys would have only poverty and misery to face on these shores. Her mother came from a long line of landowners reaching back to the time of the Revolution. Her father had moved his enterprises from Cap-Haitien to the capital some years ago and maintained his progress. Yet both women seemed to believe in the African spirits still haunting the Americas, ancestral and mythic. There was something she needed to learn from these women, but Carmen was at a loss to understand precisely what she was searching for, what indeed she needed for her own return, one that would eventually take her back to Canada to birth this child in her belly, to live her life with some sense of rootedness.

"Mother, I'm pregnant," she says.

"Why does the hen come home but to lay her eggs?" her mother replies as they are enveloped in complete darkness.

They sit in silence beneath a blanket of stars.

The next day, her grandfather sits at the breakfast table and watches them both eating in silence. "Louise," he says to his daughter, "I think it's about time that you show Carmen something of the country. It's not good for her to stay cooped up in the house or at the restaurant." He waves aside his daughter's protest. "I've arranged for one of my driver's to take you both from here to Le Cap after the weekend. He's reliable, trustworthy. You have a reservation at the Hotel du Roi for the week." He smiles at them, satisfied with his surprise. "What do you think, Carmen?"

She is thinking it will be a good occasion to extend the conversation she had begun with her mother the other night. She is thinking also that she might see Léah again. They had called the ice cream shop in Le Cap but received evasive replies as to her whereabouts. She is thinking that the thought of traveling out of the noise and stench of the capital pleases her and that she wants to see this land she has still not allowed herself to claim as her own. "Yes," she says, "I would love to."

"Louise?"

Her mother frowns. "Why don't we send her on her own?"

"Louise!"

Her mother's delicate hands dance like birds in flight above the white cloth laid out on the wooden dining table where they had all their meals served. "Papa," she continues, "she's a big girl. Send her on that trip your friend Julius is going on. It's after the weekend also. He can keep an eye on her."

Carmen looks back and forth between her mother and grandfather. They are talking as if she has suddenly disappeared. She clears her throat, "Well, mother, if you don't want to go . . ."

Her mother interrupts her sharply. "It is not that I don't want to go with you. This is a matter for your spirit to undertake. I am not your guide. I brought you into the world. I took you as far as I could. I have taken my own journeys. My roads are not yours."

"Louise," Papi says softly, "Don't leave the girl hanging like that."

"Papa. This is her one and only chance. If I go with her, I will be like a shadow falling on her foliage. We've given her the foundation. Let her go. Let her go and grow."

Carmen's heart contracts against itself. Is it fear she feels? Or something altogether new? She cannot put a word to the sensation. She feels great pain. She is reminded of the day her mother left for Haiti, the divorce finalized, watching her walk through the security gates at the airport in Montreal with something like defiance in her gait holding her steady as she moved away from Carmen, away from her old and bruising life, away from all the sorrows Canada had rained upon her head. "I'll see you on the other side," her mother had said before parting. Was this the other side? Had she finally reached her destination? She looked at her mother across the table and understood that she would have to find her mother on her own, that she would have to go on this journey of her own will, her own strength of spirit. But it was weakness, or so she felt, that had brought her to her mother's side, her failure in assisting Gladys— Gladys who walked presently in her mother's old shoes, the ones she had discarded a week before her final departure five years ago saying they hurt her toes and why hadn't she taken better care of herself all those years?

"I have to get to the restaurant," her grandfather finally fractures the silence, "Louise, I'll talk to Julius and see what he says." He smiles at Carmen, "Whatever happens, you'll be fine. We'll take care of it."

She nods and her mother gets up from the table and leaves them both staring at the skins of mangoes in their plates, crumbs of bread and guava jelly sticking to their knives. "She knows what she's doing," says her grandfather then looks at her, "and you will too. Like mother, like daughter."

It takes only the length of the day to arrange for the trip. A business friend of her grandfather's, from the USA, is on his way to Le Cap with a hired car and business associates—tourists looking for a diversion from the capital and its incessant unrest. The weekend passes quickly and Carmen finds herself saying goodbye to her mother on the porch they had just recently occupied with their silence and resentment. Her grandfather says, "N'ai pas peur." Don't be afraid. And suddenly she isn't afraid. She is looking forward to whatever lies on the other side. She knows it will feel like nothing, no, be nothing she has experienced before. Yet on some other plane of existence she knows she has felt it all before, in some time lost to her memory, lost to history.

Alexis

For days now, it seems, I have sought freedom from nights filled with nightmares, dreams that reveal their purpose not at all, and mornings taken up by talk of the bloody events unfolding in Ayiti. The rumors spreading from one man to the other tell of a secret plot against the president. I do not know what to believe. There is nothing in the papers, and I have received no letters. I decide to take Darren up on dining at Miss Eulah's. I find myself there almost daily. We play dominoes or card games when all four of us are there and not too tired or else Louis and I head over to the Blues bar and listen to music with his friends, who continue to welcome me. Louis, I find out this time, is a permanent fixture around the house, Miss Eulah's unofficial companion. I have never seen older folks keeping such good company. In Haiti, so many of us die young, it is a rare and precious thing when an elder survives the ravages of the country, a rare and precious thing. Many of those who survive do so alone, like Mamie Leila, who has survived both her husband and her children and raised a grandson all on her own. When Darren takes off for the club scene or some secret rendezvous, no questions are asked and I stay behind, talking to Mr. Louis or helping Miss Eulah with things she needs done around the house, helping with the yard, putting up a string of white lights around the porch in honor of the solstice arriving soon. Most of the time, the night ends with me sitting on the front porch, Miss Eulah retiring for the day in her back bedroom, and Mr. Louis smoking one more rolled cigarette. A week has gone by quietly and uneventfully.

But all times of quiet are ransom for the unforeseen, the unexpected, the accident waiting to happen. In the next week, a night comes that alters everything, for me, for Darren. That night loosens everything in my brain, opens every door I have tried to close to the spirits, to my own, fragile soul. It is Louis, in the end, who saves us both.

126

That night, everything seems as usual. I have dinner with Darren, Miss Eulah, and Mr. Louis. We play a game of cards and then Darren excuses himself after taking a brief phone call, saying he will be back in less than an hour. He leaves, a black fedora perched cockily on his head. The hour passes. Miss Eulah goes to bed and I sit talking with Mr. Louis on the porch. He is in good spirits.

"Feels like you been here forever, son," he says to me as he smokes his cigarette.

I nod.

"How are things going at the store?"

"They're okay," I reply. "Darren helps me out a lot."

"You two are good friends, isn't that right?"

"Yes, sir."

"You know where he gone to tonight? You know what that call's about?"

"No, sir, can't say that I do."

"Hummh," his brow crinkles into a frown. "When Darren first brought you here, I thought you two had something going, you know? That you were funny like him, you know?"

"Hanh," I murmur, not knowing what to say, my shoulders tensing.

"Yes sir," Mr. Louis laughs, "thought you'd fooled me that night we first met and I took you to the Blues place."

"Mr. Louis," I say. I had begun to call him "Mister" as a sign of respect. I could not call him or Miss Eulah anything more endearing than that or else I might feel homesick or untrue to those I'd left behind. "Mr. Louis. Are you ashamed of Darren?"

"Well, what do I have to worry about? He's not my grandson."

"But he is Miss Eulah's."

"Yes, I know," Mr. Louis pauses. "I'll tell you what I think, Alex. I'll tell you true what I think. It's like this. Things like that, people can't control it. Some of us are born with blue eyes and others with blond hair. Some of us are dark as sable! Doesn't make us any less worthy of calling out to the ancestors before we go to sleep at night, does it? Doesn't make us any less African or brothers and sisters. So, the way I see it, Darren's a good kid. He works hard. He loves his Grandma and treats old folks like me with some respect," he laughs, "rolls me a cigarette when I ask him to, and just like I like it! What more can I ask for at my age? Yeah, he's not my grandson, but he's just like if he was. Whatever he does is his business. If he doesn't harm himself or others, then that's okay by me." He punctuates the last words by taking two breaths from the cigarette and pushing his feet off the porch a bit more quickly to make his rocking chair move back and forth briskly.

I listen to the creaking of the chair, the floorboards, and the calm beyond us. The summer has ended long ago and fall is beginning to give way to winter in so short a time. I had supposed that Mr. Louis shared my sense of shame, that he would have had the same reluctance to accept as I had when faced with Philippe's life, both its joys at discovering his identity, and its hardship in having that aspect of his identity exploited by transient tourists. I was as ashamed of that as I was of the bond that connected us, a bond I resisted and did not want to understand. Was I "funny"? It was a question I left unanswered.

We sit in silence for some time. Mr. Louis hums a song under his breath. The night grows cooler. Time passes.

I finally prepare to leave.

"You leaving," Mr. Louis observes.

I stand up, "Yes. Tomorrow's another work day."

"Un-hunh," Mr. Louis says, not moving from the rocking chair. "You going to stay at that job forever? You have plans? Guess now's not the time to go back home from what I see in the newspapers."

I nod, though, in truth, I haven't given my next move much thought. Then I remember my Uncle Kiko, my mother's older brother who had fled Haiti before I was born, over twenty years ago, during the Duvalier years. "I have an uncle in Canada."

"Do you now?" Mr. Louis comes alive once more. His eyes sparkle behind the glowing tobacco of his lit pipe. "My sister Alberta lives up there. She sure does."

"Alberta?"

"Yep. Named after one of our great-grandfathers who fled slavery by way of Canada. Ended up in Alberta, homesteading. Came back after Jubilee but never forgot the freedom he'd known in that cold land, even though there was still racism up there. They just called it something else, xenophobia, I think, or some such thing. So Grandpappy named his oldest daughter after the land that gave him refuge and taught him to become a man. He named her Alberta and the name stuck and has been passed down ever since."

"Nice," I say, "That's nice, Mr. Louis."

"Haven't seen her for going on ten years now," He chuckles, "You'll have to look 'ol Alberta up and say hello for me when you get there."

"Canada's a big place, Mr. Louis," I smile. "Where is she at?"

"Montreal."

"Ah, then I can say hello. My Uncle Kiko is in the same city."

"Small world," Mr. Louis replies, tapping loose ashes from the tip of his cigarette over the railing of the porch into a bed that bloomed roses in summertime. "I think the Good Lord made it that way so we wouldn't always wander this earth like lost souls."

I nod, "Well, Mr. Louis. You have yourself a good night."

"All right, son. Take it easy."

I am barely off the porch when I hear Miss Eulah calling out my name. I turn back to see her standing at the door of the house in her bathrobe. She looks flustered, and older than her already advanced age. Her grey hair glows in the moonlight.

"Alexis," she says, voice quivering and low, "is my grandson back? Is he out there with you?"

Mr. Louis stands and goes to her, grabs hold of one of her arms. "What's wrong, Eulah? What's the matter, honey?"

I step back up on the porch.

"I've had a dream, more like a nightmare. Oh my Lord," Miss Eulah begins. "Oh, God. Didn't he say he'd be back in an hour?"

"We haven't seen him, Miss Eulah."

"He's not back yet," Mr. Louis enjoins.

"Something terrible has happened. I can feel it."

"Now, now," Mr. Louis pats her arm. "I'm sure it was just a bad dream, Eulah."

But I take one look at Miss Eulah's eyes and know that she has seen something terrible in her dreams that cannot be denied. "I'll find him," I say. "I'll look for him. You just stay here. Mr. Louis will stay with you."

Mr. Louis tries to stop me but I have seen too many things in the land of my birth to doubt the clarity of Miss Eulah's eyes at the moment of her greatest fear realized, even in dream.

I make my way through the now familiar city streets, talking to the older men with twisted hair drinking out of brown paper bags. I stop in the mom-and-pop stores Darren has taken me to on nights Miss Eulah needed a special spice or ingredient for a dish. She refuses to give her money to the large supermarkets and makes do with what Darren is allowed to bring home from the Kroger. Otherwise, she invests cash hard earned as a domestic in white people's homes in an area of town called Green Hills back into the Black community which surrounds and sustains her. But Darren is in none of the usual places. I finally decide to go to the club, remembering the name he had given that first night I had declined the invitation, less than two weeks prior.

The parking lot of the club is full despite the lateness of the hour, and the music loud. I am let in and make the round of the dance floor and back rooms. No sign of Darren. I make my way into the back alley. There is a fight underway.

Apparently, the police have not been called. I try to stay calm. There are empty cartons of beer, empty packs of cigarettes littering the alley. A fedora lays muddied in the gutter.

"Darren!" I cry out.

He tries to see who is calling out to him from beneath an avalanche of falling fists. I make out his bloodied face.

"Darren!" I cry out again and rush toward the melee. I want to get help but cannot stand by to see the fists falling on Darren's back. Philippe, I think. This is what they will do to Philippe. Perhaps in my absence, someone has. It is as if Philippe is in Darren's face, turning toward me for help, and my heart leaps into my mouth. I cannot help myself. I remember holding Philippe against me in a rainfall after I had spent an evening in the company of a school friend of ours, a girl named Marthes. I had an inkling then of Philippe's feelings for me, that it was no ordinary love that bound us together, but I had wanted to prove that I could and would live my own, separate life. The night of our high school graduation fête, Marthes and I had stolen away and made love beneath the natural umbrella of a flamboyant. It was only later that I realized that Philippe had been looking for me and seen us there, his heart breaking at the sight, tears mingling with rain as thunder tore the veil of sky in two. Later that night, I had held him close and in the holding understood everything I could not then put into words. Filled with anger too late, I lunge at the men holding Darren down.

"Damn nigger," I hear one of them say.

I try to advance and pull Darren away. I try to walk through the flying arms but they form a wall and all I hit is skin and bones. The next thing I know, the trees have sprung arms hard as baseball bats and they are swinging at my body. Their branches hold long, sharp knives that tear at top layers of my skin like fingernails. The wind has lost its voice. My ears are emptied seashells. And the fists keep coming at me from every direction because the trees are everywhere, a forest of trees. They grow mouths that spit tobacco juices in my face and I drink them in like sap, forgetting that we are far from the tobacco fields. The trees grow teeth that bite down into my bones and try to chew away my flesh. My body is suspended in air, spinning wildly out of control and even if I close my eyes and try to concentrate on staying in my body, I find myself floating away because my body is raging against my lack of tears, the scream that refuses to push itself out of my lungs and into my throat, past my lips and into the foliage of the mad trees.

My body is a cyclone of bursting blood vessels, a rainbow of pain. I long to part with it. The trees will not let me go, and the more they choose to make a wreckage of my body, the more I awake to the knowledge that I will not let them make of me a corpse. Sound rushes back into my ears and I hear a scream loud enough to pierce the heaven's arc itself over the forest. My spirit falls back into my body and my body falls to the ground with an empty thud. The trees lose their knives, bats, and teeth and grow quiet. The wind returns with its whispers. I lie there with my ear to the ground, listening to the echoes of the men's footsteps receding into the club or down the alley, blood seeping from my mouth like water from a fountain.

When I finally awake, it is to see Darren on the ground next to me, bleeding from the mouth. His eyes are closed but he is still breathing. The man with the fedora is gone. The lights of the club have gone out. "We're going to be all right," I tell Darren, not knowing what bones, if any, are broken. I can move all of my extremities, though not without pain. I am going to be all right, I tell myself, as I look out at the pine trees and see that they are staring at me quietly, their needles brown with shame for having witnessed my unmaking. My body lies on those needles as on a bed of feathers. I am thankful for their presence, their faded, green smell. An owl howls from a tree across the street and I use its voice to guide me to my feet which sway beneath my weight. There is mist everywhere, hiding the buildings, the white stripe down the middle of the road. I check Darren for broken bones. He seems all right. I gently wake him and pull him to his feet. I hold him at the waist and pull one of his arms around my neck. He sinks against me and we almost fall back to the ground.

When I raise my eyes to look at the tree housing the owl, what I see is a man, a Black man, hanging from a noose. His feet dangle off the ground. His clothes are rags, ripped to shreds against a skeletal body.

His feet are shoeless. I step back, bump into something stiff but light. There is another body behind me. I turn to see it. This one is a woman, chestnut skin, a frozen smile on her face, the noose hung beneath ruby lips. The mist hides her body but it appears to be naked. I start to run down the street, dragging Darren at my side, running away from the hanging corpses, forgetting the pain in my own body. Everywhere we run, there are bodies up and down the street, all hanging from trees: bodies of red-skinned children, women the color of coal, men the color of plums. All sway without life, the mist enveloping their wilted bodies. None with shoes. We run and run down the street, hoping to find someone, anyone, who can take us out of the forest, give us a ride home. And then I hear them: the dogs.

The dogs are traveling south of us but their voices are coming from the west. They are tracking us up river by scent. We have run all the way downtown to sink into the riverbed, wanting to become part of the soil. But the dogs are coming and so I redouble my effort to keep Darren awake and running beside me. We run the length of the river toward a cave where the Natives had hid from the white men who had killed the people of their villages over three hundred years ago. I crouch inside the cave and I hear the dogs coming closer. I want to cry but a noise behind me keeps me from shedding a single tear. I turn around and inside the darkness of the cave I can make out the forms of human bodies. Someone reaches out to us, puts a hand on my bloodstained jeans. It is a small hand, a child's, or maybe it is a woman's hand. I cannot tell. But the hand is reassuringly brown like mine and I hold it until the dogs move past us overhead. When the dogs are gone, the hand in mine pulls away into the darkness and I think I hear the shadow to which it belongs say, "Thank you, brotha," the last word made long and thick like molasses poured over hot mush. I want to stay there in that cave. The dogs are gone and the quiet is peaceful like a grave. I turn to look at the people behind me but they are skeletons with chains hanging loosely from their wrists and ankles. I want to scream again but I hear the wind calling my name and we flee once more. I feel the lumps of bruised pain rising beneath my skin, wanting to break free.

We stumble once or twice into the river. The water soothes me. My steps become slower and slower; Darren's body becomes lighter. He is beginning to regain his senses. I can smell flowering magnolias in the air, flowering in the dead of winter. How can they flower in this place? They smell of warmed-over death. We crawl through the forest on our hands and knees, kissing the cold soil with torn knuckles and knees, our heads hanging just below the mist.

I am going slowly mad with the voices bouncing in and out of my brain. *Strange fruit hanging from poplar trees.* Billie's voice. *What is Africa to me?* Countee's voice. *Help me to shatter this darkness, to smash this night.* Langston. Proud Langston. And then the voices without names: *What have we done? Won't you take my hand? We gonna jump the broom, baby. Mama, what they want with us? Hush, hush. The dogs, Papa. Hush. Won't you walk a piece with us brother? What're you 'fraid of, brother? Them chains ain't on your legs are they? Walk then, Child.* I listen. Listen hard. *Walk then, Child.* I rise to my feet and I lead Darren through the forest of limbs, the shoeless feet swinging by our shoulders. *Sometimes I feel . . .* I see Billie singing at the forest's edge with a white magnolia in her hair . . . *like a motherless child. . . .* "Billie," I say to her, "how can you stand that smell, so close?" She sings a wistful song in response . . . *a long way from home . . .* We keep on until the mist has lifted and the darkness has given way to light . . . *but I can hear my mother's voice calling me back . . .* I see white lights glittering before me and follow them to safety.

We find ourselves on Miss Eulah's porch, solstice lights brightly lit. She lets out a gasp when she sees us, and Mr. Louis takes Darren into his arms and pulls him into the house. I leave for my room to spare them the burden of my wounds, even though I hear Miss Eulah calling out my name from the kitchen, where she is filling plastic bowls with warm water for the cleansing of Darren's bleeding gashes.

I walk to the apartment and wave away the fear in my brothers' eyes. Yes, I know they are my brothers then. I am no longer afraid of their weakened bodies, their hearts made hungry with longing for home. All the doors in my mind have been thrown open in that one night's walk by the river. I am tired of walking, dream-waking. I am tired of the past haunting me like shadows of dogs trained to kill Black folks, wherever we are.

I sit at the kitchen table and pull out the address of my mother's brother who lives up in Canada, what they once said was the promised land. The kitchen table stands before me, still and stable, and I write on a piece of clean white paper the Jesuits have given the others for their spelling lessons. The paper is lined with thin, faint lines of pink. I do not care. I pull out my uncle's address. The paper it is written on is wrinkled and the writing in my mother's hand appears shaky although I know her hand had been quite still as she had written it out on the scarred tabletop of her own kitchen table. I can see just where her pencil had been guided over a deep gouge in the wood, a crevice opened by a knife held in a hasty hand. I can see her smiling at me. *For when you are ready.*

I smooth out the paper in front of me. I bring the pen to my tongue and lick it to loose the ink. I am ready now because my eyes are opening and I want something different in my life than days at the Kroger bagging groceries, pretending that I am going to go to college someday. There is no such promise in sight. *For when you are ready*, she had said, writing out her brother's address. I have been dreamless of my mother's voice for so long and it has come back after one night's hell. And so I begin my letter:

Dear Uncle Kiko,

My mother has given me your address. I left my mother and father not long ago with the help of some missionaries. I speak English well and so have been working. I have been living in Nashville, Tennessee, for some weeks now. This is a hard place. I am not complaining, mind you. But this is a hard place. The trees speak to me, Uncle, and what they tell me is to walk north like the ancestors. Will you help me, Uncle? I do not have much money. I would not be too much of a bother. Can you help me, Uncle? I will eat very little and I will do whatever you tell me. My mother has given me your address. "For when you are ready," she said when she gave it to me. I need you now.

That first letter, I rip it up. I want my uncle to know that I am as strong as any man. I do not want him to think I am begging. So I start again:

Dear Uncle Kiko:

I am your sister's son, Alexis. I have been working in the southern United States for some weeks now. This is a hard place. I know that it must not be any easier where you are, but I long for familiar faces. Can I come to you, Uncle? I hope you will answer this letter. My mother sends her best wishes.

Sincerely,

Alexis

That letter pleases me. I have it wired by the Jesuits in the morning then go to see how Darren is doing.

He is sleeping when I arrive. Miss Eulah thanks me.

"I don't know what we would have done if you hadn't gone after him," she says.

Mr. Louis looks deeply into my eyes and reads the horror of the previous night in my pupils. "You leaving?" he asks.

I nod.

Miss Eulah hugs me to her. "Be safe," she says. "Let us know exactly when you plan to leave so we can send a little something with you."

"You going to Canada?" Mr. Louis asks.

"Yes, sir."

"I thought so. It's a good idea. Things are going to heat up here for a while."

"Yes siree," Miss Eulah says, "Louis is going to send Darren to stay with his brother out east after the holidays, so he can be with more young folks his age, like him." There is pain in her voice, "where he won't be the only one."

"I understand, Miss Eulah, I do," I say, "I'm sure Darren will do well."

"You come spend the holidays with us, all right? I mean, if you're still here," Miss Eulah says. Then her eyes well up and she retires inside the house to see after Darren.

Mr. Louis takes my hand. "You did us a good turn," he said. "And I can see you put your life at risk as well." He glances at my lumps and bruises. "Look," he says. "I've written down my sister's address." He hands me a folded, yellow piece of paper folded with some money. "If you need anything, and I mean anything at all, you call her. She runs a rooming house up there. She'd be glad to have you. And there's some money there. Hold on to it after yours runs out." He smiles, "Save it for a rainy day, all right?"

I nod, touched by the gesture. "I wrote to my uncle, Mr. Louis. I think everything will be fine. But I'll look her up."

"Like you did me?" he chuckles.

"No, sir," I will attempt not to wait for fate. "I'll make a point of paying my regards, and yours."

"That's good son. That's good." He sighs heavily. "Don't worry about Darren. He'll be fine." He grips my shoulder tightly and I feel all the weight of his sixty-odd years pour into me. "I've seen a lot of things in these parts in my life, son. Lots of things. I thought by now lynching would have come to an end, you know?"

I nod, "Yes, sir." I had read about lynchings in Pè Joshua's library. Pè Joshua had pointed out that lynchings had taken place when the Americans had invaded our island in the early years of this century.

Mr. Louis nods back and looks at me with red-rimmed eyes, "It takes all manner of forms." He lets go of my shoulder. "You need to remember to take care of yourself, now. You take care when you get up there. Keep remembering."

I nod again and turn to leave, his last two words echoing through my head. They are words I've heard before, from my mother. It feels to me as if my entire journey has been made up of a mosaic of memories, some personal, others ancestral. And there is nothing I can do to stop the deluge of images but to hope that it will bring me to a safe shore.

When an answer comes to me from Canada, a day or so later, it is in the form of a couriered plane ticket.

With shoes on my feet, my bag in my hand, I head North.

September 22, 1991

Carmen

The road leading out from Port-au-Prince and north toward Le Cap is uneven—sometimes paved, sometimes cut out of the mountainside with broken rocks—each stretch of road marking a specific moment in history, a president's glory or dream. It is said that each leader of the country has contributed to the building of the road in some way, sometimes to link a department that had been his mother's birthplace to the main arteries of commerce, sometimes only to make a show of a promise not to let the country fall into disrepair. Each broken leg of road inscribed in the soil the map of their failure.

The roadside enchants Carmen despite the poverty evident in all the villages they pass. Her eyes, which have expected only to see the evidence of deforestation, a soil turned brittle and dry by the rays of the sun, are assailed by the variegated blankets of green: rice fields, grass, trees, canopies of flamboyants interrupted by the rouge of their flowers waving in the wind. Women on donkeys ride their wares to market while others carry baskets set on their heads. One woman, wearing the traditional blue dress of Haitian peasantry, carries two baskets, one atop the other. One is filled with pale yellow-green heads of lettuce, the other with radishes. The woman walks stealthily through the broken piece of road, feet steady against the pebbles and rocks; her orange kerchief outlines the crown of her head and soaks in her perspiration.

When the car slows down as they make their way through small villages set up by the side of the road, Carmen wonders if the road has cut through the communities of farmers and unskilled laborers or if the houses made of odd pieces of wood, colored pale pinks, yellows, blues, have sprung up by the side of the road like mushrooms in a forest at the base of old trees. But all the people she sees in the yards, the dirt streets, the makeshift stands waiting for vehicles like theirs, are relatively young.

Their age is betrayed by facial wrinkles brought on by the sun, gnarled hands and feet distorted by the work that keep their lives afloat. Where are the elders? Have they been lost already, or forgotten? The car slows and the other travelers extend their hands out of the windows to exchange currency for *tablette pistache* or a nectarine plucked not long ago from a family yard. The people are thin, many sickly. Carmen wonders aloud what would happen if they kept their fruit to themselves.

"You have much to learn," Julius, her grandfather's friend with whom she has arranged her voyage north, laughs at her thought. He eats the peanut tablet in the palm of his hand with gusto after offering a piece to Carmen, which she declines.

What would happen if they kept it all? She wonders still as the car picks up speed. Wasn't it Hegel who once said that those enslaved had only to withhold their labor to break the chains of their enslavement? A college professor had once told her that Hegel had not believed in the human rights of African slaves. If anything, Haiti proved Hegel's theory wrong. There were those who had no choice but to continue to be enslaved while there were those who refused their enslavement and were left to wander the streets aimlessly, worse off than the supposed modern slaves, those who continued to labor for the industries of the North with little return. The latter were truly the most wretched of the earth.

Still the roadside unfurls and reveals its mysteries. Carmen sees huts eerily resembling those of Western African peoples, thatched on top, walls built of mud. She watches rice peddlars fill burlap bags at the side of rice factories, stocky buildings made of concrete painted white. In other villages, there are sacks of multicolored beans for sale, and always, in front of them and behind them on the road, there are trucks heavied with human loads. Some are tap-taps carrying workers to hoped-for new jobs north of the capital, others are filled with workers returning home from a month or two away with small amounts of hard currency to bring home to their families. Army trucks speed past them, sending dust flying.

Once, the car slows suddenly as an army truck pulls a tap-tap off the road, the occupants made to spill out one by one at rifle's end. A woman stares at Carmen from the side of the road, plastic bags propped up against her legs, straw hat on her head, a crying child swathed in her arms. Carmen tries hard not to look away but eventually she does, aware of her comfort in the hired car, the ease of the chatter among the other passengers. The men in the army fatigues are Haitian. She wonders what is going on. They are all silent in the car, watching.

"Something is going on," Julius says when the tap-tap and army truck are finally out of sight, "I see the army everywhere now." He looks away, a distracted look in his eyes.

Carmen wonders at his words, remembers her mother saying something about a rumor that the president was about to be toppled as she pondered whether or not to purchase her ticket to visit.

When they enter Le Cap, it is to crumbling walls marking the periphery of the old city. Heaps of garbage crowd the street, and the car goes around each mound. Street workers gather the debris into wheelbarrows with rusted shovels. Their work will never end.

The car makes its way through the narrow streets, many still covered with cobbles; the houses rise up on both sides of the street, wooden edifices painted all hues of bright colors, French colonial styles. Multiple families share dwellings that once used to house well-to-do merchants and their progeny. Doors open and close at the sound of the car speeding over the cobblestones, revealing one-room dwellings, small cots set against naked walls, light bulbs hanging from ceilings, lit tentacles in the darkness, foot-high stools for chairs. Worlds are contained behind those doors. Carmen looks away.

Julius sighs, "I can breathe again. This place is nothing like the capital. It is magical. So much like it used to be."

But Carmen sees nothing of the city she knew so long ago, ten or twelve years ago. The dwellings at the side of the roads are visibly brittle, second floors closed off. Stray dogs skitter sideways down long corridors. Old men beg by the side of the road. The heaps of garbage are everywhere. She does not recognize the streets leading to the dwelling her mother once called home. Nothing is familiar.

The car stops at L'Hotel du Roi. After thanking and saying goodbye to Julius with promises to join him at the poolside sometime in the next days, she begins to plot out what she has seen since coming back into the country, what riddles she hopes to solve.

She sits at the desk in her room and goes over the scribblings in her notebooks. She has been keeping a journal since her arrival, so she will have something to say to her daughter when she is old enough to absorb the sights Carmen is taking in for her, for herself. What has shocked Carmen most since her arrival is the way in which everything has changed from what she remembers of her childhood years. Or perhaps it is that nothing much has changed but that the memories she has carried from childhood are filled with gaps and holes that make nostalgia what it is, a safe harbor. Carmen knows her childhood escapades to Haiti with her mother must have been sheltered ones even at a time when the Duvalier regime was still ravaging the countryside and the poor with its death squads.

Carmen's family, on both sides, are professional people, lawyers, engineers, teachers. They hung on as they could under the regime. They did not get involved in politics and so survived from year to year. Carmen always wondered, later, when safely in Canada, what the lives of the rest of her family members must be like in the homeland; she wondered most of all how avoiding politics could be done. She wondered if it meant turning one's eyes away at the most obvious and pretending not to see when things got too bad. If it meant walking over slain bodies and pretending not to see the corpses; if it simply meant creating a whole and complete life behind high walls (or even small ones, for that matter) or within a wall made of the flesh of sisters and brothers and cousins and seeing nothing else but their survival and your own before you. This is a question she cannot answer. Her grandfather had built his fortune in restauranting for tourists in the capital and survived the '86 ousting because reporters and troops kept flooding into the country despite the lack of infrastructure or, perhaps, because of it.

How could things have gotten worse since the departure of the Duvaliers? Carmen writes this question to herself in her journal and underscores it with two broad pencil strokes. This question has haunted her since her arrival at the airport, since her grandfather's words as he waved off the begging children. This is something she must understand if nothing else. She pauses to look out into the courtyard. It cannot be that things have gotten worse for the masses in terms of safety, though it is clear that the poverty is worse. It must be that power is up for grabs and there are too many greedy hands reaching out to grasp it, not many looking out for the poorest among them. This is why Aristide had been thought such a godsend but his leadership was in question.

There is hardly a breeze in the air, and the flowers in the garden below Carmen's window are wilting from the heat. She fans herself as if in response to their plight. It is still early in the morning and she has yet to see if water is running for a shower.

She hears a knock at her door. Carmen rises from her desk and opens it. One of the cleaning ladies is there, smiling.

"*Bonjou,*" Carmen says in her French-accented Kreyol. "*Koman ou ye, sè?*"

"*M'byen*," the woman answers. "*M tande ou bezwen yon gid?*"

"*Oui*. Yes. I do need a guide," Carmen says and explains that she wants to know more about the history of the area since her mother's family is from these parts and that she wants to see the Citadel and surrounding area.

The woman continues to smile and tells her that there is someone in town she should speak with, an old blind man by the name of Léogane. She can arrange for the man's granddaughter to come and fetch her in the morning. Carmen smiles in agreement. "*Oui*," she says, "*Ça serait super.*"

Then the woman's voice drops an octave, "I have to warn you," she says in a deep, quivering Kreyol, "they call the granddaughter one of the undead." With that said, the woman quickly departs.

Carmen stands there at the door and wonders what the woman could mean. She shrugs to herself and steps back into the room, wondering what to do with the rest of her day. After changing into a light, white cotton dress, she decides to walk down to the pool to see what the tourists look like. She spends most of the morning there, lounging by the side of the pool, in a state of semi-consciousness, writing notes to herself for the coming day. After taking time to eat a quick lunch in the main dining room, she decides to return to her room for a nap. As she unlocks her door, she bumps into a young man coming out of a neighboring room. She excuses herself. He does not seem to hear her and turns away from her, hurrying down the hall. Carmen stands there for a minute, something about the young man striking her as important. She watches him as he goes, taking note of the lightness of his footsteps as she then enters her room, closes her door, and lies down to sleep.

The next morning, the same cleaning woman brings a young woman to Carmen's door. Carmen is again at her desk, sorting through her notes on the whitewashed square table set against the wall below the window looking out on the flower-lined courtyard.

Standing before her is the grown woman she had met as a child so many years ago. The face unmistakable: the still eyes deep as wells, the smooth skin, short cropped hair, the body so sure of itself as it moves through the corridor of the hotel.

"So," Léah says quietly, "You have returned."

Carmen is speechless. How does she know it is her? How does she know?

Léah smiles. "I've known all along," she says. "All along. Only, you did not want to know your fortune when we first met."

Carmen remembers that Léah had offered to tell her fortune that summer so long ago. "No," she acquiesces, "I did not want to know."

"Come," she says, "We have work to do."

The cleaning woman reappears. "*Ou pral mennen'l wè Léogane?*" Léah nods. Voicelessly, quietly, Léogane's granddaughter indicates that she will escort Carmen to the family's business.

"Her name is Léah," the cleaning woman says to her as Carmen locks the door of her room behind them.

Carmen nods. Léah seems indifferent, eyes looking straight ahead. The cleaning woman disappears into another guest room. Carmen follows the young woman through the cobbled roads, traces the curve of Léah's long neck, the hair closely cropped against the shapely, pear-shaped crown of the head, with an invisible hand.

September 23, 1991

Philippe

After high school, Philippe found there were many ways to make money, not all of them very righteous. Like his schoomates, he could have chosen to work on boats or sell goods in the streets. If he had, he would have been able to hold up his head as he walked through the streets of Le Cap or his own village. But there were other ways to make money, more lucrative ways. Under Bébé Doc, François Duvalier's son, the drug trade had increased: delivery boys were needed at all ports of entry. Even after Bébé Doc left that spring of '86, the drug trafficking went on. The tourists had long been gone but the drugs kept a steady flow of wealthy men, who were always in need of a little bedside comfort, traversing the country's best hotels. A number found that comfort with local boys. Girls or boys, it didn't seem to matter. Often the poorest girls, especially those without an education, did not seem to have other choices but to prostitute themselves. If you were a boy, then as long as everyone knew you were not *makoumé*, that otherwise you liked girls, it was all right to make a living this way. As long as you were doing it for the money, and only for the money.

It took Philippe some time to begin working the hotels in the port city in this way. He had heard the rumors that many of the other young men making a living this way had got *move sans* that way, bad blood, or what others called SIDA, or AIDS, but others maintained that it could be contracted only through a *bokor's* spell. For a long time, Philippe had believed that his only skill had been to trade pieces of history for language lessons with the tourists. He knew what to tell them. But often what he could do for them in the privacy of their shaded bedrooms would make more money flow. From the *vodou* circles to the *carrefours*, the crossroads where young boys waited alongside young girls to be picked up by someone in a fancy car and taken to rooms that were hardly what they had dreamed of when they thought of the rich, the rumors about Philippe widened into a circle that buffered and contained him from the tongue wagging. Then, only a year or so ago, the days of his illness started, manifested by a dry and hacking cough. Shortly thereafter, he was told by the local doctor that he had contracted tuberculosis by way of AIDS.

In the wake of illness, Philippe convinced himself that one day one of those tourists would lead him to cross the sea to that other land he had never seen, where too many of the people he had grown up with had disappeared. Philippe did not really want to leave. In truth, he missed too many people. He missed Alexis most of all.

On his way to Le Cap's Hotel du Roi to do what tourism had taught him to do, to give himself away while giving nothing of his inner self, Philippe remembers Saut d'Eau and the high school graduation dance that had given his love for Alexis away. He remembers Alexis looking away from him in the school bus on their road home from the waterfalls as he enters the dark room of a man they say knows how to cut fingers from hands right through the bone with a sharp hunting knife; that knowledge had been retained since the days of the Revolution, since the days of Dessalines' dismemberment. But today, those who could commit such deeds were fighting for no cause but their own. He enters the room and remembers everything that he has lost and wishes to gain as he stares up into the man's spidery, pockmarked face.

The room has emptied of sun, and Philippe begins to dream as the man enfolds him in a tight embrace of hands and thighs until Philippe's body is pinned against the mattress like a fly would be pinned by filaments of white thread spun by a spider in its web.

In his dream, the sky drips blue light into the ocean, a painter's brush being run clear of its paint. Philippe's toes touches water lightly. The sunlight skimming across the surface of the sea makes the water shine like diamonds or like a mirror in which he can not see himself too clearly. He raises his head and squints at the men working on the ship cradled in the half-moon dip of the harbor. They are all gathered at the prow of the ship looking out toward the ocean and the wide expanse of sky. Philippe follows their gazes. He hears what is coming before he sees it.

Philippe rises to his feet as he listens to the whir of the engine of a hydroplane approaching the harbor. He places a hand over his eyes to block out the sun. He hears the propellers beating the air. The motor hums harshly; he can tell by the sound that the plane is old. Finally, he sees it approaching: a white-, blue-, and yellow-streaked metal body shaped like a bullet descending from the sky. Despite age and the constant creaking of metal hinges, it hovers above the harbor. Suddenly, a hatch opens and multicolored balloons fall from the belly of the plane into the air. Philippe watches the balloons falling, oversized raindrops suspended in the air. The balloons are weighted down by small squares to which they are attached with white strings invisible against the clouds that have drifted from the mountains over the harbor. In a matter of seconds, the sky darkens and the balloons reach the water. The packages make small splashes in the ocean and are then buoyed by the balloons.

"What is it?" Philippe asks in Kreyol of a man standing to his left, also watching.

The man shrugs and strokes his moustache nervously. Philippe notices that he is wearing expensive-looking leather sandals on bare, calloused feet. His jeans have a pressed seam running down both thighs and are tied below a pale pink shirt with a soft leather belt matching the sandals, ". . . not supposed to be happening this way," the man mumbles.

"What?" The question slips out of Philippe's mouth involuntarily. He notices the bulge of a gun beneath the man's shirt, stuck into the belt of his pants.

The man looks Philippe over with exasperated, bloodshot eyes. "You need to make some money?"

Philippe shrugs back. He has learned that there is no need to rush into any job even though there are few that come his way here. He is useless on a boat, always has been.

"Look, your buddies out there are going to get those packages for me, see. And I need someone to wait here for the packages. I'm needed at the hotel in town. So, do you need some money?"

"Yeah, sure. How much?"

"I'll give you fifty for waiting and another fifty for taking it down to the hotel, all right?"

"That's a lot of money," Philippe laughs, "What's in those? Drugs?"

The man comes so close to him that Philippe finds himself looking into a sea of tiny scars. The man's breathing is labored. Philippe tries to turn away but the man holds his gaze then grabs his arm at the elbow. The man's fingers press through Philippe's flesh to the bone.

"Never mind what's in the packages. There's a hundred in it for you if you do it. And, if you don't," the man puts his hand on the bulge swelling the pink fabric of his shirt, "there can be something else with your name on it. Your choice."

"Not much of a choice," Philippe tries to laugh again, but his throat is dry.

The man releases his arm, "Then we understand each other?" He steps back. From a distance, his skin looks smooth, pristine.

"Yes," Philippe nods, squinting his eyes against the sun.

"It shouldn't take long, maybe a half hour. I'll be waiting for you at the gates of the hotel. D'accord?"

"D'accord."

The man walks away, his hands thrust deep into the front pockets of his jeans.

Philippe waits, anxiety weighing him down like a stone on the shore.

In the dream, he walks away and never sees the man again.

In the dream, he is still walking away.

In the dream, he never turns back.

Coming to in the dingy room, the man's labored breathing bringing him back to reality, he remembers how the world around him had suddenly shifted in tone in that moment when he had realized he could not walk away. There had been drugs falling from the sky like small, dead birds. There had been no exchange over the nature of their encounter. There had been money promised if he would just walk through the hotel's vestibule as if he belonged there and make his way to the room number he had been given, twice a week, for as long as the man was there.

The blue of the sky, masking a deeper shade of crimson, had been oppressive. Philippe had made his way to the hotel, walking hurriedly as if pursued. He looked over his shoulders every few minutes. If anyone had had the time to pay him mind, they would have thought that he had thieved a Lotto stall. Philippe's venture through the streets was nothing new. The way he looked every which way as if he were being hunted down was no surprise. If those who looked and took notice of the man thin as a rail darting in and out of traffic, if they did not know what he ran from, if those eyes had been able to watch him arrive at his destination, they would have had no need to even consider the question. The hotel had become a refuge for tourists, embezzlers, people of all stripes who were benefitting from the renewed global interest in the small country. Philippe stopped at the open gate, lost in time, thinking of the lines he had read in his history book of the days when King Christophe had arrived at this very hotel to wash dishes, to do whatever had been necessary. Then he had become a revolutionary. Were such days over?

Philippe stepped over the threshold, metal plates soldered into the weathered stones, and forced each of his steps to hold him up as he advanced. He was sweating now, large, uncomfortable drippings staining his shirt at the level of his chest and under his arms. Surely it was worth a hundred dollars to make it to the front desk, to ask for the man with the sandals squeaking of new leather.

He had not had to walk far. The man from the beach stepped out from under a parasol hanging low over a table set out by the pool for those tourists who insisted (against advice) to sit out under the sun so they could bronze and become deep shades of brown like their Haitian hosts. He was talking to a young woman by the side of the pool. The young woman was dressed all in white from head to toe, a big straw hat sheltering her head from the sun. They both smoked long, thin cigarettes. They were both the same nutmeg-brown color. The woman turned toward Philippe but he could not catch her eyes, as she was looking through dark, smoked glasses. She turned her head back to the interior of the hotel, looking toward a barred window with a bust of Marie-Louise, King Christophe's wife, sitting on the sill. In her white robes, she could have been Marie-Louise's ghost walking through the halls of the old hotel. The man stepped away from both the woman and the parasol, curled stubby fingers around Philippe's right forearm, pulling him into a chair. Philippe found himself staring at the buckle of the man's belt before he realized he had been forced to sit.

"Don't say a thing," the man said. His voice had lost all traces of a Haitian accent. He sat down in a chair opposite Philippe.

Philippe did as he was told.

"Here's your money," the man said, pushing green bills across the table.

Philippe hesitated before putting his hand over the money. For one thing, the other man's hand was still resting on the bills. He wore gold rings on three fingers, one ring studded with small diamonds. Philippe wondered how much each cost. Certainly more than a hundred dollars each, maybe thousands.

"Don't you want it?" the man asked.

Philippe took the money quickly, then pushed the bills into the right side pocket of his shorts without making sure that the two bills were indeed fifties.

The man sat back in his chair and fished in his shirt pocket for a cigarette and a light, both of which emerged a few seconds later as if by magic. He smoked in a languorous manner; Philippe watched the circles of smoke he blew into the air. Philippe looked back to the pool. The young woman in white had disappeared. He looked across the table and the man smoked with a too-contented smile on his face. "I must go," Philippe said.

"So soon?" the man purred. "What about a drink?"

Before Philippe had a chance to refuse, the man's fingers were snapping through the air, calling the bartender to the table, a smallish woman with long braids framing her round face.

"*Deux rum*," he told her. She came to their table with two shot glasses of golden liquid set in the middle of a small metal tray decorated with a pastoral French countryside scene. "*À la votre*," he said to Philippe as he drank the liquid back in one, long, gulp.

Philippe followed suit. The rum tickled the back of his throat. He coughed.

"If you are interested in more work," the man said, arching an eyebrow over his glass, "there's plenty to go around. And we could use someone like you. We could use your innocent look." He laughed, "Of course, we all know you aren't that innocent." His hand slid under the table and found Philippe's thigh, squeezed it. Philippe closed his eyes. The rum rushed to his head. He attempted to calculate how much more money he could get for whatever would come after this. He opened his eyes, stared straight into the eyes of the man sitting across from him.

"I must go," Philippe said.

A flash of anger brightened the man's eyes then disappeared to be replaced by a stone coldness. "You know you aren't going anywhere." He laughed without reason.

He had been right. He had led the way back to the room without a look back to see if Philippe was following.

The man snores next to Philippe. Philippe dresses quietly and takes the money waiting for him on the night table. As he eases himself out into the hallway, he bumps shoulders with the woman he had seen earlier by the side of the pool. He excuses himself hurriedly and rushes off. She has no time to respond.

He finds himself wandering out of the main gates and into the congested streets, stumbling over debris left burning on the sidewalks. Philippe's mind plays over and over again the scene he has just left. Some part of him is convinced that it has all been a mirage, the bag under the table, the woman in white floating by the pool as if enveloped in her own private cloud. But Philippe can still feel the pressure of the man's fingers against his thigh and everywhere else on the surface of his skin. The night sky looks so blue that only a storm can be approaching.

Alexis

Uncle Kiko's house stands in the middle of a long row of dingy-looking, whitewashed wooden dwellings. His is distinguished by lime green painted accents around the windows and a forest green door. The windows are cloaked with thick, off-white drapes. The black metal mailbox hangs from one nail above rusted railings. A beige mat sits on the chipped cement steps, its "welcome" greeting worn away. A silver chain-link fence surrounds the house, the only thing that seems to shine under the cold rays of a Canadian sun. The yard is filled with piles of fallen leaves. Four dented garbage cans stand firmly next to the house, on the left side, hiding from complete view a garage with a broken door at the far end of the yard. There are two bicycles and a tricycle, all upturned in the driveway as if they were left there in a hurry. A rubber skipping rope hangs loosely from a square in the fence where it has been left, a skinny orange flag knotted to the metal wiring.

I stand in front of the gate and call out my uncle's name.

"*Oncle Kiko*," I repeat softly, wondering if this is the right house. I check my mother's note and compare addresses. I am standing in the right place. I wonder if my mother feels my movement north, if she can imagine that I will soon be meeting her younger brother. My mother's memory of Kiko is that of a young man who left Haiti in the late sixties, before I was born. The family had to practically have him smuggled out. He had got into some trouble with the government. The Duvaliers were still in charge then. He had been taken to prison, and for three long days there had been agonized phone calls to all the family members who might be able to help. No one knew exactly what Uncle Kiko had done; there was a rumor that he had accepted to take up arms as a Macoute but wasn't playing the game quite right. They had wanted to scare him into submission. The whole family was scared. In the end, someone had the right connections and got him out of jail before any real damage was done to him. Then they sent him to Canada, where there were friends who would help him get set up in his own business. I remember nothing of Uncle Kiko except that there were letters once, many of them. They appeared like the movements of the moon, slowly, steadily. They never said much: working, well, traveling. Sometimes a photograph. The last one showed Uncle Kiko in an undershirt wiping his hands on a greasy cloth. My mother assumed he'd become a mechanic, but at Kiko's side you could see the length of a midnight blue car with fins on the side and half a sign on its roof that read "Taxi." How difficult could it be to maneuver through the traffic after driving tap-taps up the winding roads from Port-au-Prince to Le Cap, roads that had barely been cut out of the ground, let alone paved over? Eventually, the letters came to an end. Nothing except an address and a note to my mother: "If you and mine ever need anything." My mother had kept the note, the photograph, and rarely spoke of Kiko except in those moments, like the New Year, when memory fills with absence. She would remember then when, in his youth, before the days of the Macoutes, he came home from driving the tap-tap for thirteen hours straight and then promptly fell asleep with his head on her kitchen table. Or she would remember the way his laugh sounded, like chicken bones being thrown in the air, she would say, like dice.

"*Oncle Kiko,*" I say louder, wanting him to be there, to open the door so I do not have to suffer the cold any longer, so I can hear his laugh for the first time at the sight of me shivering. "*Oncle Kiko, c'est Alexis.*"

I watch the front door. I hop on one foot, then on the other, trying to warm up. I have taken a bus from the airport and walked the rest of the way to the house. I look down the street. All is quiet.

"Uncle . . ."

A car horn interrupts my call. The car is midnight blue like in the photograph my mother has kept all these years. The taxi sign flashes on and off as the car comes to a stop along the curb. I step over my bag which I have set down on the sidewalk and walk over to the passenger side of the car. A short, bald-headed man steps out and, with the door still open, crosses both his arms on top of the car and rests his head. He wears tan leather gloves on his hands that he adjusts from moment to moment absent-mindedly.

"Alex?" the man asks.

"Alexis," I correct, and smile.

"Hm-unh. Alexis. Good name. Good name."

151

"You're Uncle Kiko?"

"The one and only, son." Uncle Kiko brings his hands together in a solitary handshake. "The one and only." He shakes his head and smiles a toothy grin, "Why aren't you inside the house? Door isn't locked. Nothing to steal."

I look back at the house, flustered, then shrug at Uncle Kiko. "I called out your name but there wasn't any answer."

"People here know me by the name of Carl," Uncle Kiko says, "even my wife. Must've of thought you were some kind of lunatic." Then he laughs and his laughter is just as my mother had described except there is something broken in it, something I would not have heard had my mother not been so precise in her descriptions over the years. Of course, it has been a long time since she has heard that laugh, and she has never in her life called him Carl. "Let me walk you in, son." He slams shut the door to his cab and comes around the car. He is wearing overalls, the kind worn by train conductors. They make him look like a child even though he has acquired a thickening of the body that comes only with a certain age. He puts one arm around my shoulders, opens the gate with the other, and steers me down the path toward the green door of the house.

Behind the first door, there is another door. It too is green, a forest green that seems darker because of its place in the shadows between the bright outdoors and the shadowed interiors, where dust floats on prisms of light coming through the windows. It is a striking door, odd as well because it has an oval stained glass window set in its center that shows a pink and brown hummingbird posed above the open flower of an incandescent white gladiola. The rest of the glass is a tarnished gold color. I can see shapes moving behind the glass that almost makes the hummingbird seem as if it is in flight, as if its wings are actually moving so rapidly that I can hardly see their movement.

"Nice, isn't it?" Uncle Kiko says as he pulls off his boots. I follow suit.

"Yes," I reply, "I didn't know there were hummingbirds in the North. I saw some in Tennessee. I didn't know their wings could move so fast."

"Ah, yeahhh," Uncle Kiko drawls. "Haven't seen any myself but I hear there're some around here too." He stands up straight and stretches out his back. I am looking at his thick, gray socks pulled out of shape by his boots. His feet are smaller than I'd expected.

"Ready?" he asks, as I pull off my second boot and take my bag in both hands. I nod. "Come meet the family."

He opens the door and what is finally revealed there is even more of a surprise to me than the stained glass window. A chandelier hangs low above our heads in front of a winding staircase that leads to the second floor of the house. There is a dining room to the right of the entrance with matching lights attached to the walls that are designed to look like candlesticks. The dining table is a long oval, its surface smooth of marks and water stains; it is a dark chestnut brown and surrounded by matching chairs with stuffed yellow pillows tied to the seat backs. All of it sits on an embroidered rug that looks like an heirloom. The shadows of the table hide areas that have been worn down to the basic threads. There is a china cabinet at the far end of the room holding place settings with pink roses trailing thin borders of gold. Six clear wine goblets stand in a middle shelf that also holds a square crystal decanter that I guess is for rum punches. A fern hangs from the ceiling on the left side of the room, close to where we stand on a runner of brown plastic that extends down the hall to the staircase and into a room on the left where the blinds have been drawn and a body with swollen feet in nylons lies on the bed snoring softly.

"The wife," Uncle Kiko says, "Gladys. She'll be up in a while. Just got off her shift at the sewing shop."

I peer into the room with a frown on my brow.

"Don't worry," he continues, "she'll be up. Working, you know, that's how it is." Uncle Kiko shakes his head back and forth and proceeds to take me on a tour of the house.

The upstairs holds two bedrooms, one has been turned into an office, the other is shared by the children, two boys and a girl. The girl's bed is neatly made and covered over with stuffed toys of every kind with eyes pulled out and noses slightly left or right of center. One coffee-colored bear holds the place of honor on her pillow. He is clearly the oldest toy there, with one arm that has been sewed back on with a different color of thread. I smile at the sight of her crayons on the floor strewn over unfinished pages of coloring books that show gardens in bloom.

The boys have bunk beds covered with blue comforters that have clearly been thrown on for effect; the lumps beneath the covers reveal that the beds have not been made. The boys have to be somewhere between the ages of eight and twelve. They have old trucks tossed in a heap in a corner while a round rug in the middle of the room is occupied with the winding trail of a race track complete with a gas stop and miniature cars. The children, though, are not in their rooms, and the place is still with their absence.

"They're in the basement," Uncle Kiko says, reading my thoughts. "They're probably tearing it up."

Uncle Kiko swings the door to the basement open and clambers down the steps as I wait on the landing wondering what my cousins look like and if I have literally stepped out from a nightmare into a dream. He returns and introduces me to his sons, Paul and Eric. The boys mumble hellos and run off to their room. "Don't forget to help your mother with dinner when she gets up," Uncle Kiko yells after them. He shakes his head. "My daughter Anna is around here somewhere. She's still small, you know. Likes to hide when I get home. Well," he looks up at me with tired eyes, "I'm going to sit down and have a beer. Make yourself at home. The couch will be yours in the evenings to sleep on. Just make yourself at home." His eyes take on a suddenly distracted look and he leaves me standing in front of the door to the basement as he heads for the kitchen.

I am both relieved to be with family and afraid of Uncle Kiko's manner, his distance, the absence of Kreyol or even French on his tongue. The children are being raised without knowledge of either of the other two languages. I am again on foreign ground. There is something worn-down about him, thick like his body, that I do not recognize as belonging to the man my mother revered most of her young life, a man who had shattered her vision of him when he had served his brief jail sentence and admitted to involvement with the Macoutes. It was a great shame to the family but, worse than that, it had broken a piece of my mother's heart.

I stand there and wonder what will come of this encounter.

"Who're you?" a voice asks me from behind. I turn about and see a familiar face, a halo of thick curls encircling a little girl's face. For a minute, I think it is the girl I drew in Tennessee. The little girl who had come to me in my dreams. The hair is so similar but the lines of her face are different. She rubs sleep from her eyes and reveals a set of clear, dark blue eyes.

I put out my hand and she stares at it with curiosity. "Alexis," I reply, "your cousin, from Haiti."

"I don't have cousins," she says.

"Well," I withdraw my hand and tussle her hair instead, "you do now."

We stare at each other for a while and then she scampers away, hair flying behind her like the trail end of a comet.

I move through the house with light steps, fearing that any noise I make will be some sort of intrusion. I listen to the house creaking its pains against the cold outside. I am happy to be inside the walls even though something in me longs for the moment of indecision I had felt behind the front door waiting for Uncle Kiko to appear. I long for the ignorance that buoyed my hope.

I stop in the dining room and sit in one of the cushioned chairs. I can feel a breeze whistling through the windowpane at my back. I stare at the smoothness of the dining room table. The smoothness of the wood beneath my fingertips pleases me even though it reminds me of what my mother does not have and the permanent curve that work has put in my father's thin, muscled back.

The woman in the front room stirs. I hear the sheets moving, her feet dropping to the ground with a soft thud, then a resigned sigh. I can imagine her stretching, straightening out her clothes, throwing a sweater over her shoulders. I hear a brush pulling through hair and then I hear Anna's voice: "Mommy, there's a strange boy in the house."

"Is there now?" Mother Gladys, as I was to call her from that day on, replies.

"Uh-hunh," Anna mutters. "He's this big." I can imagine her throwing out her arms to the sky as if she is reporting on a fish she has just caught from a lake.

"That tall," there is a laugh in Mother Gladys' voice but she suppresses it. I can also hear that she is tired and that every ounce of patience in her soul is finding its way to the words coming out of her mouth, a small miracle she is giving her daughter so that years from now she will remember not just her mother's swollen feet on top of the bed but her mother's quiet voice listening to her, talking to her, reassuring her with its measured tones.

"Uh-hunh," the little girl seems content. Then I hear her light steps running out of the room and toward me even though she still manages to surprise me with her appearance, thin cotton bows coming undone in the tangle of her hair. "Mommy's coming to get you!" she screams and runs off up the stairs, where things have grown quiet.

A svelte woman follows her daughter's path. She is clothed simply in a gray dress with a pattern of white flowers running wild on the fabric. Her hair, which I can see would be long if let to cascade down to her shoulders, is swept up in a bun at the back of her head. It is streaked white in the places I imagine it was once a brilliant auburn like the flash of red streaming through her daughter's hair. Her skin is an orange-brown and glows as if the sun has left a permanent imprint upon her so that she can survive the cold north. Her feet are unceremoniously tucked away in frayed slippers that bulge against the swollen tissue. If I am embarrassed at seeing them, she herself has no time for shame and puts out her hand in a gesture of welcome.

"So, you're the strange man Anna has been telling me about," she says.

I stand up quickly, a little too quickly, so that the chair beneath me rocks back and forth against the back of my knees. I put out my hand as well and catch her palm in a soft handshake, "Yes, I'm Uncle Kik . . . I mean Uncle Carl's nephew, Alexis."

"Good to meet you," she says, her voice suddenly filled with the warmth that she had been pouring out to her daughter minutes before, "You must be tired. Let me take your coat."

I am still wearing the jacket given to me by the Jesuits in the South. I had forgotten it on my back as I walked through the house that afternoon, some part of me perhaps afraid that I would not be wanted here after so arduous a journey.

The South has put a fear in me I cannot shake. I realize as I hand my coat to the brown woman with deep, bluish circles under her soft, maroon eyes that the fear stems from something else besides the night of the beating that had torn my body and soul into a million reflecting mirrors in the night. It is a fear that began when I realized not only that I was far from home but that all the faces looking at me from place to place were strange faces, foreign faces, not because I had never seen those shades of white before, whites like eggshells, whites that are actually not really white but tinged with touches of yellows, pinks, the occasional flurry of rust-brown freckles. No, I had seen all of that before in faces at the *marché* or at the library or in the more expensive sections of Port-au-Prince—though money didn't mean everything, because those pale faces could just as well exist in the *lakou-foumi* where most children died before they reached Anna's rambling age. It is a fear born out of the fact that the faces I encounter here *think* they are white, which means that I am black despite the tinge of honey in my own skin that reveals that somewhere along the bloodlines, someone had walked across a room and paired their white body with a black one and changed the course of history. It is a fear born out of knowing that unless a face—my face—can be identified as belonging to one side or the other, I am not safe. I had never thought that to leave home would mean to leave the familiarity of those rainbow faces behind, that all the faces I would peer into or those who deigned to look at me from this point on would be measuring my black blood against the white.

Mother Gladys' eyes hold mine with a rare tenderness. "Make yourself at home," she says. "I'll be in the kitchen," she smiles, "making dinner."

I wait a few beats after I hear her coming back from the hall closet, where she has hung my coat, before following her into the kitchen.

The kitchen is homey; soon it is filled with the noise of the two boys. They tear through the house with abandon though they stay away from the living room, where their father sits watching television with the volume on too loud. Anna sits on the floor behind her mother, coloring in one of the books I had seen earlier on the floor of the children's room.

"Can I help?" I ask as I watch Mother Gladys clean a whole chicken with a piece of lemon after reaching into the carcass to remove the sweetmeats.

"No, no, child," she hushes me. Her voice holds a tiredness that can no longer be denied so I stand at her side and take the chicken from her and dress it as my mother had taught me in our own small kitchen.

Mother Gladys does not push me away. She just moves on to other things with a smile playing on the edges of her lips. A smile that creeps there from gladness.

The boys, both dark like Uncle Kiko, with his soft black hair, come in every half hour or so to get a cold bottle of beer for their father, who never moves from his armchair in the living room even though the light streaming through the thick curtains has long disappeared. He is bathed in the blue rays from the television, enveloped in his own thoughts, which seem to have locked him away from the rest of us.

"Don't worry," Mother Gladys touches my arm as I watch one of her sons go into the living room with a new bottle midway through our preparations. "He's always like this after a long day's work. Fares must have been thin today. He'll snap out of it." She calls out to Uncle Kiko, "Won't you?" He shifts in his chair in response, acknowledging only that her gesture has disturbed his peace.

After dinner, Uncle Kiko stares at me from across the table with a toothpick in his mouth. He seems to be reading my features. Mother Gladys is back in the kitchen, cleaning the dishes, standing on her still-swollen feet, and I wonder if I shouldn't be helping her. Something in Uncle Kiko's alcohol-glazed eyes keeps me in my seat. I have nothing to say, and as I wait for him to speak the first words of our conversation, the children's footsteps falling like soft rain above our heads, I think about the meal, the first Haitian meal I have eaten in months.

The boys had set the table, with Anna yelling orders from beneath the fern, while Mother Gladys had placed the bowls of food in its center: there had been long-grained rice with kidney beans cooked with sautéed onions and pieces of ham; *mirlitons*, the green squash that looks like a mouth that has been sewn shut, stewed with smallish shrimps; fried plantains; the roasted chicken, plump and golden. I was like a man stranded in a desert who had finally crawled to an oasis but could not drink the water out of sheer gratitude. The look on my face must have spoken my thoughts because Mother Gladys had paused before she took my plate to give me a first serving. "Well," she had said, "it's not much." Then she laughed, "But it's what I know how to cook for Carl."

Uncle Kiko had laughed for the first time since he had set foot in the house, "That's my Gladys. She keeps trying 'til she gets it right!"

I looked at Mother Gladys. Her eyes were bright with something I could not read. "All right," she had said after leaving before me a full plate of food, "everyone eat, eat."

And we had, without words, because words have a way of getting in the way of the tongue and the food flattening itself against your palate, a way of refusing the throat its swallow.

Uncle Kiko lets out a loud belch in front of me, shifting my thoughts back to our present stalemate. I can hear Mother Gladys singing softly in the kitchen.

"So, why have you come?"

I am startled by the question. Hadn't he sent me a ticket?

"Well, you answered my letter, to begin with, and . . ."

"You should know Gladys convinced me to send you that ticket."

"Well, sir," I throw the "sir" in for good measure, realizing that I do not know this man, my uncle, at all. "I . . . I . . ." I start to stutter. What can I say?

"Have you ever killed a man, Alex?"

"Sir?" I am confused by the question.

"I asked you if you'd ever killed a man."

"No, sir." I am aware of my body stiffening in the chair, all my muscles at attention. Mother Gladys is being very quiet in the kitchen. The children's feet are heard running overhead.

"Well," Uncle Kiko looks up at me with red eyes, "I have."

"Yes, sir," I reply, "I mean . . ."

"So, you know the story?"

"No, I didn't mean to say . . ."

"What did my dear sister tell you, boy?"

Fear grips my belly and I feel cornered, afraid, though I do not know the reason why I should feel this way.

"I'll tell you the real deal," Uncle Kiko continues. "I've killed people. Yes, I have. I was young then," he squints at me, "not too much older than you are now. The Duvaliers . . . you know about them, don't you?"

I nod.

"Well, they were offering all the young men, especially out in the country, guns and blue shirts and red-striped pants and power. There wasn't much pay in it but you could make money hand over fist if you wanted, if you knew what to do with the power the gun you carried gave you."

He pauses. I sit and stare. Who was this man?

"Am I shocking you, Alexis?" Uncle Kiko laughs his empty laugh. "I don't mean to shock you but if you're going to stay under my roof you might as well know the truth. And the truth is that our family was poor but not so poor as some others. We had a bit of education and we were expected to go to school. Your mother, well, your mother she went far, didn't she? God knows why she chose to marry a laborer, a *pov typ*. But so much more was expected of me, and school was never my thing. I didn't know what I was getting into, I really didn't." Tears fall from Uncle Kiko's eyes.

I sit still and wonder if Uncle Kiko is really telling the truth. In my childhood, the Macoutes were feared, more than feared. We spoke of them as devils. I look at Uncle Kiko, short and soft, not at all muscular, not frightening in the least. There were always those few we saw carrying the gun but who did nothing with it, but that was rare. Those few were the only ones who survived the *dechoukaj*, and even then . . .

"I didn't know what I was doing," Uncle Kiko continues, "I just wanted to get away from the family, do something all my own. Who knew? Who knew? I found myself breaking into houses in the name of the Nation," he laughs, "the great Nation, the first Black Republic this hemisphere has seen, to be reduced to the name of Papa Doc. Our Father who art in the National Palace . . ." Uncle Kiko's laughter turns to more tears. "But you wouldn't know any of this."

"I know, Uncle Kiko," I say, but he is not listening to me. My fear has turned to bitter bile as I remember all the stories of torture in Fort Dimanche, the corpses we would see by the side of the road in the city when I was still a child, the innocents killed just to prove that the government could do whatever they wanted. I do not need to know that my uncle has been a part of this world, part of the world that crushed us Haitians beneath its heels, part of a world so unforgiving it reveled in our misery, our despair.

"I tell you, Alexis," it is clear the alcohol is wearing him down, "I tell you, it was horrible. I found myself killing people. Once, I killed a pregnant woman with my hands wrapped around her throat and was told to tear the fetus from her belly. I tried to do it but I couldn't. I wish I had been able to because I was more afraid of what they could do to me if I didn't do it than what I was capable of doing. Do you understand?"

I do not.

"Because if the orders I was receiving were so *horrible*, then what would they do to one of their own who disobeyed? Can you imagine? I was too afraid to take the risk."

"But you did, Uncle Kiko, didn't you?" What of the story I had been told of the family smuggling him out after a jail sentence? "Weren't you sent to prison?"

"Prison?" Uncle Kiko's head seems to be growing heavier by the minute. He looks up at me. "Who told you that?"

"Isn't that why you were sent out of the country? To escape the Duvaliers?"

"Who told you such a story?" Uncle Kiko attempts to get up from his chair, "it was the damn family, yours and mine. They saw I couldn't get out of it so they pulled some strings with the Jesuits, people who taught at the school. They pulled some strings, Alex," Uncle Kiko nearly yells out the last words of that sentence, "They pulled some strings, I disappeared from the barracks for three days, and then I was on my way to Canada, a place I'd never seen or wanted to see. I've been here for over twenty years. Twenty years of my life gone."

"Isn't it better here, Uncle?"

"Better?" Uncle Kiko spits out, "You smell the sea here, boy? You feel better being in my house?"

After those revelations, of course, I cannot. I catch a glimpse of Mother Gladys in the kitchen, putting away bowls and plates, looking tired and worried. My heart goes out to her. Uncle Kiko must have reformed his ways to have such a woman in his life, and a family with her.

"You need to understand," Uncle Kiko rants on, and, as if reading my mind, "I was never a bad person. I never wanted to harm anyone. I just wanted to contribute in some way, to get out from under the family's control. And things just turned bad. I didn't know they were already bad. I was young and in over my head. The family was probably right, getting me out when they did. But I see how things are now, how some of the people who did worse things than I did got rich and stayed even after the Duvaliers left. And what have I got? This broken-down house," he pats at himself with both hands, as if searching for cigarettes, "this broken-down body."

"You could go back sometime," I venture.

"They're in the middle of another goddamn dictatorship waiting to happen. Don't you watch the news? I know what's going on. Isn't it why you're here?"

I left Haiti because I too wanted to get away from my parents' pressures, high hopes, but I also wanted to get away from all the poverty and despair. I left to get away from Philippe and watching his life disintegrate as his SIDA became more apparent, his body growing thinner day by day while a persistent cough invaded his lungs. So many things had taken place since I'd left that I could only keep going, refusing to ask why.

I leave Uncle Kiko's question unanswered.

"I don't want you creating trouble for me or for my family," he manages to stand on unsteady feet.

"I don't intend to, sir."

"How old are you?"

"Twenty, sir. Almost twenty-one."

"Twenty-one. Look here, the world may say you're a man, but in my house," he strikes his fist on the table so hard that the remaining dishes rattle. I jump. "In my house, you are still a boy. Raise a hand against me and you are on your own. Understood?"

"Yes, sir."

"We'll have papers for you soon and then you can be on your way, do whatever you want. Don't get me wrong now . . ." We both listen to the dishes dancing against each other in the kitchen's water-filled sink. "You're my sister's son and I'll do everything I can for you. We'll feed you, house you, but you have to earn your keep. Kapish?"

I nod, and something in my chest crumbles, reminding me of the piece of paper on which my mother had scribbled his name and address. My mother had not known that his silence had been a blessing in disguise.

"Now," he says, "tell me about your mother. How is Dora?"

There is no real interest in his eyes that I can detect but I tell him how my parents seemed to me the last time I saw them, content in their lives but tired. I talk slowly, with deliberate casualness. I know with every nervous gesture of my uncle's hands as I speak, his heavy breathing leaving streams of alcohol suspended in the air between us, that the fear I had fled in the South lives in this house. It is lodged deep in my uncle's chest, a flower that long ago bloomed its discontent.

When the interrogation is over, Uncle Kiko goes to bed in the front room. "He's drunk," Mother Gladys says to me then. "And those stories he told you, I don't know if they're all true. He talks like that when he's been drinking. He's seen a lot, your uncle. But he's a good man, at heart. I think he's a good man still wrestling with his conscience. There's still goodness in him. When he's sober he's perfectly all right, you'll see."

Laid out on the couch in the living room later on, yellow light streaming in from the streetlamps, I listen to the house creaking.

Sleep skirts my weary flesh, a ghost that has yet to know rest.

"*Frè, ou la?*" The question comes to me in the form of a whisper I hear murmured in my ear.

It is a question I find myself choking down from screaming after a nightmare refuses to release me from the grip of its cold fingers.

In the nightmare, I am walking with Philippe from the schoolhouse down to the village where we grew like wild weeds together from infancy to young manhood. He is speaking to me but his voice comes to me from far away. It is as if we are underwater. He is speaking of all the money the tourists come to leave in our mountains and how he will be a rich man someday. And I, I am quiet, watching his thin frame dancing in clothes that are too large for him, that make his body disappear from view. He is wearing a gray flannel shirt, fraying green and white shorts that have been made from old school pants. Then I realize that I am not walking with him. I am a bird, *une hirondelle*, flying above him, glancing past his shoulder to hear him more clearly. He is talking about the endless cycle of time, how he is caught in time and can never break free. I fly in front of him and see that his face is creased like an old man's. He is at least sixty years of age but with the body of the young man who was once my only true friend in this world.

I am myself again but years younger, a child sitting in my mother's kitchen eating a hot *akasan*. I can hear her singing, if I listen well, a soft murmur that reminds me of flower petals as they fall to the ground in decay. Sadness surrounds me. The room is dark. Every piece of furniture is a dark brown, so unlike the bright yellows of my mother's kitchen and, still, it is the same place. Philippe is suddenly at the door—a rectangular square of light frames his silhouette—calling to me: *Frè ou la?* And I do not respond.

The most fearful part of the dream, a moment I have difficulty revisiting, is the moment when Philippe's face comes to light. There are two deep and bleeding gashes running along the angular plane of his left cheek, a scar in the shape of a scorpion's claw etched on his chest, and tears running from his eyes that turn into pieces of blue stone as they fall. He lays the stones by my dish, and it is then that he vanishes before I have the opportunity to respond. The last time I see Philippe before waking he has turned into a lizard and escaped through a hole in a wall.

I do not know what to make of the dream. I wonder if Philippe is all right, if he has been injured.

I stare above me at the gray spiderwebs of cracks in the ceiling, a broken layer of paint bubbling down toward me, threatening to fall. I welcome the fissures, the flaking dust descending each time one of the children tramples overhead on the way to the bathroom. I welcome them because they prevent me from trying to paint the features of Philippe's face on that ceiling, an angel fallen from heaven suspended above me. They prevent me from trying to conjure him up in this too-small place, a closet of a room that feels smaller than the corners we inhabited together like crayfish in wet sand in our village—a room he has never seen, and will probably never see. Strangely, it is his absence from my world that allows me to believe he exists still, and that all must be well.

September 24, 1991

Carmen

Nou la! Nou la! Nou la!, the voices brushing against the wide branches of the banana and palm trees whisper. You can hear their words in the rustle of the leaves hitting each other in restless agitation. *Almost two centuries, two hundred years gone. Still, the voices speak, we remain.* They gently coax the heart-shaped blooms of butterfly vines as they crawl along the forest ground. *We are here.* The voices course through the forest greens singing unheard songs to the disheveled mountain ridges, throwing their stories over the rounded backs of gales. *Wild river of memory.* Spirit voices. The stories of the long dead but not departed: *Nou la! Nou la! Nou la!*

Carmen hears a rush of noise, a sound similar to that of water filling her ears, as if she has dived into a deep pond. She is wading through a shroud of blue, gasping for air. Underwater, the voices encircle her, multicolored, of different shapes, sizes. They surround her, trap her in a vortex. She is still.

One voice, Léogane's, tells her the story of Léah. Tells her how they had held the baby girl against their chests and hoped that she would be sighted so that her life could be different from those of her grandfather and great-grandfathers before her, so that she would not have to suffer through the compensation of an occult gift of divining the past and future. Léogane tells her how the eyes had stayed closed for long weeks finally to open, vacant. They waited to see what the gift would be, the gift or the curse.

We didn't have to wait long, Léogane mutters into her tape recorder, voice crackling as if from a distance. *Léah, she walk up and down that beach by the time she three. A beautiful something, that girl, stopping in her tracks, the sun washing over she face in sheer joy, all sweetness. Her brown, brown skin deepened to the color of blue-black wild berries in no time at* all, in no time at all. Sometime, we lose track of her. She walk away so quick and she so small, you know, disappearing behind rocks and fishnets. She take to doing that so often and reappearing, we not worry too much. *Ou konprann mwen? Ti fi la li fò*, strong as an ox, even so little. There is laughter in the background. Léah's sister laughs. Léogane chuckles. *Ou panse mwen fou? Mwen pa konnen pou ou* (he switches to French for her benefit), *moi, je me souviens*. Three years old!! She go walking away from us on the beach and disappear as she usually do. Fishermen come talking to us, complain about the fish not being aplenty that year. Hard times, you know. Hard times and Macoutes demanding more money for 'em to be left alone, do their work in peace. They go out on their boats. No sign of Léah. She usually like to sit and listen with me. They out for a long time. Léah older sister been to school and back, and me still sitting there, watching. No sign of Léah. Then them fishermen they start yelling at me to come up to the dock, something about Léah. I run so fast, it not believable. *Et, mwen pa gen je!* No-eyed-man running. Must have been quite a sight for all with eyes them. But I follow the voices and know the beach like the back of this hand here. They pull me up on dock and say Léah, she dead. She all tied up in the net with fish everywhere around her like she some kind of mermaid, *la sirène*, they bring up from the bottom of the sea. Them fishermen tell me they never see so much fish at one time. They say it must be Léah brought them all in for them. And she just lying there, no sign of life. I scream for them to cut her out of the net, breathe life into her, anything. As soon as them human hands touch her skin she start shivering and then she giggling like mad. Fishermen, them startle, then go back and cut her out. I laughing too and she come to me and I take hold of her.

That when they start calling her undead. People come to the house when they need healing of some sort. She does best with things unseen like anxiety, you know, fear. And when they fish they not come aplenty, she help with the catch. The fishermen take her out sailing and the only sound she make when she still a child is a high-pitched squeal as the prow of the boats hit by high waves and the spray wash overboard, sprinkling her with foam. She something else, Léah. She don't say much. But she a powerful something, that one. A powerful something. Léogane clears his throat, his voice softens. *She a gift from the gods.* Léogane's voice fades away.

Carmen thinks of that moment earlier in the day when she had opened the door to her hotel room to find the tall, slim woman standing there, dark brown eyes staring at something invisible over her shoulder.

Léah. She followed her into the streets and began to hear something in the wind playing with the length of their long dresses. The voices. She followed her to Léogane to hear about the secrets hiding in the shadows of *the mornes* . . . she heard Léogane speak of things passed down from father to son over generations, as far back as the time of the king's court in the north of Ayiti, as far back as the days when Sans Souci was a palace with no equal in the Caribbean basin. She asked questions when stretches of silence offered themselves, windows opening to more unveiling of stories. She wanted to know about Léah's blue stone necklace. Léogane and Léah smiled when she asked, dark eyes staring off into the distance. They tell her nothing. Léah's sister caught Carmen's eyes and for several seconds weighed and measured the width and depth of her goodness. Then there were smiles and talk of the king's journal log forgotten. Léah put a hand on Carmen's right arm and she felt a heat radiate between their skins, the same pulsating she had felt when arriving into the country.

The voices that had followed on their heels from the hotel to the café by the seashore where they had sat to conduct the interview returned, and stilled Carmen to silence, to the beat and measure of the intake and letting go of each of her life-sustaining breaths.

Afterward, Carmen followed Léah up a winding street to a blue indigo door. Inside, a cross made of twine used for the braiding of baskets hung above the doorjamb. Carmen advanced into the dimly lit room as Léah lit oil lamps in its four corners then lit two candles on an altar devoted to the figure of Ochún, sea goddess and protectress of children, along with her sisters. In the center of the altar, a calabash rested, filled with flower petals, hollowed blue pigeon's eggs, mangoes, and seashells. Around the calabash, palm nuts, cowrie shells, and blanched pieces of bone had been set as if awaiting the moment of divination, as if awaiting Carmen's appearance before them.

Léah continued to move quietly through the room now warmly bathed in orange and yellow. Light streamed in from the backroom, separated with a swatch of translucent blue cloth. Carmen made out the shadow of a woman's shape moving about behind the cloth curtain but held her tongue.

"Sit," Léah told her as she pulled out a wooden chair from beneath the table in the middle of the room. "Sit, and you will hear your fortune."

"I don't understand," Carmen began.

"There is nothing for you to do. You left here once before without your fortune. Now you will hear it."

Carmen sat, half-frightened, half-delighted by the turns this adventure was taking. She watched as Léah brought a red and white cloth to the table and laid it across the girth of the wood. Then she brought a small calabash filled with lit oil, and some palm nuts and cowries from the altar.

"Hold this in your hand," she said and slipped one of the pieces of bone into Carmen's outstretched palms. "Hold it tight in one hand and then the other. It will give us all the answers to your questions."

"But," Carmen began to protest, "I have no questions to ask."

Léah smiled, her eyes seemingly fixed on a gourd hanging to their right, alone in the middle of the wall. The gourd seemed to glow beneath Léah's emptied gaze, its crown of cowries shimmering in the oil lamp light. Léah turned her face toward Carmen. "Come," she said, "it is time for your fortune to be told."

Léah rolled the palm nuts in her palms until they were warmed by her touch. Her lips moved imperceptibly as if reciting an incantation. Her eyelids were shut. "Ask what you will of the goddesses," she finally said and threw the palm nuts against the cloth on the table. They scattered among the cowries. Léah spread her palms out over the seeds and shells, divining where each had landed and mapping their placement in her mind. "*Oui*," she said, "they have spoken."

"But I haven't asked . . ." Carmen said bewildered.

"Have you not?" Léah asked sharply. "Your first question was: Why am I here? To which there is no answer, as you yourself have brought yourself to this place."

"Yes," Carmen said, surprised, "I did wonder . . ."

"The second question: Will I survive this sojourn? Open your right hand."

Carmen opened her right hand. It was empty. She felt the bone digging into the flesh of her left palm.

"Empty?" Léah asked.

"Yes," Carmen answered.

"Good," Léah sighed. "You see, there is nothing to be afraid of. Nothing to be afraid of but your own self."

Léah bent over the seeds strewn on the tabletop again as if drinking in their powers. Carmen heard movements coming from the backroom and was about to take a look back when Léah took the bone from her hands and placed three cowrie shells in their stead. Léah closed Carmen's fingers around the shells. "Now I will tell you what the shells say." She held Carmen's fingers in her own, and the strange throbbing that Carmen had experienced intermittently since arriving in Haiti returned to the centers of her palms. She closed her eyes against the faint burn she felt there; the shells clanged against one another in the warm encasement of their entwined fingers.

"They say two things," Léah resumed, voice calm, quiet.

An eternity seemed to pass by as they sat quietly hand over hand over hand. The glow emanating from the backroom seemed suddenly more intense.

"The goddesses tell you: *You know what is at the bottom of the sea.*"

Carmen felt the baby girl inside of her moving against the lining of her stomach.

"They say: *Fire is your friend.*"

Carmen thought then of Gladys and her story of the woman who set fire to Montreal. She wondered at the woman's promise to burn her house down if it ever came to that. She wondered at the fires within this woman she had left behind in a cold country and an even colder house. She began to weep.

"When you came here as a child," Léah continued to speak, "you were anointed at Saut d'Eau. It took this long for your possession by the water goddess to manifest itself."

Carmen felt the baby move once more.

"Yes," Léah said, "The gods planted a seed within you that took fourteen years to grow. Fourteen years for you to realize the power of fire that is within you."

"But," Carmen began to protest. What of Nick? What of the fractured life she had led thus far, rootless?

"*Tu es une racine,*" Léah answered, reading her thoughts. You are the root. "You are carrying one of the daughters of Ochún in your belly. The sea goddess has seen the future and she has planted a seed of herself in you for that future."

"*Je ne sais pas,*" Carmen mumbled, suddenly frightened at the prospect of raising a child unlike all the others, a goddess-child, an undead. Then she realized that this is why her daughter had been able to appear and disappear at will, why she had been able to make out her face behind bookstalls and standing in doorways. Hadn't her mother told her that doorways were conduits to the gods, modern crossroads? Yes, she remembered being told so those summers so long ago when her mother had steered her away from all things North American, Catholic, and had her baptized in the waterfalls consecrated to Damballah, the serpent god, and Ayida Wedo, another version of the sea goddess. She had not felt any different after the baptism except for a strange tingling in the solar plexus, a strange tingling that she realized now was the same as the feeling she had felt since disembarking on Haitian shores. She had been chosen long ago.

"*Oui*," Léah said then, interrupting the flow of Carmen's thoughts, "Long ago you were chosen. This is why our paths crossed." Léah suddenly seemed to glow from within. Her aubergine purple skin tones became translucent. Her eyes appeared to suddenly be lit by a smoldering fire, as if she could see. She looked deeply into Carmen's eyes and uttered a string of words into the air.

At first, Carmen heard nothing.

Léah let go of her hands and the cowries held within spilled out onto the floor. *I am Ochún. I carry your fortune in my belly.* Léah stood and crushed the cowries beneath her feet. They turned easily into a fine mist of powder.

Follow me.

Carmen followed Léah into the backroom. As they crossed the threshold, the room became bathed in a white light. Carmen could see nothing in front of her. Nothing beside her. She reached out to cling to some piece of furniture which might be nearby but nothing found her fingertips. She became afraid and pulled back her hands but they were grasped in midair.

Child, do not be afraid. You are home.

Then the floor beneath her feet disappeared and her body was submerged in salt water. She found herself wading in the sea, sinking beneath waves.

All sound disappears and she has visions of armies advancing through the Haitian *mornes*, sees Papa Dessalines in his time of victory waving the newly made blue and red Haitian flag above his head, then the fires ravaging the cane fields, smoldering in the damp rice fields. She sees Papa Dessalines falling from his horse in mud, his dismembered body dragged into the capital, the woman with the red kerchief following with the flower petals folded into her apron. How is it that she sees all this? The unborn child in her womb swims within her as if with the current of the waters surrounding her. *I was here before.* Carmen hears the words and knows in the instant they fall into her ears that she has heard the unborn daughter's voice for the first time. She was here before. She is Ochún's daughter. How can this be?

Before she can begin to fathom the meaning of what is happening to her, Carmen finds herself face-to-face with a chained woman, hair rising like serpents to reach the light above the waters, arms and legs chained to the ocean floor. Hadn't she read about this in a manuscript her mother had sent her in Canada? Wasn't this the vision Christophe had seen before his departure for Ayiti so long ago? What had this to do with the daughter? With her?

Suddenly, she can no longer breathe. It is as if she has just discovered herself underwater, drowning, pores clogged, heavied with salt. Léah's words of divination return to her mind: *You know what is at the bottom of the sea.* Carmen forces herself to look at the apparition before her. The goddess is moving slowly in the water. Her face is veiled with a white-striped blue cloth. Carmen makes out white and blue beads fastened about the woman's neck. They resemble Léah's. Carmen understands. She is being warned that something must die for this child to be born. The goddess before her is Ochún's sister. She rises from the cemetery that is the ocean's bed. Carmen understands finally that her child is to bring a rebirth to these shores even as she grows far from it all, in the safety of the North American continent. Something must die. Is it her?

Is it her? As soon as she allows herself to think this thought, Carmen's body rises through the water in an upward motion. She is blinded by the speed of the water's movement and reaches out for some footing. There is nothing to hold on to. She sees her mother waving to her at the foot of two immense waterfalls. She sees Léah as a child sitting by the edge of the river with her flasks of water waiting to be filled. Léah speaks to her in her adult voice: *Usually the gods possess the chosen one after their baptism. We have waited fourteen years for your possession.* She sees her father slumped in his armchair in their living room so many years ago, a look of defeat spanning his brow. Her father of whom she has so little. Her father's image is superimposed with Olokún's. Death. Must she forget? Olokún nods. Only in forgiveness is there a new beginning.

"No," she says, "I cannot forget what he put us through." She thinks of Gladys and all the women and children who do not survive. How to forget?

The voices come again: *If you do not let this pain die, you cannot move toward the future. It is not in forgetting that we begin anew but in forgiving.*

Has she enough forgiveness in her?

She sees Léah smile at her. Another woman she does not recognize, a young woman, reaches out for her.

She finds herself in a bathtub filled with rosewater and lavender essence, flower petals from violets, African daisies, hibiscus, and orange orchids. A honey-based wash is poured over her hair, and she feels Léah's fingers massaging the oils into her scalp. The other woman cleanses her body with a sea sponge. Carmen closes her eyes. Has she gone over to the other side?

Je suis la.

Carmen opens her eyes to see her daughter standing at the base of the bathtub dressed in soft yellow with matching ribbons tied in her hair. Her daughter smiles. *You are still with the living,* she says, then laughs, then disappears. The baby moves within her again.

She smells the lavender rosewater, the flower petals. She remembers the palm nuts and cowrie shells, the piece of bone that answered to questions of yes or no in the palm of her hand. She looks at her hands. They suddenly seem immense to her, larger-than-life. She closes her eyes. When she opens them again, she finds herself dry and robed in a white nightgown that glows in the darkness of the room, where she is lying on a bed of straw mattresses. She looks about and recognizes Léah's calabashes and gourds hanging from the walls. On one hook, her familiar necklace of seven beads hangs loosely.

"Sleep now," she hears Léah say to her from the other room. "Sleep now."

Carmen falls fast asleep. It is a deep and restful sleep, entirely dreamless. When she wakes it is to the sound of the roosters in the neighboring yard. She stretches and finds that she feels light, lighter than she has ever felt in her life. She tries to remember the events of the evening prior but all she remembers is interviewing Léogane, Léah leading her to her home, and the lighting of the candles on the altar as someone moved in the backroom. She recognizes that she has awoken in that backroom and looks around for her clothes.

"All rested," a voice calls in Kreyol from the front room.

"Yes," Carmen stumbles on the word, not recognizing the voice. "Yes. I'm well thank you."

"Your clothes are in the cupboard there, next to the bed. We cleaned them for you. You went very far."

"Yes," Carmen says, not fully understanding, "I thank you."

"There's breakfast when you are ready," the voice continues, "Léah will be back soon."

"Yes. Thank you."

Carmen dresses hurriedly then folds the nightgown and leaves it on the made-up bed. Where did she go? She is only aware of a lightness in her spirit. She walks into the main room and finds a honey-hued woman standing over the stove. The woman turns to her and smiles.

"Léah has told me very much about you," she says.

"Ah," Carmen says, as she makes to sit down at the table.

"Yes, please do sit down," the woman smiles again broadly. "*Café?*"

"*Oui*," Carmen hesitates, "What happened?"

"It is not for me to say," the woman says. "Léah will be here shortly. She can answer your questions." With that said, she places a tin cup filled with coffee in front of Carmen and a bowl of steaming *akasan*. "Bon appétit," she says and disappears through the front door. "*A plus tard.*" See you later.

Carmen sits in the kitchen, the altar next to her cloaked beneath a blue cloth, and sips at her coffee. She has either entered into a madhouse or she is beginning to find the answers to her questions.

Léah

Léah slips her clothes on before crossing the road. The heap in her hands unfolds into an ankle-long, indigo-blue dress, sleeveless, a seam running tightly above the waist, lifting up the breasts into two bare brown mounds peering above the low-scooped neck. The dress falls over her, a light cascade of cloth. Léah pulls the fabric down. Her hands flatten out the seams over the curves of her body, her fingers arc themselves out over her hips like two wide brown fans. She does not care who is watching. She does not fear for her safety. She makes her way through the rubble at her feet, her feet remembering what her eyes cannot, where each piece juts out or pulls to the right, or where another has come loose and trembles underfoot. At the curb, ten paces away from where she rose from the sea, she pauses, cords of muscles straining beneath the smooth skin of her neck, and listens for the slow whir of a motor. Hearing none, she makes her way across the street, taking small and measured steps, one foot sliding before the other to make sure that nothing new has changed the landscape of the surface she has walked since childhood or, if something has changed, to make sure that she can carve out a new path in her mind for the next time.

Léah has never been afraid of stumbling, or of awkwardness. Over the years, she has learned that what she lacks in vision, her body has replaced with other, deeply set sensors that set off alarms when necessary and always prevent unforeseen disasters. She has learned to trust herself and her body above all else, as well as the powers the sea had given her even before her birth.

Just as fish swim in water, Léah has learned to swim through air. The stumbling blocks set in her path are like coral reefs or thick seaweed demanding only that they be felt out and contoured. The voices of her neighbors sometimes guide her through as if they are lighthouse beacons. She has the baker's voice memorized as it wafts down the cobbled streets in the early morning, with the scent of the freshly baked bread he carries in a two-foot-wide basket balanced upon his head, knowing from the way he yells out if he has had to move through the street differently because of an upturned cart or parked automobile. At noon, she hears Lucie calling her sons in from their playing in the street and knows from the way their feet fall against the ground how many people are crowding the street at high noon. She listens for clues in the change of routines, if a voice from the right has suddenly moved to the left, is weaker or louder. Listening, Léah knows the shape of the roads she travels, both by virtue of her own slow gait and by the shape of change among those she has lived with for so many years.

In this way, Léah walks the half-block to the alleyway where the brightly painted, azure door leading to her rented rooms stands in wait. She knows her companion, Fernande, has left the door unlocked. She pushes it open.

"*Ou leve?*" she asks, voice low, reedy, a hint of affection hidden in the breathing space between the words.

Carmen, her breakfast eaten, has made her way back to the bedroom to scribble some notes in her journal and record some thoughts.

"*Ou leve, chè?*" she asks, more quietly this time.

Léah sits on the edge of the bed next to Carmen.

"He's going up the mountain," she says cryptically.

"Who?"

"Ah, it is up to you to find out."

"I don't understand," Carmen says.

"You will in time. I told you yesterday that the answers are all within you."

Carmen begins to remember.

"Fernande and I helped you to cross to the other side yesterday, to visit with the ancestors, the water goddesses that haunt our shores still . . ."

"Are you one of them?" Carmen asks, her eyes fixed on the smoothness of Léah's skin, the shortly cropped hair. Was she truly one of the undead?

"People who do not understand the spirit world will make up one of their own, Carmen. This too you must come to see. I am no zombie. But I, like your daughter, have been sent from the sea."

"Am I going to be late . . ." Carmen pauses, ". . . for this meeting in the mountains?"

176

"No. They always wait for the tourists."

"I'm not a tourist," she replies, slightly piqued.

"Yes, of course you are."

Carmen sighs, "Of course I am."

"Of course," there is a smile in Léah's voice.

Carmen takes her jewelry, left for her at the side of the bed on a wooden table painted a muted green, into her hands. She slips rings onto her fingers, a watch around her left wrist, a gold Saint Christopher medallion on a gold chain about her neck. She fiddles with a hand-held recorder, rewinding the tape to see where the last voice left off. *If these hills could talk.* Léogane, the grandfather, telling a story. *They would tell you about the triumphs of war, the failures of greed. The wind carries the dreams of our ancestors, their memories. You'll listen, won't you?* She smiles. Would she listen? What would she hear?

"You can leave that here," Léah says.

"Leave it?"

"They'll think *ou CIA*, or something. *Ou pa bezwen'l.*"

Carmen sets the tape recorder back reluctantly on the table, worries about it for a moment. What if someone steals away with it? What if she loses all those stories?

"Yesterday," Léah resumes quietly, "we opened up a channel for you. You will hear the voices of the spirits in the mountains and they will recognize you. You must not be afraid. The guide you will meet in the mountains hears them too. He will be able to help you."

"What am I to be helped with?" Carmen cannot help but ask.

"This is as much for you as for your daughter," Léah replies. "Listen to what the voices have to tell you about the land. The guide's name is Philippe. I told you about him before we helped you to reach the other side. You will not remember until later. Such are the ways of the spirits. He can tell you much about the land. He is the next link in your destiny. He will guide you from this point on." Léah rises from the bed. "But you and I will meet again. You and I are linked through your daughter across the ages. We will meet again."

"Yes," Carmen says, certain this time that they will. A deep sadness wells up within her. Léah, such a small part of her childhood yet always remembered. And here she stands in her house, having slept in her bed, having met her companion, a sweet woman whom others feared because the two shared their quarters and Léah had the gift not only of second sight, making her way as she did through the streets, but the gift of a spiritual third sight. "We will meet again." She embraces Léah, and Léah holds her tightly. They stand breastbone to breastbone, the one's breath against the other's neck. There are no words left to speak.

Léah is the first to let go. "Go," she says. "Listen to the voices of the mountains." She places a small corked bottle in Carmen's hands. "This is the dust of the cowries. Take them with you. They are like bones whose dust is to be read at a later time. They will keep your fortune safe for you."

Carmen looks at the bottle and feels tears welling up into her eyes. So much has happened in a fortnight. How will she know Philippe?

"You will know him," Léah says. "You will know him as I knew you the first time of our meeting. Your powers have been unblocked. You are ready for the journey."

Not understanding completely, Carmen nods.

"*Bon*," she says finally, "*m ale*." She stands to leave; she suddenly feels awkward, notices the rustiness of her Kreyol.

Léah puts a hand against her stomach. The child moves beneath the layers of their touching skin. "You will find stories for your child," she says cryptically.

"*M ale*," Carmen says again.

Léah says nothing in reply. Seemingly unmoved, her eyes stare ahead of Carmen, toward the front door. Its inner façade is painted red.

Both see the mountain paths in their minds' eyes.

Alexis

When Uncle Kiko drinks, everyone walks around the house as if on eggshells. On such nights I take long walks in the neighborhood, to clear my mind and reclaim my spirit.

As I walk, I hear Kreyol drifting out toward me from open windows, and Jamaican *patwah*. At the dinner hour, the streets and alleyways between the houses and squat, brick apartment buildings are redolent with cooked beans and pawpaw, oven-baked chicken and fried plantains. Some older neighbors sit out on their porches wrapped up in thick coats. They wave or yell out a hello. How strange that on a street lined with garbage cans, trees stripped of their green plumage, not a coconut or palm tree in sight, that we would recognize each other and make ourselves at home. "Make yourself at home." Both Mother Gladys and Uncle Kiko had used the phrase with me that first night of my arrival. Yet now I felt more at home wandering the streets of the neighborhood than I did sitting in their living room.

I recognize that much of Kiko's daily anger has something to do with my presence. It doesn't matter that I have given him all the money the Jesuits allowed me to keep. Or that because I have not been in the country long, I can not work for my keep. I am just one more mouth to feed, a grown one at that. In short order, things finally come to a head.

We have just finished dinner. The children have been excused from the table after clearing their plates and, as usual, Mother Gladys is in the kitchen, cleaning up after the meal she has herself prepared after a long day at work standing on her feet.

"Gladys," Uncle Kiko calls out to her from in front of the television in the front room. "Gladys. Bring me a beer."

"I'll get it," I offer, wanting to spare Mother Gladys more work.

"She can get it, damn it," Uncle Kiko snaps back.

I am making to stand when I feel Mother Gladys' hand push me gently back down into my seat. She must have heard us talking and brought the beer. "It's okay," she says to me and hands Uncle Kiko a brown glass bottle, "Here you are, Carl." She returns to the kitchen.

It is clear to me that Uncle Kiko is an alcoholic. Why Mother Gladys supports his habit is beyond me. I follow her into the kitchen.

"Need any help?"

"No, son," she smiles toward me wearily, "Don't mind him, Alex. His bark is worse than his bite."

I want somehow to have a conversation about what I am witnessing in the house but do not know how to begin. "Mother Gladys," I try, "I think . . . I think Uncle Kiko needs to drink less."

"I know, Alex," Mother Gladys replies.

"You know? But . . ."

"You don't have to tell me. I shouldn't be giving him the bottles. I've heard it all before, Alex." She looks at me pensively, "You just haven't been here long. Things can be much worse. At least he's here drinking and not out at some bar. And I have the children to consider. He stays calm this way."

"This is calm?" I ask. The house has all the warmth of a morgue. "How can you raise Paul, Eric, and little Anna under this kind of cloud?"

"It's easy to criticize, Alex. I know you mean well. Lord knows I know you mean well. But I have been with your uncle for over twenty years and have shared my life with him. You're his blood but you haven't laid eyes on him for all your living days until this last month. You just have to let me handle it. Just go back in there and keep him company. Everything will be all right."

I do as I'm told. Uncle Kiko has already finished the bottle of beer and is beginning to drift off to sleep. He starts when I sit down and open up the paper to the want ads.

"You back?" he asks.

"Yes, Uncle Kiko," I reply. "I'm here."

" 'Bout time someone kept me some company," he says loudly as if to make sure Mother Gladys can hear him.

"You don't have to yell, Uncle Kiko. I'm right here," I say.

"Carl. Didn't I tell you my name was Carl?"

"Yes, sir."

He squints over at me, eyelids heavy. "You reading my paper?"

"Yes, sir."

"Give it to me here."

"I'm just reading the want ads."

"Didn't I say I wanted the paper?"

"I'm almost done, sir."

"Don't 'sir' me. Hand it over."

I fold the paper and hand it to him over the coffee table that sits between us. He takes it and fumbles with the creases. Pages come loose and fall onto the floor.

"Goddamn it," he says, "Look what you made me do."

"Maybe you should go to bed, Uncle Kiko," I say, making to gather up the pages.

As I do so, Uncle Kiko slaps the right side of my head. I am struck dumb. Mother Gladys stands at the door of the kitchen. She has heard the slap. I wave her away.

Uncle Kiko sits straight in his chair. "What did you say to me?"

"Nothing, sir," I mumble. My skin tingles from the slap.

"And why don't you, sir," he says sarcastically, "get a job?" He brings his face close to mine and I can smell the stale beer on his breath. I give up gathering the newspaper and move away from him,

"I'm going to go for a walk."

"Oh no you're not. You're going to fold that paper and hand it to me."

"I'm going," I say, not looking back.

I hear Mother Gladys before I feel Uncle Kiko behind me. "Please Carl," she says, "No."

Uncle Kiko tackles me in front of the door. I fall against the stained glass and it fractures under my weight. We wrestle on top of the broken slivers. I try not to hit Uncle Kiko but his fists are pummeling my face.

"No," I hear Mother Gladys say again, and then, "You promised."

I let Uncle Kiko hit me over and over again until I hear ringing in my ears. Then my mind clears. My blood runs cold in my veins. I lift myself up from the ground, bringing Uncle Kiko to his feet with me. I push him toward the screen door and we fall down onto the porch, down the steps and into a leaf pile. Holding his head in a vice with one arm I pummel him with the other. He breaks free, charged by adrenaline, and then stumbles before he comes at me again, this time throwing me back onto the porch steps. I feel the pain before I feel the sharp edges of the steps crowding against my spine. Still, I rise and lunge at him again, but his fist smashes my nose and blood spurts against the scattering leaves leaving imprints against them like broken flower petals. He is ready to break every bone in my body, but I am too tired to keep fighting. Like Mother Gladys, I too feel defeated.

"Okay, Uncle Kiko," I reach a hand up toward him, palm facing out in surrender, the other hand holding my nose, "You win."

He teeters toward me, the adrenaline in his alcohol-filled blood sapping him of energy. He leaves me in the leaves and stumbles up the steps. I hear him walk over the broken glass and into the house. Things collapse to the floor in the front room and then I hear him crash onto the bed.

"Are you all right?" Mother Gladys asks. She kneels at my side and smiles to the neighbors, waving them away as they try to ask her about what has just happened. "Everything's all right," she says before she has even heard my answer. She helps me back to the house and helps stop the bleeding.

"I can't stay here," I tell her, my nose throbbing. I am sitting on the toilet, seat down. She is sitting on the rim of the bathtub, lips trembling. "I can't tell you how sorry I am," she says. "I can't tell you."

I nod and leave her there, ready now for my quotidian walk even though the hour is growing late. "I won't be long," I tell her as I grab my coat and walk over the broken glass and to the porch. Soon I am in the street and walking toward anything that may offer me some answers.

I walk for what seems a long while. When I feel I can walk no longer, I find myself standing in front of the local Haitian community center. I read the billboard posted in their window announcing their programs for the month: workshops on teen pregnancy, a new after school program, a workshop on domestic violence, another on AIDS prevention. Surely providence has sent me this far. My feet are like lead before the door yet I summon the strength to enter.

"Hello," I venture, "anyone here?"

No answer.

"Hello?"

"Hi. What can I do for you?"

I turn around and see a young woman sitting behind a gray steel desk littered with papers she is sorting, with both hands going at once.

"I don't mean to disturb you," I begin, "I was just walking and I read your billboard."

She looks up from her work and takes in my swollen nose and bruised cheek. "*Jésus!*" she exclaims in French, "What happened to you?"

"I . . . I don't know where to begin."

She hears the serious note in my voice and stands. "Sorry I didn't get up before," she says as she extends a hand toward me. I shake it. "It's been a long day and I spent most of it on my feet."

"Take a seat," she says, "I just need to lock up and then you can tell me your story and we'll see what we can do for you. Would that be all right?"

I nod silently and sit. She puts the closed sign in the window and speaks to a couple of people in the back rooms before returning to her desk.

"Just saying goodbye to the cleaners," she says to me and smiles again her easy smile. "Now tell me the story, from the beginning."

As I begin to tell her how I came to the city, about my uncle and his family, and how we fought earlier in the evening, she turns her full attention to me, even as her elbows sink into the piles of unsorted papers on her desk. There are deep bluish circles beneath her eyes.

"I should let you go home," I say to her at the end of my tale, "Your husband must be very worried."

"Husband?" she laughs. "I've only just met you and I shouldn't be telling you this but I don't have one. And thank God for that!"

I stare at her. The community center services a mostly Haitian and Jamaican neighborhood. I wonder how she can work in peace here in such a state. "Well," I say, trying to cover up my shock, "Can I at least walk you home?"

"That's very kind of you but my girlfriend is picking me up," she says, "I don't even know your name."

"Alex. I mean Alexis."

"Alexis," she says, "I'm Yannick. I'm familiar with your case."

"What do you mean?"

"Gladys has come to see us before but she refused to leave your uncle. We've turned over everything to government agencies. There's nothing else the community can do."

"Nothing?" I slump into my seat, feeling deflated and discouraged.

"Nothing."

I stand. My hands gesticulate helplessly in front of me like weak limbs on a tall tree whipped by unseasonable winds, "Well then, I think I've wasted your time."

"No," Yannick says. One of her hands flies up to her neck and she massages a tight muscle there. "No, the least we can do is listen. Perhaps you can convince your aunt to return and we can try again."

"Perhaps," I nod. "I think I should go. I think . . ." I am suddenly at a loss for words. "Thank you for listening." I turn to walk out when a picture on a nearby desk catches my eye. "Who is this?" I ask.

"Oh," Yannick stretches her neck to take a look at the picture past him, "A coworker. Her name is Carmen. She should be back at the end of the month."

"She looks like one of my cousins," I try to cover up my astonished interest. It is as if I have just seen the girl I have been sketching from my dream visions all grown up. I leave the center filled with a vague and distant sense of renewed hope.

Outside, the air is crisp and leaves crackle underfoot. As I bound up the porch steps, I make a mental note to talk to Mother Gladys first thing in the morning. For now I am looking forward to the couch as I never have before, to sleep and rest from this long day.

I enter the house and find that the debris of broken glass has been swept away. Everything is quiet. I tiptoe to the couch. Light filters through the curtains and I make my way through from living room to bathroom to get ready for sleep. I prepare my makeshift bed, spreading out my folded sheet above the cushions. I pull out the picture of the girl I had drawn in Tennessee, and as I unfold it, a piece of yellow paper falls out. I hold the fallen paper in the palm of my right hand and look at the picture. I am not mistaken. The features of the woman in the photograph I saw earlier are in this girl's face. I smile, the mystery beginning to be solved. I put the picture away and unfold the piece of yellow paper in my palm: it is Alberta's address and phone number written in Mr. Louis' hand. I resolve to call her in the morning and move to her rooming house if I can. The sooner I leave, I think, the better.

Philippe

The Jeeps form a jagged line beneath the twisted trunks of the flamboyants; their putrid line of yellow, green, and lavender disrupts the beauty of the dense bush surrounding their metal casings. Las Vegas in Cap-Haitien. Miami Beach in the mountains. Scream of neon in the forest. Philippe has seen it all. Once, even a limousine owned by a famous African American singer whose great-grandparents, it was said, had been Haitians. The limousine had stayed in the lot for a good hour, engine turning, keeping the air conditioning in motion in the summer heat. The star emerged, halfway through the hour, took the short walk to the foot of the Sans Souci palace, and had his picture taken. He wore a pink suit that harmonized with the rose-dust of the crumbling walls and sunglasses that wrapped around his eyes like a shield. These foreigners, always protecting themselves from harm. Philippe remembers seeing his picture in a magazine from the mainland. *L'étoile* had come and gone. The boys had laughed in the store, looking at the magazine picture, doubled over by the bitter bile of their laughter.

Philippe surveys the Jeeps, looking for an appropriate target. He tries to match each vehicle to its owner. The more gaudy the vehicle, the more distant the traveler. He can recognize the tourists who are the most afraid of their own adventures by the lengths they take to seem as if they have seen everything before, as if they have no need for a tour guide, a hand-holding. These are the people with the straw hats decked with flowered cloth bands, the Hawaiian shirts (all islands are the same, aren't they?), fatigue pants (to wander in the jungle), hiking boots made for colder, harsher weather. Philippe wonders at times if these costumes are the doing of guide books or if the people just simply have no common sense. A pair of jeans, a cotton shirt, sandals, what more is necessary? This is what he wears to work, alternating the jeans with shorts, depending on the weather. The only good thing about their stupidity is the money they will give so freely, mostly out of guilt—not Haitian money, which is worth little more than the ink worn away by hands made slippery from the sweat of long hours of work. No—they will give their precious Deutschmarks, French francs, Japanese yen, and, most coveted of all, American dollars. It doesn't matter what the currency, as long as it comes from out there, from beyond the island; it's all good, but not so easy to make. It means having to play games and, often, having to trade things too personal to be spoken. All that work and betrayal of self in order to take the crumpled, foreign-looking bills to the moneychangers in the market who give a fair deal, better, at least, than going to the bank. Each of them have to look out for themselves. Family ties break down over currency. Community means less and less: only the fittest will come out of the fray alive. Philippe has known this since the moment he learned to walk.

Philippe stands in front of the crumbling, rose walls of Sans Souci. He squints in the sun, pulls out a folded, worn baseball cap he keeps stuffed in the back pocket of his faded jean shorts, and adjusts it on his head. He pulls at a thread hanging loose from the visor, blocking his view of the tourists. Holding the thread between forefinger and thumb, he pretends to inspect it with the closest care as he listens to the deals being made all around him. The tourists bargain down, the tour guides bargain up: ten dollars for a tour of the Citadel, twenty on muleback. A group with small children settles on the mules for fifteen dollars. Philippe smiles at the tour guide leading the mules up the trail. Fifteen American dollars: good deal. Philippe watches as the rest of the tour guides rally around the remaining foreigners.

Finally, Denis, the official tour guide for the Citadel, knowing that the tourists will amble up the path on their own as if they own the place, speaks up, "*Bon, nou pra'l fé un* deal. *D'accord?*" He lays one hand flat on his chest with earnestness meant to inspire trust, "Myself and my colleagues will take you up the trail, point out the historical facts, take you through the Citadel, and then you can pay us what you like. Good."

"You like?" he asks two men in gaberdine shirts.

The men nod, consult each other over their wallets. They nod again, and the tourists and guides start splintering off onto the path in groups of two and three. Denis turns to the groups once or twice to point out a flowering hibiscus shrub or to point out when different parts of the path they are now walking was built by a new president or military leader hoping to leave his mark before being ousted by a junta or the US government. There have been too many of these interim leaders since the coup of '86. Baby Doc Duvalier had fled so hurriedly from the country that he forgot the bones of his father. They remained rattling in their coffin, buried in the graveyard facing the white palace where Papa Doc had ruled with his iron fist and kept enemies in the basement for hours of torture. Duvalier-son was a creampuff by comparison. Perhaps he had left Papa Doc's bones behind on purpose, fearing the evil they could bear again if taken to a new land. As it was, the masses intent on the *dechoukaj*, the necessary uprooting of all the evildoings that had served to oppress them for so many years, had forced open the grave shortly after the son's ousting, found the decaying bones with Papa Doc's signature black-rimmed glasses (a decoy?), and toppled the contents of the coffin to trample on the remains, shouting, *"Libere! Nou libere!"* Free. We are free at last. Philippe nods his head as he remembers watching the frenzied scenes on the black-and-white television of the local Lotto store.

He watches now as the clusters of tourists advance up the path and chooses his target, a young nutmeg-brown woman in her twenties. She is wearing a pink sleeveless shirt, tight, knee-length jean shorts that have been tailored with odd-looking fringes. Philippe smiles inwardly, recognizing a good mark.

He has seen her before. It takes him the minute of going toward her to remember where, and then, as he does, he finds it is too late to turn away. He had bumped into her as he hurriedly made his way out of a hotel room just a day ago, trying to make it out of the building before anyone saw him and recognized his face. Philippe decides to keep calm. He continues to make his way toward her until his footsteps fall naturally side by side with that of the young woman's. Their feet keep time like drumbeats against the soil—one beat, counterbeat. For a few moments, Philippe forgets that he is walking with the woman for a purpose; he is enjoying the pattern of their footfalls and listening to the wind. *This is going to be a fine day*, he thinks to himself.

Carmen

Carmen's fingers close over an imaginary tape recorder in the back pocket of her jeans. She cannot believe that she has left it behind. But Léah is right, showing up with it in an open space would send off signals about her trustworthiness. She would have to depend on her ability to ask the right questions and remember the answers, just as she had at home, talking with her grandfather late into the night about the events of the last year on the day he brought her home from the airport. Duvalier may have left eight years ago, but the shadow cast by his dictatorship was a long one.

The evening before, before everything in her life had suddenly turned upside down, when she and Léah had sat on opposite sides of the small square dining table with one leg shorter than the other in the café, once Léogane had been interviewed, Léah had grown quiet as Carmen laid out her plans for her family research. She had explained about her grandfather and the family's move to the capital in search of a better future some years ago. She had talked about not knowing enough of her past to piece things together and of how she truly desired to leave something behind for her daughter. She knew all there was to know about Canada, her father's land, but knew too little about her mother's land, the land of her own birth, shrouded as it was in a nostalgic veil of absence. Her memories had been *trouées*—pierced—by the years of silence and fear that surrounded life under the Duvaliers. Léah, eyes closed, had listened, the flat and open palm of one of her hands holding her chin up in a thoughtful posture. Carmen glanced at the blue-brown skin, followed it from chin to wrist, to elbow, to its disappearing trail beneath the cloth of her dress and faltered in her explanations. Léah's skin seemed to glow as if it was, perhaps, a celestial body fallen to earth. Carmen could not explain why this was so. She listened to the quiet of the house, looked across the table at this remarkable woman who had led her through the streets seemingly without sight and helped her along on her journey.

Léah's hand moved slowly away from her chin. To Carmen's eyes, it seemed as if the gesture had taken an eternity to occur. She wondered as the arm moved through the air where the fine, long fingers would come to rest. She wondered for a moment if they would light upon her own, and a spark went through her stomach, a spark like nothing she could remember having felt before. When the hand finally settled, open palm resting against the wood, Carmen exhaled slowly, in relief.

Léah smiled, "I can hear you, you know."

Carmen flustered, looked around as if Léah must have been speaking to someone else. "What do you mean?"

"Just that," Léah repeated, "I can hear you."

Carmen held herself with arms crossed against her chest. It was hot, as usual, her underarms wet with sweat, but she felt a shiver come over her.

"There is someone else who can help you," Léah continued.

"Who?"

"Someone I've known since I was a child, really."

Carmen leaned in closer toward the table, hands still clasping both her upper arms. The table held her. "Who, Léah? Who is it?"

How had the space between them become so close all of a sudden, Carmen remembered thinking just at the moment that her thoughts were being pulled away from the attraction for Léah she could not deny, an attraction that had been there from the moment that Léah had led the way from the gates of the hotel out through the narrow corridors of Cap-Haïtien? How had the space between two virtual strangers become so filled with intimacy as they shared this first cup of mint tea in the café by the sea, filled with trust? "Who?" she asked again, wanting to know what other secrets Le Cap, King Christophe's city, might release to her on this brief, brief journey.

"Well . . . ," Léah took in a small breath so that her words seemed to have the lightness of clouds suspended in the sky, or perhaps it was that, to Carmen, they seemed just as magically beyond any explanation. "His name came to my mind as soon as you spoke about your grandfather and the things you are trying to remember that cannot be remembered. There are so many things that we have forgotten, Carmen, as a people, and so many other things that are being forgotten for us. Those of you who left," Carmen cringed at the words, wanting to interject her lack of choice, "I hear you Carmen," Léah continued, "Those of you who left took some things with you, but you also forgot a great many other things, like the voices in these hills, the voices of the ancestors. If you want to hear these, and I think you want to hear them, and by the time this is evening is through, you will be able to hear them, then there is someone who can help you, up there, on mount Laferrière, a tour guide. He is about your age, early twenties. He has lived in Millot all his life."

"How can he help?"

"I tell you, he can hear things that even I can't hear, that even Léogane cannot remember."

Léogane had lived a long and full life, and as one of the best known storytellers of the region, he had amassed a huge arsenal of tales that told the history of the country, a history that was at once truthful and beyond comprehension, that needed to be believed to be understood rather than the other way around. How could a young man in his twenties have acquired such powers? Carmen wondered. Then her thoughts turned to the voices Léah had mentioned, that Léogane had also talked about when she had interviewed him a day earlier. Why did Léah think she could hear anything of the kind? She had told her nothing of the way in which, for years before her death, she had thought she could hear her grandmother speaking to her from across the ocean. She had never spoken about the communications to anyone or in any way. This, because the sounds she heard consisted of a language she could not have described. They would wash over her as she walked to catch a bus or tried to drift off to sleep, and they intensified after the Duvaliers had been ousted and the army and neo-Duvalierists fought for control of the small country. Over the years, Carmen would write letters to her grandmother in response to the sounds she heard, to make sure everything was all right with the family, to make sure her grandmother knew she had not forgotten them or where she herself had been birthed. The answers came by and by on odd pieces of paper that never matched their envelopes. The letters shaped by her grandmother's arthritic hand retained their schoolgirl grace, leaning more than slightly to the right, the *s*'s curved like the necks of swans. Every letter Carmen received was brief and sought to console her. *Yes,* her grandmother would write, *we are doing as best we can and we hope that God is with us. It is very kind of you to write and let us know how much you are thinking of us. Only God can say what will become of us. But we remain. I love you very much.* To read the letters, Carmen would have thought that she had never heard a sound even though she knew she had. Her grandmother's recourse to a Christian God always left her perplexed as well, and she sought out more information on *vodou*, the religion no one had taught her about, that no one would speak of in the family. She wondered what her grandmother would have thought about her research. But she knew that she could hear her across the distance because of something that was alive in those hills, even if camouflaged, even if trampled beneath the feet and drowned out by the beating of drums.

"He can tell you more about the spirits of the hills," Léah said to her quietly. She had not revealed his name until this morning, after the evening of the divination and other rituals that were only beginning to surface in her memory.

Carmen nodded even though she knew Léah could not see her.

"I can't see you," Léah whispered again, "but I can feel you."

And that was how it had all begun. The *all* of it: what Carmen can not yet understand and still utterly believes in, despite herself. This is how she has been brought to walk the hills carrying so little fear in the blooming place of her solar plexus that she feels that, like a leaf fallen from the limb of a tall tree, she can be carried away to safety by a small gust of wind. She is following Léah's advice despite herself, despite what she does not know, because she trusts something about Léah's hands that can not be measured by time, something about the way they move through air, against wood, and skin.

Phillipe

Philippe listens to the wind and to the sound of the echoing fall of their footsteps.

"*Je m'appelle Carmen*," Carmen says as if she has said it once before. He smiles at her through a fog of sounds.

She is trying to size him up. He looks familiar to her, not from what Léah has told her earlier, which remained quite vague, but from a sighting a day or two ago while she was lying out in the sun by the pool at the hotel waiting for Léah to come by, waiting to be led away to speak with Léogane.

"Oh," he replies, remembering his own tongue, "Philippe." He produces his right hand for shaking. He holds her hand firmly, in silent communication palm to palm. He learns all he needs to know from a handshake, its firmness or lack thereof, the way a palm feels, dry or sweaty. Her handshake is firm, noncommittal, but friendly. Her palm is cool, no trace of humidity even though it is a hot day that will get even hotter once the sun is directly overhead, beating down upon their heads. She is wearing a hat like his, though hers is brand new, with a sports logo on the front he cannot place at the moment. He does not know much about sports even though he watches the *télé* with his friends in the Lotto store and jokes with them about the scores. It does not hold his interest the way the tides do, the way Léah appearing out of nowhere from the spumes of the sea can, and the wind, always the wind and its many voices. Philippe smiles at his ignorance. It makes him feel free. He can ask as many questions as he wants from these tourists that way and still get what he wants: money, information about the continent.

"Carmen," he says in his most charming manner, all smiles, trying to make sure that she does not remember him from the quick exit he made from the hotel, bumping into her in the shadowed hallway.

"How can I be of help to you today? What languages do you speak? I can guide you in any language." He says all this to her in French, since she has introduced herself in that language. He is hoping he can impress her with the many tongues that can fly from his mouth. He says hello in Spanish, American English, Kreyol, German, and Dutch.

"*Anglais, français,*" she says, surprised. Léah had said nothing of his linguistic abilities. "*M pa pale anpil kreyol.*"

Philippe sizes her up. The kreyol is Frenchisized rather than Haitian, but she must be Haitian to know any of it at all. He figures she must be from the tenth department, one of those who was born overseas and never came back until the Duvaliers were ousted. And here she was, a tourist in her own country, trying to find her way back to the core of her native land by visiting the historical sights, the massive monuments that could justify her existence as a Haitian in whatever countries she now called home without ever feeling at ease, where no one ever took her in and said: you are home, no need to look back.

Carmen is thinking about the woman she has left behind in the city: the beautiful, handsome Léah. She is thinking about the twisted sheets of the bed, remembering lying there after the bath of lavender and rosewater, the visions returning in snippets, Fernande making her breakfast in the narrow front room, the blue/red door opening and closing behind one or the other of the two women who had opened up a path for her soul.

"Where you from?" Philippe asks.

Startled from her thoughts, she nods, then smiles, "Here. I mean, I'm visiting from Canada. But I was born in Port-au-Prince." She notes his slenderness, reminding her of her grandfather with that same wiry, birdlike build.

Philippe nods back. What does a birthplace amount to, he is thinking, if one never sees it, breathes it, knows its fears and deaths imprinted in membranes of memory? He hears Carmen breathing in small waves of effort.

Carmen marches behind, thankful that she has been hitting the gym at home at least three times a week. The climb reminds her of muscles she has forgotten, dormant at the back of her legs, along the sides of her waist. She glances up at Philippe, marveling that he found her before she sought him out. Léah had described him to her as the wizard of the mountain, a young man made wise by a life spent conversing with the spirits. She feels the desire to speak to him of those voices; she wants to know what her grandfather had fled those many years ago in moving his enterprises from Le Cap to Port-au-Prince. Suddenly, all thoughts of her father have disappeared; it was he that she had been asked to surrender, to forgive, in order to provide her daughter with a whole sense of spirit. Her father's spirit was broken, but he was gone, like the ghost of the Duvalier regime; he would fade with time and leave behind a place for healing. She is singly focused on the task ahead: getting to know the land beneath her feet.

"What kind of tour would you like?" Philippe asks over his shoulder, sensing her eyes on the small of his back, "I can point out the historical details, the local color, talk about the days of Christophe, whatever you like."

"Uh-hunh," she murmurs to herself, a frown forming between her eyebrows. She is calculating how much his talking to her is going to cost. She appalls herself at the thought, amazed that in this country, her country, one of the poorest in the world, she would, like a tourist anywhere, count her pennies when everything—the sea, the *fruits de mers*, the tours—is handed to her, practically for free, on a silver platter.

"You can pay me whatever you like," he says, "when we come back down. Whatever you like." He smiles to give her every assurance of his goodwill.

"Okay," she says, aware that she has been read in an unflattering way. She wants very much for Philippe to like her, not just so that he will tell his stories but also so she can show him something of herself, reveal layers of her past, her Haitianness. She wants him to understand that they really are on the same side. "My grandfather is from here. His family used to live here. I just want to know about the ways things used to be, or still are, for myself, and," she hesitates, "my daughter."

"Ah yes," Philippe says, a false tone of interest in his voice. The group ahead is now being led off the paved area to paths obstructed by dense bushes lying low against the ground. The paths are worn but filled with crumbling stones. Philippe offers his hand to Carmen to help her up some loose ground. She brushes it away. To cover up for her rudeness, Philippe moves a branch out of the way instead, as if for himself. "I have a friend who went to study on the continent," he offers in the silence that has been building between them.

Carmen does not respond. She is too busy looking up at the shadow of the Citadel against the blue sky. It looks like a hard piece of solid granite that has risen whole from the belly of the mountain. She is too busy trying to figure out how she will have Philippe tell her the stories buried in the crevices of this mountain. She stops and holds a hand above her eyes against the glare of sun.

"So where do you live?" Philippe tries again.

"Oh, I've been around," she replies, suddenly evasive, "How about you? Where did you learn to speak all those languages?"

Just like a tourist, thinks Philippe. Ask them about themselves and it's as if you've asked to be taken home with them, room and board included. He wonders if she has already done just that. She glows as if she has just stumbled out of someone's bed. But he does not feel attraction coming from her. She is very still. But what is it with the questions? Acting like a tourist? Damn tourists! Never stop throwing their questions at you, never once thinking that perhaps you have your own desire for privacy. Still, the thought of Alexis in that other place, on the other side, moves him to want to peel back layers of emotional tissue. It isn't as if he will ever see her again, after all. "Look there," he has her turn around to look, "you see that little house on the hill there, beyond the palace . . . we go to school there. I mean . . . I . . . I went to school there." He measures her glance and can not read it. Unsure, he adds, "It's a good school."

"They teach you all those languages there?" she asks, a touch of wonder in her voice.

"No," he laughs and the sound emerges from deep within his chest.

It is the laugh of an older man coming from a thin, frail, adolescent body, Carmen thinks. Then she realizes that he does not look well.

"I learn from the tourists," he says, laughing still. He turns back to the Citadel, "You know, this is a world treasure." He feels a strange pull in his stomach, suddenly nervous with her at arm's length. He is trying to move back into the safe armor of his tourist guide skin, trying to give her some of the information he is certain she should know, that she is surely resisting in order to put up this front of being a full-fledged Haitian, "It has been classified by the United Nations as one of the modern world's treasures. It was designed by German engineers who perished within the walls because Christophe did not want his monument duplicated anywhere else in the world. It was built by Haitian hands through forced labor and no one knows really how such a feat could have been achieved, you know, back then." Proud of himself, Philippe walks ahead of Carmen.

She is remembering the afternoon of the day before. Léah sitting across from her in her family's café in the main square, spoonfuls of peanut ice cream moving from bowl to mouth. Her lips a plum rouge. She remembers Léah laughing in the same manner as Philippe as she asked about the mountain's history. Her relaying, "You'll have to see for yourself." Léogane nodding in the background, sitting on a stool at the long counter behind Léah. Léah's sister wiping down the table beside them, cleared of a family of four with a crying child.

"I know!" she calls to Philippe's back, "I've studied all this on my own. About Christophe's reign, you know, the pros and cons. Your school back there is one of the things he did right."

The muscles in Philippe's neck tense up in reaction to Carmen's last words. What does she know about right and wrong? What does she know about the king and what it means to have been born and raised at the bottom of this hill in shacks that resemble dollhouses to people like her who have never lived in such small quarters with other human beings piled body against body? He feels himself ready to defend the king. He knows the statistics, the time it took to build the palaces, the Citadel, the lives lost. He knows these things, but he feels they belong to him only, and to the other guides working the mountain. They certainly do not belong to her and those who left them all behind to grab their fortunes from the whites who had thrown their country into disrepair, crushing them all beneath their heavy boots.

"So," Carmen says, sensing that she has tampered with the lines of communication between them, "tell me about your friend. What was his name?"

"Alexis," Philippe says dryly. They are now at the foot of the Citadel's massive prow. The sharp edge of the main façade of the building makes it look like a ship stranded against the mountain after the waters around it have receded. "He studies," he says finally. "He is an artist, a painter," he adds proudly. "He has drawn everyone in the village and me more than once. But I haven't heard from him in a while. He was going to Montreal."

The thought of Alexis flushes out all the anger Philippe feels toward Carmen and the other tourists marching ahead. He grows silent with his own thoughts and memory.

Carmen

Carmen stands on the path leading to the entrance of the Citadel, squares of roughly cut rose and orange stones cemented together recently to give the Citadel a face-lift now that tourism has come alive again. She has listened to the gaps in Philippe's story, the things that are moving through his mind alone, the secrets there. She wants to tell Philippe about meeting Léah, that she knows about his ability to hear the spirits.

The village can hardly be seen from where they stand. Small squares of yellow and blue peer through the dark foliage below. They are far above sea level. She can see the harbor and the red-tiled roofs of Le Cap.

Philippe follows Carmen's gaze. It is always breathtaking, this sight. He extends a hand to help her up a scraggly incline in the footpath. She brushes his hand away, impatient.

"Oh," she says, distracted, a response to finding out that Alexis is an artist, that they live in the same city, Montreal. Intriguing, she thinks, how many Haitians become painters. Dreams painted on flimsy pieces of stretched canvas made of sacks, odd materials. The colors always brilliant, so much more so than the daily struggles for survival. To enter a Haitian painting, Carmen felt, was to enter hope itself and to return to a distant, distant past when Ayiti was truly the one and only pearl of the Antilles.

Carmen's thoughts turn to the Citadel. This place she has heard of for so long. She thinks of Léogane telling her about the soldiers marched off the high walls to impress military company in King Christophe's day, his voice sagging as if he himself had been one of those men, telling her about his great-great-grandfather and all the things he had heard as he stood by the door of the palace, guarding it, listening to the men plan their mutiny, listening to the men groaning against their hunger. For her, this is a pilgrimage to the roots of her existence, this march toward the Citadel. In whatever way is still possible, Ayiti remains home to her. She can feel it in her bones. She has come to pay her respects to the ancestors.

Philippe watches as Carmen joins the others and inspects a bottle of Kola from the bottom to see if there are any pieces of matter floating in the yellow liquid, banana flavor. She goes through three bottles before settling on a fourth, while Denis presses her to buy. Philippe holds back a laugh. She opens the bottle by pulling the cap off against a large rock. She swigs back the bottle in a masculine gesture, drinking quickly, her Adam's apple moving back and forth like a small fish swimming against the current of a stream.

Carmen breaks away from the group and rejoins Philippe. She has decided she likes him. Philippe, in another time and place, could well have been her brother. She has already decided that she will give him five dollars for his troubles when this is all over. She has forgotten all the questions she wants to ask him. She is suddenly growing restless, her thoughts straying again to Léah. Léah, who had placed the flat palm of her hand on the soft, bare skin of Carmen's stomach and told her that she was carrying a child of Ochún in her womb. Like all the women on her mother's side of the family, she would not show until later in the pregnancy. Carmen's hands hover over her stomach in wonder; then she remembers she is not alone.

"So," she resumes their conversation in an attempt to regain her concentration, "how did you say you learned all those languages again?"

"From tourists . . . like you." Having removed his cap, Philippe rubs his head absent-mindedly. "They come from everywhere," he says, "But a lot of them are American, like you."

"Haitian," she says, "I'm Haitian with a Canadian passport."

"That's what I said," Philippe replies, taking off his cap to wipe off the sweat on his forehead, "American."

Carmen follows him with her eyes as he leads the way into the Citadel, disappearing behind the thick walls. She wonders what will become of him, if talking to tourists in exchange for a few dollars will be enough to lead him out of this place.

She assumes he would want to leave. She assumes that with all those languages tripping off his tongue, he could do anything he wants in another place, another time. But it is this time, this place. This place, Haiti, that she left as a child to see again only as an adult who feels continuously displaced. Could Philippe withstand that kind of distance? Was it enough for him to know the outside world through these foreign tongues, the line of loud-colored jeeps stationed on the outskirts of the village, tourists looking for a moment of redemption from the role they played in the poverty surrounding them by climbing a mountain? Carmen shakes her head. There seems to be no way out.

Inside the walls of the Citadel, the tourists stand in a small group like a herd of sheep. They are miniaturized by the black stones. Denis leads them past a low-lying building that looks like a bunker. It stands empty.

"Le Roi Christophe built the Citadel to defend himself against aggressors coming across the channel," Denis says, "but he never used the fort. These cannonballs are the original ones brought from Germany. Some are from France."

The crowd of tourists hold their chins, bemused at the wonder of it all. Carmen finds her way to Philippe, who is watching something at the far wall of the Citadel.

"What are you looking at?"

Philippe points to the bottom of the wall. Hidden in a clump of bright green grass, a small, mottled goat sits sleeping. How odd, Carmen thinks.

"Don't let him fool you," Philippe says, "he's only hiding from the slaughter knife." He pauses, "As we all are."

"Will you tell me more about your friend? Alexis, is it?" she says, wanting to know how he got out, how he fled the knife blade.

Although she is standing very still beside Philippe, she feels as if her body is swaying and might, at any minute, fall over the wall into the precipice below. She has forgotten to bring water, and the Kola she had earlier has turned into a nauseous stew in her belly. Her feet ache from walking up the incline to the monument. A sound rides the wind, a low sound; a moan. It reaches Carmen's ear like a tidal wave, making her even more unsteady on her feet. She impulsively grabs for Philippe's arm to steady herself.

"Vertigo?" he asks.

She cannot explain what she has just felt. At first, yes, it did feel like vertigo. A nausea created by lack of habit, a sort of tourist disease. But the wind has carried something even stronger than discomfort with it, voices from the past she hardly hears anymore, that she is no longer accustomed to hearing far from Haiti. She hears the wind rustling through the plastic windbreakers of the other tourists tied around their waists. "Did you hear?" she asks Philippe.

"What?"

She looks at Philippe inquisitively. His eyes reveal nothing. She is looking into two dark, round marbles that can only be made to shine by the sun. He gives nothing of himself away. "Nothing," she laughs to cover up her embarrassment at wanting him to open himself up to her fear. "Nothing, just vertigo."

"You should go back to the group," he says.

She nods, removes her hand from his arm, which she just then notices has never moved under her touch. Philippe holds both arms firmly crossed against his chest, a shield of soft flesh, hard bone. He looks years older than what she assumes are his early twenties. She notes the soft stubble on his cheeks. Still, barely old enough to shave. A man not old enough to shave. She is suddenly conscious of the gift her parents had offered her, taking her back to Canada to escape the strife, the poverty, the fear of the Duvaliers: a childhood. She did not have memories of walking over corpses on her way to school as her mother did. The bloodshed she knew was fictive, fixed in the still shots below headlines announcing the latest news from the capital after the elections of 1987. A childhood. It was no small gift in the face of all there was to lose.

Philippe suddenly doubles over with a hacking cough. The tourists turn around to stare. Carmen quickly walks back toward him but he waves her back. She sees a small splatter of blood between his feet. She walks away reluctantly. Philippe straightens up, wipes his mouth with a cloth handkerchief stuffed in his pants pocket, and waves ahead to Denis to signal that everything is all right. He senses Carmen moving away toward the group behind him without taking a second look at her. Her touch lingers on his arm like a tattoo.

Of course he hears the voices gliding on the wind. Of course he hears them. But how had she? He breathes in deeply, does not want to think about it too much. He places the flat of his right hand against his aching chest. He feels he is getting worse. He does not even have the breath it takes to climb the mountain trails. He will have to cut back on his trips up to the Citadel and do more things around the hotel. It is as if his fate is locked.

Philippe looks across the crests of the mountains hemming them in. There are live things sprouting between them, hidden, their multitude of scents rising to fill his nostrils. The red, red soil, regenerating. He closes his eyes, feels his body pulled into the earth. He is losing a sense of time. The voices come back to him on swift wings of wind and his body suddenly feels light as if he is being picked up whole and swept into the air. As the voices flood his mind, and he begins to feel that he will not return to solid earth, he suddenly remembers that he is not alone. He forces himself to snap his eyes open, to look at the mountains, to turn around and compel his feet to move forward, back toward the group of tourists, who are becoming restless and demanding to climb the high walls.

"Not the children," Denis is telling them. "All the children must stay here." He offers in the way of explanation, "No guard rails."

Philippe watches Denis climb up ahead, agile as a panther, showing the tourists where it is safe to walk.

The older tourists clamber up the uncovered wide steps behind Denis, walk nonchalantly across the top surfaces of the Citadel as if they are walking in a toy maze. One teeters, almost falls. They are inebriated with their curiosity. Philippe is glad to see that Carmen is not one of them.

Carmen is walking the length of the inner courtyard, thinking to herself, counting with her feet the depth of the field within the walls. She is thinking of the voices. Léah had told her that Philippe was one of the only ones who could hear them clearly, distinguish one from the other, communicate with them, understand their yearnings. Léah could see without eyes but she could not hear all the voices in the wind even though she had her powers that made it possible for her to leave her door unlocked, that made it possible for her to bathe tranquilly in the sea. She was protected by the spirits, was rumored to be one of them in the flesh, but she spoke of them as if they belonged to another world, a world she had left behind some time ago.

"Okay. *Tou' la li fini*," Denis says waving the tourists back down the main steps, signaling the end of the tour. Philippe understands that Denis does not want to be held responsible for a white tourist falling off the Citadel at this time in history. Tourism has just recently been reborn. There is no need for adverse publicity.

Philippe catches up with Carmen outside the walls on their way back down toward the jeeps. They are at the front of the group this time, retracing their steps through the bush on a dirt shortcut that has been carved into the soil by hundreds of feet before them. This time, Carmen lets Philippe help her over unstable ground. She hardly thinks of the gesture of reaching out; finally, unexpectedly, it has become natural. She wonders how it is that another human being who has existed in her consciousness only so slightly, could, in a matter of minutes, a moment in time, seem so important, take up all of her interest. She wants to hear about Alexis; she wants to know the pieces of Philippe that will make him real to her forever.

"I'm a friend of Léah's," she tells him, finally letting him know that she can be trusted. "She told me that you could tell me something about these hills."

Philippe looks at her from the corners of his eyes. *Léah?* This changes everything. Even though he does not know Léah well, a meeting long ago, beneath the waterfall at Saut d'Eau, one of the sacred *vodou* worshipping places, had sealed something between them, something which had no name and no contours but which had everything to do with understanding and respect. Léah had known his secret since that time and had tried to help him. She had been the only one, the whole of his life, who had looked at him and understood his difference and not held him up to ridicule. For that gift of acceptance, he had always been grateful. He had not seen Léah since that time long ago, until he had come across her a few mornings past, as she made her way home from the sea, clothes folded in her hand, as he made his way to the shore in search of work that had led him back to the dank hotel room and his sealed fortune. Philippe learned long ago not to ask the universe for explanations to things that seem beyond his immediate understanding. "You know Léah," he says finally.

"Yes. She told me about the voices."

"She did?" Philippe stares at Carmen. Then the voices in the hills had been sent to them both. "Did she tell you that it is a rare thing to be able to hear them?"

"She told me you would tell me what I needed to know."

Philippe hesitates. "You should speak to her grandfather, Léogane."

"I have, Philippe. And I will some more," Carmen says quietly, then feels bold, "but there are things only you can tell me. I know this to be true, even if Léah had not told me to look for you here."

Philippe smiles despite himself. "I saw Léah for the first time in seven years this morning."

"Really?" Carmen is surprised. They live in such close proximity but then she realizes that without proper roads to cities a village in the mountains is far, when one has to work for transportation.

"I know what you're thinking but even here people lose each other from sight. Besides," he adds, "we are both solitary people. And I live in the hills and try to make a living here, and she lives down in Le Cap. I try to stay away from Le Cap." He remembers the hotel and wonders how much Carmen knows about the activities that go on in the tourists' rooms. "I've had to start going back into town to make more money. My grandmother isn't well and we are living on very little."

"You aren't well, are you?"

Philippe looks away.

"I heard you coughing. I saw blood. You can get help . . ."

"No one can help with what I have," Philippe makes a gesture of futility with his hands. "My blood has been cursed."

Carmen grows quiet. She does not know what to say.

"It's all right," Philippe says to ease her discomfort. "I'm not well, but you have not come here to talk about my troubles. I will tell you something about the voices.

"When I was a child, I would walk these hills by myself, in the dark, even though I should have been in bed, sleeping, and resting for the next day of school or work. I would walk these hills and after some time, the voices came to greet me from another place. I would sit upon rocks or on the soil of clearing places where sometimes the villagers would have gathered and celebrated the feast day of one of our spirit keepers, and I would let them come into me, talk to me, share themselves with me." Philippe closes his eyes, and when he opens them, the darkness Carmen had looked into before has turned amber with a golden light.

"I was telling you about my friend Alexis, before." A distant smile appears fleetingly on Philippe's face. "We used to walk together but he was afraid of the voices, afraid of what it would mean to his life to hear them and hear them well. So I began to walk alone."

Philippe goes on, telling Carmen about the way the voices appear as dim lights between the branches of trees and then become people of solid flesh that only he can see, of how the voices speak to him of the ways their lives have been cut short and all for the greed and lust for power of others. They continue walking down the footpath as Philippe talks, stopping only when he has to turn away to cough into his handkerchief. He apologizes with embarrassment every time he does so. By the time he is done talking about the spirits, the silence between them is charged with electricity. It seems to Carmen that the voices are there between them, telling them to keep their ears open, even to silence.

"Tell me about Alexis," she finally says, as the tourist cars come into sight. She knows her time with Philippe is coming to an end and senses also that this absent man has a hold on Philippe, a hold as strong as the voices of the mountains.

Philippe smiles as he points out a root protruding from the ground, a bare, dusty, knotted white growth. "Yes," he says, "how well do you know Montreal?" He would like to know what the place looks like. To know would make him feel closer to Alexis. He misses him.

"Pretty well. I don't like it much. You know, it doesn't feel like home. But there are some great universities there."

"Ah, yes. Alexis plans to go to university. I don't know," Philippe's hand flutters about his head, a butterfly unsure of its flight, "we parted on . . . how shall I say . . . difficult . . . terms." How much more is he going to reveal to this woman he hardly knows? "Alexis was . . . is . . . my best friend. We went to the same school. The school up there on the hill. I showed it to you. His parents sent him to school and to tutoring like he was a *blanc*. He never had to work as a tour guide or in the fields like the rest of us. Never. His family is of a different class than most of us. He didn't get a scholarship, but the missions—they still come here, you know, like the tourists, in waves, from everywhere, especially the Southern United States— they took notice of him. And he went . . . with them . . . in a plane . . . to the other side. Just a few weeks ago. Not long ago at all."

"Must have been difficult for you to see him go," Carmen says, thinking of her own comings and goings, how difficult it will be to leave Ayiti this time, reconnecting as she is, glimpsing into her mother's past. And now, of course, there is Léah. How will she leave Léah behind even though they have only known each other for a short while, a short while that feels like a lifetime?

The half-built road leading down the mountainside to the jeeps comes into sight.

"Oh, yes," Philippe says, "but that is how it is here."

"I know," Carmen says, stomach turning to knots.

"Well," he says, "Alexis will do well. What does it matter?"

Carmen senses that it matters. That there is a world to uncover there but she does not have the tools to do so; and she is growing tired from the walk and the heat of the day. It has been too much for her. She yearns for her small cot at the Hotel du Roi at Le Cap even though there will be no running water until morning. She wants only to lie on the cot and stare at the patterns thrown against the ceiling by the fan whirling in circles, sending the dust in the room flying from corner to corner. She wants to hear Léah knocking at her door, like the very first time.

"I'll go too one day. It's just a matter of time, and money."

"Yes," Carmen laughs, "*ou gin anbisyon*. You speak all those languages, too. Of course you'll leave. Find your friend. Be well."

They laugh, both of them knowing that the chances of his leaving are slim to none.

"If I gave you a letter to take to him, would you do so?" Philippe finally asks. "Would you do me this small favor?"

Carmen wonders how she would find Alexis in a city as large as Montreal but then considers that Yannick might be able to help her. "Yes," she says, "I'll try." At least she can give him this hope, even if she does not find him.

"Good," Philippe smiles. "You are staying at the Hotel du Roi, yes?"

She nods, wondering how he knows this fact.

"Then I will bring it there later, perhaps in a day or two."

"Make it soon, Philippe. I'll be leaving by the end of the week."

"I will then," Phillipe responds.

When they come to the end of the path, two women large with child, standing there with three small children holding on to their skirts, come to greet the tourists. They have set out a few bracelets and necklaces made from seedlings against the posts of their wooden fence. Carmen looks over the necklaces made of seeds artistically combined to form a harmonious pattern of colors. She thinks of the seeds against her skin, warming her in the winter days of Canada. She asks for their cost. Two dollars, one of the women says to her. Carmen figures out that they mean Haitian dollars, which would make the necklaces no more than a few cents. She plays the tourist and pretends not to understand, giving them the equivalent of two US dollars in Haitian currency. A normal mistake, every tourist makes it. She looks past them and sees the shack they are living in, thatched roof, torn clothing washed and drying ceremoniously in the sun. A puppy rolls over in the dirt at the front of the house. She wonders if the two women live there together or if they are married to tour guides. One of the little girls hanging on to the skirt of one woman smiles at her from behind her thumb, which is split open at the base from the constant sucking, the collision of her new front teeth with her still-baby-soft flesh. Carmen smiles. The little girl reminds her of the daughter she has always wanted to have. Hand against her stomach, she thinks now of how she has revealed next to nothing of herself to Philippe. She turns to him and smiles as they walk away from the women. Still, there is a connection between them. It, like the voices in the wind, will survive the day.

Behind them, the tourist children on muleback are galloping toward the parking lot. The children screech, fearful that the mules will throw them off their backs. The tour guides laugh. The parents join in, though their laughter is more nervous, filled with the knowledge that anything could go wrong, filled with the fear that their power might break at any moment, though they all know that nothing of the sort will happen. The tour guides relish the havoc the mules' running out of control has created, the few minutes of uncertainty the tourists must live through until they lift their children off from the mules' backs.

Carmen slips a ten dollar American bill into Philippe's hand, knowing that it is twice what she had calculated. It means that she will eat a little less on her way back to the capital. It does not mean that she will go without. For, after all, she is on a vacation of sorts. But this is Philippe's life, and she wants, in some small way, for him to understand that she knows the difference between his life and hers, between what Alexis' life might become and his for staying behind. "Thank you," she says, still holding his hand, the money separating their palms. There is a heat between them; her heart clenches with unfathomable sorrow.

"Pa' de quoi," he says in his best French accent. He touches the rim of his dusty cap with the tip of two fingers and watches her walk away to climb into one of the jeeps heading back to Le Cap. "A bientôt!" he yells out after her. I will see you soon.

There is a slump of defeat in her shoulders that mirrors his own as he walks back toward his village, the money a soft fold of paper in his pocket.

Carmen

In her hotel room, which, after the day's long walk, suddenly seems spacious and welcoming, when it had appeared on first arrival cramped like an unventilated closet, Carmen lies the length of her bed trying not to move too much in any direction. She has taken a cold shower, quickly, since the cleaning lady had told her as Carmen unlocked the door to her room that the water would be available only for a half hour. For some reason that is unclear to her, the three-star hotel has water only twice a day, usually at hours when no one is in need of it, midafternoon and in the early morning hours before anyone awakes. It is a challenge to figure out when the water will pump through the pipes. Carmen receives this information because she is on good terms with the domestics in the hotel. They know her family, her grandfather's family, more precisely. She makes a point of stopping to say hello and to exchange a few words before going on her way in the narrow alleyways of the city or to sit by the pool, kept lit for nocturnal bathers, in the cool of the evening. Carmen never plunges into the pool, cautioning herself that most people staying at the hotel are using it for their private bath. She prefers the cold water tumbling abruptly into the taps of her room and fumbling in the dark with her towels, to a public bathing. And, anyway, she is here to explore Haiti's north coast, not to indulge in the trappings of tourist consumerism. Yet, she is, she admits to herself, a North American, as her family in Port-au-Prince observe whenever they have occasion to see her. She has become accustomed to climate control—surroundings that are never too hot or too cold—food that is well-seasoned but not spicy. It surprised her to leave the comforts of her room to follow Léah out into the cobbled streets in search of Léogane. It surprised her more when she found herself in Léah's rooms, tape recorder in hand, her hands trembling at the thought of what was to come. She could not have imagined in advance what occurred.

Arms flung wide open to both sides of the bed, Carmen looks up to watch the blades of the fan throwing shadows in the air like a puppeteer.

She wears a dress made of thin muslin; the fabric flutters in the breeze created by the fan. The fluttering cools her. The room is hot but Carmen pretends otherwise with the lights turned off and the window shutters closed against the light of day. She wonders what the rest of her stay will bring. She feels that she can return to Canada whole, for herself and for her daughter. The meetings with Léah and Philippe have been only the beginning of the rest of her journey. The rest is in her. She has made her pilgrimage to every Haitian's Mecca in making that climb up to the Citadel. Carmen feels alive just at the thought of the sight of the mountains, though she is quite content to find herself back in her room, tucked away from the heat of the sun's rays.

Her thoughts rest a moment on Philippe. She wonders if she has given him enough money. It worries her to be participating in the very poverty she decries when she is in Canada, fighting for her life, caught between two worlds, fighting for the right to carve herself a place, however minute it might be, in the footnotes of history.

She realizes she has met a powerful man in Philippe, and she wonders if, indeed, he can be a man, out there, in those mountains. She thinks about all the languages he can speak and how that ease with so many tongues will waste away in the hills, given to tourists who would be only too glad to hear their own language coming out of that black body, a body they revile and yet exoticise to assuage their own pleasures.

Her thoughts turn to Léah: Is she taking advantage of her, like the tourists? Could she be as unthinking, as greedy? Her thoughts return to Philippe, his frailty, that lean adolescent body betraying the hardness of his life. She remembers now having seen him the day before, as she lounged by the side of the pool in the afternoon, trying to keep from being burned by covering herself from head to toe. He hadn't seemed to recognize her. She thinks that perhaps that has been a blessing. That way, she did not need to ask what he was doing talking to a man who was reputed to have been a Tonton Macoute in the bad old days of the Duvalier regime, a regime that seemed never to want to die. It haunted the country, all Haitians really, like a plague that had yet no antidote. What if her grandfather had been stuck out in the country, dependent on tourists for his livelihood, watching friends leave never to return? Philippe was like a ghost of what-could-have-been. It was like seeing the life that could have been her grandfather's, that could have prevented her own coming into the world.

Carmen has to believe that all these things are meant to be, the crossing of lives, of memory, of unfinished stories and stories yet to tell. What else can she do? Carmen closes her eyes and lets go of a deep breath. She can not be responsible for Philippe's life any more than she can be responsible for decisions that have been made long before either of them came into the world. She can only be responsible for herself. She had given him as much money as she could spare. To spare, of course, there was the problem: she has put herself at no risk.

Carmen thought then of the day she had calmly packed away Nick's belongings in his old ash-gray Samsonite and left them by the door for him to pick up on his way back from work at the radio station uptown. It was a last and simple gesture, accomplished with calm and resolve though nothing of what had led to that final moment made much sense to Carmen's mind. Not the coming home the day before to music on too loud and hot soup left to blister the bottom of a sterling silver pot. Not the walking through the apartment to clothes strewn about and left bunched up across the threshold of the bedroom. Not standing at the foot of the bed where they had made love only a day ago, to see Nick in the arms of someone else whose face was not unfamiliar to her, a mutual friend. Not the banal, clichéd scene of watching that friend hurriedly dress and, still clutching socks and shoe, fumble for keys on the key stand by the front door to make a quick exit. Not waiting for Nick at the kitchen table and having her hands held in his as he explained that it was just nothing, nothing at all, a small slip, nothing major, and that they could go on as they always had. And she, sitting there, knowing it was all over because hadn't she given up just the very same liberties in order to bring together their two lives, and perhaps, some day, make a third, even a fourth? Hadn't they been like mirror images then, not so long ago, describing themselves as free spirits, and yet, and yet, ready to commit themselves to each other and try to make things work like no one before them had ever done? How naive she had been! Sitting at the kitchen table, seeing every familiar groove and stain in the maplewood as if for the first time, Carmen was unmoved by Nick's tears and sweaty hands.

"We can make it work," he had said, over and over again. "We can. We really can."

"It's over, Nick," she'd replied finally, dispassionate. Rain had begun to fall outside and she turned her eyes to the sight of the pale drops pelting the windowpane.

The dream was over.

"You should go," she quietly told him. "I'll pack up your things."

"I can do it," Nick interrupted.

"No," she said firmly, "I don't want you here one minute longer. I'll have it all packed and ready to go by tomorrow morning. You can pick it up while I'm at the library."

Nick nodded his head, yes. Carmen could not even look at him. There were worse things, weren't there? Worse things than infidelity. He'd never hit her or screamed at her like other men could have. There were worse things. He wasn't addicted to anything and was hardly a drunk. He was a talented musician. But he was dreamless. Nick drifted from one job to the next and she tried to dream all his dreams for him or give him hers. Like the dream of her daughter. It hadn't worked.

Carmen continued to watch the falling rain and waited for Nick to go before gathering herself up and walking into the bedroom to strip the bed of its sheets. After doing so, she methodically went through the rooms and gathered up his belongings until she was satisfied that she had left hardly a trace of him in any corner of the flat. It seemed to her that Nick had needed her dreamless in order to move through his own days, to give them a shape he could not give them himself. She had needed more than this but she had not known what she was looking for—until Léah.

Until Léah, she had not been looking.

Carmen shuts her eyes. The voices from the hills drift in on the breeze, soothe her mind . . . the same voices she had heard in the Citadel and, for a moment, had thought she shared with Philippe. She remains convinced that he too heard the voices, the very same voices. Why he denied it to her was a mystery. Perhaps he feels she can not be trusted with the secrets of those hills. Perhaps Léah also feels the same wall of mistrust? How mysterious their crossing of paths, as mysterious as that mark on Philippe's chest that looked like a scraggly outline of the Haitian coast. She sighs again. It is too hot to think. It is too hot to write.

Carmen has scribbled a few words on torn pieces of paper for a poem she has in her mind to write, to remember these hills: *The revolution has ended.* The words are struck out with two, three, thin, scraggly lines. *Where has the revolution gone?* she writes. The day before, she had jotted a few thoughts in her journal, thinking that the myth of its privacy would somehow allow her to unleash words that she was too afraid to commit to the scraps that, if found in the wastebasket, could lead to an unfortunate chain of events for the finder that she would not be able to control. In the journal, she had written: *They may have pruned the tree, but the roots live on.* These, the words Toussaint had spoken when he had boarded the ship, *Le Héros,* or so Léogane had said to her after she had told him of her grandfather's refusal to journey with her to Cap-Haitien, to the past—their common heritage. Her grandfather had refused, saying that he was too old for such meandering. *Do you see this body,* he had said, *it is staid like rock. It no longer flows like the tides of a river.* He had laughed, showing a gap-toothed grin that resembled Léogane's. She had held his hand in hers and smiled in return, feeling the ridges of his hardened skin against the softness of her palms. She was then suddenly made aware of the vast gulf that distanced their lives. Her mother's migration and marriage had severed the vital current of their lives. And yet, there she and her grandfather had been, one hand in the other's, still as statues, the wind whipping through their clothes with a determination known best to fingers seeking gold along the underbellies of rivers.

Carmen writes: *My blood channels generations . . . I lament the loss of the first fires. Do you remember?* She puts her pencil down, stops her mind from ensnaring itself in an endless cycle of unanswerable questions, and drifts off to sleep.

211

Philippe

Philippe has regained his grandmother's house, his room, his aloneness. He lies on his bed with his hands locked behind his head, staring at the ceiling. His shirt clings to his body, hot with sweat. He wishes now that he had not talked of Alexis to Carmen. It brings back the intense grief he felt for months after his friend's parting, a grief he had thought impossible to break until the days began to grow longer and his mind began to drift into new places that anchored him to the present. He has to survive whether Alexis is here or not and he has to wring some joy out of every day even if only to bring a smile to his grandmother's face. But now, after the long day of climbing the mountain he and Alexis had made into a third friend, after speaking and not speaking of the one who he had, in his short life, held closest to his heart, he finds a strange pain gripping him from within.

Philippe turns over on his stomach and fishes beneath the pillow for the letter he has hidden there to keep his dreams flowing in the evenings that sometimes seem endlessly long. He pulls it out, wrinkled, writing faded, and smooths it against his pillow with the flat of his hands. He stares at the writing for a long time before he focuses his eyes on the shape of the letters and begins to read.

Friend, the letter reads, *my dear friend*, the writing politely, gracefully curlicued. It is best to read slowly so that each word can be taken in, savored, swallowed whole. *My. Dear. Friend.* The letter went on: *It has been a very long time, yes, a very long time, since the days when we walked along the path to our futures, has it not? There is not a day that goes by that I do not wonder about what has become of you. I am sorry I did not have the chance to say goodbye to you. I am sorry we did not part well. My. dear. friend. How long shall it be? Won't you come to see me? I do not have a lot of room here to myself but what is mine is yours, no, brother?* (Were they still brothers?) *It is cold, cold here. But I get used to it. I get used to so many things because none of it is quite as bad as what I left*

behind. And still, there is nothing here quite as good as what I left behind:
I miss you brother. (Philippe has to take those words apart, understand
them, read them over and over again.) *I. miss. you. brother. One day, all
that went on between us will be repaired. You will see. All of it. Until then,
I remain, yours, One love, Alexis.*

Philippe puts the letter away, tucks it back underneath his pillow.
He has had this letter for some months now; it soothes his spirit when it
seems that there is no reason, no shape to the long days of sun.

He still does not know if he will answer it. He has written many
fragments of letters on old scraps of paper. He brings them out now and
looks them over. There must be eight or ten pieces of paper with notes
scribbled on them, responses and reproaches he never mailed. He pulls
out an old workbook from beneath his bed, finds the stub of a used school
pencil, and begins to piece together a letter from the fragments.

Frè, the letter begins. Brother. Philippe continues to write, the stubby
finger slipping from his fingers once or twice. He grips it firmly and copies
the passages that have been closest to his heart. He will give the letter to
Carmen when he sees her next, so that she may give it to Alexis when
she finds him, out there in the city of Montreal.

Frè, my heart is empty of you who have walked so far from
my arms. A heart can only feed on its own pain for so long.
My heart is eating away at my soul, brother. I look for you
in the crevices of my body, a hair fallen here or there, in
remembrance of another time, an eyelash that speaks of the
love your eyes once held for me. I do not find these things,
these fragments of your body. To whom do you give yourself
now in those cities that love you not? To whom do you speak
your sorrows if not to the rivers of our childhood? You and I
are like sea and shore, water and air. Brother, do you see me
when I fly overhead like a bird looking for its nest? I am flying
high, high above you in the clouds looking for my resting place.
Will we meet again? Will you find your way home? These are
the thoughts that eat at a heart that longs like worms in rotten
fruit. I am still living, *frè.* My heart, still beating. But for how
long? I give my ears to the wind waiting for the day when you
will speak to me again.

Frè, m konnen vwa ou. I have thought of you and left
your name unspoken. I have fought your presence in my

dreams. And yet there you are; I will find your voice again. Can you hear me, brother? I speak to you in your dreams. Can you see me, *frè*?

Brother, can you see me dancing at the mouth of the Citadel defying the empty space before me? Can you see us here, when we were children, playing hide-and-seek among the thick, hundred-year-old walls? Can you feel the wind on your cheek, tender fingers of hunger? Yes, I envy your freedom. I envy your flight from these walls. Can you feel warmth beneath your feet? The blood of our fathers spilled on this land is still hot underfoot, a poignant reminder that you must return, someday. For this is where you live, brother. This is where you are most alive.

Can I lead you home, *frè*? Will you listen to my voice? Yes, I can feel you moving against the cold winds of that northern land you thought could embrace you better than I. Ummm, I close my eyes, *frè*, and I can see you, truly see you. I see your eyes, round like the marbles we lost among the rusted cannonballs in the Citadel that summer long ago when you began to speak of leaving. Your eyes are rounds of fire, sparkling amber and jade. Your eyes are open, brother. Ummm, I open my eyes to drink in the sea, and all that greets me are your sighs. Do not forget me. Do not forget your homeland. We await your return, patiently, like mothers tending the fires of their hearths on cold nights, high in the mountains.

I await you. My voice will be with you always.

Love in all and many ways,

Philippe

Satisfied with the letter, Philippe encloses it in a self-made envelope and leaves it beneath his pillow with the others. He walks out onto the porch and is bathed in the yellow light of the setting sun. His skin glows. Mamie Leila groans. He stands indecisively on the threshold of the house. He absorbs as much sun into the pores of his skin as he can, like a fruit needing warmth to grow, ripen. He thinks he should return to the city to give Carmen the letter. It would take a few hours to get there and return. It would take up the night. Mamie Leila groans once more. Philippe hears her bed creak against her weight. He imagines a thick elbow straining to hold up her fleshy body. The image forces him back into the half-light of the interior. Dust hangs like flecks of gold in the air, choking all his best intentions. He stifles a cough. His chest radiates pain. From the corner of his eye, to his left, something flaps. It is the square of burlap dyed red, faded from heat and sun to a rusty orange, dangling from the heads of thick black nails holding it into place above the square opening of a window cut out of the wooden slats forming the wall. Philippe feels a chill go through his spine: it anchors him to the floor through his heels. Rust red filters through his mind, promise of a migraine. He shuts his eyes, hears Mamie Leila stir again. He should make her come out to the porch, sit in her rocking chair, breathe fresh air. The colors leave his mind: blinding white light. He loses balance and throws an arm out to steady himself against the doorframe. He feels the weight of his diseased lungs, wishes he could cough out the disease in them. His body wracks against itself as he resists a cough. Paint slivers stick to the palm of his hand, which is suddenly wet with perspiration.

"Philippe!" Mamie Leila calls out.

Her voice sounds so far away to his ears, so far away. His head is bent down. His eyes, unseeing, stare at the floor, one foot in front of the other at weird angles, bones floating against the fabric of his clothes. He is not feeling well.

"Philippe?" she says again, a hint of worry shaped into the question of his name.

"*M vini*," he says, swallowing the bloody phlegm brought up by the coughing to the back of his throat, but his feet do not move and the wood grows hot beneath his fingers.

He raises his head. His body is cold now, a stone exposed to the elements. He removes his hand from the doorframe and rubs off the flecks of faded yellow paint, places his feet parallel one with the other. His center of gravity has returned.

Philippe lets his hands fall to his side and walks down the narrow corridor leading to Mamie Leila's room. Her bed linens smell faintly of hair oils, sweat, urine, rosewater. She smiles at him as he takes one of her pendulous arms and wraps it around his neck. He pulls her out of bed to her feet and, holding her up, they walk back through the corridor following the outline of light rimming the curtained window. They make an odd coupling, he stick-thin and angular, she tall and round. The room is bathed in yellow-red light.

"No," she says when they reach the threshold, line between outside and inside, chaos and safety. "No." The word slips through her teeth like a fish gliding through water, scales grating against shale at the bottom of a shallow riverbed. *No.*

Alexis

All the lights are out when I arrive at Ms. Alberta's early, before daybreak. But once I knock on the door the porch light comes on with the lights in the foyer and the door opens to reveal a small, plump woman.

"Miss Alberta?" I ask, almost shyly, my duffel bag sagging at my feet. I am sure I am a sorry sight to behold. I extend the crumpled yellow piece of paper toward her, "Your brother," I start again, "Your brother Louis told me to look you up."

She smiles and my fears begin to fade away.

"Yes," Ms. Alberta says with a bit of a drawl accentuating her speech. "My brother described you to a T! You must be Alexis." She peers up at him behind horn-rimmed glasses. "I was just reading in the back with Mr. Gillespie and he told me someone would be knocking on the door. I had no idea it would be you though, child. No idea." She clasps her hands together in delight. "Well," she says warmly, "You just come right in. I've even got a room free for you. It's all the way up in the attic, though," she frowns, "I hope you won't mind a walk up?"

"No, Ms. Alberta." I venture a smile as I take up my bag and walk into the foyer after wiping my feet on her welcome mat. "I could use the exercise."

"I think you need something to eat is what you need!" she says and leads him back to the kitchen after closing and locking the front door. "You can meet Mr. Gillespie."

Could life be this simple? I think. Could the nightmares be coming to and end? From that moment forward, Ms. Alberta takes me under her wing, offers to let me have my rent free until I find myself some sort of job. She has no doubt my landed papers will be in the works soon. She makes me feel right at home. I try to give her the money Mr. Louis has given me; it is all that I have left but she refuses it. "Buy yourself something that will help keep you busy!" she tells me as Mr. Gillespie, her cat, looks back and forth between us. We eat breakfast together and I tell her about my uncle and his family. She knows the story already. Some communities are so small that you can hardly turn around to face yourself in a mirror before someone tells you what you look like. She tells me everything will work itself out as it should.

Later on, I take her advice and end up in an art store on the large boulevard running perpendicular to our street; I buy paint and stretched canvas. I feel ready to unload all the images my nightmares and dreams have brought to me. I feel certain they hold the key to those things I still do not know or understand.

Once I return to the room in the attic, I lie down on the bed, fully clothed, and turn on the radio at the side of the bed. Top of the news: Haiti. I sit up and listen intently, turning up the volume.

"Today, news from Port-au-Prince has come that president-elect Jean-Bertrand Aristide is under house arrest in his villa on the outskirts of the city. He is reportedly being detained by members of the Haitian army corps. Our correspondent in the field has more to tell us."

I listen as the voices drone on. How can this be? I feel as if a fire is in my brain.

I remember well the day Duvalier left Haiti in his black Rolls-Royce, his girth a gross insult to all those in the country from whom he had stolen millions of dollars, from whom he is stealing still in faraway France with the contents of the country's coffers.

That day was one of celebration. Haitians on the outside planned to return, sold their homes, cars, quit their jobs and took planes back home even though there was nothing left there for them, even less than they remembered from childhood or their parents' memories. It had not occurred to me then, sitting in Millot, hearing about the flight operation, that it had been televised for the world to see. Our shame for the world to see. But then came the *déchoukaj*, our anger spilling out in the dirt streets. That too was televised and then I was happy to hear it. I was happy to know that the world had seen us defend ourselves, seen us screaming out our cries of "No!" with full force on the bodies of the infamous Tonton Macoutes, Papa Doc's secret, notorious militia, who did not seem to know better than to leave their blue uniforms at home. They were killed in the streets like dogs and they deserved no better death. They had been to us so much like the Cuban dogs the French had brought to gnaw on our flesh at the turn of the century, during the Revolution.

I do not want to know that nothing has been resolved even though bitterness has forced me to flee this far without a look over my shoulder, seeing ghosts wherever I turn, even in my own family. I think about Uncle Kiko sitting in his armchair in his living room, drinking, his family living in fear of his heavy hands. Would his life have been different had there been no Duvaliers? If we could have somehow taken the reins of our destiny as had the other islands despite their bondage to Europe, then to America? Would this bitterness have turned into anger, or from fear spoiled like meat?

And Philippe. Would his life had been different? Would he have needed to prostitute himself for so much less than a living wage, just to make ends meet? Would he have had to hide his shame in the *vodou* circles? Could he have lived a full life, even with another man, in a different Haiti? A free Haiti? Every night, for months now, I have seen Philippe's face wiped clean of happiness, the wounds on his cheek, on his chest. I walk with him through the nightmare and every single time he asks, *Frè, ou la?* And every single time, I fail to answer that, yes, I am still there, standing with him in the hills of our childhood, walking over the crevices in the soil.

I sit on the edge of the bed, holding my head between the palms of my hands.

I see myself walking in my village to my mother's house. I can smell the beans my mother has simmering with bay leaves on her stove, a pot of sticky rice steaming next to it, a chicken roasting in the oven.

My mother is not in the kitchen, but a woman in a yellow dress is striding through the kitchen toward the stove, checking on the rice, the beans, opening the door of the stove to pierce the side of the chicken with a knife point to see if its juices will run clear of blood. I hear my mother's voice in the distance. I hear her humming a song of my childhood, a song that speaks of these hills and their history, my history. It is a sad song, words full of longing and hope, shattered dreams . . . *sorrow on their tight skins . . . My feet are drums . . . my spirit sprouts wings . . .* I look around the room as if my mother will be there but there is nothing but myself, and my hands, and the art supplies begging to be opened.

I paint from morning to night until I can see the moon rising overhead emptying her full self into the empty gourd of the sky's darkness.

Philippe

"*Embargo*," Mamie Leila says from the cavern of her room. She has pulled the shutters tightly against the sun. She wants nothing of light. She believes hope is gone. Last week, the news has reached her, in the capital, men dressed in army fatigues killed her sister's daughter and son. Her sister, suffering from *une attaque de nerfs*, a nervous breakdown, was taken to a public hospital. Alexis' parents came shortly thereafter to say their goodbyes. Soldiers had paid them a visit, asking questions about Alexis' involvement with the presidential election. They had chosen to seek refuge in the home of a public official in Port-au-Prince who would see that no harm came to them. The village was being stripped bare of its protective barriers and daily customs. A sea change had occurred. "Embargo?" Mamie repeats, "Explain it to me."

"*M pa konnen*," Philippe responds. He sits at the kitchen table, separating kernels of corn from their husks to make the evening meal. He is worrying about the letter he has yet to deliver. The knife keeps sliding out of his hand dangerously, threatening to splice open the fleshy underside of his thumb. He cannot concentrate. What does he know of embargoes? There is a rumor that if President Aristide goes to the Americans, trade will come to a close. All Philippe understands is that it means fewer ships will come in, less food. It means that those the Americans are trying to stop with their trade rules will simply get into their fancy jeeps and cross the border to get their fuel in the Dominican Republic. It means, in short, a slower death. Unless—unless you are doing anything at all to survive. Then embargo means money under the table, black market. "You aren't doing anything you shouldn't?" Mamie Leila's tired voice creaks through the floorboards, tickling his feet with the shadows of her underthoughts.

Philippe looks at his bare feet, wiggles his toes as if to push away Mamie Leila's worry-thoughts back down under the floorboards and into the earth where they can lie still and burrow into the roots of vines lain to waste. He turns his attention back to the ears of corn piling up on the table. He thinks about yesterday, seeing Léah rising from the sea, talking to Carmen, and making enough money to buy a sack of food for the house. Yesterday was a good day. The day before that, well, the day before that was not so good.

"Child," Mamie Leila drifts toward him again, "*ou tande m?*" The voice is weak, weaker than earlier. Mamie Leila asks the questions she must ask but in her heart she already knows the answers. She wants to hear a lie so that she can rest her head against her thin pillows and begin to dream again, to let go of this life. She feels she has done all she can. Her heart would break to hear the truth.

"*Oui M'an,*" Philippe says, concentrating on the husks of corn, his knife sliding against the cores without slipping, broad stroke after broad stroke. "*Ti gason,* you keeping out of trouble?" Mamie Leila's voice snaps Philippe out of his dream state.

Philippe plunges his hands into the pile of corn he has made in the bowl before him, corn husks discarded at his feet. He will make Mamie the best meal she has ever eaten. That much he can do.

"*Oui,*" he answers her. He does what he must do in order for them both to survive. That word again: survival. He does what he should so that he does not have to break a human heart in his life.

"*Bon gason,*" Mamie Leila responds. Her voice is filled with the soothing aloe of a devoted love.

Philippe stares at his hands, covered over with yellow kernels.

Feet run through the foliage of the yard. He looks up. A young man runs through the yard. Denis. "*L'armée,*" he says. "They're coming."

Phillipe runs into the house to gather his grandmother up and out into the light of the porch.

"No," Mamie Leila mutters, in shock.

Philippe half-pulls the grandmother to the rocking chair. Her body does not resist. She is staring at Denis, clothes torn in odd places as if he has been chased by demons, rocks cutting cloth to ribbon as he went, pursued.

"I must go see what is going on," he says to her. She reaches out for Philippe but he slips away. She catches air in her palms. She is tired. She sinks into the rocking chair, buries deep within her flesh and waits. Philippe leaps off the porch. He must get his letter for Alexis to Carmen.

"*J'reviens!*" he yells back toward her. "Don't move," he says, as if she has any intention of pulling herself back on her feet.

What is done, is done. She breathes in the mountain air, free of golden dust. She is sitting in the shade. The falling reddish-hued light plays with her bare toes seductively.

Carmen

The voices from the mountain slip under the locked wooden door to Carmen's room and filter through the flesh and bone matter of her body. She has spent the last few days of her stay in her room waiting for Phillipe and his letter but he never arrives. Her grandfather's friend, Julius, is anxious to get back. There are whispers about the military. All Carmen can do is listen to the voices visiting with her daily. She walks with them into the mountains: her body is light as air, as transparent as a tear, peaceful. But the voices are not at peace. They clear a furious path through the forests. She follows, feeling the heat of their frustration licking her feet like flames. The voices take hold of her, hug her to themselves and then abruptly depart, lumbering ahead, heavy giants, through the foliage. They are burdened with their sadness, an emotion deeper than despair. They lead her through the trails back to Christophe's Citadel, to the very stones where she had stood, only days earlier, feeling the earth shift beneath the soles of her feet as the voices called her name for the first time in this country she called her own but had seldom seen. *Who are you?* she asks. The voices are still.

Carmen sees Léah as she had been the day before, her blue dress flitting in the breeze. Sees Léah calling her, asking her in her dreams, *Do you know who you are?* Her laughing in answer, laughing to keep from crying, fingering the blue stones, one by one, eyes asking, timidly, *From where? How?* Léah's refusal to answer except with laughter. And then, later, telling her about an ancient log, written in King Christophe's own practiced hand, telling the story of the stones emerging from the turbulent belly of the sea from the forgotten shores of his Grenadian childhood. Then the deafening silence between them, charged with a language that knew no words but was filled with the images that made of remembrance a live and teeming thing, like a stream or river flowing through forgotten backwoods.

Carmen walks through the memory of her first meeting with Léah, walks through it to a clearing in the forest, on the tail end of the whirlwind of voices; her face feels the words trickling through the layers of branches, leaves, bark, her flesh, her bones bleached by time. Her feet leave the ground; she enters the swirl of voices and begins to ask the questions she has carried with her since childhood. *Nou la!* the voices tell her. She detects defiance, then sorrow, then, again, the flashes of ochred anger, memories of the ocean waters never recrossed. Enslavement. The tragic law of no return. The voices, tormented, speak of loss. *L'Afrique n'est plus à nous. Africa is no more. What are these hills if not our Africa?* She hears obstinate pride. The remaking of home. Women's voices, hard like coral turned to stone. *They took our bodies, tore them to pieces with leather switches. They took the fruit of our labors, from our hands, our wombs. They took it all with insatiable hunger, fruit of their hate, their anger, ate our breasts, our private parts, then threw us to the dogs to be torn limb from limb for their sport. The landowners, they saw in us acres of verdant fields . . . cultivated and reaped us.* The voices buckle against the hard trunks of trees, bewildered. The voices muddle. Carmen listens, then asks more questions. A woman, younger than the first voices, returns to answer: *During the Occupation, I watch the Americans feed my son to the flaming pyre. I watch him burn. I smell his burning flesh, flesh of my flesh burning . . . worse than meat turning foul on a hot day . . . I cannot tell you.* The voice departs. Carmen's spirit turns within the vortex, touching over voices with the edge of a soft, yellow glow that is her place of memory. New voices: *Sister, where have you gone to? Have you come back to listen, to hear, to take in what you are told?* Her questions answered with questions. She does not know and tells them so. The vortex is heavy with apprehension. Sadness returns, winged hope.

Carmen plucks a feather from the wings and softly opens a new space: *Tell me.* And it is then that she hears the voice that pushed her off-balance in the fortress. A boy-man's voice, soft with the beginning of a hard edge encircling the childhood innocence. She thinks of Léah emerging from the sea in the fishnets. *Sè, what songs can i sing you?* She thinks of Léah sitting at the table with her pistachio ice cream, Léogane sitting behind telling the story of her childhood disappearances. She asks for a name. *José.* She takes his name on her tongue like a rare delicacy, like the sweet, staining orange flesh of a *quenêpe* held against the teeth for tomorrow's dreams. José speaks of his life in the mountain . . . *remember mother like yesterday, like butterfly wings . . . the desire for more than survival . . . Dessalines' fire in her breast . . . cleaning the house of the mulatto Innkeeper's wife . . . myself living in Christophe's Hotel across the way . . . watching the candles burn out at her window . . . the corvée . . . all able men working on the Citadel . . . the punishment of work . . . beasts of burden for the king's glory . . . legacy of hope for those despairing . . . we died to leave an imprint upon the soil . . . have you noticed how red the soil? have you noticed how dark the Citadel against the sky . . . have you noticed that the bay is shaped like a scorpion's claw closing in on L'Ile de la Gonâve like a prey biting into the flesh of its pursued victim . . . Christophe . . . Sans Souci . . . Will you bring us to rest? Song, won't you sing us to sleep?* Carmen weeps against the voices, tears turning to rain over the canopy of a wide flamboyant, red flowers turning slick from wetness.

The voices ride the wind. Horses. Carmen feels them ahead and behind, on all sides. She is walking in two worlds. Her body has materialized . . . she follows her feet, sees the tips of her shoes faltering. A hand steadies her . . . a large hand with wrinkled skin . . . a young hand made old with work . . . Philippe. He smiles at her. She smiles back. He takes her in his arms and they dance along the thick wall shaping the eastern corner of the Citadel. José laughs overhead. His laugh sounds like thunder claps. The voices crash against the walls. Philippe steps back from Carmen. Her arms fall to her side. Emptiness. He falls, disappears into the abyss behind. Silence. Carmen sings words she has never before heard: *Nou la. Qui nous délivrera? Who will sing the songs of the mountains, and touch the sky with fingertips that leave no prints upon the clouds?* Her song-words whistle in the air. She sings a melodious aria: *Ha, hi, ha, ha, hummmmm.* On and on. Then. Silence. Léah's silence.

How was it that she had come to know Léah's silence, had chanced to move, cocooned, within its protective walls? It had happened so quickly, or so it had seemed, the interview with Léogane finished, the short walk across the way to a colorful, unlocked door, leading into Léah's rooms. It had happened too quickly: Léah setting the table for two in quiet, pouring tea into two blue mugs. Léah asking her, *Do you know who you are?* Carmen bursting into tears at the table because she could not find the words to answer, because in the moment that Léah lay a brown hand over hers, she knew that she had come one step closer to home, to her self. *Do you know who you are?* Following Léah into the backroom. Hand over hand over hand. Brown skin over, under brown skin. Losing herself in the silence, in the still dark eyes. Breathing in a faint scent of cloves in Léah's hair. *Do you know who you are?* Whispers in ears. Then sinking beneath the surface of clear blue water. Trembling to. coming. home. Time collapses.

Carmen's muscles twitch into wakefulness; she is in the befuddling state of half-sleep. Her eyelids flicker open. The room is dark. It is not yet five in the morning. She finds herself staring at a strange shape floating on the ceiling, milky blue, thin outline of pink. She thinks she can make out a face—José, Philippe, Léah? No one. A murky shadow refusing to be identified. It passes by then another appears in its stead. She hears the fall of boots then the light step of bare feet. She opens her eyes wide, muscles coming back into control. She feels her right arm fold at the elbow, fingertips rubbing the edges of her eyelids clean. The shape against the ceiling is a shadow slipping from the corridor and past the narrow sliver over the door. Rough outline of light. A knock at the door. Léah? Carmen smiles to herself and rises slowly from the bed, her limbs still in a state of half-sleep. She opens to find Philippe there, back turned to the door, looking down the corridor, his neck muscles tense with worry.

"Philippe," she says, "you came."

"*Wi*," he turns around. He ventures a smile. He feels suddenly embarrassed at her door, seeing her in her white nightgown.

Carmen looks down at herself. "Oh," she says, "I'm sorry. Please," she waves him in. "Come in. I'll just get my bathrobe."

"I'm not here for long," he says, hesitating at the door. "Have you noticed there are soldiers outside?"

"Please," she repeats herself, "come on in." She grabs her bathrobe from the edge of her bed where she had thrown it the evening prior, too tired to make much sense of the room or to remain orderly. "Soldiers you say?"

"*Wi*," Philippe whispers. "They seem to be everywhere suddenly. *Toupatou*."

"Did they stop you on the way up?" Carmen remembers the trucks of soldiers they had seen on their way to the port city, remembers the woman who had stared at her across the car's windowpanes after she had been forced to descend from the tap-tap careening down the highway ahead of them. She wonders what happened to the woman, if they had all gotten away without too much abuse from the soldiers. She quickly moves toward the window and looks down into the courtyard. A man dressed in green fatigues strides across it and then looks up her way. Their eyes lock and Carmen feels a chill paralyze her spine. She forces herself to turn toward Philippe and disguise her sudden fear. "There doesn't seem to be much going on."

"No," Philippe says, "There is something going on. They are searching the rooms. I came by night and the military was already here, crawling in the shadows. I had to wait until morning before coming up. The sun has yet to rise, as you can see. I could not go without giving you this letter for Alexis." He pulls out the envelope tucked behind the elastic waist of his shorts, beneath his shirt. He has made an envelope from the remains of a rice burlap bag. "It is in this," he says, embarrassed again, "my letter for Alexis."

Carmen takes the letter from him. She holds it as preciously as Philippe gazes upon it, understanding, without knowing its contents, the importance of the words contained within. "I will deliver it," Carmen says, not knowing if it will be easy to find Alexis but knowing now as she has never known before that anything is possible. If the gods can come to life, she thinks of Léah, her unborn daughter, then surely the living can be tracked down.

"Merci," Philippe says, "I am most thankful."

Carmen does not know what to say. His appreciation is almost too much for her to bear. "Philippe," she begins again, "before I went to sleep last evening, I heard those voices, those voices I heard in the mountain before, with you." She searches his eyes for a clue that he understands what she is talking about and finds the eyes understanding, compassionate.

"Yes," he says, "I heard them too. I hear them all the time."

"There is nothing to be afraid of then?" she asks.

"No," he sighs, "Carmen, there is nothing I can tell you about the spirits that they can't tell you themselves. You are one of the chosen of this land. It makes no matter that you are the daughter of a *blanc*. Many of us are here as well. You were born to this land for a reason. The ancestors are here for you." He sighs again, then coughs, using the tail end of his shirt to wipe phlegm specked with blood. "I, however, will not be here forever."

She looks at him with concern. What can she do? "Can I give you some more money?" she asks, not knowing what else she has to give.

He waves her off. "*Non*," he says shortly, "Money will not help me where I am going." He heads back toward the door. "Just make sure he gets the letter."

She nods and puts it away immediately in a fold of her journal where she keeps odds and ends of paper she has collected since leaving

Canada. No one will think twice about it stuffed with her receipts and business cards. "It is safe," she adds.

"I must go," he says. "I left my grandmother alone in the village and she is not well." Philippe walks out of her room tentatively, looking furtively left then right. He exits the hotel quietly, swiftly, and only as he steps over the threshold do the men in the fatigues take note of his departure.

"*Éh!*" one of the men yells out after them, "*Ki moun ki la?*"

Philippe continues through the streets hurriedly, trying to pretend he hasn't heard a thing and makes his escape through the throng of people herding in the middle of the street, looking at the military men with horror, demanding to know the why of their presence.

In her room, Carmen closes the door, looks out into the courtyard, wondering herself why the men in green have descended like locusts upon the hotel. She hopes Philippe makes a clean getaway. She lies back down in her bed, pulling the covers up around her. The room is dim. It is still early morning. Even though the room is warming to the rising sun, her whole body shivers. She listens intently for signs of difficulties beyond her door. She continues to hear the steady fall of boots in the corridor, the cleaning women speaking shrilly among themselves. Within minutes, a shadow falls again across her door. There is no knock at the door before it bursts open.

Carmen makes out the bulky shape of khakis, thick-soled boots, the butt of a rifle held close against the body.

"*Debout! Debout!*" The shape yells.

The rifle pokes through the covers to find her body. Carmen leaps out of bed. Her feet shudder at the cold of the linoleum. She trembles in her nightgown. Pale outline of breasts, quiver of stomach. She folds her arms against her body: a shield. She cannot make out the face. She wishes she were still dreaming. The voices have remained. They whisper into her back: *Sè, will you sing your name to better tell our stories?* She does not answer. The shadow at the door advances into the light.

September 30, 1991

Carmen

Carmen is an angel in her robe. Light streams into her room from the open green shutters of the window. Her nightgown billows, giving her transparent, blue-tinged wings. After checking her room—sliding his hand between the mattresses and box spring, turning the contents of her suitcase out onto the floor until he finds first her journal, emptying its papers—he ignores the burlap envelope Philippe had entrusted to her. He is looking for her passport, finds it, flips through the pages lined with swirling colors resembling paper money, sees the place of birth, that she is one of them, in a way, then—the line for citizenship, Canadian—the Haitian military officer throws the passport at her. It bounces off her chest. She catches it with clasped hands as if in prayer.

She watches him move through the room like a frenzied panther, golden skin glistening from sweat, the sweat accumulating under his armpits and blossoming dark green patches through the khakis. The khakis are caked with mud, patches of purple depths, reminding her of blood. He throws open the window shutters, yells to someone below, in the courtyard, then departs as abruptly as he had entered the room.

Carmen is blinded by the light streaming into her room, the morning opening her like a flower in full bloom. As she advances toward the window, she wishes she could disappear or be enveloped in that blue hue. Her nightgown flattens itself against the brownness of her skin. She feels suddenly luminous, black hair streaming full-length against her back like dense webbing, light working its way through it like fingers turning the topmost hairs into auburn filaments. It is there that all her fears lay dormant, trapped among the fingers, the loose strands. Before departing, the soldier had taken a thumb and moved it down a cheekbone, outline of face, like a blind man who needed to remember her later, create a picture in his mind where nothing looked as it did in the sighted world. Or, she pauses, resting her stomach against the window frame, the gesture had been made for her, so she would remember the curve of his thumb, the flatness like the smooth head of a small rubber mallet. It had still been dark in the room then; he had not yet leaped from one end of the room to the other in search of god-knows-what. His thumb had caught in a tangle of hair, yanked at it, then his fingers had plunged in to catch the curls in the back of her head down to the stem of her neck. She had felt a chill, fear. The thumb seemed to register the current of her thoughts and, mercifully, had withdrawn.

At the window, Carmen looks out onto a courtyard filled with men clad in greens, unlikely browns. *San maman*, they are called, some of them. Motherless brood. Too impossibly brutish to have been born of a woman's womb. Carmen lays an open hand on her flat though fleshy stomach. Each of them had a mother who brought them into the world, someone who patched up their wounds after falls and carried them over unstable ground. She wonders what kind of mother she will make to this daughter. Carmen feels a luminous heat pressing from within her and out against the palm of her hand. She overhears the cleaning women in the corridor telling each other of rapes taking place countrywide, women's bodies used as pawns or spoils of war, young boys forced to copulate with their sisters or, worse even, with their mothers. She hears them speak of the young men, orphaned by mothers and fathers with wanderlust in their hearts put there by the force of poverty, the effort to keep despair at bay . . . young men killing the grandmothers who had raised them from their crib, who had taught them how to count by using the seedlings of fruits, who had taught them how to listen to the ancestors riding the wind in order to guide their feet along the narrow streets of the cramped cities. So that they would know how to turn deaf ears against the whispers that might lead them down unknown alleys toward the emptiness of dust-filled pockets and metal casings.

Carmen feels the thumb of the soldier who had entered her room uninvited, against the nape of her neck again, a phantom limb. Looking down into the courtyard, she sees the soldier as he had been when he had first entered the room, a shadow outlined by a sudden burst of yellow light, a halo in human form. At the moment, he is gesticulating toward the window, talking with another soldier who seems, by his posture and features of face, a superior. She cannot make out their words. The hand moves through rays of sun, a wingless bird swooping, making strange maneuvers left to right, high and low. There is an exchange of harsh words, deep tones, resonance of displeasure from the superior who stands, strangely unarmed, in the middle of a swarming beehive of rifle-clad young men whose booted feet are most likely swelling in the heat like the boiled flesh of crayfish. The hand drops to the man's side. Suddenly, they all look up at her, eyes marbled, hard, unflinching. She becomes solid, wooden, aware of the presence of her body, the transparency of the cloth against her flesh, the absence of curtains over the window. The faded green of the shutters wavers like a mirage. Carmen's hands leap to attention, stretch out in front of her, and pull the shutters toward her against the eyes which have brought a hush to the space that now stretches itself between them.

In the time of only a few minutes, everything has changed. She has been spared by virtue of a passport, but the cries coming from beyond the courtyard stir her to awareness: the army is invading the city, attempting now, by force, to lift the thin skin covering the currents of terror that has been running through the populace for months.

As Carmen dresses, packs her case to return to the capital, she listens to the voices of the domestics outside her door. *Lame*, they are saying, then, strings of names, worry over the dead-to-be. She yanks the door open, startling the groups clustered in the hall. They quickly separate as if there is still thought of work on their minds. The cleaning woman who reintroduced her to Léah walks toward her across the tiled floor, heels of shoes clicking against the tiles in a peculiar double-rhythm.

"You must go," she says, voice harsh, barely above a whisper.

"I know," Carmen shows her packed overnight bag. She pulls some money from a breast pocket in her jacket and presses it into the woman's hand. "This is all I have left," she says, remorseful that she had not given it all to Philippe the day before, in the mountain. She wonders how he is, where he is, whether the army trucks have made their way to the villages above the city already.

The woman nods. They touch each other's cheeks in understanding. "Come," the woman finally says, splintering their connection, the silence between them, with her anxious voice, "let me show you the way."

Carmen is led out of the hotel through a side door, a path that finally leads to the street. There is a truck waiting, a taxi on its way to the capital with others who have been staying in the hotel. She kisses the young woman on both cheeks and then steps into the back of the vehicle to sit squeezed between the knees of two old men who seem blanched by the turn of events; their eyes are bloodshot from lack of sleep. She lets her back rest against the seat cushion. What is happening? What of Léah? Léogane? Philippe? She tries to think of nothing. But the voices in the corridors haunt her.

They have the president.
They've arrested Aristide.
President Aristide has fled the country.
Where is King Christophe now?

Alexis

At twilight I am left surrounded by two or three finished paintings. I drop my paintbrushes in a tin can filled with turpentine and survey my work.

The first painting shows Philippe as I remember him as a boy, just as he appears in the nightmares I have been having lately, with the fresh cuts marking the left side of his face, the healed-over scar in the shape of the outline of Haiti's coast on his chest. The wind is playing with the soft collar of his flannel shirt. In the painting, Philippe is staring into space: his eyes are reflecting the brilliant purplish blues of a Caribbean sunset and the outline of an ebony-skinned woman. The same woman also stands behind him, to his right, emerging slowly from the sea. On his left, his grandmother sits on her porch, bathed in shadows. I do not know why that section of the canvas is so dark. I do not know.

The second shows Philippe as I believe he might look now, though still in the same tattered clothes. He is standing on a far wall of the Citadel, looking out to the mountain ranges that hem our village in its valley. Above him looms the shadow of a man that should reflect his own face but instead shows the murky outline of a ship in the harbor, a ship our friends navigate as they try to make a living at being fishermen. The ghost figure is transparent: I have painted the mountains so that they shine through, almost as if to defy the apparition of this mask of a man. To the right, moon, stars, and sun form an unlikely congregation. To the left, floating in sky: the outline of Haiti and the small dot of land that makes up the island of La Gonâve. Philippe is standing up on the large black stones of the Citadel, his hands thrust into his pockets, his head bare. I have tried to imagine him standing there, alone, all of his concerns projected into the expanse of sky and sea that captured both of our imaginations when we used to sit together in the mountains.

The last painting is unfinished. It is a portrait of the woman I saw in the picture at the community center, the woman who looks so much like the little girl who has come to me in dreams. I have painted her, eyes closed, blue stones wrapped around her neck, her body thick with pregnancy (this, I do not know why), a hand outstretched toward no one, a small female angel robed in the white dress of a *vodou* initiate, blue wings sprouting from her shoulder blades, whispering into her ear.

I close my eyes. If I could only sleep dreamless. If I could only find some answers. I believe some of them are there, in the paintings.

Suddenly, a knock comes at the door. "Alexis!" Ms. Alberta is screaming, voice muffled by the heavy door. "Alexis!"

I jump to my feet and open the door. I stand face-to-face with Alberta, her aged face fissured with worry. She grabs both my arms and pulls me out of the room. "It's your uncle, Alexis," she says, "Didn't you hear the fire trucks?"

I am bewildered. "What?"

"The house," Alberta says, "it's on fire!"

I look at her with terror. Am I dreaming again? Is this another nightmare? I fly out of Alberta's house without a coat and run as fast as I can down the streets until I reach my uncle's home. She is right. There is a crowd of people assembled outside. I search for the children, Gladys, Uncle Kiko. I break through the crowd, pushing and shoving people to the side. I am pushed back. "*C'est ma famille!*" I cry out. Finally, a path is made for me and I find myself standing at the edge of the circle of onlookers, watching the fire crew hosing down the house. All that is left is its charred skeleton.

Someone takes my arm and pulls me to the side. A police officer faces me. "You live here?"

"I used to," I say, not taking my eyes away from the fire.

"Everyone made it out safe. Everyone, that is," the officer pauses and searches my face, "everyone except a forty-five-year-old man. Do you know who that could be?"

"Kiko. I mean Carl, my uncle," my heart sinks. "Where are they?"

The officer points back toward the crowd and it is then that I see them, Mother Gladys, little Anna, and the boys.

"We may need to ask you some questions later," the officer says. "It may be a case of arson."

I look at the officer square in the eye. "I doubt it, sir."

He asks for my present address and phone number. I give him Ms. Alberta as a contact. I look back at the family, the crowd, and move to join them.

Philippe

Philippe watches a small boy in gray frayed shorts and a light brown shirt running through the crowds in a crazed zigzag. Denis is pulling on Philippe's shirt, trying to lead him in another direction, toward the harbor and the docked ships. They need to see what will be confiscated or burned down by the water. Philippe watches the boy's feet, running, barely touching ground. They remind him of something. He does not know what. He turns to point him out to Denis, so they can both see, but the boy is gone.

They run down to the harbor. As they had feared, there are ships burning, sending tongues of flame across the surface of the water turning sooty with ash. The fishermen stand dumb on the shore, hands hanging limply at their sides. The men clad in khaki, guns slung over narrow shoulders, laugh. A group has set up a table and are playing cards.

Philippe leaves the shore and walks through the crowds, listening to the *teledjòl*, the word on the street. What has happened remains unclear. Something about a change in government, another coup, the army trying to keep the masses in line. The people speak of market stalls torn down, doors to their homes broken, some men killed in their beds while sleeping at the break of dawn, old women with their throats slit from ear to ear, children lying naked in pools of blood. It reminds them of the days of Duvalier. How could anything be again so terrible? Philippe does not know, does not dare to imagine what strange and malevolent spirits are devastating the city. Whoever they are, they are on their way to the mountains. Philippe hears the *teledjòl* and looks for the messenger, Denis, but he is gone. He needs to find a way back to the village. He moves through the crowds quickly, eyes searching for a truck, a car, anyone with keys in their hands. He pushes arms out of his way, steps over bodies, sees a reporter holding a small block of paper, pointing to the hills. Philippe shadows the man until he is close enough to snatch the paper from him.

"I need to get home," he gasps into a soft shoulder, gripping the man's elbow.

The man looks him over, a protest at ready in his throat. He looks into Philippe's eyes and sees the tumult there, a deluge of pain. The man nods, makes space for Philippe in the back of his truck, and they wind their way into the mountains in silence.

When they reach the village, Philippe runs to his grandmother's house. There is no need to check on Alexis' house. It stands lonely and empty at the end of the winding dirt road. The gate in front of his grandmother's house swings open on its hinges. The tall grass has been trampled beneath many feet. Philippe can make out the rocking chair: it is moving slowly back and forth. He can make out Mamie Leila's feet against the worn wood of the porch. He slows his own feet as he makes his way up the walk. He slows the rhythm of his heart and breathes the air in deeply. The rocking chair is moving back and forth—all is well. As he is about to stride up the creaking steps, two men dressed in army fatigues exit the small house. Philippe quickly jumps off the porch and hides beneath it.

"*Madanm*," one of them says to his grandmother. "*Ki moun ki la avèk ou?*" Who lives here with you?

"*Ti gason mwen*," she responds, voice small, tired. She had not had time to see him there, with the tall grass of her yard rising on both sides of the path, hiding him as he made his way toward the porch.

Philippe listens intently.

The men continue to speak in Kreyol.

"What is his name?"

"Philippe."

"What does he do?"

"He is a tour guide. *A la Citadelle*."

"Ah. Does he have a friend name Alexis Dominique?"

"*Oui*," the grandmother replies.

"Do you know Dominique was involved in politics?"

"Not that I know of," the grandmother says. "They are both good boys. No trouble all their lives."

The men rock back and forth on their heels. The boards of the porch creak above Philippe's head.

"If you see your son, send him to see us. We are going to be down that way."

Philippe sees one of them pointing to Alexis' old house. They have seized it. It is perhaps the best home on the street. Philippe wonders what

Alexis' parents must have done to secure their safety. Alexis is too far to know that any of this is happening. Philippe feels the pain in his chest rise again. He feels the need to cough. He holds his mouth with both hands. Fever rises through his body. The soldiers depart. The grandmother makes a strange sound as if she is holding her breath. He is below the porch. Her rocker no longer moves back and forth. Philippe waits awhile. He finally crawls out from the porch once the soldiers have turned the corner of the street and are out of sight. He coughs into the red dirt beneath him, red blood. He cleans his hands in the dirt then rises to the porch.

"Mamie Leila," he whispers against the wind whipping his face as if it is trying to push him back, back, back to the road. The man who had driven him up to the village is long gone. "Mamie Leila," he says again, finally hesitating.

Mamie Leila is sitting in the dark. The sun has moved in the sky and cut a swatch of light on the other side of the wooden deck.

Philippe lets his eyes grow accustomed to the gray shapes in front of him. He is no longer in a hurry.

"Mamie Leila?" Philippe almost whimpers. He sees her.

She is smiling.

There is a line cut into her neck, red like a cartoon clown's smile. The flesh is strangely puckered, purplish.

Philippe steps forward, kneels at the side of the rocking chair, and stops its rocking with two fingers. The shadows on her dress are made of her own blood, soaked through. He stays there, hands clutching the sides of the rocking chair as if in prayer, until night falls, until the villagers come to pry him away, taking the body to bury with the other dead, one by one.

After the burial, Philippe finds himself thinking of the young boy running through the streets in the city that afternoon of mayhem. He finds himself running barefoot like that boy through the forest, voices in the wind pursuing him. He will not let them catch him. He will defy them all. He will even defy the SIDA that has made it impossible to fight off the tuberculosis afflicting his lungs, his very breath. This tourist disease which, in time, will sap his muscles of their remaining strength, drain his body of its seasoned youth, and deliver him prematurely to his grave.

Anger drives Philippe through the paths leading to the Citadel. Once there, he stands atop the Citadel's majestic walls and screams thunder into the sky. The sky is dark, starless. He remembers Alexis' departure and how he had fled to the mountains rather than say goodbye, tears spilling from his eyes involuntarily. He hears his mother's words to him from so long ago: *Don't try to grasp too much out of life.* A torrential rain begins. Philippe closes his eyes. There is nothing left for him in this world. All he sees at present is a dense white light. It is a light better than dreams; it is better than wakefulness; it is grander than despair, brighter than hope. Philippe flings his arms out into the night, out toward the light, and lets his body fall.

The whiteness cradles him as if in the arms of a new mother. And, like those of the ancestors who had gone before him—weightless—his voice rides the wind.

October 1, 1991

Carmen

Carmen watches out of the car window as she, Julius, and the others with whom she had traveled north less than a week ago make their way out of the city under a harsh, orange ball of a sun. There are corpses lying in the streets, women and men howling over them in desperation. She sees a young boy in gray shorts running wildly, blood stains on his small hands. She wonders if he is running to or from home. She has an urge to reach out and hold him in her arms as if she can heal something of what is going on. She is confused. Everything is surreal. She feels the men's knees pressing against her. The man on her left is trembling. She can feel it through his slacks; his bones swimming in a terrorized flesh. She is the safest among them, crouched down low and out of sight, sitting on the floor. But she can see out. There is confusion, many people running. For an instant, she thinks she sees Philippe running along the jagged edge of the harbor. She looks again. It is him. She swivels her head to take a closer look. Their eyes connect but she does not know if there is any recognition. She wonders what he is still doing in the city and, as she wonders, the car comes to a jolting halt.

They step out to a barricade at the gates of the city, old gates that no longer have a real function. They are searched, their passports scrutinized. Her Canadian status holds her safe, as does her brown skin, nonchalant air. The men have a harder go of it because they are intent on defending themselves. The soldiers are willing to let them go if they will leave their passports behind . . . they are worth a mint on the black market. Carmen sits in the car and waits as the driver negotiates for the return of the men's passports. She watches out the window again.

Carmen starts at the sight of Léah standing in her long, flowing blue dress, skin a radiant shade of aubergine, the blue stones wrapped tightly against her neck glistening in the sunlight, walking along the shore of the sea. Carmen's thoughts turn wild. An overwhelming fear churns her stomach to knots. She feels a sudden nausea overcoming her and her head spins as it had when the voices had come to her in the mountains and she had feigned vertigo. She feels the desire to warn Léah to go home, to hide. She is too late.

Two of the soldiers have surrounded Léah on the beach. Léah seems not to hear their words. "*Madivinez*," they call her, injurious, man-woman. One soldier pushes her with the butt of a rifle. She stumbles but remains silent. The other does the same. They have no shame, the *san maman*. Léah remains still. They tear the dress from her body and she stands there, naked. The men strike her. Carmen, panic-stricken, seeks help. She speaks quick, urgent words to the driver, who waves her to silence. She looks back to the soldiers beating Léah into submission. Léah has fallen to her knees; her skin has ruptured in thin lines across her body; blood seeps from her wounds. The men suddenly step back from the body and walk away.

Carmen leaves the car and runs toward Léah, who is bleeding from the mouth; her eyes roll back in her head. Carmen holds Léah's frail body in her arms. Her homecoming. Carmen's body is a raging torrent, water-filled, tears spilling from the eyes, rivering her cheeks. Is this how it all ends? She holds Léah as if she is holding her own child.

The driver appears at her side followed by Léogane and Léah's sister. Léogane is quietly weeping; he knows that unlike the time they had found her as a child laughing in the net of the fishermen, Léah will not soon rise again. Carmen will not let Léah go but clasps her closer to her chest.

"I am sorry," she whispers slowly to the sister. The sister says nothing, pries away Carmen's fingers from the stiffening body, eyelids open to the sky.

The fishermen come toward them, their boats burned down to nothing on the placid waters of the bay, fishnets hanging from their gnarled and tired hands. They begin to wrap Léah's too-still body in the fibrous netting. When they have wrapped the body, Léah's sister presses something into Carmen's hands and turns to leave with Léogane leaning against her. With the help of the fishermen, the body is carried off. Later, much later, when the chaos in the city has died down, they will return her to the sea.

The driver leads Carmen back to the car and makes the man sitting up front wedge himself between the knees at the back. Carmen is thankful for the space; she cannot breathe; she cannot think.

For what seems much longer than the five hours it takes to reach the capital, Carmen sits in stillness, tears spilling furiously from her eyes, holding whatever Léah's sister has laid in her bloodied palms. She can speak to no one, not her grandfather, not her mother. They seem to understand her quiet. Her mother was right, she had much to behold. She has beheld and become one with the land and its people, its magic and its nightmares.

Only when Carmen finds herself alone, in the room she occupies in her grandfather's villa, does she dare to look and see what Léah's sister has pressed deep into the hollow of her palms.

Seven bloodied blue stones stare back at her in defiance.

October 4, 1991

Alexis

Today, the day of Uncle Kiko's funeral, the woman in my painting emerges from nowhere. She steps out from a yellow taxi cab sitting in front of the house dressed fully in black, from head to toe, as if she anticipated the fire that took his life. I too am dressed in black today and I open the front door for her and help her with her things. Then I leave her to herself and walk out into the fresh air, trying to get my bearings. Kiko is dead. His family will go on. A part of the past is beginning to die. President Aristide was allowed out of the country by the military men who organized the coup. He is gone from Haiti. What will become of the beloved country?

As I walk that afternoon, little do I know that days later I will meet the young woman of my dreams in the offices of the community center where I had first seen her picture sitting lonely on a desk. We will stand in the office, Yannick looking at us both in amazement, and recognize something in the other. Yannick will tell me again her name. And I will remember from somewhere deep in the recess of my mind that this name means "song." Yes, song. She will hand me word from my soul-brother, Philippe. And in the moment of touching the burlap roughness of the envelope, I will understand that he is already gone, journeying back to Ginen, the land of our ancestors. In the moment of this exchange, the grief in my heart will turn to a song of hope as my eyes meet Carmen's to read there the sorrow of a loss I have yet to comprehend. I will read in them my own tears. I will recognize my self.

For so many of us Haitians, sorrow is part of our genetic code. We drink our tears in our mother's wombs.

I will read the letter in that office with Carmen and Yannick nearby and I will hear Philippe's voice echoing far off in the distance:

Everything will be all right.

The world will keep on turning.

Time will not keep still.

I believe in him. I believe now in his words in the same way that I believed in the power of Shango when Philippe and I called upon him in the hills of Haiti. For when the skies thunder in the hills around Millot, the ground absorbs the flashes of lightning like rods of steel. The trees sway and tremble with anticipation, their feathered leaves break away with abandon, twirl to the ground.

I remember Philippe and I when we used to dance in the rain within the walls of the Citadel. We would walk the narrow paths through the dense bush of the mountains, lizards scurrying beneath the rough soles of our feet. Philippe, as usual, walked ahead. I measured my own steps by his imprints as I followed. The rain would fall against our bodies like the hands of the musicians at the dances and *vodou* gatherings strumming out rhythms on their tight drums. We would make our way to the rough walls and, hidden away from sight, we would dance as if possessed on top of the stones. Our laughter would be drowned out by the falling rain. Our feet fell against puddles the size of small pools. The mud flew against our clothes like we had worked in the rice fields. We did not care. The Citadel was ours: the skies overhead, the mountains protecting us like our mother's arms, the sea crooning to us from afar. We were free.

The thunder I have known, that I have fled with all my soul and now return to, humbled, is nothing more than the light contained in the distant murmurings of an unforgotten land.

The dreams I have had since I left Haiti wanting never to look back will finally make sense. Philippe has been announcing his death to me every night since I have been able to hear the voices, willing to draw again. It is as if he has been letting me know that he is now a part of that world I refused to know when we were children. The dream of the blue tears finally make sense as I recognize the beads coiled around Carmen's neck. She is the one I am to follow now, the one my heart will cleave to. Her child will be my child. I will teach her all I know. I will no longer be afraid of the voices that haunt the jaundiced history of our Haitian hills.

Frè, I will say to my brother, *frè, listen, my eyes are finally open. Rest in peace.*

Epilogue

Awakening: February 1992

Her bathrobe sinking to the floor in a pool of soft blue terry cloth, Carmen balances her weight onto her right foot as she extends the left into the water-filled bathtub. The water is warm, just right, and she sinks into it until she is completely covered save for the roundness of her belly. She closes her eyes and places a hand on the taut brown skin which, with its stretch lines and uneven colorings, reminds her of a large gourd. She sings to her unborn daughter lines from a song passed down from earlier generations . . . *I wear yellow* . . . *like the sun* . . . a song belonging to the land of their ancestors . . . *a signal to the tree spirits* . . . *that I have not forgotten* . . . the baby moves against her belly lining, beneath her hand. Carmen smiles. This child will be strong.

Carmen lets the water of the bath hold her. She is exhausted beyond words. Each of her muscles has catalogued the events of the past, tumultuous, mind-numbing weeks. She lifts a leg up into the air, hears the droplets hitting the water below, and stretches a calf muscle tight with the story Gladys had told her that first time they met in her office, of her great-great-great-grandmother, Marie-Angélique, and her burning down of the city of Montreal as she tried to flee her slave master, a man who owned her body and the flesh of her flesh but not her will. Carmen sinks her leg back into the water then lifts the other to stretch out a knot in the back of a thigh. As the muscles lift, pull, and contract, she feels the burning sensation that comes from standing too close to a fire and remembers hearing the news of the house burning down, shortly after her return, of Carl's death. More lives lost. She thinks of Haiti and those who have perished there.

Carmen arches her lower back. Her chest hits a wall of cold air. She stretches out the aching muscles between neck and shoulder blades, all along the spine. Small spasms of pain sear into her brain. She remembers the log and Christophe's words, words filled with such fear, power gone mad. He too had set fire to a city once, in the name of liberty. But that fire had lodged itself into his brain, a maniacal fever that the land itself had absorbed, like heat from the midday sun, and not yet extinguished. All those men who died building the unused fortress. *La Citadelle.* All those men who had been walked off the immense walls. Carmen remembers walking within those walls, the honed pieces of rock beneath her feet covered over with wild blades of grass. And the voices. The voices. *Do you hear us, sister?* It is as if they are with her now, in the small space of her bathroom. *Do you hear me?* A child's voice. Carmen lets her body sink back into the warmth of the bath water. She opens her eyes.

A young girl of nine or ten stands beside the tub and smiles at her. The girl's hair is long, black and auburn, full of unruly curls. *I am here,* Carmen hears her say. Carmen nods. Her daughter is almost here. The young girl disappears and Carmen feels a sharp pain in her belly. Tears flow from her eyes, flow down her cheeks and into the corners of her mouth, warm, salty.

She puts a hand to her throat and touches each of the seven, olive-sized blue stones, eyelets draped there like witnesses for the life to come. Carmen thinks of Léah. She closes her eyes again and the tears flow more plentifully. She remembers Léah's hands on hers, those hands that helped fishermen bring in nets full of catch in the off-season. Hands that felt their way to safety across familiar terrain daily. Hands that reached out to help whenever they could. Hands that held her as no one else had and brought joy to her spirit. Carmen feels the hands traveling across her body like ghosts, anointing the breasts rounded by pregnancy, traveling across the soft stomach, sharp points of hip bones, and sinking as if to sand between her thighs. Carmen feels a pulse between her legs and weeps more deeply.

She misses the still, clear eyes, the voice, deep and reassuring. Then, more difficult to remember, are the last moments, witnessing the army men batter Léah's beautiful, sable body, risen just minutes before from the depths of the ocean bed, her true home. Léah's hands stayed still at her side, never coming to her own defense, as if she knew her time had come, as if she had, in fact, been in their midst far longer than she had hoped possible. Carmen remembers holding Léah's body—that moment of never wanting to let go, a willingness in her to die in that moment—despite the new soul growing then in her belly, despite all the words that she had yet to write, about the ghosts haunting the Haitian *mornes*, the stories of the undead, people who, like Léah, or even Philippe, were really from some other world entirely, a world they could scarcely access for fear of its powers. She remembers the torn skin, the blood, blood she carried tattooed in her palms as she clutched the stone necklace entrusted to her by Léah's family. The blood it took hours to wash away and weeks of tears not to see every morning, upon waking.

Carmen feels another pain in her belly, water freeing itself from her insides and mixing with the bath. She opens her eyes and looks down toward her thighs. The bathwater is pink. Her baby daughter is on her way.

Carmen lifts herself out of the bath, fighting against the pain as the contractions come, wraps herself in the terry robe and calls Alexis, who had fast become like a surrogate father to the unborn child once they had met and talked, Philippe's letter delivered, their stories exchanged, a connection between them forged, of necessity, and a destiny, they knew, fulfilled within the hour of their first meeting, especially once she saw the portrait he had painted, the woman in the painting unmistakably her even though they had not yet met.

While she waits for him to arrive, she breathes and listens to the air filling and emptying itself from her lungs. She holds her belly with both hands. She knows that her daughter will remember all their stories, all of them. She will name her Aurore after the dawn breaking on a new chapter of Ayiti, as they struggle to free themselves from the clenched fist that their history has become—almost two hundred years after the Revolution had made of them a free people.

Carmen understands then that it is Léah who is the angel Alexis has painted perched on her shoulder in her unfinished portrait, the angel who has brought voices back from the dead. It is she who has been helping them all along—along with Aurore, her unborn hope, newborn light.

I am here. Carmen hears Léah's voice for the first time, strong, free. She breathes deep between contractions and decides that her daughter's middle name will be Léah, in remembrance.

When Alexis arrives and they head for the hospital in a taxi driven by a Haitian originally from the southern Haitian city of Léogane, who regales them with stories of his own son's delivery years ago in the back of a tap-tap bouncing down an unpaved road on the outskirts of his hometown, the two leave behind a bathtub filled with red waters and blue memories.

All three, along with the whispering ancestors following on wings of wind, place their faith and hope in the new life about to be born, and the amber of the rising sun at their backs.